PRAISE FOR LO[...]
MOONGLOW BAY NOVELS

"Page-turning and passionate, Lori Wilde's novels are always a delight!"

—Jill Shalvis, *New York Times* bestselling author

"The resilience of the bond between sisters is tested on a rocky path toward healing in this engrossing tale of secrets and betrayals. Lori Wilde's infinitely relatable characters make *The Moonglow Sisters* a must-read."

—Julia London, *New York Times* bestselling author

"*The Moonglow Sisters* is everything I love in a book. It's emotional, funny, tender, and unforgettable. I couldn't stop reading until the last wonderful page. Lori Wilde writes characters who always speak to my heart."

—RaeAnne Thayne, *New York Times* bestselling author

"Every now and then a book comes along that touches every emotion, from heartrending tears to belly laughs. *The Moonglow Sisters* is a one of those rare books. From the first line to the last sigh, it was amazing."

—Carolyn Brown, *New York Times* bestselling author

"Wilde reunites three estranged sisters in this powerful tale. . . . Wilde's fine characterizations and pulsating plot will please readers who enjoy family sagas."

—*Publishers Weekly* on *The Moonglow Sisters*

"Wilde's second novel set in Moonglow Cove is a redemptive story of the healing power of unconditional familial love and the potential to grow through life's struggles. It's sure to please the author's many devoted readers and fans of similar authors, like Susan Mallery and Kristan Higgins."

—*Library Journal* on *The Keepsake Sisters*

"Fans of Jill Shalvis and Susan Mallery will relish the complex family relationships Wilde creates."

—*Booklist* on *The Keepsake Sisters*

"*The Keepsake Sisters* grabs your attention and heart right from the start. . . . Mesmerizing."

—Fresh Fiction

The Lighthouse *on* Moonglow Bay

Also by Lori Wilde

THE MOONGLOW, TEXAS SERIES

The Keepsake Sisters

The Moonglow Sisters

THE STARDUST, TEXAS SERIES

Love of the Game

Rules of the Game

Back in the Game

THE CUPID, TEXAS SERIES

To Tame a Wild Cowboy

How the Cowboy Was Won

Million Dollar Cowboy

Love with a Perfect Cowboy

Somebody to Love

All Out of Love

Love at First Sight

One True Love (novella)

THE JUBILEE, TEXAS SERIES

A Cowboy for Christmas

The Cowboy and the Princess

The Cowboy Takes a Bride

THE TWILIGHT, TEXAS SERIES

The Christmas Backup Plan

The Christmas Dare

The Christmas Key

Cowboy, It's Cold Outside

A Wedding for Christmas

I'll Be Home for Christmas

Christmas at Twilight

The Valentine's Day Disaster (novella)

The Christmas Cookie Collection

The Christmas Cookie Chronicles: Carrie; Raylene; Christine; Grace

The Welcome Home Garden Club

The First Love Cookie Club

The True Love Quilting Club

The Sweethearts' Knitting Club

AVAILABLE FROM HARLEQUIN

THE STOP THE WEDDING SERIES

Crash Landing

Smooth Sailing

Night Driving

The Lighthouse *on* Moonglow Bay

A Novel

LORI WILDE

WILLIAM MORROW
An Imprint of HarperCollins*Publishers*

This is a work of fiction. Names, characters, places, and incidents are products of the author's imagination or are used fictitiously and are not to be construed as real. Any resemblance to actual events, locales, organizations, or persons, living or dead, is entirely coincidental.

HarperCollins books may be purchased for educational, business, or sales promotional use. For information, please email the Special Markets Department at SPsales@harpercollins.com.

FIRST EDITION

Designed by Diahann Sturge

Lighthouse images © Tetra Images / Adobe Stock

Library of Congress Cataloging-in-Publication Data has been applied for.

ISBN 978-0-06-313594-9

22 23 24 25 26 LSC 10 9 8 7 6 5 4 3 2 1

This book is dedicated to Suzanne. I'm so sorry I couldn't have done more to protect you. I love you with all my heart and I treasure the relationship we have now. Be free and happy, little sister.

CHAPTER 1

Harper

SOURDOUGH STARTER: Composed of fermented flour and water, a sourdough starter is a leavening agent that uses naturally occurring yeasts and bacteria to make baked goods rise.

For over one hundred and fifty years, the Lighthouse on Moonglow Bay had been haunted and everyone in the sleepy seaside town of Moonglow Cove, Texas, knew it.

And avoided the place.

At 116 feet, it was the second-tallest lighthouse on the Texas Gulf Coast, and the third oldest. Adorning the roof was a wooden widow's walk outside a small, enclosed, glass cupola. The lighthouse sat at the farthest tip of a ten-mile curve comprising the charming, half-circle inlet. As many lighthouses of that era were built, it was made of bricks brought from New Orleans by schooner in the late 1850s and covered with white plaster.

But what made the structure singularly unique was the odd forward jut that gave the eerie illusion the lighthouse was about to fling itself into the ocean.

Despite its beguiling exterior, dark secrets lurked inside. Only one family had ever owned the property—a once large and prosperous family that was now almost extinct.

Beside the lighthouse stood the keeper's cottage. The house was two-story, eighteen hundred square feet with a square-box floor plan. A high-pitched gabled roof, gingerbread trim, twin chimneys, and window dormers lent the utilitarian design a whimsical air. Entry through the front door led to a living room on the right and a parlor on the left, which in recent years served as the master bedroom. The back door led through a mudroom straight into the big country kitchen.

At four thirty on a sunny afternoon in May, a black SUV pulled to a stop at the end of the road three hundred feet below the craggy bluff where the lighthouse stood.

Harper Campbell stepped from the Uber, cell phone in hand, and gazed out across the sea oats shimmering in the wind. Shading her eyes with the flat of her palm, she blinked up at the bizarre obelisk overlooking the water. As she studied the imposing structure two questions popped into her mind.

Why wasn't there a drivable road that went all the way to the lighthouse and caretaker's cottage instead of this cul-de-sac that ended at the ocean? And seriously, why had she worn stilettos?

Why?

She had no answer for the first question, but as for the second? She'd wanted to look professional and believed the trip would be a quick in and out. Arrive, hear the reading of the will, grab a car back to the airport, and return to the spiraling mess she'd left behind in Manhattan. No need for an overnight stay.

Um, unless you want to mend things with Flannery.

At the thought of her younger half sister, Harper's chest tightened, and she closed her eyes against the onslaught of complicated memories.

Breathe.

Behind her, she heard the crunch of gravel as the Uber drove away, leaving her stranded alone in the middle of nowhere.

Goose bumps lifted the hairs on her arms, and she shivered, unnerved by the strangest feeling that she'd just come home after an eternal journey, even though she'd never set foot in Texas.

Frankly, the sensation was creepy.

She wouldn't mythologize this place, even though as an advertising and marketing expert that was exactly her job—to manipulate and polish reality into something more palatable. But while she often used nostalgia to her advantage in her work, it wasn't a place where she personally cared to dwell.

She wasn't Flannery after all.

Wincing, Harper rubbed the pad of her thumb between her eyebrows where a headache had started gnawing as her plane took off from LaGuardia that morning. She should have had the Uber driver stop for aspirin.

This wasn't going to be easy, no matter how she stacked and sliced it. The estate executor, a Mr. Grayson Cooper, had called her two days ago, measured and enigmatic.

"Your grandmother," he'd said in a placid tone, "has passed away and I've been tasked with sorting out her affairs."

The *real* shock of that news?

Growing up, Harper's mother, Tia Campbell Dupree Johnson McGillicuddy Evans Pinkerton Blanks, had told her that Grandmother Campbell had died long before Harper was born, walking into the Gulf of Mexico with a cinder block tied around her neck, and drowning herself. Not that her mother's flexible relationship with the truth was an anomaly but the information that, until recently, her grandmother was very much alive was a lot to absorb.

"Mrs. Campbell has left a valuable inheritance for you and your half sister, Flannery," the executor had continued.

Harper pressed for details. He was straightforward but stingy with information, dancing around her questions and saying she could contact Mrs. Campbell's lawyer directly if she wished for more information. Harper knew *that* evasive waltz. She was an expert at deflection and sleight of hand.

"You'll learn everything at the 5 P.M. reading of her will on Friday, May 20, at the lightkeeper's cottage next to the Moonglow Lighthouse," he'd continued.

"This seems highly irregular," Harper said. "Why can't you just give me the particulars over the phone?"

"I'm simply obeying your grandmother's wishes."

The phone call had been such a frustrating exchange that if she hadn't been in a serious bind, Harper would've ignored the whole thing. Who needed to jump through hoops to please some controlling, dead matriarch she'd never met? Who needed this white elephant lighthouse on the Texas Gulf Coast? Flannery was welcome to it.

Aww, but Harper *was* in a bind, wasn't she?

A very serious bind.

Worst-chapter-of-her-life bind and she needed a contingency plan, no matter how far-fetched.

Her cell phone buzzed. She would have ignored it as she had the sixteen voice messages, forty-seven texts, and seven hundred eighty-one—and counting—Twitter notifications that had popped up once she'd deplaned.

But this was her boss, and she was already in hot water up to her back molars.

"Hello, Roger," she answered, keeping her tone light and neutral, belying the boulder in her belly.

"Harper, we need to talk."

"Can it wait? About to go into the meeting with the executor of my grandmother's will—"

"No, it can't."

Why had she answered the freaking phone? "Rog—"

"I just got off a Zoom call with Crenshaw and Merc."

That pulled her up short. "And?"

"They want you gone."

Confirmation of her fear was a hard karate chop to the throat. "Roger, you know Kalinda wrote that tweet, not me—"

"Doesn't matter."

"What do you mean it doesn't matter? Of course, it matters."

"Kalinda did it through your account. You're the one who gave her carte blanche access. To the world, you're the author. This is all on you."

"I don't get a chance to defend myself?" Harper tried to pace, but her heels kept sinking into the soft sand. Fine. She'd start walking the paved incline leading toward the lighthouse. "I need to set the record straight. I don't want people thinking I'm—"

"It doesn't matter," he repeated. "You hired Kalinda because you were determined to recuse her. I warned you against hiring someone with her background, but you were adamant that you could save her. I feared all along you were projecting your qualities onto her, but you gave me your word that you could handle Kalinda. Clearly, you could not. Now it's blown up in both our faces."

From this angle, palm trees blocked Harper's view of the lighthouse, but she could feel it looming, sucking her in. Her scalp tingled and intensified the pounding at her temples. She felt as if she might puke.

"You're saying I'm responsible for Kalinda's actions?"

"I'm saying there is enough blame to go around." His voice roughened, and in her mind's eyes she could see his myopic squint. She adored Roger. He'd taken a chance on her when no one else in the business would, but now he was throwing her to the wolves.

"You're in the hot seat too," she said, finally getting that he must save his own skin.

"This is bad, Harper. There's no other way to say it. Crenshaw and Merc are threatening to walk with their billion-dollar account—"

"If my head doesn't roll," she finished for him.

There it was. The truth she'd been running from since the Twitter mob came after her like Frankenstein villagers with pitchforks, shovels, and bayonets. She'd thought that by removing Kalinda's inflammatory post and lying low this would all blow over. Had hoped that the Twitterverse would quickly find someone new to bully if she just refused to stir the pot.

There was a long silence.

"I'm fired, aren't I?" The headache worsened.

"You shouldn't have gotten on that plane to Texas. It makes you look guilty as hell. You should have stayed here and pled your case," Roger said, sacrificing her at the altar of the almighty dollar.

Could she blame him? Wouldn't she do exactly the same thing in his position? The belly boulder shattered into a million sharp shards, slitting her gut wide open. She was fired for something she hadn't done without ever being given a chance to defend herself.

"My grandmother just died." Harper latched onto the excuse like a lifeline.

"Look at it this way. Now you have all the time in the world for your grief."

Now that was just plain tacky. "Up yours, Roger."

"*Aww*, there it is. That simmering, indignant crusader anger that got you this far in life. Although your do-gooder anger does give credence to the idea that maybe you *did* write the post yourself."

"You don't believe that!"

"Not really, but I'd be a fool not to consider it."

"Why would I purposefully sink my own career?"

"That's it. Give in to anger," he egged her on. "Let the rage fuel you on your next venture. I wish you nothing but the best."

She almost brought up the fact she'd donated bone marrow to his four-year-old daughter, Lacey, after the child had been diagnosed with leukemia last year, but she was immediately ashamed of that impulse. She'd given the marrow because she loved the kid and wanted her to have a happy, healthy life. She wouldn't hold that over Roger's head.

Rubbing her hip, Harper said, "This is bullshit and you know it. Crenshaw and Merc need a scapegoat and I'm it."

"Sweetie, you're in advertising. You know good and well the truth doesn't matter. Perception is everything."

In the distance, seagulls cawed, and waves crashed. Happy

vacation sounds amid her own personal Shakespearean drama. She wondered what Shakespeare would make of Twitter. Harper stared at the leaping lighthouse, pondering the idea.

"Hey, I'm out on a limb too," Roger went on. "I had to eat crow and a lot of it to keep *my* job."

Okay, fine. She was out of a job. Big deal. She'd been looking for a job when she'd found this one. "No due process? No way to clear my name and hold Kalinda accountable?"

"There might have been if you hadn't bounced."

The firm expected her to be at their beck and call 24/7, and until now, she'd had no problem with that. Her job was her life.

Was.

Harper leaned forward against the weight of the oversized tote she used for airline travel and pushed harder up the steep incline. Her thigh muscles bunched with the effort, but she barely paid attention. She did notice the pinch of her pointy-toed Christian Louboutins. They were built for red carpet galas, not seaside hikes.

"Wouldn't a public apology and demotion work just as well? I *am* truly sorry this happened."

You're begging. Stop it.

"The public outcry has been too great." Roger grunted. "The post went viral, Harper. You're screwed. Crenshaw and Merc see you as a liability and rightfully so."

"I could sue for wrongful termination." She wasn't trying to intimidate, just pointing it out.

"Not if you ever want to work in this business again. My advice? Take your lumps, rest, and regroup. Come back in a couple of years when everyone has forgotten you."

"But I didn't post that tweet!"

"Doesn't matter. All that matters is perception, and the perception is that you accused Crenshaw and Merc of unethical and possibly illegal practices."

He made a stellar point. She was a brand strategist for one of the biggest advertising agencies in the world and that single, inflammatory tweet—accusing Crenshaw and Merc of suppressing evidence that one of their most popular products was defective—could seriously undermine the medical device company's brand of integrity and service.

A brand that she'd spent three years cultivating.

"I didn't—"

"Your Twitter account did and there is zero proof that C&M is doing what the post accused them of. Thank your lucky stars they aren't taking you to court for libel . . ." He paused. "*Yet.*"

"Is that a threat?"

"It's reality. You brought this on yourself."

Indignation was a finely woven cloak and she wrapped herself in it. "Excuse me? How do you suppose I did that?"

"Good question. Now you've got the time to figure out how your actions landed you where you are."

Panic closed over her, clammy as the humid breeze. Last night, she'd knocked back a few whiskeys to chase off impending doom, and the alcohol had worked to temporarily pacify her mind. She'd slept like the dead.

But now the worst had happened. She teetered on the verge of losing everything—her apartment on the Upper West Side, her friends, her career, everything she'd built since she'd crawled out of the muck of her abusive childhood.

Roger was right. About all of it.

She had to own her part in this. She'd trusted the wrong

person—yet again. Why did she keep doing that? She kept loading the bullets, handing the gun to people, and then got surprised when they shot her.

"I'm sorry," he murmured. "If it helps, you were an exemplary employee."

"Other than that, Mrs. Lincoln, how was the play?"

"Yeah," he said. "I know. I really will miss you."

"Please, just shut up."

"That's it, champ. Own the anger. Let it strengthen you."

"You're taking the fun out of insulting you."

"No," he said. "I'm issuing you a challenge. I know it's the one thing you can't resist. Think of what a terrific comeback story this will make one day."

"Roger, you can blow that out your—"

But he'd already hung up.

Leaving her feeling completely abandoned and utterly rudderless. Everything she'd worked a lifetime for was dust in her hand. In the span of twenty-four hours, cancel culture had slaughtered Harper Campbell's hard-won career.

But that wasn't true, was it? Cancel culture hadn't killed her life, she'd done it herself by trusting someone she shouldn't have.

Again.

She'd let down her guard. This was all on her.

The anger Roger had urged her to cultivate kindled inside her, and she ran the rest of the way, uncaring that she was in designer shoes and toting a handbag that weighed over twenty pounds. She did CrossFit. She figured she could do anything.

Panting, she rushed higher, faster. Sweat collected on her brow and at her cleavage. Her heels made machine-gun *rat-tat-tats* against the cobblestone path. She could feel her phone vibrating in her hand, hear it dinging more messages. She should drop the cell into her bag, but she couldn't seem to let it go.

In fact, she curled her fingers more tightly around her phone. It was her lifeline, connecting her to everything. She crested the bluff, huffing and puffing, sprinting on empty, toes on fire from the shoes.

Up close, the lighthouse was so much more imposing. She halted and dragged in a ragged breath. The tower stood like a stern guardian glaring down at her, judging her.

You're worthless. You messed up. There is no forgiveness for the likes of you.

She'd heard those words before. Knew them by heart. They were the whip with which she'd beaten herself to do better, be better, but where had thirty-three years of self-flagellation gotten her?

Crashed on the rocks. Unsaved by a familial lighthouse.

Ding. Ding. Buzz. Buzz.

Filled with rage she couldn't restrain one second longer, Harper gave a guttural warrior cry, raced to the edge of the bluff, drew her arm back and flung the offending cell phone into the Gulf.

Heart in her throat, she leaned over the drop-off to watch it tumble onto the rocks, instantly regretting launching it.

But somewhere on the back shelf of her mind, she felt something else, too. Something she hadn't felt since her mother had died six years earlier.

Relief.

CHAPTER 2

Flannery

GERM: The part of grain that, given the right conditions for germination, will sprout.

Flannery Franklin drove along Moonglow Boulevard, eyeing the western sky and working up her courage to face her estranged sister.

Thunderclouds erased the separation between surf and air as if a melancholy artist had dragged a blending brush along the horizon, muddling colors and shapes. She couldn't recall ever seeing such a moody landscape. It possessed volume and heft with varying shades of shifting gray so complex it felt as if her fifteen-year-old Toyota minivan was barreling straight into a quirky Tim Burton-esque nightmare.

She almost pointed out the unusual panoramic vista to Willow, who was sitting in the back seat behind her, but her five-year-old daughter was mesmerized by a game app on Flannery's phone, and during the long drive down from Kansas City, she'd grown tired of her mother's impromptu art lessons.

Honestly, Flannery was tired too. Exhausted to the center of her bones. Running away from home was a lot less exhilarating than she'd supposed.

All their belongings were crammed into the minivan and Flannery could barely see out the back window and had only the side mirrors to guide her. Nibbling her bottom lip, she clutched the steering wheel tighter.

She was broke, on the run, with no place else to go. This inheritance better well work out; otherwise, Flannery had no idea what she would do.

"Continue forward on Moonglow Boulevard for one half mile," said the robotic voice from the GPS.

Flannery swallowed her anxiety, checked her mirrors, and changed lanes. *Almost there, almost there.*

The worrisome part of her brain whispered, *But where?*

"Turn right on Stardust Lane." The recorded male voice was British, programmed by Alan, who enjoyed the pretentiousness. She should figure out how to change it to the default setting.

"Turn left on Comfort Circle."

Moonglow. Stardust. Comfort. What romantic names. But Flannery had learned long ago that romance was for pipe dreamers and self-deluded fools.

She took Comfort, but the road just dead-ended without warning into a paved cul-de-sac. There were no houses, nothing around, just sand and sea and in the distance, high on a bluff, a walking path that led to the Moonglow Lighthouse.

It had to be at least a half mile away from the road, and the thought of pushing Willow in her wheelchair up that steep incline sapped every last bit of Flannery's flagging strength.

Why wasn't there a drivable road to the keeper's cottage? Why wasn't the place wheelchair accessible? What was she supposed to do with her car? Just leave it parked here unprotected?

That didn't seem wise. Too many questions. No answers. Then again, she should be very used to that.

She stopped the car and stared up at the lighthouse. Was it her imagination, or was the thing angling toward the ocean as if it was a jumper unsure of whether to leap or not?

Squinting, she canted her head. By gosh, the structure *did* tilt. Weird. Was the design intentional? Or had someone goofed? Or was it simply crumbling?

The Leaning Lighthouse of Moonglow Cove.

This was her inheritance? Just her luck.

Sighing, Flannery cast a glance in the rearview mirror. Willow was still deeply engrossed in her game. Thank heavens.

Feeling utterly wretched, Flannery rested her forehead against the steering wheel and killed the engine. There was no way she could get Willow, the wheelchair, and their suitcases up to the lighthouse by 5 P.M.

No way at all.

Common sense told her to call the executor and ask for help. But even the thought of wrestling the phone away from her daughter to make the call felt monumental. Getting this far had taken all the courage Flannery could muscle.

Her gaze fell on her arms resting in her lap. To the four finger-shaped bruises just above her left wrist. On the back side of her arm was a corresponding thumbprint. She'd do best to keep the bruises hidden until they healed.

Raising her head, she reached for the threadbare brown sweater that she'd draped over the big cardboard box that was buckled into the front seat and tugged the cardigan on. All right. Time to tackle that incline.

Overwhelmed, Flannery raised her head, familiar despair gnawing at her. Through the gathering gray murkiness, and overgrowth of sea oats, she saw it.

Appearing like a miracle just when she needed it the most.

A sign.

The sign read ELEVATOR TO THE TOP and there was an arrow pointing around the side of the bluff.

Exhaling pent-up air, Flannery gave thanks, her relief so complete that tears burned her eyes.

"Mommy, why are you crying?"

"I'm not crying." She injected pep into her voice and swiped away the tears with her knuckles. "I just had something in my eye."

"Where are we?" In Willow's voice, she heard an excited tremor as if her child was a canary and had awakened to find the cage door standing wide open, but she was too afraid to fly free.

Flannery totally understood. "Well," she said, turning her head to peer into the back seat. "We're here."

Willow's wide blue eyes seemed to engulf her entire face. "At the ocean?"

"At the ocean," Flannery confirmed.

Blinking, Willow peered out the window. "It's gray."

"It'll look less gloomy when the clouds part. C'mon, let's get you unloaded." It was almost five. They were going to be late.

It's not like they won't wait for you.

It was Alan in her head, smothering her. Her husband enjoyed making people wait but tardiness stoked Flannery's anxiety.

Keep it together, for Willow's sake.

To lighten things, she started humming. "I Gotta Feeling."

Willow loved the bouncy Black Eyed Peas song and her daughter immediately started singing and waving her hands about, just as Flannery had hoped she would.

Mood shifted. Good job, Mom.

Still bebopping in time to her own music, Willow unbuckled her seat belt and waited for Flannery to unload the wheelchair and help her transfer into it.

"Can you smell the ocean?" Flannery spooned half a cup of honey into her voice.

Sweet and peppy. Sugar rush. That imagery reminded her of go-go-go Harper, and the temporary buoyancy drained right out of her. Soon, she and her half sister would be face-to-face for the first time in six years and she had no idea what to expect.

"Mommy," Willow said, "you sound weird."

Yes, yes, she knew that. Dropping the manic smile, she plucked her cross-body purse from the front seat and looped it over her shoulder, then rummaged in the back seat for their overnight bag.

"May I put this in your lap?" she asked her daughter.

Willow held out her arms and Flannery settled the bulky bag onto her thin thighs. Willow wrapped her hand around the tote, anchoring it. She was such an accommodating child. On that account, Flannery had been supremely blessed. She unlocked the brakes on Willow's wheelchair.

Standing here with the wind whipping through her billowy floral dress, Flannery couldn't help wondering what fresh kettle of rotten fish she'd gotten herself and her daughter into.

But she was all out of options. Nothing to do now except put on a perky face and push through.

"Here we go," she sang out, hitting the lock button on the car remote and sticking the key into her sweater pocket.

"Where are we goin'?" Willow asked.

"To the lighthouse." Flannery pointed, then wrapped both hands around the wheelchair handles and started pushing.

The small stone path leading to the elevator was covered with sand and it was difficult to navigate. The wheels seized up and refused to roll. Flannery ended up just shoving the thing ahead of her. One of these days she would buy Willow an electric wheelchair. She'd been saving up for it since Alan's insurance wouldn't pay for the expensive wheelchair, but she'd turned that squirreled money into her escape fund.

"We're stuck."

"I just have to wipe off the wheels." Flannery crouched at the front of the wheelchair to brush sand from the casters.

It was futile task. The wheels would just fill with sand again. Hopefully, the elevator was just out of view where the path curved, or it would be midnight before they made it to the cottage.

"There," she announced, back to the falsely cheerful voice she'd been using far too often to convince Willow that all was well. Could her daughter tell she was putting on a front? She hoped not. Willow was far too young for the truth.

Eventually you'll have to tell her we're not going back home.

Yes, well, she'd sort that out later. Dusting off her hands, she stood and straightened.

"Mommy!" Willow said, her voice full of awe. "Lookee, a pelican. Just like at the zoo."

Last week—had it really just been a week ago when they'd done something nice and normal as a family?—they'd gone to the Kansas City Zoo for the first time and Willow had been besotted and begged to spend the whole day there. Alan had been in such a good mood that Flannery lavished him with praise for being so kind and patient and such a wonderful stepfather. Flattery had worked and it ended up being one of the best times they'd ever had.

Memories like these drove her guilt. Maybe things weren't as bad as she'd thought they were. Maybe she was making mountains out of molehills. No one's marriage was perfect, right?

She pushed up the sleeves on her sweater and stared down at those four bruises. No. She was done lying to herself. Now that she had a way out, she was staying gone. This inheritance was her saving grace. She needed to get up there and claim it.

"He caught a fish! He caught a fish!" Willow's glee tugged at Flannery's heartstrings.

Her gaze tracked to where her daughter pointed, just in time to see the pelican perch on a pylon and gulp down the fish. Even though she shouldn't take the time—they were going to be so late—she paused to inhale and look around.

There was a short apron of beach underneath the bluff, but it was rocky and the posted yellow sign warned, NO SWIMMING.

Goose bumps raised on her arm. Was this place dangerous?

Only if you swim where you shouldn't.

"Mommy, this is awesome! I love it here!" Willow said, her sweet voice high and melodious.

That lifted Flannery's spirits.

Smiling wide, Willow curled her hands into fists, tucked them underneath her chin, and rounded her shoulders forward in that adorable gesture she used when she was happy, and lately, she was so rarely happy.

Flannery felt a sharp pang of yearning in her heart.

What would it be like for Willow to grow up in a place like

this? In a quaint lighthouse by the sea? Hope turned into true excitement as she thought of the possibilities. Moonglow Cove was an hour from Houston, which had excellent doctors and facilities in pediatric medicine. The town itself was so pretty and she could find a job. Maybe working in day care since she'd never been anything but a daughter, sister, wife, and mother.

Getting ahead of yourself, Flan. No one said you've inherited a lighthouse.

That thought shook her out of her daydreams. She needed to get up this bluff for the reading of the will and find out what she had inherited. After that, she could start making plans.

Leaning over the wheelchair, she kissed the top of Willow's head. "Hold on, puddin' pop, this path is pretty bumpy."

Half rolling, half shoving, Flannery pushed the wheelchair toward the metal birdcage-style elevator installed onto the side of the stony bluff. From the look of it, an antique engineering feat. The elevator was at least half a century old. The metal cage was rusted and looked untrustworthy.

Flannery's claustrophobia kicked in. Oh man. The distance up to the lighthouse had to be at least three hundred feet. She gulped. It was either this or the incline.

Which was safer for Willow?

Bigger question. Did she really want to inherit a place where the only access was up a supersteep incline or traveling in a Tower of Terror elevator?

You're letting your imagination run away with you. An old lady lived here alone for years. How dangerous could it be? Get in.

Drawing in an extra deep breath to bolster her courage, Flannery pushed Willow toward the open door. She turned and backed into the cage so that the wheelchair was facing forward.

Her pulse thumped in her throat, bounding so hard she felt light-headed and put a hand to her neck.

Calm down, calm down.

Without prompting, Willow locked the brakes on her wheelchair and glanced over her shoulder at Flannery, who was quite frankly cowering in the corner. "Let's go, Mommy!"

Briefly, Flannery closed her eyes, gathered her courage again, and then looked for the control panel to send them upward. Willow beat her to it, leaning over to press the up button.

The cage door closed, but not all the way. There was a six-inch gap. Panic took hold of Flannery. She wanted out. She darted forward desperate to stop the thing from moving, but it was already jerking upward.

"Fun!" Willow giggled and clapped her hands.

The elevator chugged, headed to the top, gears creaking and grinding. Bile rose in Flannery's throat, and she sank back against the cage. She didn't want to infect Willow with her fear. Her knees were trembling so hard, she feared they'd collapse beneath her, and she jabbed her fingernails into her palms.

Hang on, hang on. Not far.

They were halfway up. She closed her eyes again, unable to look down. Willow, the brave little thing, was singing the Black Eyed Peas again.

That's when the elevator groaned, uttering a loud screech that scraped the inside of Flannery's skull. *Oh no!*

"Mommy?" Willow's voice grew worried.

The elevator groaned again, lurched harder, and then stalled to a teeth-jolting stop.

CHAPTER 3

Harper

MOTHER DOUGH: Dough reserved from an earlier batch and allowed to ferment before being combined with fresh dough, used especially in making sourdough bread.

Inside the keeper's cottage, Harper waited with the executor. It was ten minutes after five and her sister still had not appeared.

Would Flannery show up? It wasn't like her to be late.

Restlessly, she thought about calling her sister, but they hadn't spoken in six years, not since that major blowup at their mother's funeral. How did you start *that* conversation? If she'd known how, she would have called long before now.

Maybe just text?

It occurred to her then that her sister might not even have the same phone number. That's how little she knew about Flannery these days. Then she remembered she'd flung her own phone into the ocean and felt instantly adrift. What in the hell had she been thinking? First thing on her to-do list. Get a new phone.

"Your sister said she would be here," Grayson Cooper said, reading Harper's mind. "And so will your aunt Jonnie. I saw her today at the hardware store."

Harper had never met her aunt Jonnie. According to Harper's mother, Tia and Aunt Jonnie had had a falling-out before Harper was born. Over what, Harper had no idea. Tia had rarely talked about her family, or where she'd come from, and Harper knew next to nothing about her mysterious aunt. The few things she did know were this: Aunt Jonnie was fourteen years older than Tia, she'd been Grandfather Campbell's favorite, and Tia hated her older sister with a purple passion.

Purple passion.

Her mother's catchphrase for intense emotions. Tia's expressive language and love of words and literature had colored Harper's entire childhood. Her mom had passed on her penchant for storytelling that had served Harper oh so well in advertising and her job as a brand strategist.

The executor sat serene, his energy bland and accepting.

Harper wondered if he meditated. He seemed the type to meditate. Her mind was far too zippy to sit still and think of nothing for minutes on end, but she admired the heck out of people who could do it.

"Is anyone living in the cottage at the moment?" Harper asked, desperate to fill the silence stretching across the kitchen table between them.

"No," he answered simply and then didn't say anything else.

It was so frustrating, this doing nothing with a stranger.

Part of the problem was that Grayson Cooper was the most gorgeous creature she'd ever set eyes on. Midnight black hair with only a sprinkling of gray, high cheekbones, broad shoulders, flat belly, the works. He had eyes the wickedly cool, pale ice blue of a glacier.

He'd been polite, but professional, and declined to speak about her grandmother's will until her sister and aunt arrived. Instead, he talked about the lighthouse, giving her far more background than Harper cared to know. He told her that he was a high school history teacher, volunteered for the Moonglow Cove Historical Society on the weekends for fun, and in his spare time wrote books on coastal Texas for a university press. Then he announced, with not a small measure of pride, that he was a fourth-generation Moonglow Covian.

Like big whoop. Was it an attribute that his ancestors had gotten stuck in one place for so long?

As he talked, Harper tuned out his words, instead admiring the masculine slant of his nose and the bemused arch of his eyebrows as if he found the world perpetually entertaining. He was tall, well over six feet, with muscular biceps visible through the sleeves of his crisp white business shirt.

He'd taken off his suit jacket and draped it over the back of one of the wooden kitchen chairs and rolled up his sleeves, revealing ropy tanned forearms liberally sprinkled with dark hair. The man was seated directly across from her, a closed briefcase on the floor beside him, and a manila file folder on the table between them.

He was just too damn pretty. Like a young Rob Lowe.

She searched for flaws, and under close scrutiny, found them. His mouth was just a tad too big for his face, his chiseled chin just a smidge too angular, and he had teeth so shiny they had to have been professionally whitened. He looked like many of the businessmen she'd encountered on a daily basis in NYC—a smoothly polished professional. She had not expected to find anyone of his ilk in a pastoral place like Moonglow Cove and she wasn't sure if his familiarity bothered or comforted her.

"You may not know much about the people in Moonglow Cove, but we know about you." Grayson's eyes diamond-glittered in the late-afternoon sun falling in through the partially opened plantation shutters.

"Well, that sounds minorly creepy." She laughed inappropriately. Something she did whenever she was nervous. Flannery did it too. Harper hadn't even realized she did it until the therapist she'd been seeing to help her cope with work stress pointed it out.

Grayson seemed to take note of her odd laugh as well, his eyes narrowing and his chin tightening. He drummed his fingers against the table, his Zen slipping a bit. "Did you know you're a fourth-generation Moonglow Covian as well? Our families helped settle this town together."

Oh, dear lord, not more ancient history. "I don't know anything about that."

"Too bad." He made a clucking noise and shook his head.

Harper frowned. "Are you history-shaming me?"

"No, no." Both eyebrows shot up. "Not at all. I think it's sad that your mother never told you about your heritage."

Besides being stunningly gorgeous, he had a voice that went down easy on the ears. Like expensive whiskey, dark and rich. Barely a hint of a Texas drawl. He might be from four generations of Moonglow Covians born and bred, but he'd traveled, and seen the world. He'd lived somewhere that had whitewashed the accent out of him, and now Harper was more intrigued than she should've been.

So what if he was good-looking and even-tempered? So what if he wasn't wearing a wedding ring? She wasn't in the market for any kind of relationship, not even a casual hookup.

Although if she *had* been interested, he'd head the list of potential candidates.

Unnerved, Harper glanced around the farm-size kitchen that she'd barely paid attention to upon her arrival. The room was huge, with acres of cabinets and counters and clearly the hub of the house. Butcher block surface mixed with white subway tile. Farmhouse sink. Not retro. Original. A chef's dream with plenty of room for baking, cooking, measuring, and chopping.

Not that she knew how to cook. No need for learning how in Manhattan where excellent food delivery was a text away.

The flooring was black-and-white checkerboard linoleum, a throwback to when the kitchen was last renovated sometime in the 1950s, according to Historical Database Cooper. The flooring hadn't aged well. The wooden table and chairs they sat at were from the same era. Dust lay thick all over.

When she first arrived, Grayson had wiped down the chair for her to sit with a handkerchief—who carried handkerchiefs these days?—that he'd pulled from his jacket pocket.

"How long has it been since the house was occupied?" she asked.

"Since your grandmother went into the nursing home five years ago."

"No one has looked after it?"

"There's a caretaker who lives down the road. Hank Charbonneau. He's a former firefighter who got injured in the line of duty. Hank takes care of general maintenance, but it seems he doesn't bother with dusting."

"I see." Harper bit her bottom lip. She had so many questions, but now wasn't the time. It was fifteen minutes after five according to the electric wall clock. "How come you're the executor of my grandmother's will?"

"She asked me if I'd do it."

"Why you? Why not a family member?"

"I admit, I charmed your grandmother when I was researching *Lighthouses of Texas*."

"One of your books?"

"My fourth," he said. "It comes out next spring."

"What do you mean by 'charmed'?" Harper asked, feeling suspicious of this stranger.

"Your grandmother was one of the oldest people in Moonglow Cove and until her stroke, her mind was razor-sharp. She was a historian's dream. I enjoyed talking to her and came up here several times a week for six months as I interviewed her. She didn't get many visitors and seemed pretty lonely. I listened and she talked. She seemed to enjoy the attention. At the end of our time together, she asked if I'd be the executor of her will and because I cared so much about the lighthouse and Moonglow Cove, I agreed."

Harper studied him for a long moment. That bemused smile seemed permanently affixed to his face, as if he found everything entertaining. "Are you sure Flannery is coming?"

"She said she was." His tone was noncommittal.

"She's never late," Harper murmured.

"No one is *never* anything," Grayson said mildly. "It's a long car trip from Kansas City. I think we can cut her some slack."

He was right. She was exaggerating. But that didn't stop her from getting irritated with him.

He offered up a faint smile. "I try to avoid black-and-white thinking whenever possible. It puts people in boxes."

Well, good for you, Mr. Fourth-Generation Moonglow Covian.

Restlessly, Harper dropped her gaze to the chicken-shaped salt-and-pepper shakers sitting on the lazy Susan in the middle of the table. The dust was so thick she couldn't see the holes in the tops of the shakers.

The back door opened, and a torrent of wind blew in along with a tall, rangy woman in her early sixties. A shock of steel-gray hair stood out from her head, tangled and frizzed. She wore a yellow rain slicker, even though it wasn't raining yet, and snazzy rubber boots imprinted with Van Gogh's *Starry Night*.

Her sudden appearance was so startling, Harper sucked in a gasp. Although she didn't look at all like the young woman in the only photo her mother had of her older sister, Harper knew this had to be her aunt Jonnie and she appeared a force to be reckoned with.

But then again, so was Harper.

Or at least she had been before her epic crash and burn. Her body tensed and she curled her fingers into her palms, making two fists against the table.

The woman stepped farther into the room, running one hand like a rake through her unruly curls. Tucked into the crook of her other arm, she carried a white ceramic crock with periwinkles printed on it, and for one horrified second, Harper thought it might be an urn.

Please, don't let that be Grandmother Campbell's ashes!

Harper got to her feet. In the distance she heard the sound of a child's voice. She must be imagining things; there were no children around here, high on a solo bluff, overlooking the stormy sea. A chill went down her spine and she shuddered involuntarily.

"Harper?" The woman tilted her head.

"Aunt Jonnie?"

The woman nodded.

Neither of them moved.

Harper wasn't sure what she felt. There was an odd combination of sensations rolling throughout her body. One small part of her, the part she usually tried to ignore, felt a keen sense of loss that she couldn't rush into the arms of one of the few relatives she had left in the world.

A relative who was a complete stranger.

Where was this urge to merge coming from? She'd never needed people. She'd always been good on her own.

Never. Always.

Extremist words that Grayson Cooper would pooh-pooh.

"Welcome to the Lighthouse on Moonglow Bay," Aunt Jonnie said, as if welcoming a curious tourist. She offered a smile, but there was a touch of overwhelming sadness in it.

Not knowing what else to say, Harper muttered, "Thank you."

Amid the awkward tension, she and her aunt turned simultaneously to the executor.

Grayson sat with impeccable posture, studying them with unruffled aplomb. Seriously, did he have to look so hot?

"Flannery has yet to arrive." He waved a hand. "Please, Jonnie, have a seat. She should be here soon."

Moving with a strong determined gait, her rubber boots squeaking against the linoleum, Jonnie joined them and settled the crock on the table in front of her.

Collectively, the three of them exhaled. In the quiet space, the sound was deafening. *Yeesh.* Harper wanted so badly to jump up and pace.

"Look at that," Aunt Jonnie said, "we sound like heavy breathers on a phone sex line."

Her aunt's salty analogy took Harper by surprise and she couldn't help grinning despite the eerie ceramic crock between them. Icebreaker. It's what the situation needed. *Thank you, weird Aunt Jonnie.*

The sound of a child's voice came again, high-pitched, and ghostly.

Harper shifted her attention to Grayson. "Did you hear that?"

"I did." Grayson stood, his chair scraping against the floor. "That must be Willow."

"Willow?"

The executor seemed startled that she didn't know who Willow was, but he adroitly camouflaged his surprise. "Willow is your sister's daughter."

Like a punch to the gut, it took a minute for the impact of his words to register. Harper felt her jaw unhinge. Flannery had a daughter? How had she not known this? How had Flannery not told her?

Hurt and resentment caught Harper by the throat and strangled her. She wanted to leap to her feet and bolt from the house. She felt blindsided, dumbfounded, and so very hurt.

"Flannery has a child?" she whispered.

There was a knock at the front door, and the effervescent sound of the child's giggle. Willow.

Her niece.

The sudden rush of love that raced over Harper was just as

overwhelming and perplexing as her resentment. She had a niece and the last thing she expected was to feel giddy about it, but damn if she didn't.

"Who should get the door?" Aunt Jonnie asked.

Grayson was already standing. "I will."

He left the room.

Harper met Jonnie's gaze and then she shifted her attention to the urn to keep her mind off her ricocheting emotions. "Wh-what's in the crock?"

A sly look came into Jonnie's eyes, accompanied by a mischievous grin that unnerved Harper. "Why, it's your inheritance."

She'd inherited her grandmother's ashes? No. Please no.

"I-um-I," she stammered, "thought that . . . well . . . Mr. Cooper made it sound as if Flannery and I had inherited this place."

"Oh no." Aunt Jonnie shook her head. "It's not that simple."

"What do you mean?"

In the foyer, on the other side of the house, came the sound of Grayson opening the front door and greeting the new arrivals. Harper's pulse quickened.

Aunt Jonnie patted the urn. "I'll let Grayson read the conditions of the will, but if you want a sneak peek, I don't mind opening the lid."

Did she want to look?

No.

Silently, Harper nodded.

Aunt Jonnie crooked a finger and lifted one corner of the rounded lid.

Compelled, Harper leaned over to peer inside, bracing herself to view human remains. Instead, she saw a blob of pasty beige doughlike substance that smelled faintly soured.

"Wh-what is that?" Harper plunked back down into her chair and blinked rapidly at her aunt.

"A treasure beyond measure."

Huh? Harper resisted rolling her eyes. "Okay, but what *is* it?"

"Why, my dear, it's the Campbell family's one-hundred-fifty-year-old mother dough."

CHAPTER 4

Flannery

ACETIC ACID: Refers to a type of acid produced by the bacteria in sourdough starter and is responsible for giving the bread its characteristic tangy flavor.

Flannery eyeballed the gorgeous guy who'd answered the front door and immediately her guard shot up.

She did not trust good-looking men. Not to mention, she was still shaken from the bumpy elevator ride. Just when she'd been about to flip out, the ancient elevator had chugged upward again. Okay, fine, she spooked too easily. It was something she needed to work on.

"Mrs. Franklin?" Mr. Tall, Dark, and Handsome asked with an extended hand. "I'm Grayson Cooper, the executor of Mrs. Campbell's will."

Gingerly, she shook his hand and then quickly curled her fingers around the handles of Willow's wheelchair again. "Pleased to meet you."

"And you must be Willow." He crouched in front of the wheelchair, surprising Flannery by paying attention to her daughter. Most adults didn't bother to get on her level. "How old are you?"

What was his angle? Why was he buttering up her child? Flannery furrowed her brow.

Willow cast a glance at her, looking for permission to answer.

Flannery nodded. She'd taught her daughter to be careful with whom she shared personal information.

"I'm five." Willow held up her palm, fingers spread. "How old are you?"

Grinning, the lawyer said, "I'm twenty-seven years older than you."

Willow looked puzzled. "How many fingers is that?"

"More than I have on two hands."

"Wow," Willow said. "You're old."

"Willow, don't be rude," Flannery chided gently.

Grayson chuckled. "Truly, I am ancient."

He was nice and Flannery certainly didn't trust that. In her experience, when someone was too nice, it usually meant they were up to something.

The man straightened and offered Flannery a generous smile that made her feel both sucked in and even warier.

"Come on into the kitchen," he invited. "Your sister and aunt are waiting for us."

That sense of impending doom, the dreaded family reunion that had weighed her down since Kansas, strangled Flannery's stagnant heart. Forcing a smile, she followed Grayson into the kitchen, propelling Willow in the wheelchair ahead of her.

The second she spied Harper sitting at the kitchen table with an older woman that Flannery didn't know, everything inside her melted and she wanted nothing more than to run to the older sister who had protected her so many times in the past, wrap her arms around her, and hug her tight.

But those hugging days were long gone.

A lump of tears blocked her throat, and her knees trembled, and she was so grateful to have Willow's wheelchair in front of her.

Harper stood. They locked gazes.

Flannery forgot to breathe and tasted the salt of her unshed tears.

"Hello, sister." Harper's voice was soft but firm. The steely hand in a velvet glove. Flannery's half sister was so much stronger than she was. "I see you have a child."

Flannery nodded, unable to speak, emotions rolling over her like ocean waves. In this moment, she regretted not contacting Harper and telling her she'd had a baby, but well . . .

Alan.

Her husband had forbidden her from having any contact with Harper after he heard what had happened at their mother's funeral and Flannery had learned the hard way when to pick her battles with him. She'd had to let her sister go, allowing the estrangement to fester when she'd wanted nothing more than to mend those battered fences.

Harper's tone saddened. "And your little girl is in a wheelchair."

"Don't feel sorry for me," Willow said fiercely, knotting her little hands into fists.

"I-I . . ." Harper sputtered.

"My wheelchair is my superpower." Willow proudly raised her small chin. Flannery's daughter didn't need no stinking pity. "I roll wherever I go. Don't you wish *you* had wheels?"

Profound love for her precocious child pressed against Flannery's chest. Willow didn't let anything, or anyone, hold her back, including the severe form of spina bifida that had relegated her to the wheelchair.

Frankly, Flannery was a little jealous of her daughter's resilience. How different might her life have been if she'd been born with just an ounce of Willow's innate courage?

Harper's eyebrows went up, but her eyes twinkled, and a slight grin tugged the corners of her mouth and suddenly, Flannery could breathe again.

"I *do* wish I had wheels," Harper said. "You are a lucky girl."

Flannery studied her older sister's face. If anything, Harper was even more gorgeous than when she'd last seen her. She looked a decade younger than her thirty-three years. Younger even than Flannery, who'd just turned twenty-six.

Her sister's blond hair was styled in a sleek long bob that skimmed the top of her shoulders, not a single strand out of place. Harper had stick straight hair, whereas Flannery had an unmanageable mess of curls. Their mother used to say that when it came to hair, Harper got the gold mine, and Flannery got the shaft.

Feeling self-conscious, Flannery reached up a hand to pat down her thick unruly dirty-blond hair, frizzed and matted by the wind and humidity. She felt dumpy in her brown floral print dress and oversized worn-out sweater.

We're not in Kansas anymore, Toto.

An uncomfortable silence settled over the room. Flannery darted a glance at the older woman standing to one side, a lidded ceramic crock cradled against her elbow.

Offering a timid smile—damn her for being so meek—Flannery said, "You must be Aunt Jonnie."

The woman barely gave a discernible nod, her blue eyes watchful. Aunt Jonnie wore round Harry Potter glasses that did not camouflage her wariness and not a lick of makeup. Underneath a yellow rain slicker, she wore faded jeans, and a chambray shirt. She looked like an older, weathered, countrified version of their mother.

Tia would have resented that comparison. Looks had been very important to her. In that way, their mother and Harper were very much alike, pressed, polished, and perfect. Glamorous and gluten-free. Cool and colorful. Skinny and sociable.

Although that had all changed in the end.

Whereas everything about Aunt Jonnie warned, *Don't tread on me.*

Flannery glanced back at Harper, who was watching Willow, who was staring at Aunt Jonnie, who was looking at Grayson Cooper.

The executor took control of the emotionally charged situation, and smooth as oil, he indicated the old farmhouse table with a wave. "Shall we all sit."

The man said it as a statement, not a question. That ruffled Flannery's feathers. She was tired of being ordered around by men.

Grayson's gaze latched on to Flannery's and he added, "Please."

Harper took the seat she'd vacated when Flannery and Willow had come into the room. Aunt Jonnie moved to the opposite side of the table, pulled out a chair, and sat down. Leaving Flannery to maneuver Willow's wheelchair around the sideboard. Grayson moved one of the chairs so that Flannery could park Willow next to the remaining empty seat on that side of the table.

The only sounds in the room were wheels against linoleum, rustling papers, and Aunt Jonnie drawing in an audible breath.

Feeling jittery, Flannery locked Willow's wheelchair and took the seat beside her daughter.

Flannery looked across the table at Aunt Jonnie who was still clinging tightly to the ceramic crock. It looked similar to the crock she used at home to make kimchi and sauerkraut. "What's in the pot?"

"We'll get to that." Grayson cleared his throat.

At the same time, Harper said, "Our inheritance."

"Please tell me it's not cremains." Flannery pressed a hand to her stomach, willing away nausea.

"We'll get to that," Grayson repeated, leveling Harper a look that said, *I'm running this show.*

Whew, there were a lot of strong personalities in this room and all Flannery wanted to do was pull out her e-reader and dive into the latest Kristin Hannah book. She undid the clasp on her purse, quelled the urge to read, and snapped it back up again. Just knowing the book was there if she needed to escape was enough to soothe her.

The executor shuffled the documents. "This is the reading of the will of Penelope J. Campbell." He paused, looked up, and caught Aunt Jonnie's eye.

Willow, already bored, was fiddling with the zipper on her windbreaker, moving it back and forth on a track, slowly speeding up. A sure sign she was anxious.

"Sweetie." Flannery put a hand on her daughter's arm. "Would you like a juice box?"

Willow bobbed her head. "Fruit punch, please."

Flannery reached for the overnight bag she'd shifted from Willow's lap to the back of the wheelchair when they'd gotten out of the elevator and glanced around.

"Anyone else want a juice box? We have fruit punch, strawberry kiwi, and lemonade." Holding up two juice boxes, she waggled them in the air.

Harper shook her head and Aunt Jonnie put up a stop sign hand.

Grayson smiled kindly. "I'll have lemonade."

Flannery passed him the juice box and opened Willow's for her, poking the straw into the box and passing it to her daughter. She took one for herself, then gave her cell phone back to Willow with a game app open to keep her occupied during the adult conversation. She wished she had somewhere to leave Willow during all this, but she did not.

"Everyone ready?" Grayson asked.

They nodded and Willow took a big slurp off her juice box. Aunt Jonnie grinned, and Flannery liked her a bit more.

While Grayson read aloud through the legalese, Flannery pressed her palms against the tops of her thighs to keep her hands still and stared across the table at the white ceramic crock with periwinkles on it.

Harper rubbed her thumb across the back of her knuckles of the opposite hand. The gesture told those in the know she was itching to punch something.

Aching to reach out to her sister, Flannery kept her hands clutched in her lap. There was so much resentment and animosity between them that she didn't know if they could ever work through it. Didn't know if she even had the energy to try.

A familiar yearning for something she could never have welled up inside Flannery. She knew coming here would be emotional, but she was thoroughly unprepared for the roller coaster of feelings plunging and rising inside her—anger, sadness, grief, longing, and hope, oh that desperate stupid hope.

"To my granddaughters, Harper Lee and Flannery O'Connor, I leave the Campbell family one-hundred-fifty-year-old mother dough," Grayson read.

Sourdough? Their inheritance was sourdough starter? If it hadn't been so ludicrous, Flannery would've burst out laughing.

Here she thought this insane inheritance was going to be her salvation. Her key out of her crappy marriage. Instead, she inherited sourdough. She didn't even know how to bake. What was she going to do with sourdough? It wasn't even hers alone. She had to share it with her sister.

Harper rubbed her palms together. "Get to the good stuff, Cooper. What else did we inherit?"

Flannery admired her sister's spunk. Instead of waiting patiently, Harper plunged ahead demanding answers.

"I'm getting to that." Grayson looked more amused than irritated, as if he was sitting on some sly secret.

"Who gets the lighthouse? Who gets the caretaker cottage?" Harper asked.

"Patience." His arctic pale blue eyes crinkled at the corners. Seriously, it ought to be illegal for a man to be that handsome.

Flannery noticed Harper rubbing her knuckles harder.

Grayson cleared his throat and kept reading. "As far as the keeper's cottage and the lighthouse go, my granddaughters will inherit *only* if they complete a series of challenges in the allotted time frame. Otherwise, the property passes to the Moonglow Cove Historical Society."

"Excuse me? A series of challenges? What does that mean?" Harper snapped.

"Give him a chance to explain," Flannery urged, leaning forward in her seat.

"This sounds like a distinct conflict of interest for Mr. Cooper. He works for the Historical Society." Harper glowered. That familiar scowl when things weren't going her way.

She looked so much like their mother in that moment that invisible icy fingers wrapped around Flannery's stomach.

Harper pressed her lips together and settled back into her seat. "And by his own admission he cozied up to dear old Granny to gain her confidence."

"What?"

"Your sister is referring to the fact that your grandmother and I formed a bond when I was interviewing her for my book about lighthouses," Grayson explained. "That's why she made me executor of her will and wanted to pass the estate to the Historical Society if you two don't complete the challenge."

"See," Harper said with a dramatic flourish of her hands. "What did I tell you? He's nice to Granny and now he stands to inherit."

"I work as a docent at the Historical Society as a volunteer," Grayson corrected. "It's not as if I'll personally inherit this place."

"No, but for a history buff, getting your hands on the lighthouse must have you salivating." Harper narrowed her eyes.

"I'm not even getting paid as executor." Grayson shook his head as if Harper had disappointed him in some fundamental way, and Flannery felt a strange pang in her gut. She hated conflict of any kind, even if she wasn't involved in it.

"You're getting something out of it." Harper's eyes were mere slits.

"The conditions are in a codicil." He ignored that last comment and shifted through the papers. "Your grandmother asked me to laminate two copies of the codicil for you." He looked at Jonnie and then passed the documents to Harper and Flannery.

Flannery skimmed over the document, her eyes drawn to the bulleted list of rules and regulations, and her throat tightened as she read.

1. The mother dough must be kept alive at all costs.

2. The sourdough must be preserved the same way it was 150 years ago when Levicia Ellis Campbell began the starter after her husband, Ian, built the lighthouse. The mother dough must be stored on the counter and fed at least twice a day, although every eight hours is preferable. No refrigeration allowed.

3. Tending the dough in this way will produce a lot of discard, but the discard must not be thrown away. It is to be used in food preparation. There can be no waste. Jonnie Campbell will supervise the process and provide discard recipes.

4. The challenge will last for six weeks, culminating in the annual Moonglow Cove Fourth of July Bake-Off, during which time my granddaughters must live here on the property and bake together. No exceptions.

5. They cannot accept help from anyone.

6. My granddaughters must enter the bake-off and compete against each other for the winning prize of five thousand dollars.

7. If, at the end of the six weeks, any of these rules have been violated, the inheritance is forfeited, and the property will automatically pass to the Historical Society.

8. However, if my granddaughters successfully complete the six weeks, whoever scores highest in the bake-off inherits it all.

Flannery finished reading and glanced over at her older sister. Harper scowled at the copy of the document in her hands, almost as if she could change what was written there with the intensity of her frown.

Tinny noises of a clashing electronic battle drew Flannery's attention to Willow, who'd unmuted her video game. Flannery put a hand on her daughter's shoulder and leaned over to whisper, "Turn the sound off."

Willow silenced the game but kept playing.

Raising her head, Harper pinned the executor with her stare. "This is manipulative, and I won't be a party to it."

"Flip the document to the back," Grayson said.

Flannery turned the laminated codicil over and read the ninth and final stipulation.

9. Both of my granddaughters must agree to accept the conditions of the will, or neither shall inherit.

"If you walk away, that's fine for you, but it means Flannery can't inherit either," Grayson explained.

"This is bullshit!" Harper exploded. "I've had enough of manipulation and deception!"

Flannery cringed, curled into herself. She had a feeling Harper was talking about far more than this will.

"Mommy," Willow whispered, "that lady cussed."

"She's your aunt Harper," Flannery murmured.

"Sorry," Harper mumbled and looked pained. "I shouldn't have said that."

"I agree with you about the manipulation," Grayson said, locking gazes with Aunt Jonnie. "I told your aunt as much when she brought me this handwritten codicil she found among her mother's things."

"I smell a rat," Harper said. "How did our grandmother know she would die just in time for the six-week period before the bake-off?"

"She didn't." Aunt Jonnie cleared her throat. "She knew it would take about six weeks for you to learn how to work with sourdough bread. That's the reason for the time limit. If she'd died in August, you would have had to wait a whole year to compete and inherit."

"This sounds very unorthodox." Harper's mouth pressed into a hard, straight line.

"There was nothing traditional or orthodox about my mother," Aunt Jonnie muttered.

"So legally, if we challenged it, we'd stand a decent chance of overturning the will?" Harper asked Grayson.

He shrugged. "I'm no lawyer, but my guess? Fifty-fifty odds.

In my understanding of Texas inheritance laws, if you challenged the will and won, then the properties would have to be sold and split down the middle. Jonnie would get half, and you and Flannery would split your mother's half since she is deceased."

"And no one could get the place?" Harper rubbed her chin with a finger and thumb.

"That's right. Unless . . ." He caught Jonnie's eye again. "Any of you wanted to just walk away from the inheritance."

"So we follow the rules laid out in this crazy will, or we can contest the dang thing, waste time and money in court costs, and still lose."

"Yes."

"And even if we win, the property will have to be sold?"

"That's right. One of you could buy out the other two and purchase the place that way. But double-check with your grandmother's lawyer just to be sure I have that right."

"You can bet I'll do that," Harper said.

Flannery's heart was pounding so hard she could hear it in her ears. She wanted no part of this dicey situation, but she needed the inheritance. It was the difference between starting a new life or returning to Alan.

She suppressed a shudder. She simply couldn't allow Willow to grow up in a toxic environment the way Flannery had. This inheritance was her only way out.

"Are you okay with this?" Harper stabbed Flannery with a hot gaze.

"I don't like it," Flannery told her sister. "But I need this."

"You seriously want to go up against me in any kind of competition?" Harper asked.

"I do not."

"Neither one of us knows how to bake, unless you've learned how since the last time we spoke."

"I haven't."

"We'll be on a level playing field." Harper tapped her bottom lip with a chicly manicured fingernail.

"You're considering doing it?" Relief took dread's hand and waltzed across Flannery's stomach.

"If dear old Granny can play dirty, so can we," Harper said. "Whoever wins, we'll agree to split the inheritance with the other. How does that sound?"

"You'd do that?"

"Flannery," Harper said, her voice turning surprisingly tender—the sound of it did CPR on Flannery's dying hopes, the hope that somehow she and her sister would find their way back to each other—"You're my baby sister. *Of course*, I would do that."

Tears pushed at the back of Flannery's eyes again and she blinked hard willing them away. She and her sister had caused each other so much pain, but maybe, just maybe they could get past their differences. If this competition could bring them closer, bring it on.

Harper met Grayson's gaze. "Can we do that? Or did the old bat find a way to muck that up too?"

A bark of laughter burst out of Flannery.

Everyone turned to stare at her, including Willow.

"Sorry," Flannery apologized and ducked her head. "I laugh inappropriately whenever I'm nervous."

"Just like your sister," Grayson said, looking noncommittal, unflappable, and mildly amused. "It's my understanding that you can do whatever you want with the property once you inherit. But again, please double-check with the lawyer."

"You're okay with this?" Harper stabbed a glare at Aunt Jonnie.

"Which part?" Jonnie asked.

"The part where you don't inherit the house."

Their aunt lifted her shoulders in a slight shrug. "I don't want this property. Never have. Too many bad memories. You're welcome to it."

Flannery wanted to ask about those bad memories. She didn't. Instead, she leaned over to kiss the top of Willow's head, her mind filling with the repercussions of accepting this challenge.

"Mommy," Willow said proudly holding up the phone, "I won the treasure chest."

"Look at you," Flannery said. "I knew you could do it. You're so smart."

Willow beamed. "It was easy."

"Maybe it's time to put the game on a harder level?"

Willow extended the phone to her. "Yes, please."

Flannery was so proud of her daughter. Willow wasn't afraid of challenges. She wished she had half of her self-confidence. She reached for the phone and realized everyone was staring at her again.

"What is it?" she asked.

"We're in the middle of something here." Harper cleared her throat.

"Yes," Flannery said, feeling defensive, hope ebbing. "I know that, but my daughter needs my attention. She will always and forever come first."

Harper held up both hands and leaned back in her chair, before folding her arms over her chest and tipping up her chin defiantly.

Oh, Flannery knew that look so well. She felt the tension to the center of her bones. Six years had passed without speaking to her sister, and the old hurts still simmered. She'd been so stupid to think that time and distance might have resolved things. How in the world was she supposed to work with Harper for six weeks, tending some ancient sourdough, without them ending up at each other's throats?

The thought was enough to send her fleeing back to Kansas.

Almost.

But then she thought of Alan and said, "I'm in."

CHAPTER 5

Harper

ACTIVATION: The process of creating a lively, vibrant sourdough starter either through refreshing refrigerated starter or rehydrating and awakening a dehydrated starter.

Harper was furious.

How dare the grandmother she'd never met pit her against her sister? Tia had done enough of that nonsense. She ground her teeth. How badly she wanted to walk away, call an Uber, and fly straight home.

Except she'd thrown her phone over a cliff and Manhattan was a hostile place for her right now.

"What happened to Grandmother Campbell?" Harper asked Aunt Jonnie. "Where is she buried? When was the service held?"

Flannery looked slightly horrified, as if she feared Harper wanted to go find the old lady's grave and spit on it.

Tempting. But Harper wasn't *that* petty. She was just trying to understand the machinations behind her grandmother's actions. She'd spent her life trying to figure out an illogical mother, and now it seemed, the apple hadn't fallen far from the tree. Learning about her grandmother's manipulative behavior went a long way in explaining Tia.

Yes, she was angry. Not an attractive quality, but there it was. She was angry at her mother for lying and telling her that their grandmother was dead when she hadn't been. Now, however, she was starting to understand her mother a little better. Something had made Tia the way she was, and it seemed that something was Penelope J. Campbell.

"She was cremated a week ago," Aunt Jonnie explained. "There was no service per her wishes. I have her ashes whenever you're ready to scatter them. We can do it together."

"I want no part of that." Harper shook her head. "She was your mother. You deal with her ashes."

At the same moment, Flannery said, "How lovely. Thank you for thinking of us. I could write a poem to recite as we scatter them."

Of course, Flannery wanted to write a poem. She'd always been the sweet, gentle one. If she was a book character, she'd be Beth from *Little Women*. Her sister was the kind book nerd that everyone ran over, Harper included. Growing up there had been two ways of dealing with their mother, either fight like hell, or lie down and let her walk all over you. Harper had chosen one path, Flannery the other.

"You two don't present a united front, do you?" Aunt Jonnie asked.

"We're out of sync," Flannery murmured, sparing a glance at her daughter. "Harper and I haven't seen each other in six years."

Or talked to each other. Or written to each other. Or texted. Or told each other some monumental news, like, oh, maybe they'd had a child. A child who needed a wheelchair.

Resentment grabbed a ride on the back of anger. How could Flannery not have told her she had a daughter? Willow's birth should've ended their squabble. It would have if Harper had known.

"It'll take us a while to get our mojo back." Flannery offered a smile that chipped at Harper's stony heart.

Aww damn. She felt like an ass for being so harsh with her tender sister. *Straighten up, Harper, you're no longer on cutthroat Madison Avenue.*

It occurred to her then, how difficult it must've been for Flannery. Raising a baby with no mother or sister to help her. Really no family at all, except for whoever Willow's father was. Hopefully, Willow's dad was a good guy. Hopefully, it wasn't that irresponsible, daredevil Kit.

Harper's gaze dropped to Flannery's ring finger. It was bare. She was an unwed mother? What had she been through all alone?

Suddenly the anger and resentment Harper wore like a cloak turned into grief, pure and raw. Sorrow was a tight fist in her throat. Over the past six years, she'd looked for Flannery on social media, but found no accounts. She tried to call once, but her sister's number went to voice mail and she hung up without leaving a message and Flannery hadn't called her back. Briefly, she'd considered consulting a private investigator, but she'd decided to let things be. If Flannery didn't want any contact with her, she had no choice but to honor her wishes.

Sorrowful tears wanted to crawl down her cheeks, but Harper would not let that happen. She would not cry. She hadn't cried in years and years. Not since she was a small child, when Tia mocked her emotional distress after the death of her pet hamster, calling her a titty baby and telling her to toughen up, because the world hated wimps.

At the time, she'd been five. Willow's age.

So she'd developed an emotional fortress. No one got through. No one hurt her. Years of unshed tears formed a border wall inside her heart. *Never show weakness.* She'd made that her motto. It was the way she got through life. Tough as nails. Hard as concrete.

She wanted to leave. Did not want to face the past or stir up hurt feelings. She wanted everything to go back the way it was. Her ideal life in New York City, where she had it all.

Had.

It was gone now.

Harper bit her bottom lip. Okay, maybe she couldn't go back to New York, but she could get the hell out of Moonglow Cove.

And go where? Do what?

She had a few thousand dollars tucked away, but not enough to start a whole new life from scratch. What would she do for a living? Her reputation was shot. The timing of her grandmother's death and finding out about the inheritance had been uncanny. One day before the Twitter kerfuffle Grayson had called with the news. In hindsight it seemed like a sign.

Yeah, a sign of the apocalypse.

Okay, running away wasn't a real option. She was stuck here, and she had to sort things out with her sister.

New goal. Learn to bake bread, win a bake-off, claim the lighthouse and cottage, sell the property, split the proceeds with Flannery, and *then* get out of Texas.

Harper glanced up from where she'd been staring sightlessly at the codicil and saw Grayson studying her. His eyes were wary, as if she were a suspicious package that he'd found abandoned in a corridor.

"Mommy." Willow tugged on Flannery's sleeve. "I need to go to the baffroom."

Flannery looked at Aunt Jonnie. "Could you direct us?"

Jonnie stood up. "I'll do you one better. I'll show you the way."

"Are the facilities wheelchair accessible?" Flannery's voice held a note of worry. Nothing new about that.

Aunt Jonnie sized up the wheelchair. "Maybe we can maneuver through the door. If not, we can carry her inside."

Getting to her feet, Flannery wrapped her hands around the wheelchair handles and waited for Jonnie to lead the way. They disappeared, leaving Harper and Grayson alone in the kitchen.

"Question," Harper said to him the second they were out of earshot.

"Yes?"

"You knew her. You interviewed her for your book. Why would my grandmother do something like this?"

He shrugged. "Penelope could be eccentric and dramatic. My guess? She wanted to get your attention."

"Or manipulate the hell out of us."

"Distinct possibility with Penelope. The lighthouse and cottage are the final way she can pull the strings."

"Is there any money beyond the properties?"

"Not that I know of, but, again, this is a question for your aunt or your grandmother's lawyer," he said. "To my understanding as executor, Penelope's savings went to pay for her health care. She was in a facility for the last five years. If she'd lived much longer, this place would have been sold to fund her care."

"To your knowledge did she ever ask to see us or our mother?"

"When I visited her, your grandmother didn't talk to me about you."

Ouch. But honestly, why was she surprised?

"But most everyone in Moonglow Cove knows about you and your sister."

That felt unsettling. "They do?"

"Well, mainly as gossip. They know about you to the degree of the hearsay that Tia left town when she got pregnant at seventeen with you, and later had another daughter."

"I see." Harper drew circles in the dust on the table, but honestly, she didn't see. She had a grandmother who'd been alive, but who'd never reached out to her, and an aunt she had known little about beyond being told by her mother that Jonnie was a terrible person. From what she'd seen of Jonnie Campbell so far, that was another of Tia's fabrications.

It was all too much. *This* was why Harper distanced herself from her family. She had the overwhelming urge to fix everything and make it all better and when she couldn't, she felt responsible and broken. It had been much easier to shut them all out. Including the one person she loved more than anything in the world—her sister.

"Are you going to accept the challenge?" Grayson asked.

"I don't know yet."

"Fair enough."

Silence. It did not feel golden.

Harper cleared her throat.

Grayson smiled. It seemed genuine. *He* seemed genuine. All the more reason to steer clear.

"May I ask you a question?" She held his gaze.

"Sure."

"In general, what do the townsfolk think of my family?"

He didn't answer right away, instead running a hand over his jaw. "I try not to pass on other people's opinions."

"That bad, huh?"

"Everyone likes Jonnie."

Ahh, enough said. "Tell me about her."

"She's down-to-earth and minds her own business. She's generous to a fault and would give you the shirt off her back. She's fair and honest, but she doesn't pull any punches." He studied Harper. "You remind me of her."

"Are you buttering me up?"

"Why are you so suspicious?" he countered.

"Because, hey, I don't know any of you people."

Grayson looked so steadfast, so self-assured, Harper felt like a jerk. *Apologize for being snippy.* She was going to, she was about to, but then he spoke.

"I heard about the Twitter thing."

Harper groaned and buried her face in her hands. "I suppose I'm hot gossip around town. You must think I'm horrible."

"I don't believe everything I read on Twitter."

"You're in the minority."

"Sadly, social media seems to have killed the capacity for critical thinking."

Harper sighed. "So you know I don't have much of an option but to stay and see this through."

"We usually have more options than we think. It just depends on how much we want to tell ourselves a victim story."

"Are you telling me off, Mr. Cooper?" She smiled at him, liking him more than she should.

"Is it helping you to pull out of your pity party nosedive?"

"Probably not."

"Yeah, I get that. You gotta find your way out by yourself."

"Are you always this philosophical?"

"You're really attached to absolutes, aren't you? Never. Always."

Was she? Maybe.

More silence. What was taking Flannery and Jonnie so long? Harper squirmed in her chair.

Grayson sat there blandly, saying nothing.

"Are you married?" Harper blurted and was immediately embarrassed. Good grief, why had she asked that?

"No."

"Why not? I mean c'mon, you're gorgeous."

"I was married," he said. "Once upon a time."

"What happened?" she asked, more fascinated than she should have been.

A wistful look passed through his cool blue eyes. "She passed away."

Aww shit. Harper jammed her fingers through her hair. *Open mouth, insert Christian Louboutins. Red soles and all.*

"I'm sorry. That was rude of me," she apologized, unable to meet his unwavering gaze.

"It was a long time ago." His tone was soft, but she heard no pain in his voice.

"What was her name?" *Stop it! Stop asking questions. Leave the poor man alone.*

"Stephanie."

"Such a pretty name."

"She was a pretty person."

"Look," she said, desperately wanting him to like her, even though she had no idea why. "I'm not normally such a jerk."

"We're all jerks sometimes." His eyes were so kind she felt two inches tall. "Being human isn't easy. The Campbells know that more than most."

"Meaning?"

"Drop by the Historical Society sometime and I'll show you around. I'm there from nine to twelve on Saturday mornings."

"Every Saturday?"

"Most of them."

"You're really into history, huh?"

"Those who cannot remember the past are condemned to repeat it," he quoted.

"Who said that?"

"George Santayana."

"Who's he?"

"Drop by the Historical Society and find out."

"Do people ever get tired of you pushing history on them?"

"Quite often."

"And yet, you persist."

"I'm passionate when I'm fully invested in something." His eyes stayed locked on her.

I wish you were fully invested in me.

Seriously? She was losing her marbles. Her skin suddenly felt too tight, and she had an overwhelming urge to shed it. Snakes were lucky, she decided. They could just shuck off their restrictions when they got too tight.

The sound of raindrops pattered against the windowpane, and they both turned to look at the panoramic view of the sea. This place was worth something. The sun was edging closer to the horizon, sending a few golden rays arrowing through the gathering clouds.

"I love rain," Grayson murmured. "It washes things clean."

"What about storms?" Harper asked. "What about hurricanes?"

"All part of Mother Nature's cycles."

"I don't like rain," she said. "It's gloomy."

"It rains a lot here in the spring." His gaze didn't leave her face.

"Just like my luck."

"You should stay through the summer," he said. "Even after the competition is over. It rarely rains after the first two weeks in June."

"What do you do for fun?" she asked, wishing Flannery and Jonnie and Willow would return. "When you're not historying."

"Historying?"

"I'm in advertising. We play fast and loose with words."

"I've noticed." He paused. "I like long walks on the beach."

She almost rolled her eyes at that. "And getting caught in the rain?"

"Please, do not sing the 'Piña Colada' song."

"Aha, did I find something you hate?"

"I try not to hate."

This time she did roll her eyes. "Okay, I'm starting to see why you're single. You're not real."

"Want to know the reason I don't like the 'Piña Colada' song?"

"Besides the awful lyrics? Yes."

"My office is on the seawall near Paradise Pier."

"Paradise Pier?"

"It's the amusement park on the waterfront and that damn song plays on a continuous loop from the Ferris wheel."

"Ooh, you cussed."

"I told you I was passionate when I'm fully invested in something." His pupils widened as he raked his gaze over her.

"And you're fully invested in hating the 'Piña Colada' song?"

Grinning, he nodded. "I am."

"Me too. It truly is a wretched song and your hatred of it makes me like you better already."

He laughed. "I've never met anyone quite like you, Ms. Campbell."

"Ditto, Mr. Cooper."

He pulled a business card from his front pocket and passed it to her. "It's got my personal cell on it," he said and paused before adding, "In case you ever need to talk . . . or want to grab a drink."

"As long as it's not a piña colada."

"Heaven forbid."

They grinned at each other.

She shouldn't feel flattered. But he was a handsome man, and she was a single woman with physical needs. Perhaps he could provide a nice distraction for her during the next six weeks.

Yeah, but did she really want to get involved with a widower?

It's just sex, honeybunch.

And now that she'd actually thought about sex in conjunction with this marvelous hunk of man, she couldn't think about anything else. Her gaze fixed on his mouth and she wondered what he would taste like. Most likely juice box lemonade.

She moistened her lips.

His gaze fixed on her mouth.

Bingo.

He was feeling it too. It had been a while since she'd experienced this kind of chemistry.

Smiling, Harper pocketed his card. Maybe she'd call him, maybe she wouldn't. For now, it was just fun to spin fantasies.

CHAPTER 6

Flannery

HARD WHEAT: Wheat with a high protein content. Suitable for bread baking because of its ability to develop gluten.

The bathroom door was barely wide enough to accommodate Willow's wheelchair, but Flannery and Aunt Jonnie managed to roll it into the tight space.

"Mommy," Willow said as she settled onto the toilet. "Privacy."

Her daughter was serving her words back to her as Flannery had been teaching Willow about boundaries. Her goal had been to keep Willow from constantly following her to the bathroom, but she'd never thought about it in reverse.

"You sure you don't need any help?"

"*Mommy!*"

"Okay, okay, we're going." Flannery motioned for Aunt Jonnie to follow her, collapsing the wheelchair so they could squeeze by it on their way out.

Once in the hallway, Flannery shut the door behind them. The corridor was long, narrow, and dark with wood paneling. It smelled musty. A seaside cottage closed up for far too long.

If it were her house, she'd paint everything white and banish the darkness.

"How are you holding up?" Jonnie asked.

It had been quite some time since anyone had asked how she was doing. The kindness of the question pierced her heart. She wasn't like Harper. She was no good at tamping down her tender feelings and she considered it a personal failing.

"Flannery?"

Looking into the kind eyes of the aunt she'd never had the opportunity to know, a single tear slid down her cheek.

She'd been robbed of family in so many ways. Their mother severing ties with their aunt before they were born and lying about their grandmother being dead. The nomadic childhood. The revolving door of men coming in and out of their lives. Her own father finally giving up on seeing her because dealing with Tia had simply gotten too much for him.

But the hurt ran far deeper than that.

The pain of the past six years was like a sudden bullet. All the stark power of Flannery's suffering condensed into one tiny metal casing of grief pierced her heart. The loss. So much raw loss.

First there had been Tia's fatal heart attack, quickly followed by Harper's angry explosion and the fatal rupture that had ended their relationship.

Harper.

The one constant in Flannery's life was gone in an instant over ugly words, harsh accusations, and miserable misunderstandings. She could still feel the devastation of Harper's rage as her sister had blamed her for their mother's condition.

In her mind's eye, Flannery could still see the older sister she'd adored with all her soul, shaking and red-faced, screaming in the cemetery. Harper had ranted about working eighty hours a week at two jobs for years to support her and Tia. Saying that the least Flannery could have done was make sure their mother hadn't eaten herself to death.

"It's all your fault!" Harper had yelled. "She's dead because *you* fed her Twinkies and french fries."

It was true that Harper had been their only means of support—Tia had lost Flannery's child support money when she'd turned eighteen—and Flannery couldn't deny that. Plus, Flannery couldn't work because someone had to look after Tia who had gotten so obese she couldn't even get out of bed.

But Harper made it sound like Flannery had intentionally fed Tia unhealthy meals. She'd tried her best to offer nutritious food, but Tia had a cell phone and a credit card, and the grocery store delivered. Flannery had only been nineteen and groomed from infancy to meet Tia's needs. How was she supposed to fight those odds?

From Flannery's point of view, Harper was to blame. She'd abandoned them. Taking off to make her fortune in New York when Flannery was just fifteen, sending home money to appease her guilty conscience for not visiting nearly often enough. For not sharing any of the physical and emotional burden of caring for their difficult mother because she thought money got her off the hook. Harper had been the golden child. She had no idea what it was like to be the scapegoat—the butt of their mother's disdain and disregard.

Shocked by her beloved sister's verbal assault, in that emotion-fueled moment, Flannery had done what she needed to do to protect herself. She'd told Harper to never contact her again.

What she hadn't expected was that Harper would take her at face value and completely disappear from her life.

Then there'd been Flannery's starry-eyed union with Kit, the wild young man who'd infatuated her, then had promptly gotten himself killed in a drag race. Without anyone to fall back on, pregnant at twenty, she'd then stumbled into her foolhardy marriage with Alan.

And then Willow being born with a serious form of spina bifida, a congenital condition that would in all likelihood leave her in a wheelchair for the rest of her life.

Flannery drew in a breath and flicked the tear away.

"Life's been hard for you." Aunt Jonnie touched her hand.

All this time, she could have had the comfort of a caring auntie. That feeling of being cheated swept over Flannery again. How badly she wanted to fling herself into the arms of the woman she'd never known.

Another one of Flannery's failings. Seeking validation from others. She nodded, unable to speak. If she started talking about it, she might never shut up.

"Stoicism," Jonnie said. "It's the Campbell way."

Oh, but she wasn't stoic. Not at all. She was hypersensitive. A crybaby. In case she ever forgot, Alan listed her failings on a daily basis.

"Where do you live?" Flannery asked, shifting the topic. From the kitchen she heard murmured laughter. At least Harper was enjoying herself.

"On a houseboat in the Moonglow marina," Aunt Jonnie said.

"That sounds like fun."

Jonnie shrugged. "It's just like any other house, except it rocks."

"Do you ever get seasick?"

"I'm a Campbell, of course not. We have sailor DNA."

"I don't know if I get seasick or not. I've never been out on the ocean."

"Huh?" Jonnie grunted. "For real? We need to fix that while you're here."

If she stayed in Moonglow Cove. Then again, where else would she go? Not back to Alan if she could help it.

"Who's going on a boat?" Willow called from the bathroom.

"Are you eavesdropping?" Flannery called back.

Willow giggled.

Flannery lowered her voice, "I have to be careful. She's sharp as a tack."

"That's in the Campbell DNA too. Smart but . . ." Aunt Jonnie broke off, shook her head, toed the floor with the tip of her rubber boot as if doing so could erase the thought in her mind.

Flannery wanted to ask what else was in the Campbell DNA but was afraid to hear the answers. Instead, she said, "I really need this inheritance."

Her aunt studied her. "It's just for six weeks. All you have to do is keep the sourdough starter alive, learn how to bake, enter the competition, and get along with your sister."

Was Jonnie being sarcastic? "That's like saying climbing Mount Everest is easy-peasy."

"You sound like Tia." Jonnie gave her a tender smile. "Your mother had a flair for the dramatic."

"Another understatement, Auntie." Flannery smiled back.

"Your mom stomped all over your tender heart, didn't she?"

Again, Flannery nodded silently. Her aunt knew her mother

in a way Flannery never had. Maybe, during the course of this trip, she could figure out why Tia had been the way she was.

"Thank you for writing me when she passed away." Jonnie's voice caught a little on the last word. "I should have written you back. I just . . . well . . . it had been decades since I'd seen my . . ." Jonnie's voice thickened with emotion. "Sister."

Flannery felt the echo of the word resonate inside her. Sisterly estrangement was awful. Empathy for Jonnie sent a fresh tear trickling down her cheek.

"I shouldn't have waited so long to write to you," Flannery said. "Mom asked me not to ever tell you if she died, but in the end, I couldn't honor her wishes. I mean, I'd want to know if something happened to Harper. I'd be devastated if she passed away and I didn't find out for years."

"You and Harper have been apart for a long time?"

Flannery touched the tip of her tongue to her upper lip. "Since Mom's funeral. There was a horrible graveside scene and . . ."

"You haven't spoken to her since." Aunt Jonnie stared off down the hallway, her gaze fixed as if staring into the past. "I don't blame you for not telling me that Tia was sick. I'm just grateful you did let me know when she passed."

"Thank you for your understanding."

"Thank you for not hating me because I never responded to your letter."

Why hadn't she responded? Flannery wanted to ask her but didn't.

Aunt Jonnie looked as if she ached to put a hand on Flannery's arm, but she stuck her hands in the pockets of her yellow rain slicker instead. "I *am* sorry."

"Why? You didn't do anything wrong."

"That's just it. I didn't do anything." Jonnie shook her head and hunched her shoulders. "There's so much you don't know."

Her aunt's words sounded slightly ominous and in those close quarters, just the two of them standing in front the bathroom door, Flannery felt vulnerable and overwhelmed.

"I heard the executor call you Ms. Campbell. You've never married?" Flannery asked.

"No."

"No children?"

A pained expression crossed Jonnie's face, letting Flannery know she'd gotten too nosy. Had Jonnie lost a baby? Her heart wrenched at the idea.

"Mommy?"

"I'm here, Willow." Flannery pushed the door open a crack. "What is it? What do you need, honey?"

"There's no TP."

"My bad," Jonnie said. "I should've gotten the house ready for you, but I've been so busy at work I haven't had a chance to pop over."

"What do you do for a living?" Flannery asked as she dug in her purse for the packet of tissues that she always carried with her and pushed open the door to hand the tissues to her daughter.

"I'm a shrimper," Jonnie said.

That surprised her. "You own your own fishing boat?"

"Shrimping boat," Jonnie said proudly. "Actually, I own three."

"Wow, you're very successful." Flannery was impressed. A woman in her sixties running her own shrimping company? She could totally see Jonnie hauling in nets. She certainly looked strong enough.

"Modestly successful. Shrimping is a tough business. I don't work the traps anymore. Arthritis." She rotated her shoulder. "Mostly, I don't even go out on the boats these days. Just ride a desk and oversee twenty employees."

"Canna go out on your boat sometime?" Willow asked, flushing the toilet.

"You absolutely may," Jonnie said. "Fair warning, a shrimp boat is stinky, but you get used to the smell."

"Maybe let's have this conversation somewhere other than the bathroom?" Flannery said to Willow. "Let's wash your hands and get out of here."

"And then we can go eat?" Willow rearranged her clothes as Flannery positioned the wheelchair near the toilet.

"I've got animal crackers in my purse." She had to conserve her money.

"No, Mommy. *Real* food." Willow adroitly deposited herself into the wheelchair and backed it up to the sink so that she could wash her hands. "Oops, no soap."

"I really must get some supplies up here, now that I know you're going to stay," Jonnie said. "I didn't want to haul it all up if you weren't going to stick around."

"No worries." Flannery took hand sanitizer from her purse and squirted a dollop into Willow's open palms.

"There's no food in the house," Jonnie said. "Again, my fault. We could all go out to eat, or I could pop off to the grocery store and bring back supplies. You're going to need flour for sure. The mother dough should be fed twice a day. She's been stored in the refrigerator, just waiting for you girls to show up."

Flannery knew absolutely nothing about baking and even less about the specifics of sourdough. Aunt Jonnie made it sound as if bread dough was human. Something you had to feed to keep alive.

Something with an identity.

"How about we all four go to the grocery store," Harper asked from behind them. "It'll be our first outing together as a *family*."

They turned to see Harper standing in the hallway. It could've been a sweet moment, except for Harper's sarcastic tone.

Flannery chose to ignore her sister's inflection and roll with the sentiment. She wasn't looking forward to the time she'd be alone with Harper and wondered how long she could put that off. "I think that's a great idea."

Harper eyed her.

Flannery had forgotten how intense her sister's stare could be. Turning to Aunt Jonnie, she said, "Do you have a vehicle that will haul us all? Including Willow's wheelchair? My minivan is loaded down with everything I own and there's not enough room for everyone."

Eek, should she have admitted that? Did it matter? They'd find out eventually she was on the run from her former life.

"Yep," Aunt Jonnie said. "I do."

Flannery thought about taking that darn elevator back down the bluff and felt her stomach fly into her throat. When they got outside, she headed for the incline that led to the cul-de-sac with Willow in her wheelchair and everyone else just followed.

The executor included.

She noticed Harper kept glancing over at Grayson. She didn't blame her. The man was worth staring at.

Grayson went to a mountain bicycle parked outside the back door, slipped on the helmet left dangling from the handlebars. Looking impossibly dashing in his suit and tie, briefcase tucked in the handlebar wire basket, he waved good-bye, and cycled past them.

* * *

Fifteen minutes later, Flannery watched Harper glowering at the array of flour on the shelves of the baking aisle.

"I rarely cooked, and never bake," Harper muttered as if to herself. "Not with the high-quality bakeries in Manhattan."

"But this isn't New York City, is it?" Aunt Jonnie said evenly.

Surrounded by her estranged half sister, her daughter, and the aunt she didn't know, Flannery studied the offerings. There were bags of flour, bleached and unbleached. High-protein and masa. Flour made from brown rice and coconuts and almonds. Organic flour and free trade flour. There was spelt and amaranth and millet. Whole-wheat and buckwheat and rye. How on earth did you decide?

"Bread," Harper mumbled. "It had to be bread. And here I've been low carb for ten years."

Aah, that was how she still fit into a size two. Flannery put a hand to her belly; the last time she'd seen Harper, Flannery had been three sizes smaller, but she didn't feel ashamed. At a size twelve she felt sturdier, stronger, more able to hold her own than when she'd been thinner.

Plus, her weight irritated her husband. Anything to subtly get under Alan's skin. Flannery covered a smile with her hand.

"What do we buy?" Harper looked as confused as Flannery felt.

"No idea. The only thing Willow and I make are slice-and-bake cookies."

"Yum," Willow said and rubbed her tummy. "Cookies. Can we get some?"

"Not today." Flannery put a hand to Willow's head.

Willow's bottom lip pooched out, but she didn't make a thing of it.

Jonnie's eyes twinkled. "You girls are going to have so much fun learning about the joys of sourdough."

"You have wacky ideas about fun." Harper shook her head. "My experiences with baking . . . Well, honestly, a root canal sounds more fun."

"Now who has a wacky idea about fun?" Aunt Jonnie laughed. "Just you wait. Sourdough will soon have you singing a different tune."

It was the first time Flannery had heard her aunt laugh. On the surface, she seemed a serious woman. One who considered fun something of a nuisance. A woman much like Harper herself. Intense. Focused.

"Mommy," Willow asked, "can we get McDonald's after this?"

Flannery looked to Aunt Jonnie. "May we?"

Harper rolled her eyes. "Why are you asking permission? You're a grown adult. Aunt Jonnie, Willow wants to stop at McDonald's."

"We don't have a McDonald's in Moonglow Cove," Aunt Jonnie said. "But we have a Burger Box. Will that do?"

"Do they have Happy Meals?" Willow asked hopefully.

"No, honey, I'm afraid they don't, but they have the most delicious burgers, and their fries are out of this world." Jonnie's voice was tender.

"Okay, then." Willow nodded cheerfully, accepting the verdict. Thank heavens she was an easygoing child.

Whatever struggles Flannery had gone through, she'd managed to shield Willow from the brunt of it. Or so she told herself. But Willow was getting older and things with Alan were worsening. Flannery didn't know how much longer she'd be able to protect her child from his volatile mood swings. It was the main reason she'd finally found the courage to get out.

"Let's wrap this up," Aunt Jonnie said, tapping the face of her watch. "I have a meeting tonight at nine."

What kind of meeting started that late?

"I know the sourdough 'rules' say we can't ask for help baking the bread." Harper stuck a five-pound bag of bleached white flour into the cart. "But could you help us gather the ingredients, since I have absolutely no idea what we'll need?"

"That I can do," Aunt Jonnie said. "First of all, no bleached flour. It inhibits bacterial growth."

"We want bacterial growth?" Flannery asked, concerned. She was a bit of a germaphobe, and the dusty keeper's cottage had already made her anxious.

"Sourdough starter *is* bacteria." Aunt Jonnie took the bleached flour from the cart and put it back on the shelf.

"Eww," Harper said. "That's disgusting."

"It's simply the process. You really don't know anything about bread making, do you? No worries, that'll soon change."

Efficient as a machine, their aunt began pulling supplies off the shelves—baking powder, baking soda, salt, olive oil, coconut oil, sacks of sugar and unbleached flour. A lot of flour. Twenty-five-pound bags. Three of them. Along with two bags of whole-wheat flour and one of rye.

"Do we really need that much flour?" Harper blinked at the cart.

"You don't want to have to run to the store every other day for flour. Remember, per your grandmother's rules, you have to bake with the discard." Aunt Jonnie tossed in handfuls of yeast packets. "You'll thank me later."

"I thought you used sourdough in place of yeast." Flannery frowned, trying to sort this out. "What's the yeast for?"

"Some recipes, like pizza dough, still require some yeast, along with the sourdough levain," Aunt Jonnie said.

"We gonna make homemade pizza?" Willow asked.

"So much pizza." Aunt Jonnie chucked Willow under her chin. "Now, on to the dairy case."

"How are we going to pay for all this?" Flannery worried.

"My mother left a stipend to cover the cost of ingredients," said Aunt Jonnie.

"Good thing," Harper muttered.

What did she mean by that? Flannery eyed her sister. There was a tension in Harper's voice that alerted her to something going on beneath the surface. Was she having financial difficulties?

Before she could put her finger on it, Harper turned away, following Jonnie and Willow to the refrigerated section.

Flannery trailed after them, rounding the corner of the aisle just in time to see a well-heeled, middle-aged woman, dressed in a tennis outfit a size too small, racing over to her touch-me-not sister, arms outstretched to wrap Harper in a bear hug as she hollered in a frantic Adderall drawl, "*Harrrper!*"

CHAPTER 7

Harper

KNOCKING BACK: The process of knocking excess air out of the dough after the bulk proof that makes for a more even texture in the bread.

Right there in the aisle of Whole Foods, Harper froze. Legit, could not move.

Not just her body, but her brain, too, shriveling and closing as it shut down. Who was this aggressive woman and why was she folding her arms around Harper and squeezing her as if she was a long-lost daughter?

Oh, for God's sake, now the woman is crying. Not just trickling tears, but full-on, snot-dripping sobbing. Harper stiffened in the woman's embrace.

Flannery, the helpful thing, pulled handfuls of tissues from her pocket and thrust them at the woman, who finally broke the hug so she could take a thick wad of powder-blue Kleenex. "They're lotion infused."

"I can't believe it's you! I can't believe you're here in Moonglow Cove!" the woman blubbered. "Oh, Harper!"

Desperate to get out of this intrusive hug, Harper met Aunt Jonnie's gaze. Telegraphed her a message. *Help!*

"Harper, this is Missy Sinclair," Aunt Jonnie said. "Missy's husband, Ward Sinclair, is the mayor of Moonglow Cove."

"Harper knows who I am!" Missy Sinclair scrubbed at her eyes, smearing mascara and tears over her face.

No, no I do not.

The fiftyish woman, now looking rather raccoonish, studied Harper. "I am so, so sorry about Tia. I wanted to come to the memorial service, but I read in the obituary where it was family only."

How had the woman known Tia had passed away? Another mystery to add to the growing list of puzzles.

Tia hadn't wanted any announcement of her passing. No obit, no memorial service, but Harper had vetoed her mother's wishes. Death rituals were for the living and denying the survivors a way of processing their grief was pure selfishness in Harper's estimation and Flannery had agreed.

For once in her life, Harper won an argument with her mother solely because Tia had been dead.

"If people can't come see me when I'm alive, they don't need to be there when I die," Tia had been fond of saying whenever the topic arose. And then no one had shown up beyond Flannery's father, Tia's next-door neighbor, and an ex-boyfriend who'd cried harder than anyone else.

Scratch that.

Tia's ex-boyfriend been the *only* one crying and that saddened Harper more than anything else. In the end, their mother had a point about the memorial service. That was where Harper and Flannery had had their horrible falling-out. Honestly, it was the only time in their lives that they'd ever fought, and it had ripped them apart.

The flashback swept over Harper right there in the middle of the Whole Foods dairy section. She inhaled sharply and knotted her hands into fists, as her mind catapulted back to that awful, overcast day of Tia's memorial service when she'd walked into that gloomy little house Flannery had shared with their mother in Kansas City.

From the minute Harper saw how Tia and her then nineteen-year-old sister were living, anger took hold and she simply couldn't shake it off. Back then, she hadn't known how to deal with her anger. Hadn't yet been to therapy or learned to meditate.

The rooms had been stuffed floor to ceiling with books. All kinds of books. Nothing new about that. Tia had loved to read. Fiction, nonfiction, how-to. Library books bought from fundraiser events. Paperbacks with Walmart discount stickers on the covers. Hardcover remainders. Trade-size books. Garage sale finds stripped of covers. There was no order, no rhyme or reason to the stacks and shelves. Romance novels stood beside tomes on ancient Egypt. Mark Twain rubbed elbows with Richard Dawkins. *The Thornbirds* kissed *Spanish for Dummies.*

The house smelled sweetishly musty. An overwhelming odor that turned Harper's stomach. From a young age, she associated that smell with her mother, with her sudden fits of rage and prolonged crying jags, with threats of suicide and corporal punishment, mercilessly beating her young daughters with a belt whenever she was in one of her dark moods.

Harper had flown down to help Tia and Flannery move into the bungalow six months earlier, after Tia's sixth and final husband, Agnew Blanks, threw them out of his house and divorced her. They'd had a prenup, a smart move on Agnew's part, so Tia hadn't gotten much in the settlement. Harper had no idea how her mother had managed to acquire so many books in such a short time, especially since Tia didn't leave the house anymore.

Her dismay grew as she explored the kitchen. The cabinets, pantry, and refrigerator were filled with junk food. At the end of her days, Tia had done nothing but lie in bed, reading and eating.

When she'd died of a massive heart attack at age forty-four, their mother had weighed over four hundred pounds. Tia, the gorgeous fashion plate, who'd once rocked a size two, had fully lost control over herself after her last divorce and had systematically set about eating herself to death.

Seeing the freezer packed with frozen pizza and ice cream, the pantry bursting with double-stuffed Oreos and cheese puffs, Harper's anger had stewed, until finally at the memorial service, she'd gone off on Flannery for enabling their mother's food addiction. Yelling at her that she'd killed their mom as surely as if she'd supplied Tia with heroin.

It had not been Harper's finest moment.

Flannery had countered that their mother's condition was Harper's fault. That she'd run off to New York and left a teenager to deal with Tia all alone and Flannery had handled things the only way she knew how—do whatever it took to keep their mother's fragile mental health on a steady keel, even at the expense of her physical health.

Harper could still remember how her body trembled so hard, rage shooting poisonous adrenaline through her veins.

"I *had* to work," she'd roared at Flannery. "I had to make money to pay for you and Tia. No one else was going to do it."

Flannery had burst into tears. She told Harper she didn't need her. Didn't want her money. That she never wanted to hear from her again.

Flannery's words had bludgeoned Harper as a ponytailed young man pulled up to the cemetery in a Vintage Mustang rumbling loudly without a muffler. "I don't need you. I have Kit. We're in love. Never, ever contact me again!"

And so she hadn't.

In hindsight, Harper could see how they'd just been lashing out at each other. Both hurting, shoving each other away when they should have been holding each other close. Instead of clinging to their connection, they'd severed it.

Blinking, Harper came back into her body, cold air from the refrigeration units blowing on the back of her neck. She looked over Missy Sinclair's shoulder and caught her sister's eye, aching for what they'd lost.

Once upon a time, they'd been each other's lifeline. Now, thanks to Penelope Campbell's insane will, they were anchors strangling each other's necks.

Missy smiled brightly, a bit too forced, and turned to Flannery. "You must be Tia's youngest. You were barely out of diapers when I came to visit your mom in Charlottesville."

That must've been when Tia was attending graduate school at the University of Virginia, after she left Flannery's father. Harper would've been ten. How had Mrs. Sinclair recognized her after all this time?

During that period, they'd been living in a rented duplex not far from the university campus. Tia rode a pink bicycle, with a white wicker basket attached to the handlebars, to the school where she worked as a graduate assistant in the English department. Harper often begged to ride the bike, but Tia wouldn't let her. It was their only means of transportation until Tia started dating Brooks Johnson solely because he owned a Bentley and looked good in tight jeans.

Harper had liked Brooks, but he hadn't lasted long. A marriage so short, it really shouldn't have counted. Less than a year later and Tia was back on the market. But by then, Tia was driving Brooks's Bentley and sporting a newly minted master's degree in English lit.

"You look so much like your mother," Missy Sinclair said, settling that question of how she'd recognized Harper. "For a second I thought I was seeing a ghost."

"Missy and your mother were best friends all through high school," Aunt Jonnie explained. "If you want to know anything about Tia's past, Missy is the place to start."

Why would she want to know that? Harper had no interest in Tia's ancient history. And no desire to find out who her father was either. Tia would never tell her who he was, and she was good with that. Interesting question, if she *did* want to know, why wouldn't she start with Aunt Jonnie, her mother's older sister?

Flannery shook the woman's hand, murmured pleasantries, and introduced her to Willow, who Missy hugged and gushed over.

Willow got a deer-in-the-headlights look and Harper rescued her, calling Missy's name to get the woman to straighten and turn back to her.

"Yes?" Missy blinked.

Willow gave Harper a thumbs-up behind Missy's back.

She liked that kid, but now she had to think of a question to ask Missy. "Um, um . . . what clique did you and my mother hang out with in high school?"

"Oh, we were the popular ones." Missy fluffed her expertly dyed platinum-blond hair and giggled. "Tia was head cheerleader."

Yeah, Harper knew that. It's why she'd tried out for cheerleader in high school and made the squad but then Tia got all weird about it and insisted Harper quit because there'd be no one to look after Flannery while she was at work. It wasn't until years later Harper pieced together that her mother had been jealous. Super odd because Tia had been the one pushing the cheerleading.

"Tia always said she was too smart for this town." Missy gave a wistful sigh, as if wishing she'd escaped Moonglow Cove.

"Mom said that about a lot of towns." And a lot of men.

Harper toyed with the plastic sleeve around the handle of the grocery cart she'd been pushing before she got waylaid by Missy Sinclair. The plastic covering was chipped, and she dug her fingernail into the crack, widening the split and breaking off a chunk. The grocery store logo imprinted into the plastic now read *hole Foods.*

"Do you remember the four of us went out to eat at a little shack by the beach that had the best remoulade sauce and out-of-this-world crab cakes? I can still taste them." Missy sighed again, rhapsodically this time, enchanted by long-ago seafood.

Harper drudged up a fuzzy memory. She remembered a song. "Dead Skunk in the Middle of the Road."

"We sat outside and there was a live band, playing seaside music. Your mother and I drank Long Island iced teas and danced together on the wooden deck to the 'Piña Colada' song. It was a magical night."

The floodgates opened and suddenly that night came into sharp focus. It might have been magical for Missy Sinclair, but it'd been hellacious for Harper. At some point during the evening, probably after one Long Island iced tea turned into three, Missy and Tia had gotten into a spat.

The event was suddenly scratched so vividly in her mind, Harper wondered how she'd ever forgotten it. Self-protection most likely. If she could remember everything about her childhood, she would've jumped off a cliff long ago. A therapist once told her that the mind closed down trauma it couldn't deal with. She really didn't want to deal with it now, but once roused the memory was fully blown and there wasn't anything that she could do to shut it down again.

The song that was playing during Tia and Missy's fight became an earworm, playing low and steady through Harper's noggin. "Sometimes Love Just Ain't Enough," a passable cover of Patty Smyth and Don Henley's popular duet.

Harper's feet were bare, and she'd gotten a splinter in her big toe from anxiously running her foot across the weathered wood decking waiting for the night to be over. When she'd asked Tia to pluck the splinter out, her mother, sloppy-eyed and slurring, had said, "Suck it up, Buttercup."

Harper tried to remove the splinter herself, but yelped in pain.

"*Shh*," Missy had hissed drunkenly, putting an index finger against her lipsticked mouth. "I'll get it out for you, sweetie baby."

When Missy got up to come around the picnic table, Tia put a restraining hand on her friend's wrist. "Leave her be, she's got to learn how to take care of herself. No one else is going to do it for her. She needs to learn that hard lesson right now. Nobody cares about her. *Nobody.*"

Looking confused, Missy had plunked down on the bench beside Tia. "But you care about her, right? You love your kids."

"Sure, sure. We're living a Hallmark dream." Tia ordered another round of Long Island iced teas and that placated Missy.

Eventually, Harper worked up the courage to dig out the splinter herself, just in time to clean up after Tia upchucked crab cakes and remoulade sauce onto the deck at Harper's feet.

"I'm also sorry to hear about your Twitter troubles," Missy now went on, putting a hand to Harper's shoulder and pulling her back to the present. "I understand how things get twisted in translation. My husband is in politics after all. Social media can quickly mount a bullying mob. Especially Twitter."

Aw crap, Missy knew about the social media kerfuffle too? Harper supposed everyone in this small town did.

"Twitter troubles?" Flannery whipped her head around to stare at Harper. "What's she talking about, Harp?"

Harp. Flannery was the only one who ever called her that. It sounded friendly coming off her sister's tongue and for a second Harper let herself believe everything was going to be all right between them.

Missy blinked at Flannery. "You don't know?"

"Know what?" Her sister turned back to Missy.

Missy put a hand over her mouth. "Oh my, you haven't told them yet. I'm sorry, I simply assumed . . ."

"You know what they say about assuming," Aunt Jonnie said with a frosty bite in her voice. "Ass. You. Me."

"Tell us what?" Flannery rolled a tissue into a tight ball between her fingers, fuzzy lint falling to the grocery store floor. Harper could feel her sister's gathering anxiety because she had plenty of it herself.

Harper needed to get out in front of this and control the narrative. She didn't trust what Missy Sinclair might say next. "I remember you left us at the crab shack, and I had to get my drunken mother and three-year-old sister back home on a pink Schwinn, after you and Tia had a knock-down drag-out."

"I never did that. That never happened. We didn't have a fight." Missy looked a bit panicky.

"You pulled each other's hair. Tia snatched out a patch of yours, right here." Harper leaned over to touch Missy's scalp just above her temple.

The other woman drew back, flinching, and Harper dropped her hand.

"You're misremembering. I definitely gave you a ride home." Missy placed a hand over her heart to aid the denial of culpability.

But Harper saw the quick flicker of truth in her eyes. Missy Sinclair was gaslighting her.

"That's not how I recall it," Harper said, standing her ground. Going after Missy's vulnerable spots was working wonders in keeping the topic off her Twitter debacle.

"You were only ten, and you didn't even remember me until I reminded you. I'm not sure we can trust your version of events." Missy laughed skittishly.

Ooh. Missy was sensitive about leaving them stranded. Good to know.

"It's been nice seeing you again," Harper said, offering a convivial smile. She had to thank Tia for that skill. Her mother had shown her how to make nice to someone's face, no matter what she thought about them privately. The two-faced talent had served her well in her advertising.

"Oh honey, you aren't getting off the hook that easy." Missy scooted aside to let a customer go by. "You're absolutely coming to my Memorial Day dinner party, all of you and I won't take no for an answer."

Before Harper could come up with an excuse to wriggle off the hook, Flannery said, "We would be delighted to accept your invitation, Mrs. Sinclair."

* * *

Aunt Jonnie deposited them in the dead-end cul-de-sac beside Flannery's minivan parked in the overgrowth of sea oats. She helped them unload groceries and Willow's wheelchair but announced she couldn't miss her meeting and they'd have to get the supplies up to the cottage on their own. She passed Harper the house key and took off.

Dusk cooled the air and wind whipped their hair around their faces. The smell of the sea blew in strong and landed salty water on their lips.

Harper peered up at the steep incline, and then back down to the cloth bags of groceries surrounding them, trying to calculate if they could carry everything in one trip. She was still wearing her high heels. Aunt Jonnie had supplied the tote bags and they were overflowing.

No way. Not with all that heavy flour. In fact, two trips might not do it.

As if reading her thoughts, Flannery said, "I need to unload our things from the minivan, too. The essentials at least."

Never a shirker, Harper nodded. No sense standing around. They had work to do.

Harper shouldered as many of the bags as she could carry, put her head down against the wind, and headed for the steep path to the lighthouse.

"Where are you going?" Flannery called.

Harper half turned to look at her sister. "To the Leaning Lighthouse of Moonglow Cove. Where else?"

"It really does lean, doesn't it," Flannery mused. "I thought it was my imagination."

"Nope. The lighthouse definitely looks suicidal."

Flanner shot her a look and inclined her head toward Willow.

Harper lifted her shoulders. "Sorry."

"There's a better way," Flannery said.

"Huh?"

"Better than walking." She pointed in the thickening darkness toward a sign mostly hidden by brambles.

Harper squinted and read: ELEVATOR TO THE TOP. *Daughter-of-a-witch, there was an elevator? Thank heavens.*

"Although the elevator did stall on the way up," Flannery said, suddenly sounding uncertain. "Maybe we *should* walk."

"Not if there's another option." Harper changed directions, heading where the arrow pointed.

"Wait," Willow called.

Her shoulders aching from the heavy totes filled with flour, Harper paused again and took a deep breath to quell her irritation. She just wanted to get this over with. "Yes?"

"I can help," the little girl's voice was sturdy and clear.

"How?"

Willow patted her lap.

What? "Actually, that's an excellent idea."

Willow preened, tossing her head, and offering up a big smile. "Told ya' my wheels are my superpower."

"You ain't lying, kid, but are you sure? These sacks are heavy."

Willow scooted to one side of the wheelchair and waved at the empty spot she'd made. Harper returned, eased the bags from her shoulders and settled them beside her niece.

"Your child is wise beyond her years," Harper told Flannery.

"She's had to be," Flannery said.

Harper wondered what that meant, but it wasn't the time or place to dig into that conversation.

"I have an even better idea," Flannery said, glossing over her own comment as if she regretted making it. "I'll carry Willow and we can put everything in the wheelchair."

"Okay. Problem solved." Harper busied herself with getting the groceries and a suitcase from Flannery's vehicle loaded into the wheelchair. The rest of Flannery's possessions would have to wait until morning. Granted, loaded down this way the wheelchair was pretty hard to push, but it was better than making several trips in the dark.

And it *was* freakishly dark. There were no streetlamps out here and the lights of Moonglow Boulevard glimmered half a mile in the distance.

Even the lighthouse was dark. But of course, there was no caretaker. No one to switch on the light. Although they'd left the lamp on in the mudroom, they couldn't see it because the door was closed and there was no windowpane in the mudroom door. In the future, Harper would make sure to switch on the porch light when they expected to return in the dark.

Carrying Willow, Flannery led the way to the elevator and

Harper tried not to think what lay ahead of them over the course of the next six weeks. At the moment, it was simply too overwhelming.

For now, they had a singular goal. Get the stuff to the cottage, unpack everything, and drop into bed. Exhausted as she was, even that felt monumental. Where would they sleep? Were there clean bedsheets? Were they supposed to feed that stupid mother dough tonight and if so, what did they feed it and how much?

"Are you spiraling?" Flannery asked as they stepped into the creaky metal elevator.

"How did you know?" Harper asked.

"My anxiety is getting the better of me, too," her sister admitted. "I'm scared this hunk of junk will strand us again."

"One step at a time. We can do this."

"You sure?"

Harper gave a wry smile. "What's the worst that can happen? We die trying?"

"We're not gonna die, are we, Mommy?" Willow whimpered.

Aww crap. She needed a zipper for her big mouth.

"No, sweetheart, Auntie Harper is just exaggerating."

"Like Daddy does?"

"Yes," Flannery murmured. "Like Daddy does sometimes."

Harper saw Willow squeeze her mother's neck tighter and hang on for dear life. She felt like crud. She really had to start monitoring her words around the child. Willow didn't miss a trick.

Flannery pushed the button and the elevator jerked to life.

The cage was pretty small, just big enough for the three of them and the wheelchair, and already Harper could feel the creeping fingers of dread close over her spine and give her a good, hard shake.

"I didn't mean to upset her," Harper murmured.

"I know," Flannery said in that calm, accepting voice that used to put Harper's teeth on edge. There were times when she'd begged Flannery to fight back, but she never had until she'd told Harper off at Tia's funeral.

Now, she found Flannery's placidness soothing. Maybe the next six weeks wouldn't suck major buckets after all. Maybe she and Flannery could find their way back to each other.

That hope lifted her spirits. She wanted nothing more than to mend the rift, but it would take a lot of hard work and effort to get there. Not that Harper was afraid of hard work. Hard work was her default setting. Whenever things went bad, she put her nose to the grindstone and kept going.

Three days ago, she'd been living a completely different kind of life. Three days from now? Well, who knew where she'd be? Harper knew only one thing. Her life was out of control and she hated feeling helpless.

The elevator settled into place and the creaky door hinged open. Harper held back, letting Flannery and Willow disembark first, then she pushed the wheelchair filled with supplies out onto the bluff. Already stars filled the sky like scattered diamonds. Harper glanced heavenward, saw a shooting star streak across.

"Make a wish," Flannery said to Willow, pointing as her finger tracked the star's path.

"I wish for—"

"Don't tell anyone or it won't come true." Flannery gave her daughter the same spiel Harper had given Flannery once upon a time.

Harper found herself reciting the wish she'd recited for her entire childhood, every time she'd seen a falling star or blew out candles on her birthday cake or threw a coin into a wishing well. A wish that had never come true.

Please, please, let my mother be normal.

She didn't have to make that wish anymore. Tia was gone. But she didn't know what to replace the wish with.

In the darkness, they turned and headed for the house, lumbering under their burdens. Too bad there wasn't a light to guide their way. It was downright spooky with the wind whipping their hair into their faces.

They made it to the cottage without incident even without a light. A sliver of moon hung in the sky, glinting off the white paver stones leading to the door. Harper took the key Jonnie had given them from her pocket and pushed it in the lock. Together, the three of them crossed over the threshold into the eerily silent house.

And that's when a gut-curdling scream shattered the starry night.

CHAPTER 8

Jonnie

DIASTATIC MALT: Dried sprouted barley powder. Add a small amount to the dough, and it will give bread a better rise and browner crust.

The usual crowd gathering in the rectory of the Presbyterian Church of Moonglow Cove were casually dressed, and chit-chatting softly, as they got coffee and shortbread cookies from the platter laid out on the folding table positioned near the door.

The lure. Caffeine and sugar. A reward for showing up.

Jonnie Campbell spied a few new faces, but most were regulars. The place was as familiar to her as her houseboat. Jonnie was a staple in this room that smelled of old hymnals, frankincense candles, and musty carpet. She was someone people relied on and she took that role seriously, for it was hard won. She'd come a long way from the first time she'd stumbled through those doors twenty-two years earlier, her heart filled with angst and her mind tangled up in the damage of the Campbell curse.

In this gathering, she'd found salvation.

And discovered the love and acceptance she'd never known in her own family. Funny how people thought your family of origin was most important. In Jonnie's experience, family hurt you the deepest. Often with gleeful intent. She'd never had much luck squaring family with love.

Stupid as it might be, she still had hope. Harper and Flannery and Willow gave her hope. They had a long way to go, but they'd both shown up. It was a start. Where the heart was willing, miracles followed.

Or so she wanted to believe.

There had to be some magic left in the world.

Please.

The door opened and Grayson Cooper walked in. Jonnie's old heart chugged when their eyes met, and he made a beeline straight for her.

"We need to talk," he said.

At the very same time, she said, "Thank you so much for today."

"*That's* what we need to talk about."

Jonnie nodded, tippled cream in her coffee, and then blew across the surface to cool it. The coffeemaker was a throwback to the days when things were made to last, and lawsuits hadn't yet proliferated. It produced scalding coffee to such a fiery degree a yellow construction paper sign was permanently posted on the wall above the coffeemaker that read: COFFEE IS PIPING HOT! SIP CAREFULLY.

Not only was it hot, but the brew was supernaturally strong. She shouldn't be drinking it this late, but honest to Pete, she needed something to do with her hands and the coffee warmed her old bones, made colder by the girls' arrival.

No, not girls. Harper and Flannery were full-grown women. She'd do well to remember that and treat them as such. She was thrilled they were here, but the next few weeks would not be easy.

"Try the shortbread cookies," Jonnie urged Grayson. "I baked them this afternoon. Mom's sourdough recipe."

"Hallway." Grayson inclined his head toward the door. He was serious.

Jonnie glanced at the masculine wristwatch she wore on her left wrist. It had once belonged to her father, Douglas. They had a few minutes before the meeting started and Grayson seemed determined to have this conversation now.

Silently, she nodded and followed where he led.

Grayson went to the far end of the hall out of earshot of the people trickling into the meeting room. Jonnie joined him, dreading what he would say. "I'm not comfortable with what we're doing, Jonnie."

"Please don't back out on me now. You know how desperate I am. I've got to do something to help Tia's girls."

"Don't you think you're being just as manipulative as your mother was?"

Jonnie sighed. She *was* being manipulative, but not for selfish reasons. That was the difference between her and her mother. "Why are you getting cold feet now?"

"I met them, Jonnie. I like them."

"I like them too. That's the point."

Grayson scratched his chin. "We're in a gray area here. This doesn't feel right. I'm lying for you and I don't like it."

"Okay, so you can bow out now. You did your part. I'll take it from here."

"If they ask me a direct question that contradicts your story, I can't continue lying to them."

"You don't have to. If they ask you a direct question, tell them the truth. Just don't volunteer information. Please."

"If I didn't owe you my life, I wouldn't have let things get this far." A scowl marred Grayson's handsome face.

"Grayson, if I don't do something, they will grow further and further apart, and the Campbell curse will never be broken. You saw Willow. How sweet she is. We have to do something to save that little girl from ending up like the rest of us."

"You don't know how things will turn out. You're not a fortune-teller. And you understand better than most the dangers of thinking you know what's best for other people."

"I can look back and see the patterns. Once you know what you're looking for, it's clear as day what's happening, but when you're stuck in the middle of the darkness, you don't even know light exists."

Grayson chuffed out his breath and jammed his hands in his trouser pockets. He knew the truth as well as she did. He'd been down a dark road himself.

"Where would you be without me?" Jonnie pulled her trump card.

"Dead," he said with such certainty the word echoed through the hallway.

"And look at you now." She swept a hand at him. "A complete one eighty. Harper and Flannery can have that salvation too. I know you want that for them."

Grayson ran a palm over the top of his head. "I still think we're meddling in things that aren't ours to fix."

"Normally, I would agree. It's best to stay out of other people's business and let them sort things out for themselves, but I caused this, Grayson. It's my fault." She paused. "At least part of it."

"I know you're still suffering over the past, Jonnie, and that you've worked hard to let it go, but do you think that maybe you've got a blind spot about this?"

"Oh, most definitely," she agreed. "That's why I need your help."

"I don't like it."

"Noted." She studied him. "You're attracted to Harper."

He shrugged. "Why wouldn't I be? She's smart, gorgeous, and brave."

"And a train wreck."

"My kryptonite."

"I hear that."

"From a point of clarity." Grayson spread his arms wide. "I'm on record that this is a bad idea, and I won't lie for you again. Understood?"

"Understood."

"But I'll keep your secret." He paused and drilled Jonnie with an icy stare. "For now."

"That's all I can ask. I know you've compromised your values for me, and I am eternally in your debt."

"Jonnie"—a woman poked her head from the door—"We're ready to start the meeting."

"We're coming, Freda." Jonnie let out her breath and turned back to Grayson. "How are *you* doing these days?"

"I'm good." He paused. "Really good."

"I'm so glad." Jonnie reached over to give his hand a squeeze and he squeezed it back.

"Let's do this thing."

Nodding, he followed Jonnie back to the room. People had taken their seats on metal folding chairs lined up in front of the podium and were waiting. Grayson slipped into the last row while Jonnie headed to the front of the room.

Taking her place at the podium, Jonnie looked out at the faces that meant so much to her. These people had been there for her in her darkest hours. They would be there for her through this, too. She wasn't rudderless and totally without support as she'd been for so many years before coming here.

Gratitude filled her heart as she adjusted the microphone to fit her height.

"Hello," she announced as she had three times a week for the past twenty-two years. "My name is Jonnie Campbell and I'm an alcoholic."

CHAPTER 9

Flannery

FEEDING: The process of adding flour and water to the sourdough starter to keep it active and healthy.

The startled scream tore from Flannery's throat.

Involuntarily, she jumped backward over the threshold, shrinking into the shadows outside the door and tightening her grip on Willow in her arms.

Run, run, her instincts urged.

Willow burst into tears, Flannery's fears infecting her child.

Trembling all over, Flannery watched Harper charge the man who was standing in the hallway between the mudroom and the kitchen. His face was disfigured, one side scarred from his forehead to his chin, and he was holding an armful of linens. He looked as terrified as Flannery felt.

Despite her fear, Flannery had a fleeting moment to realize that the man must have been changing the sheets and had had lights on in the rest of the house to do this work, but had turned them off as he left each bedroom and came back through the mudroom where the washer and dryer were located, so that only the sole lamp that they'd left on, the lamp that no one could see from the outside of the house because there were no windows in the mudroom, was still shining.

"Who do you think you are?" Harper hollered, her face twisted into a fierce mask as she flew at him, fists doubled up and ready to punch.

It wasn't the first time Flannery had seen Harper like this—ready to defend her baby sister to the death from schoolyard bullies, the revolving door of men their mother brought into their lives . . .

Tia herself.

A surge of love for her sister filled Flannery at the same time she recognized that Harper's reaction was overkill. In a dangerous situation, she couldn't imagine anyone she'd rather have on her side.

The man dropped the linens and raised his hands over his head as if Harper was holding a gun on him. "Stop, stop, I come in peace!"

Willow's arms were laced around Flannery's neck, and she could feel her daughter's heartbeat pounding through her chest. Flannery smoothed Willow's hair and hummed a soothing tuneless sound meant to comfort her.

And herself.

"Who are you?" Harper demanded, baring her teeth, fists still raised.

"Name's Hank Charbonneau," he said in a Louisiana drawl. "I'm the groundskeeper. Your aunt Jonnie sent me to make up the beds while y'all were at the store. I 'pologize. I didn't mean to scare y'all."

His dark brown eyes looked mournful, and Flannery's empathy pulsed. The scars on his face said this man had suffered a great deal.

"I'm sorry I screamed," Flannery murmured, wanting to smooth everything over. "I thought an intruder had broken in."

"Not likely." He gave a small smile. "Everyone in town is scared of this place, but seein' as you aren't from Moonglow Cove, I can understand why you'd think that."

Why were people scared of the lighthouse? Flannery's chest tightened. Should she be scared too?

Slowly, Harper lowered her fists, but she still looked skeptical. "Why isn't it likely that people would break in? It's an empty cottage and lighthouse. Are you telling me they don't have human nature in Moonglow Cove?"

Hank chuckled. "No, ma'am, there's plenty of teenagers who would sneak up here to party. What keeps people out is the Campbell curse."

"The what?" Harper scowled.

"Not my place to tell that story," Hank said. "You'll have to ask your aunt Jonnie about that. Or that Grayson fella with the Historical Society."

Harper was still puffed up with adrenaline, her eyes so shiny they looked wet; her fists remained clenched, arms dangling at her sides, ready to spring back up at the slightest provocation.

Hank lifted his Texas Rangers baseball cap to scratch his head thick with chestnut brown hair peppered with gray. Hair that almost seemed to glow in the light from the kitchen. "I guess Jonnie forgot to tell you I'd be here. Or she figured I'd already be gone. I wasn't home when she texted, and it took me longer to get up here than expected. I do apologize for scaring you."

He was talking to Harper, but his gaze was trained on Flannery.

"Why didn't Jonnie change the sheets before now?" Harper asked. "Why did she wait until the middle of the night?"

Flannery didn't point out that it was just a few minutes after nine, still a perfectly acceptable hour.

"She didn't consult me, but I suppose she didn't know if you were going to stay or not and didn't want to go to the trouble if you decided to take off." Hank settled the baseball cap back onto his head and bent to pick up the linens. They were unfolded and wrinkled, old sheets he'd stripped from the beds.

He straightened and caught Flannery's gaze. "They weren't dirty. Just musty from nobody havin' slept on 'em in five years."

"Thank you," Flannery said, unsettled. Talking about bedsheets felt unseemly. "We appreciate it."

"Just finishing up." His eyes flicked to the wheelchair filled with grocery sacks, back to Flannery and Willow. "Y'all need help bringing anything else in?"

"I have luggage in my car," Flannery said. "It'd be nice if you could help me bring our things inside."

"Sure." Hank bobbed his head, easygoing and agreeable.

Now that she wasn't terrified, Flannery could assess him a little better. He kept the left side of his face turned away, cocking his head in an odd angle to present his unmarred cheek. She wondered what had happened to him, and how he'd gotten those scars. It looked like burn scars that had just missed taking out his eye. He wasn't particularly tall, which she liked. Tall men such as Alan and Grayson Cooper unnerved her, because they towered over her own five-foot-three-inch height. But neither was he short. Average height, five-ten-ish. With broad shoulders and a sturdy chest.

She had a sudden, insane urge to trace her fingers over his scars and plant kisses there to ease his suffering. It was a stupid impulse. The scars were years old, and she was in no position to assuage anyone's suffering, not even her own.

Their gazes touched and her heart sped up as she felt a bunch of things at once—fear and compassion, sadness and longing.

Longing for what she had no idea. There was this primal ache in the pit of her heart, and she knew it had absolutely nothing to do with Hank Charbonneau. He was just some guy sent to change the sheets.

"We can handle bringing up Flannery's belongings ourselves," Harper said, her defiant chin in the air. "You're free to go."

In that moment, Harper looked so much like their mother it both scared and fortified Flannery.

She offered Hank a small smile, proud of her own bravery. "I don't know about you, Harper. But I'm exhausted. I'd appreciate any help Hank is willing to give."

"Sure thing, ma'am." Hank raised his baseball cap again. He was younger than the color of his hair indicated, but still quite a bit older than Flannery. Late thirties or early forties.

"If you watch Willow, I'll go open the car up for Hank," Flannery said to Harper. While she was nervous about going into the dark with a stranger, she was even more nervous about giving him the keys to her car and letting him go out alone.

"We'll all go together," Harper said firmly.

"I don't mean you any harm, but I understand why you'd be skittish." Hank shook his head and replaced the baseball cap again. Was removing the cap and putting it back on something he did when he was nervous? "I'll be on my way and I'll come back in the light of day to unload your car for you."

"Thank you." Flannery took a full breath for the first time since she'd come to the house and felt the surge of oxygen relax her tense muscles.

"Where do you live?" Willow asked him, speaking for the first time since Flannery had screamed.

Hank gave her a kind smile. "Down the road a piece."

"A piece?" Willow tilted her head.

"I'm your closest neighbor." He pointed in an easterly direction toward the center of town.

"Oh," Flannery said. "Since you're the groundskeeper, could we trouble you to have a look at the elevator? It stalled on us earlier today and we were trapped in it for a few minutes. It was scary."

"I'm aware she stalls." He winced. "The sea air does a number on the mechanics. I should have put an out-of-order sign on it. I got the parts ordered, but they ain't come in yet. I'm hoping they'll be here tomorrow, and I can get to work on it. In the meantime, take the walking path until I give the go-ahead."

"May I borrow your cell phone?" Harper asked Flannery.

"What happened to yours?" Flannery asked, not wanting to let go of Willow to dig around in her purse.

"I threw it into the ocean." Harper waved a hand. "Long story. I want to text Aunt Jonnie and vet this guy."

"You must be the one from New York City," Hank said, pulling a cell phone from his back pocket. "Here, use mine. Unlock code is—"

"If you're willing to let me text Jonnie in front of you, I suppose I don't need to." Harper narrowed her eyes at him. "How much do you know about us?"

"Not much. One of you lives in Manhattan. The other in Kansas City."

Flannery experienced the old thrill-chill she'd felt in childhood watching Harper defend her. A burst of affection followed the other feeling and she wanted nothing more than to hug her sister. But a river of sorrow stretched between them. It would be a long, long time before they were fully comfortable with each other again.

C'mon, had they ever really been comfortable with each other? As a child, Flannery had been wildly in love with her older sister, while Harper had been wildly in love with getting as far away from home as fast as she could. When Flannery was little, she'd believed Harper was running away from her, but now she understood her sister had simply been trying to outrun her demons.

"Thank you again for changing the sheets," Harper said, efficiently dismissing him. "We'll see you tomorrow . . . Mr. Charbonneau."

Hank eyed the groceries stacked high on the seat of Willow's wheelchair. "I can help you put away groceries."

"That won't be necessary." Harper made motions indicating he should leave.

Flannery stepped aside and caught a whiff of Hank's scent as he walked by. It was a down-to-earth fragrance—salt and sea, shampoo, and sandalwood. Pleasant and unassuming.

"Y'all sleep well." With one last tip of his baseball cap, he was gone, vanishing into the night.

"Well," Harper said sharply, dusting off her palms. "That was an unexpected adrenaline rush."

* * *

THEY PUT AWAY the groceries in uncomfortable silence. Flannery wanted to talk but had no idea what to say. How did she start the conversation?

Amid the clatter of opening and closing cabinet drawers and doors, Willow sat in her wheelchair watching them. Flannery darted a glance at her daughter, trying to gauge what was going on in her child's head.

Whenever things turned dicey, Willow got quiet and withdrew. In that regard, she was a lot like Flannery. Whereas Harper ran, Flannery—and Willow—shut down.

She'd given Willow her cell phone to play with, but her daughter wasn't using it. The phone sat in her lap, the screen gone dark. That was not normal. Willow was a gamer. Flannery had rules around the device, so it was really unusual for Willow not to take advantage of phone time.

Biting her tongue to keep from saying something smotherly to her child, Flannery stowed the eggs, butter, and cheese in the empty refrigerator.

Just then, the cell phone buzzed. A text.

Instantly, fear-cicles pushed cold through Flannery's blood and her thoughts jumped to the worst-case scenario.

Alan?

But he didn't have this cell number. The phone was brand-new. How could he be texting? He had no idea what she was doing. He didn't even know she had family in Moonglow Cove. She barely knew it herself.

"Mommy?" Willow yawned big and held out the phone.

Crossing the checkerboard linoleum, Flannery took the cell.

The only person she'd given her new number to was Aunt Jonnie. It had to be her.

The text read: Forgot 2 tell you. Sourdough rules include feeding the dough within twenty-four hours after accepting the challenge. I'll be by in the morning 2 supervise your 1st time.

"What is it?" Harper asked. "Your face just got weird."

Flannery read the text out loud.

Harper rolled her eyes. "I'm tired of this dam—" She glanced at Willow. "Er . . . dang challenge already."

That was nice of her to monitor her language for Willow's sake and Flannery offered her sister a grateful smile. "Maybe it won't be that bad."

Snorting, Harper moved on to the next grocery bag. "It's manipulation is what it is."

"Why did you agree to the challenge?"

"Why did you?" Harper had an irritating habit of answering a question with a question.

"I'd rather not get into that tonight." She inclined her head toward Willow.

"Ditto."

Willow yawned again.

"I need to get her to bed," Flannery murmured. "It's been a really long day."

"Sure, sure." Harper bobbed her head. "I'll finish putting these things away. You go on and get some rest."

"Do you have preference of bedrooms?" Flannery ventured.

"There's only one on the first floor," Harper said. "You and Willow need the master."

"Thank you." There was so much she wanted to tell her sister, but Harper had turned away, head down, opening another cabinet, and stowing the bags of flour.

"Good night," Harper said.

"Night."

"Don't let the bedbugs bite!" Willow sang out.

"You got it, kid." Harper's voice was muffled by the cabinet door.

Flannery wheeled Willow to the master bedroom. It was furnished with antiques and old-timey tchotchkes like lace doilies, colored glassware, and figurines. It would take a lot of hard work to clean out and modernize the place once they inherited it, but she was up for the challenge.

Up for a new start.

Hope rose on shaky wings. She and hope had an off-again/on-again relationship and she knew better than to fully trust the flighty emotion, but there it was.

Manage your expectations.

Right. Gently easing hope into the far corner of her mind, Flannery helped Willow into the bathroom. After a quick sink bath, and teeth brushing, they changed into their pajamas and curled up in the full-size bed together underneath a goose down comforter.

The sheets smelled of fabric softener and camouflaged the musty odor of a house on the sea closed up for too long. She imagined the scarred man changing these sheets and a shiver ran through her. How had he gotten burned? Did he have a family? Was he from Moonglow Cove or had some odd story landed him here the same way it had her? Why was she thinking about him?

Why? Because thinking about Hank keeps you from thinking about the pickle you're in.

True enough, but while she might be in a pickle, this was the first step toward turning her life around for her daughter.

Lying in the darkness, with her arms wrapped around Willow, feeling safer than she'd felt in years, Flannery offered up a prayer of thanks. She wasn't so sure she believed in a higher power anymore—too many times her prayers had gone unanswered for her to fully believe that God had her best interests at heart—but she didn't have the fortitude to handle this on her own. It wouldn't hurt to ask for help.

Tia had been an atheist, or so Flannery supposed. Her mother hadn't discussed religion one way or the other, except in regard to literature. She'd allowed Flannery and Harper to go to church with friends and neighbors. She had neither intervened in, nor encouraged, an interest in God. Not even at the end of her life.

Flannery pressed her palms to her chest, whispered "please," and then wondered if Hank Charbonneau went to church.

Who cares? Go to sleep.

Tomorrow, the real work would begin. Learning how to bake sourdough, figuring out how to navigate the fragile relationship with her sister, fully coming to terms with the fact she'd been in an abusive relationship. It was something she'd spent the last six years denying and she needed to stop making excuses for Alan.

In the darkness, she fingered the bruises on her forearm. Alan had never gotten physical with her before, but the way he grabbed her, shook her, and left the bruises had been a bridge too far. Looking at his face that last time, feeling the force of his anger, and she'd just *known*. If she didn't escape, he would eventually destroy her.

Thank heavens, she hadn't told him about the call from her grandmother's lawyer. He believed she had no family beyond

Harper and a mysterious Aunt Jonnie she'd never met. No place to go. She could only pray with all her might that he didn't come looking for her. He had a mistress. That's what they'd fought over. The reason he'd bruised her arm. Maybe he would just release Flannery and go on to start a new life. She wondered if Grayson Cooper could recommend a good divorce lawyer since he seemed to know everything about Moonglow Cove. She liked Grayson. He had a kind face. So did Hank Charbonneau. And so did Aunt Jonnie, beneath her gruff exterior.

Yawning, Flannery couldn't help wondering if, despite the rocky start, she'd finally found a soft place to land.

CHAPTER 10

Harper

HOOCH: Refers to the liquid that can form on hungry sourdough starter when it hasn't been fed often enough.

Still on New York time, Harper woke at dawn. She wasn't someone who lazed around, savoring sleep. She charged from her bed every morning ready to tackle the day. She credited that habit with much of her success.

Not so successful now, huh?

It was Tia's voice in Harper's head as she applied makeup and got dressed, pulling on yoga pants, a CrossFit branded workout shirt and sneakers. She hadn't brought any other clothes with her because she hadn't expected to stay for six weeks. Hadn't expected to stay a full day. She'd only stuffed the workout clothes and nightie in her tote bag just in case. Once she had a new cell phone, she'd need to see about subletting her apartment for the six weeks she'd be in Texas.

Ugh. She wasn't ready to think about that now.

Maybe later she could visit some of the boutiques she'd seen on Moonglow Boulevard when she'd arrived. Perhaps Flannery and Willow would like to come along. Her heart gave a little hop. She and her sister had so much to talk about, but the topics that needed discussion were so loaded with conflict and emotion, she didn't know where or how to start that conversation. A shopping trip might be the perfect icebreaker.

She hurried into the kitchen, tugging her hair into a ponytail as she went. She searched for a coffeepot, softly opening and closing cabinet doors so as not to awaken her sister and Willow. She finally found the old-fashioned percolator and coffee filters but realized belatedly there was no coffee. They'd forgotten to buy any last night.

"Blast it," Harper muttered. She needed caffeine.

She scrawled on the blackboard mounted beside the fridge, using pink, dust-covered chalk. Gone for coffee, BRB.

Grabbing her tote, she took off for Moonglow Boulevard.

It was a two-mile walk from the lighthouse to the coffee shop and without her phone's GPS to guide her, Harper made a couple of wrong turns before she found the place that she'd seen on the ride into town. By the time she pushed through the door into the bustling store, it was 7:10 on Saturday morning, May 21.

Yay! Other early birds.

Despite her difficulties of late, Harper really did like people. She smiled at folks and they smiled right back. Nice!

It's gonna be a great day.

She took her place in line and spaced out a little, her mind making a to-do list for the day's activities, which included learning as much as she could about sourdough baking, and she barely noticed that a man had come up behind her.

"Fancy meeting you here."

She turned to see Grayson Cooper and her pulse quickened.

With the morning sun pouring through the window bathing

him in a halo of light, the high school history teacher looked like some lazy surfer dude in a romantic comedy. Today, he'd shucked the suit and briefcase in favor of beige cargo shorts that showed off spectacular legs and a forest-green polo shirt. He wore deck shoes, Ray-Ban Wayfarers, and a dazzling smile. Too bad she wasn't interested in a fling because this dude was mega fling-worthy.

"Good morning, Mr. Cooper," Harper said, charmed by his grin. In that moment, he reminded her of a Labrador retriever, all earnest and game.

"Please," he said. "Call me Gray, all my friends do."

"Oho. Are you suggesting that I might become your friend, Mr. Cooper?" She lowered her lashes.

Seriously, Harper, are you flirting with the executor of your grandmother's will?

Yep. She was. Why not? Life was short and men this handsome didn't roll into her life every day.

"One can never have too many friends."

"You sure about that?" With a saucy smile, she sank her hands onto her hips.

"Total conviction." He held up a palm like he was being sworn in.

"I thought you said that you volunteered at the Historical Society on Saturday mornings."

"I do. We don't open until nine. Are you going to drop by?"

"Maybe later. I've got sourdough starter to feed."

"Sounds like a big responsibility." There was mirth in his voice, and mischief in his grin.

"Are you always this sunny?" she asked, mesmerized by that twinkle in his pale blue gaze.

That old song by the Velvet Underground, one of Tia's favorite bands, ran through her head, "Pale Blue Eyes." Harper tensed. Whenever Tia played that tune, it usually meant she was about to break up with the latest boyfriend or husband, and if you prized your sanity it was best to duck and cover until the fallout was over. Goose bumps sprang to her arms and Harper shook her head to clear the thoughts.

"I am when I'm around someone as bright as you," he murmured.

"Is this where I groan and roll my eyes?" She did both.

"Too cheesy?"

"Cream cheese all the way, baby." Oh hell, why had she said *baby*? It sounded flippant and cute, and she did not need to encourage any of this.

"You are tack-sharp, Harper." Her named sounded like whipped cream on his tongue—soft and sweet. He added, "And beautiful. Is it wrong to notice?"

"Aww, you're making me blush."

"I'm not making you do anything. You are in full control of yourself and you aren't the sort to blush. Flannery, yes. You? No way."

"Think you can read me, huh?"

"Like a neon sign."

She stuck her tongue out at him and crossed her eyes. "You sound like a self-help book."

He laughed and shrugged. "Get used to it."

"I really don't want to like you."

His grin turned wicked. "Except you do."

"Um . . . I wouldn't call it *like* exactly."

"What would you call it?"

Lust, baby, lust. "Intrigued. You intrigue me. What's a smart guy like you doing in a backwater place like this?"

"Oh, now you're dissing our hometown?" Gray tried to suppress the smile, but it broke free and overtook his face.

"It's *your* hometown, not mine."

"Yours too."

"It's not. Just because my relatives are from here doesn't make Moonglow Cove my hometown."

"Excuse me, but you and I used to play in the sandbox together."

"No. That's not true. I've never been to Texas in my life."

"Not that you recall," he said with such certainty it gave her pause.

"I haven't been to Texas," she insisted.

"I have pictures of you and me that say differently."

Was he for real? Vigorously, she shook her head. "Okay, you're certifiable. Small-town coastal living has scrambled your brain. I've *never* been here. You and I *never* played together. I don't know who you were playing with in that sandbox, but it wasn't me."

"You sure about that?"

Was she? Doubt crept in. Tia *had* bounced all over the country.

"When was this?" She narrowed her eyes, felt her pulse quicken. Could she have visited this place as a small child? She didn't remember it, not by any stretch of the imagination.

"Thirty years ago. You were three and I was two. It *is* you in the picture. At least according to my mom, and the kid in the photo does resemble you. Same straight blond hair. Same quirky smile. Same chocolate-brown eyes."

"You think my smile is quirky?" She fingered her bottom lip.

"In a totally beautiful way."

"Who's your mom?" she asked, a weird feeling coming over her and she knew what he was going to say before the words left his mouth.

"Missy Sinclair, and my stepfather, Ward, is the mayor of Moonglow Cove."

"Next!" called the barista from behind the cash register.

"Your turn." Gray nodded with a flourish of his arm.

Ack! Now she was thinking of him as Gray. As if she was his friend.

She stepped up to the counter, feeling more confused and uneasy than ever. There was an undercurrent—*secrets*—in this town that she knew nothing about.

Harper placed her drink order, buying coffee beans and a grinder as well and adding a box of cinnamon rolls for Flannery and Willow. This would probably be the last time she'd buy baked goods. According to her grandmother's "rules," they had to bake with the sourdough discard. Whatever that meant.

Leaving the counter, she went to stand in the line of people waiting to pick up their drink orders. A minute later, Gray joined her again.

"Fancy meeting you here."

"What is this? Groundhog Day?"

"Maybe."

"Gray," the barista hollered, "your order is ready."

"What's this?" Harper asked. "You got your drink ahead of me?"

"That's what you get for ordering a blended drink," he said smugly and reached for the tall cup of black coffee the barista pushed toward him.

He turned on his heel to walk out the door, but stopped, pivoted, and swiveled back to her. "If you've got any more questions about our past, you know where to find me."

Then with a wink, he was gone.

"Damn," Harper swore under her breath. She couldn't help liking the guy when she really, really shouldn't.

* * *

THE SISTERS WERE tentative with the sourdough . . .

. . . and each other.

When Harper returned from her coffee run it was eight A.M., and she found Flannery in the kitchen cleaning like a madwoman.

"Where's Willow?"

"I thought I'd let her sleep in. Yesterday was exhausting."

"It was." Harper didn't know what else to say.

Flannery ran a damp dishrag over the counter, obliterating five years of dust.

Sipping her coffee, Harper watched her sister, who moved as if she could erase the past with enough scrubbing. She held up the bag from the coffee shop. "I brought cinnamon rolls."

"Thanks." Flannery didn't look up.

"Coffee beans and a grinder, too. Would you like me to make a pot of coffee?"

"I'm good."

Oookay. Conversation with her sister equaled teeth pulling. "I suppose we should feed the starter. Since you're such a champ at research, how about you read the instructions while I feed the thing?"

"I can do that." Flannery stopped the relentless cleaning and pulled her cell phone from her pocket.

Within two minutes of listening to Flannery read off the sourdough instructions, Harper was grinding her teeth. There were too many rules. Too many things to get wrong. She wondered what had happened to her resilience. Normally, when faced with a challenge, she rolled up her sleeves and dove right in, but there was a resistance inside her now, and she wasn't sure from where it stemmed.

Her personal situation? Her recently dead grandmother's manipulations? Her mother's deception? Her sister's meekness? All of the above?

Harper lifted the lid on the crock that Aunt Jonnie had left behind and wrinkled her nose. "It smells."

"It's supposed to." Flannery consulted her phone. "Although if it smells too hoochie you should discard all but two tablespoons and start with a fresh feeding."

"Hoochie?"

"Hang on, I don't understand it, either; let me keep reading. It says here that hooch is harmless."

"Yay." Harper splayed a palm over her chest. "At least we didn't kill the mother dough on the first day."

"I can't believe this thing is a hundred fifty years old," Flannery said, peering over Harper's shoulder to stare at the starter too. "That seems—"

"Nasty?"

"Unbelievable. But yes, nasty too."

"Back to the hooch thing. What does that mean? What do we do about it?"

Flannery read, "Hooch should be poured off."

"There's nothing to pour off."

"Maybe it's not hoochie then. Here's the picture, see?" Flannery flashed her phone screen.

"Yeah, it's not that, but it is really gummy." From the silverware drawer, Harper took a spoon and poked at the mother dough. There were hundreds of tiny airy bubbles running through it.

"Be careful," Flannery cautioned.

"What's it going to do? Explode?"

"We can't kill it. If we kill it, we don't get the cottage and the lighthouse."

Harper wondered why Flannery wanted the place so badly, but she didn't ask because she didn't want to explain why she needed it. She'd have to tell her sister eventually about what happened to her career, but it was too much to dredge up right now. Especially when they were still so cautious with each other. Honesty was a luxury at this point.

"Okay, hang on, I'm going to troubleshooting FAQs." Flannery finger-scrolled down the page. "Here we go. 'What do I do if my sourdough is too sticky.'"

"Yes, what *do* we do?"

"If your starter is too sticky, there could be insufficient gluten development," she read aloud.

"Gluten, ugh." Harper shuddered.

"Are you gluten sensitive?" Flannery asked.

"My stomach gets poochie if I eat too much bread and I can gain five pounds overnight from water retention. Is that sensitivity? I don't know. I haven't eaten bread in ten years."

"But you bought cinnamon rolls from the coffee shop."

"For you and Willow."

Flannery patted her belly. "I guess you can tell I eat bread often."

Uh-oh, land mine. Harper raised her palms. "No judgment on your dietary habits. My career places an emphasis on being svelte. It's the right choice for me. In my estimation, you look fantastic, Flan."

Flannery hunched her shoulders, turned her face away from Harper so she couldn't read her sister's expression. "According to this website, bread needs gluten development to trap gas and rise, but this process also helps the dough become less sticky."

"Did you hear that?" Harper cupped a palm around her ear.

Flannery slid her a sidelong glance, looked confused. "Hear what?"

"The sound of that sentence flying right over my head. What does it mean?"

Flannery gave a soft smile that eased the tension between them a little. "Apparently there's a learning curve to this sourdough stuff. Oh, wait, here's another explanation for why the dough might smell the way it does."

"Is it an easier explanation than the last one?" Harper asked.

"Um, I think so."

"All ears here. Shoot."

"It could be overfermentation."

"And . . ."

"A mistake that almost all sourdough bakers make at some point is simply leaving the dough for too long without feeding it."

"That makes sense, but what's the difference between that and being hoochie?"

"No idea. It says here that after fermenting for too long without food, the gluten in the dough begins to break down. Creating a thick, gloppy mass."

"This definitely looks gloppy. What does the article suggest we do?"

"Um, it says here to start over from scratch."

"Nooo!" Harper shook her head. "Surely we didn't let a hundred-fifty-year-old mother dough die already. We can't be *that* incompetent."

"Oh no." Flannery massaged her temple and bit her bottom lip. "We blew it."

Harper started pacing, hands clasped behind her back. "Keep researching. There *has* to be a way to save it."

"I'm trying, I'm trying. Ooh, here's an article. What to do with overfermented sourdough."

"Yay! Keep reading."

"Turn your overfermented dough into pancakes," Flannery read.

"Um, no," Harper said. "We have to bake bread with the starter, not pancakes."

"Hang on, I'll see what other solutions I can find."

"Look to see if anyone sells live sourdough online," Harper urged. "We can buy some and pretend that it's the original mother dough."

"Harper Lee! Are you for real?"

"What?"

"That's cheating!"

"Hey," Harper said with a shrug, feeling sheepish. "I'm trying to find a workaround. If Penelope J. Campbell is underhanded enough to set us up for failure, I'm underhanded enough to pass off someone else's starter as the family mother dough. Honestly, who would know?" Was she rotten for even entertaining the thought?

"*I'd* know," Flannery said, climbing right onto her high horse and riding it bareback.

"All right, all right. It was just an off-the-wall suggestion. We won't stoop to Granny's level, but in a pinch, it could be an opt—"

"No, it can't."

Okay, okay. Flannery was a complete straight arrow. Harper got the message. "All right then. Unless you can find some answers in your internet search, we need to call Aunt Jonnie and tell her we killed the mother dough."

A knock sounded at the back door a second before it opened, and Aunt Jonnie's voice entered the house ahead of her. "Knock, knock, y'all up and at 'em? I've brought sourdough discard recipes."

Harper leaned backward so she could see her aunt coming in through the mudroom carrying a small metal recipe box.

"So sorry," Harper said. "We've already murdered the mother dough. It's all over." She braced herself, waiting for her aunt to fly off the handle about such news the way Tia would have done.

Instead, Aunt Jonnie smiled and shook her head. "I seriously doubt that. That mother dough has survived for one hundred fifty years through much worse than you two."

"Shows what you know about our level of toxicity." Harper snorted.

"I can see why you're in advertising." Aunt Jonnie's eyes twinkled as she strolled unhurried into the kitchen. "You have a flare for the dramatic, just like your mom."

Cringing, Harper paced. The comparison to Tia brought up a

boatload of shame and her tongue wanted to lash out with something catty, but her upset wasn't about Aunt Jonnie's gentle teasing and she knew it.

"Let's see what we've got going on here." Aunt Jonnie moved to the counter and lifted the lid on the crock. "Nothing wrong. This is what dormant dough looks like. It just needs refreshing. Add 113 grams of water and 113 grams of flour and get going."

"But it's the consistency of pancake batter," Flannery said.

"That's sourdough. Once you get used to what it looks like, you'll be less afraid of it. In fact, you'll stop treating it so delicately. It's just flour, water, and bacteria."

"Are you sure?" Harper asked.

"I've been making sourdough bread since I was eight years old. It's fine, trust me."

"If you say so." Flannery looked skeptical.

"You'll want the kitchen scales." Aunt Jonnie bent to pull an electronic kitchen scale from a bottom drawer and settled it onto the counter. "Just leave the scales sitting out. You'll be using them twice a day and you'll have to do something with the discard twice a day as well, since you're not allowed throw it out."

"We have to bake twice a day?" Harper groaned. Okay, she heard it now, the whine in her voice. She dialed down the drama and raised her arms like a cheerleader waving pom-poms. "I mean yay! We get to bake twice a day! What an opportunity for personal growth!"

"That's the spirit." Aunt Jonnie chuckled. "It'll make things easier if you transfer the starter into a clear container that has measuring lines on it so you can see when the dough has doubled in volume. That'll be important for baking."

"Are you writing this down?" Harper asked Flannery.

"Got it in the notes app." Flannery held up her phone.

Aunt Jonnie rummaged around in the cabinet and brought out a tall clear plastic container with calibration levels on it.

"Thanks," Harper said. "But I thought you're not supposed to help us."

"I'm not helping you. I'm just giving you instructions. You're doing all the work."

"That's not cheating?" Flannery asked.

"Not in my book." Aunt Jonnie shrugged. "How is it any different from you looking it up on the internet, except that it's faster?"

"Good point." Flannery took a bag of flour from the pantry and settled it onto the counter beside the kitchen scales.

"Where's Willow?" Aunt Jonnie asked.

"Sleeping in," Flannery said. "Normally, she's up at dawn, but the last few days have been jam-packed."

"We ran into Mr. Charbonneau last night." Harper retrieved measuring cups from the same cabinet that her aunt had taken the plastic container. "I thought Flannery was going to have a heart attack. You should have heard her scream. She's got a great set of lungs."

"He was in the house," Flannery said. "He scared the stuffing out of me. We weren't expecting anyone to be here."

We. As if they were a team again. Harper liked that.

"My fault. I should've told you that I'd asked Hank to change the sheets and get the beds ready for you. I was rushing last night and I'm not at my best when I'm rushed. Multitasking is not my strength."

"You sound like Flannery," Harper said. "Me? I'm the queen of multitasking. The more irons in the fire, the better. I live for warp speed."

"I used to think that too," Aunt Jonnie said. "Turns out I was wrong . . . at least for me."

Yeah, well, that was Jonnie, not Harper. There was a reason she lived in the city that never sleeps. She loved being on the go, loved the hustle and bustle and constant activity. Movement kept her mind off her troubles. She wasn't a ruminator. She was a doer.

"May I ask a question?" Flannery ventured.

"Sure." Aunt Jonnie shrugged.

"What happened to Mr. Charbonneau's face?"

Aunt Jonnie flicked a glance at Flannery and said in a kindly tone, "You'll have to ask him. I don't like to gossip."

"I'm sorry." Flannery put a hand over her mouth. "I didn't mean to gossip. I was just curious."

"No judgment," Jonnie said. "I've just lived in a small town too long and experienced the terrible damage gossip can do and I want no part of it. But that's me. You be you."

Flannery looked absolutely horrified. "*I'm* not a gossip."

Aunt Jonnie laid a hand on Flannery's shoulder. "It's okay. I'm not suggesting you are. You're human. You're curious. It's normal. Be gentle with yourself. Unless you're gentle with yourself first, you can't be gentle with others."

Harper could see Flannery fighting off tears, and that churned every protective instinct inside of her. She wanted to tell Aunt Jonnie to step off and leave her sister alone.

"Thank you for saying so," Flannery told their aunt. "I do have a tendency to beat myself up."

"I know," Jonnie murmured. "I used to do that too. It's a tough habit to break."

"I have a question," Harper said.

"Ask away." Aunt Jonnie leaned back against the counter and folded her arms over her chest. She did not look at Harper with the same gentle expression she'd used for Flannery. "Although I reserve the right not to answer if it's none of your business."

No nonsense. Harper liked that about her.

"Why did you and our mother have a falling-out?" Harper met her aunt's stare.

Aunt Jonnie was the first to look away. "That's one of the questions I'm not going to answer. Your mother isn't here to defend herself and it wouldn't be fair to give you just one side of the story."

"So you won't help us clear up anything?" Although disappointed, Harper realized if she'd come looking for easy answers about her mother's past, she'd come to the wrong place, and she respected Aunt Jonnie for drawing her line in the sand.

"My telling tales about someone who is no longer with us won't ease your pain, Harper." Aunt Jonnie looked impossibly sad.

So sad that Harper felt her aunt's sorrow stirring her own emotions. *Yikes. None of that, thank you.*

She left the thread of that conversation unstitched and turned to Flannery. "Let's get going, sister. That starter isn't going to feed itself."

CHAPTER 11

Flannery

FIRST BUILD: A first starter refreshment.

After they'd done the initial feeding of the sourdough, Willow woke up and Aunt Jonnie made pancakes for them from the discard, fashioning the batter in the shape of Mickey Mouse, and she invited Willow to help.

Watching her aunt interact with her daughter at the stove, Flannery wondered why Jonnie hadn't married and had children. She had a crusty exterior but, from what Flannery had seen, a soft marshmallow center and her aunt seemed besotted with Willow. Then again, maybe Jonnie wasn't straight. Not everyone thought traditional marriage or having children was the be-all and end-all.

Flannery's anxiety kicked in. She worried that her aunt's kindness held ulterior motives, but Willow seemed to adore Aunt Jonnie right back and her daughter had good instincts about people. Flannery tried to relax, but it had been so long since she'd been able to take a good long deep breath and just let go that she wasn't sure she knew how to do it anymore.

Aunt Jonnie left at ten, and right afterward, Hank Charbonneau turned up at the back door, knocking gently. He had his baseball cap clutched in his hand by the bill when Flannery opened the door to let him in.

"Mornin'." He greeted her with a nod. "I'm here to help you unload your van. Also, if you'd like, you can park it at my house so it's not out in the open like that. Moonglow Cove is a safe place, but there's no call for courtin' trouble."

"Where did my grandmother park her car?" Flannery asked. She felt weird about leaving her car at Hank's house, but he was right. It wasn't smart to leave it parked on the isolated beach cul-de-sac.

"She didn't own one. Never learned how to drive. Jonnie took her everywhere she needed to go."

"What about when my grandfather was alive?"

"He died a long time ago, so I don't really know. I heard tell that he drove a little scooter. You don't really need a car to get around Moonglow Cove."

"What about deliveries?"

"Drivers use the elevator or walk up the path."

"That's weird that no one ever built a road for car traffic."

Hank's shoulders went up in a short shrug. "The Campbells were strange folks, 'cept for Jonnie."

"Meaning?"

"They preferred to keep to themselves."

Flannery blew out her breath. "Let me grab my keys and I'll be right back. You want to wait inside with Harper and Willow?"

"I'm good right here." Hank gave her a faint smile, settled his cap back on his head, and pulled it low over the scarred side of his face.

Flannery slipped back into the kitchen and grabbed her keys from her purse. Harper was washing up the pancake dishes.

"Could you keep an eye on Willow for a bit? Hank's here to help me unload the van, then I'm going to park it at his place and walk back."

"Sure," Harper said. "Is that okay with you, kiddo?"

Willow, deep into her video game, nodded without glancing up.

"We'll go do something when I get back," Flannery said, concerned over the amount of time she was using video games as a babysitter. "Maybe check out the lighthouse."

"That's a great idea," Harper said. "See you in a bit."

"Bye, sweetie," she called to Willow.

Willow waved, eyes glued to the screen. Most definitely, they needed to get outside and do something active.

Hank was waiting for Flannery underneath the shade of a palm. She dangled her keys for him to see and started toward the steep walking path that led to the cul-de-sac.

"I fixed the elevator," he said, jerking a thumb in the direction of the lift. "The parts came early this morning."

"Oh, okay." She hesitated. She was already claustrophobic and to be in a confined space with this man she didn't know gave her pause, but she didn't want to be rude, and he worked for Aunt Jonnie. It should be fine.

Yeah? How much do you know about Aunt Jonnie? Maybe her judgment isn't to be trusted.

Hank arrived at the elevator before she did, and it was already on the bluff level. He held out his arm, indicating she should go ahead of him. Dismissing the scar, he was not a bad-looking man. Ordinary features to be sure, but symmetrical and strong.

Heart churning, Flannery stepped inside, moving to the back left corner. In front of her she could see the ocean, hear the waves crashing against the rocks. It was a soothing sound, and the view was amazing. Such a lovely place to live. She could see why her ancestors had settled here. She hadn't lived near the ocean since Tia had married husband number four and moved them to the Midwest.

"I'm sorry I screamed last night when I saw you," she apologized.

Hank did that quick shrug again and got into the elevator with her. "No worries. I'm used to startling people."

Flannery cleared her throat, wanting so badly to ask him how his face got burned. "I bet that's difficult."

"I was a firefighter," he said, reading her mind. "A building full of flammable liquids exploded. It was a five alarm."

"I . . . er, wasn't—"

"You were, but it's okay. Figured I might as well tell you rather than keep you guessing. I was twenty-five when it happened. I spent two years in rehab and after that I lost my taste for fighting fires." He pushed the button and the elevator chugged down, smooth as silk. He'd done a good job fixing the rickety thing. "So I went into building maintenance instead."

"How long ago was that?"

"I'll be thirty-nine in September."

"I just turned twenty-six last month." *Eek, why did I share that?*

"Lot of years between twenty-six and thirty-nine," he mused as the elevator settled onto the beach.

"There are," she said, then added, "but not *too* many."

Oh, dear Lord, why did I say that? Was she flirting with him? Flannery had no idea. She'd only dated two men in her entire life. Willow's father, Kit, and Alan, Kit's best friend. Both men had chased her. She'd never made any kind of romantic overture toward a guy. Was she out of her mind? Yes, she'd gone completely bonkers.

When the door opened, she raced out of the elevator ahead of him, grateful for the spray of salt air hitting her face. She rushed to the minivan, leaving Hank behind.

"Whoa," he said in a surprised voice. "Let me catch up to you."

You're being rude. Forcing herself to stop, she turned and waited for him.

His smile was light, reassuring. "Thank you."

"I shouldn't have bolted," she said. "I'm a bit claustrophobic."

"No need to explain." His kind eyes searched her face.

Flannery hit the remote and unlocked the van.

"You weren't kidding," he said. "The van is stuffed. Looks like you brought everything you owned. It'll take us several trips."

"Thanks again," she said. "I appreciate the help."

He walked to the back of the van and opened the hatch and started hauling out suitcases with slow, easy movements.

Too nervous to stand close to him, Flannery opened the back door and took out a cardboard box filled with Willow's toys. She added a few more items to the box, bumped the door closed with her hip, then turned to find Hank standing beside her, two suitcases in his hands and a garment bag flung over his shoulder.

"You look like a pack mule," she said.

He brayed like a donkey and grinned, not the least bit worried about looking foolish. That charmed her. It was impossible not to like him.

Good grief, Flannery, stop it. Stop looking for someone to rescue you. It's time you rescued yourself.

Was that what she was doing? She didn't think so, but she had to be super careful. No more mistakes like Alan.

Laden, they trudged back to the elevator side by side, kicking up sand as they walked. She felt the grains slip through her sandals and shift against her toes. Again, Hank stood to one side, letting her enter the elevator first. She wasn't used to such gallantry and she wasn't so sure she liked it.

"You go ahead," she said feeling strangely waspish. "Your burden is heavier than mine."

His gaze crashed into her, his dark eyes pinning her to the spot, but he said nothing. Just lumbered ahead under the weight of her suitcases.

Flannery got on beside him, once more overwhelmed by the forced closeness of the small cage. "I'll get the button."

She shifted the weight of the box onto one arm, and raising her knee to help steady it, she bumped the up button with her elbow.

The metal door creaked as it slid closed.

Trapping her.

Flannery's throat tightened and her pulse spiked as she pressed her back against the side of the cage, the cardboard box clutched in front of her, obscuring her view of everything but Hank's face.

His poor damaged face.

Her own face tingled in the same spots where he'd been burned, and her stomach contracted as her empathetic imagination wallowed in the pain he must have felt, the suffering he'd endured. How dark must those moments have been for him?

"Don't pity me," Hank said, sounding terse for the first time since she'd met him.

"I'm not—"

"You are. I've had almost fourteen years of pitying glances aimed at me. I know what they look like."

Feeling chastised, she ducked her head and stared into the contents of the box. Willow's stuffed sock monkey, Mr. Chimps, stared back at her with black button-eyes. Halfway up, the elevator jerked to a stop, just as it had the day before. Flannery let out a little gasp as the suddenness threw her off balance.

"I though you said you fixed it," she blurted, hearing layers of anxiety coat her voice.

"I did." His tone was reassuring. "This is different. This is a power issue."

Her gaze flew to his face as her mind shrank against the word *power* and her thoughts jumped to fearful things. Had he arranged this? Had this been his goal all along? To get her trapped in an elevator with him so he could . . .

Could what, Flannery?

It was Harper's voice in her head now and she was five years old again, afraid to go to bed because she'd convinced herself there was a monster beneath the mattress.

There's no boogeyman underneath your bed. Come look. Harper, then twelve, had gotten down on her hands and knees and lifted the bedskirt.

No, the boogeyman hadn't been underneath Flannery's bed, because he'd been in it. She'd married him.

But that had nothing to do with Hank, who looked calm and cucumber cool.

"Wh-what do you mean?" she asked, fighting hard against the panic creeping up her body, starting at her feet and tightening every muscle on its way up to squeeze her chest until she could barely breathe.

"Someone's switched off the power."

"H-how do you know?" she asked. "It might be the thing that you thought you fixed. The thing that stalled me and Willow in here yesterday." She cringed then, wishing she'd kept her mouth shut, worried he'd start berating her for questioning him. Alan certainly would have. Where had she gotten the courage to question him?

He didn't get mad. In fact, he smiled. "The light on the buttons went off. That's an electrical supply issue, not a mechanical one."

"I don't follow."

"There's a kill switch to the elevator in the lighthouse." He clucked his tongue. "I've told Jonnie over and over that we need to put that switch on a separate fuse box. Otherwise, people can accidentally turn it off if they don't know what it is. Although I've marked the switch with neon green masking tape."

"That seems odd. Why hasn't Jonnie changed it?"

"Jonnie and I have been the only ones coming up here for years, and she didn't see fixing it as a priority. She's frugal, your aunt."

"I see." Flannery tightened her grip on the box, Mr. Chimps's sightless button eyes taunting her. "So who is in the lighthouse flipping switches?"

"My guess? Your sister."

"I suggested exploring the lighthouse with Willow, but I thought they were going to wait for me. What now?"

"Text her and ask her to switch it back on."

"Oh dear," Flannery whispered, the panic scaling to her throat. "What is it?"

"Harper lost her phone."

"Uh." Hank grunted softly, dropped the suitcases to the bottom of the cage, and shrugged off the garment bag.

"Does this mean we're stuck here?" Her voice stepped up an octave.

"Breathe," he said. "She'll come looking for us when we don't return."

Breathe.

Such a simple suggestion and yet so hard to do when she was in the talons-grip of an impending anxiety attack.

Hank reached for the cardboard box.

She clung to it. It was the only barrier between her and this disfigured stranger in the confines of a four-by-six-foot metal cage frozen on the side of a sea-swept bluff. Shades of *Jane Eyre*. She was terrified.

"Let go of the box, Flannery," he murmured, his eyes impossibly kind. "You need to sit down and put your head between your knees before you pass out."

"I-I . . ."

"It's okay to let go," Hank said. "It's okay to trust me. I won't harm you."

She shook her head, unable to speak.

"I know it's hard. I can tell you've been hurt. Jonnie's told me a little about your family history." His soothing tone mesmerized her.

Don't trust him, don't trust him. You know better.

Slowly, she eased her clenched fingers open and allowed Hank to take the box. He turned to set it on top of the luggage he'd dropped. With her belongings stacked in the only empty space, there was nothing between her and Hank.

Nothing to protect her.

He turned back to her, his scars gleaming silver in the sunlight, his brown eyes so dark they were almost black, piercing straight into her soul.

That's when she fainted.

CHAPTER 12

Harper

SLASHING: Cutting the outside of the dough with a very sharp razor or knife just before baking.

While Flannery and Hank were in the elevator, Harper opened the door to the anteroom that led into the lighthouse.

It was pitch-black inside and Harper fumbled at the wall, flipping switches until one fluorescent bulb bathed the room in a sickly yellow glow.

Willow was behind her, craning her neck to peer into the building and wrinkling her pert little nose. Her hair was parted down the middle and pulled into two braids. She wore a pink top, blue jeans, and matching pink sneakers.

"It smells funny in here," she announced.

"Musty," Harper said, stepping aside so Willow could wheel herself over the threshold. "From being closed up for so long."

"Peoples lived here?" Willow asked her in sweet, clear voice.

"I think so," Harper said, wishing she'd had time to go talk to Grayson at the Historical Society, but bread feeding had come first. "But a long, long time ago, it served as a lighthouse."

"What's that?"

"A lighthouse is a tower with a beacon in it that warned sailors away from shallow shores."

"What's that?"

"A beacon is a big light."

"At the top?"

"Yes, right, exactly," Harper said, opening the door from the anteroom into the lighthouse itself. She peered in first, making sure it was safe for Willow to enter before she moved aside to let the girl wheel in.

The room was circular, the interior walls red brick. There was one long rectangle window looking out over the gulf, a potbellied stove that vented outside, and an iron spiral staircase leading to the tower.

Harper didn't know the historical purpose of this room, but it had been converted into a living room at some point. There was a dusty old couch, a scarred coffee table, and seafaring pictures on the walls. With the right renovations it could look darling. It dawned on her if she and Flannery managed to pull off the conditions of Penelope Campbell's ridiculous will that she'd get the lighthouse because it wouldn't be reasonable for Flannery and Willow to live here.

Just sell it and get back to Manhattan.

But who would buy it? And even if someone did buy it, that would put a stranger living right next to the keeper's cottage. Harper shoved the thought aside. Plenty of time to think about that later. They had six weeks to decide what to do.

Besides, they might blow the challenge and the whole parcel would go to the Historical Society. Maybe that was for the best.

"Auntie Harper?"

"Uh-huh."

"How come I never knowed you before?" Willow was biting her bottom lip and studying Harper with a gaze so mature it surprised her. She knew what the little girl meant.

"Your mom and I . . ." How to explain this in an uncomplicated way that wouldn't cast either her or Flannery in a bad light. Harper defaulted to a fishing expedition. "Did your mom say anything about me?"

"She said you lived far, far away."

Hope pressed against Harper's chest. "She told you about me?"

"Uh-huh. She showed me pictures." Willow paused. "You didn't come visit."

"No." Gripped by sadness for all she'd lost out on, Harper shook her head. "I didn't even know about you, little one."

"Was it 'cause of Daddy?" Willow asked.

"Mmm." Should she seize the easy excuse? "What do you mean?"

"Daddy don't like Mommy to have friends."

Alarmed, but trying not to show it, Harper said, "Is that a fact?"

Willow bobbed her head. "He says he's the only family we need."

Tempting as it was to blame "Daddy," Harper wouldn't pit the child against her father. She didn't have all the facts. Had no idea what was going on in her sister and Willow's life.

"No," Harper said. "As your mother said, I live in a faraway city and I've been so busy working, I never got a chance to come and see you."

"Oh." Willow paused. "But now you do."

"Now I do."

"I'm happy." Willow beamed.

"Me too." Harper wondered if she should say more but decided to take her cues from Willow and only give her the information she asked for.

Willow rolled to the spiral staircase and peered up at the chambered nautilus effect. "Can we go up?"

"It's not wheelchair accessible."

Willow turned to Harper and rolled her eyes. Saucy little attitude. Harper liked the flair of spice beneath the sweet. "You hafta carry me."

"Oh, okay." Harper was worried she could hurt Willow. She didn't know anything about her condition.

Willow stretched out her arms.

Harper hesitated, but only for a second, as she shot back to her role as Flannery's primary caregiver when her sister was little. She reached out and scooped up Willow's thin small body, and when her niece's arms went around her neck, a helpless smile crept across Harper's face.

"Here we go," Harper sang out. "Hang on tight, these steps are tricky."

Willow tightened her arms around Harper's neck. She inhaled the child's strawberry shampoo scent and felt a strange aching rub across her heart. Memories of Flannery as a small child washed over Harper. They used to do everything together when they were young. Even though Harper was seven years older, they'd been so very close and Flannery used to pretend Harper was her mother. Then Harper left for college on the West Coast when Flannery was ten and that's when things between them changed forever.

She hugged Willow to her chest, the sound of her own sneakers against the metal echoing throughout the tower. The place needed soundproofing, for sure.

"A kitchen," Willow sang out, pointing as they passed the next room with a corresponding window like the one downstairs. The kitchen matched the 1950s decor of the keeper's cottage—avocado-colored refrigerator and all—lending credence to the idea they'd been updated at the same time.

Pausing in the doorway, Harper's marketer's mind toyed with possibilities. Converted lighthouses were so romantic. She could envision the room coming to life again with a good cleaning, fresh paint, contemporary flooring, and new appliances. What a whimsical, quaint place to build a life. Why did Aunt Jonnie live on a boat in the marina when she could live here instead?

Maybe staying in Moonglow Cove wasn't such a bad idea after all.

But how would she make a living here? She was in advertising and marketing. If she found a position in this town, she'd be lucky to pull down a quarter of her previous salary.

Previous.

The word bit into her. She hadn't had time to fully process that her career in New York was over. Maybe the cost of living in Moonglow Cove would be a quarter of Manhattan but she'd spent her life in high gear. Competition ran through her veins like blood. How did she let go of her relentless drive for success?

Go into business for yourself.

Yeah, right. Doing what?

"To the top," Willow sang out.

"Yes, ma'am."

"I'm a kid, not a ma'am," Willow protested.

"Indeed, you are and a very cute kid at that." Harper lightly tickled Willow, who giggled and wiggled.

Putting her worries aside, Harper climbed past the kitchen, headed for the lantern room. There was a closed door on the next floor. Harper assumed it was a bedroom and climbed on past. "We're almost to the top, Willow Pillow."

Willow's darling laughter rang in her ears. "I'm not a pillow, Auntie Harper!"

"You're not?"

Willow shook her head vigorously.

"But you're so soft, just like a pillow." Harper tickled her again.

Willow buried her face against Harper's shoulder, her warm breath caressing her skin. What a little lovebug! Overhead, a creaking sound caught Harper's attention.

Willow's head popped up and her big hazel eyes rounded. "What's that?"

"I don't know."

"Is it a ghost?" Willow's voice trembled.

"There's no such thing as ghosts," Harper reassured her. "Let's go see."

"I'm scared," Willow whimpered.

"Never fear, Auntie Harper is here."

The higher Harper went up the steps, the closer Willow plastered her body against hers. "Are you too scared? Do you want to go back down?"

Willow shook her head. "I wanna see the tower."

"All right," Harper said. "But if you get too scared, let me know and we'll leave."

"K."

The metal staircase ended on a landing and the door in front of them was closed as well.

"Is it locked?" Willow whispered.

"Let's see." Harper reached for the knob, turned it, and the door swung inward.

It was a cramped bedroom with a separate set of stairs that led upward to the lantern room and the widow's walk. There was a black wrought-iron bedstead without a mattress, just the frame and bedsprings. Beside it was an old chest of drawers and a straight-back wooden chair. The window was wide open, and the wooden shutters were swaying in the sea breeze.

"There's our ghost," Harper said. "A creaky hinge. Someone forgot to close the window."

Who? And for how long had it been open?

"We'll shut it on our way back down," Harper went on. "Are you ready to see the lantern room?"

"Uh-huh."

Harper's arms were starting to weary with Willow's weight. The child was light, and Harper was muscled, but she'd been carrying her up over a hundred feet of steep circular staircase.

The remaining stairs led to an overhead hatch. Harper pushed on it with one hand, and it took a bit of effort to get the swollen wooden door unstuck.

Willow cringed and brought her little fist underneath her chin. She looked for all the world like a chipmunk clutching winter nuts.

"You good?" Harper asked.

"I'm good."

"Here we go." Harper scaled the stairs, putting a hand to Willow's head to protect her from the hatch lid as they climbed out.

Inside the lantern room, they discovered a breathtaking, three-hundred-and-sixty-degree view of the Gulf Coast and the town of Moonglow Cove through the glass windows. Seagulls circled and cawed. In the distance, shrimp boats bobbed on the waves and Harper wondered if any of them belonged to Jonnie. Cars cruised Moonglow Boulevard while the Saturday brunch crowd strolled in and out of the quaint little restaurants dotting Paradise Pier.

"Auntie Harper, look!" Willow pointed in awe at the Ferris wheel on the pier. "Can we go there?"

"I don't make promises I can't keep. We'll have to ask your mom first."

Speaking of Flannery, her sister would be worried where they'd gotten off to. Surely, she and Hank were finished unpacking the van by now. Maybe the three of them could go to Paradise Pier and let Willow have an outing, grab lunch, and do some shopping. Specifically for Harper to buy some new clothes and a phone.

"C'mon, let's go ask Mommy."

"Got it, Miss Willow Pillow." The widow's walk that circled the lantern house would have to wait for another time to explore.

Back in the tiny bedroom, Harper carried Willow to the window to shut it and close the shutters. The view from this singular window looked out over the keeper's cottage. How many Campbells had lived in this room? A weird nostalgia rushed over her, and for the first time, she felt compelled to learn more about her mother's family.

She reached for the shutter banging lightly on the outside of the lighthouse and as she pulled it inward, she saw something carved into the aged wood. Frowning, she tilted her head and studied it.

Hash marks, grouped in clumps, crisscrossed the inside of the shutters. Harper counted each mark in the groups. Thirty in some. Thirty-one others. Only seventeen in the last grouping. There were eight groups in all.

Someone had been marking time.

A hard shiver ran through her. Who had lain in this bed and meticulously carved knife marks into the shutters? An eerie possibility crossed her mind. An idea she did not want to entertain. At one time, had someone been locked in this tower?

Could it have been Tia?

Goose bumps carpeted Harper's arms, and she could barely catch her breath, remembering plenty of times before Flannery had come along when Tia would lock Harper in a closet or the basement of whatever house they were living in when she was too much of a handful. Harper had preferred the frequent whippings to getting locked up.

Big leap, Harper. Reel your imagination back in. Hash marks in the shutters doesn't mean someone was held prisoner here.

But the damage was done; she couldn't stop picturing a lonesome child sealed in this tower, marking off the days, weeks, months with a pocketknife.

That's when she knew she had to go see Grayson. Not to flirt with him, but to find out exactly what kind of people she came from.

Shifting Willow to her left hip, Harper rushed down the stairs as quickly as she safely could, driven by a demon for which she had no name.

CHAPTER 13

Flannery

CRUMB: The pattern of holes inside the baked loaf.

While Harper was exploring the lighthouse with Willow, Hank was kneeling on floor of the elevator in front of Flannery.

She'd only been out for a second and now sat on the bottom of the cage floor, her knees raised, her head dropped between her knees, staring through the latticed bars at the beach twenty feet below them and trying desperately to suck in air through a spasming windpipe. She was never, ever going to get in this elevator again.

"You're okay," Hank said. "What you're experiencing is a normal reaction to a scary situation."

"I. Ca-ca-can't. Breathe."

"You're safe. I've got your back."

His words barely pierced Flannery's mind. She didn't feel safe. She felt trapped. Not just in the elevator, but in her life.

Hank didn't move. He didn't touch her. He just knelt there, solid and reliable.

You're doing it again. Romanticizing a man.

He said nothing, but Flannery heard him breathing deeply, pulling in a lungful of air from the bottom of his belly, then holding it for a long beat before letting it out in a slow, audible exhale, the sound exaggerated.

For her benefit.

Hank was showing her how to breathe.

She peeked at him. His eyes were closed, and he looked so peaceful. Just listening to him relaxed her and soon she found herself falling into his rhythm. They breathed together in a steady tempo, and she felt her muscles unwind, mesmerized and magical, fully in sync with him.

Oh, no.

Quickly, she pressed her face against her knees. She was losing herself again. Absorbed in another person's orbit.

"That's it," he murmured. "Nice and easy."

She raised her head and found him staring at her, but his eyes were kind and so very gentle.

"I get what it's like. After my injuries, I got panic attacks a lot."

She had a hard time imagining this tranquil man having a panic attack. It gave her hope that she could overcome her issues, too, and she appreciated his kindness more than she could say.

"Gettin' over trauma is a process," he said in that smooth Cajun drawl that lulled her. "Takes time and effort, but anything worthwhile does."

"What makes you think I have trauma?" she asked, fear closing around her throat.

"The panic attacks. They don't come on for nothin'."

Flannery gnawed her bottom lip.

Hank smiled at her, a soft, encouraging smile. "It's okay. Half the population, if not more, have experienced trauma of one sort or the other. Life gets rough sometimes."

"My husband is abusive," she blurted and instantly regretted it.

His dark eyes met hers. "I figured."

She smacked her forehead with her palm. "I shouldn't have said that."

"Why not?"

"I don't know you."

"Sometimes it's easier to talk to strangers."

"Why aren't you surprised?" she asked.

He seemed to possess uncanny knowledge of the inner workings of her mind and that unnerved her. Hank gave that water-off-a-duck's-back half shrug that she was starting to think of as his signature gesture and gazed pointedly at her left arm.

Flannery glanced down to see her sweater had ridden up to her elbow, exposing the four finger bruises, now a vivid greenish blue.

"I don't know who he is," Hank said. "But I wouldn't mind wringing his neck for what he's done to you."

"He's not worth going to jail over," she said. "That's for sure."

She waited for him to pepper her with questions, ask for details, but Hank didn't say a word. She met his gaze, studied his face, and worried what he must think of her.

He showed no reaction. No disapproval. No judgment. Just bland acceptance. He was right. It was easier to talk to a stranger than family. With a stranger, you had no skin in the game.

"I'd wager you have PTSD." His gaze dropped again to the bruises.

Feeling self-conscious, she tugged the sleeve down to her wrist.

"No," he said. "I shouldn't say that. I'm no therapist. I shouldn't have said that. You might act like someone who has PTSD, but that doesn't mean you do."

"You have PTSD too?"

He nodded. "I'm better. I still have a nightmare or two once in a while, but mostly, it don't trouble me much. PTSD is really treatable. If you do have it, or even if you don't, well, you can be healthy again, Flannery."

What a beautiful promise. She couldn't buy into it, though, because she'd never really been emotionally healthy. Anxiety had dogged her for as long as she could remember. Long before Kit and Alan even.

"I shouldn't have dumped my troubles on you. It was wrong of me."

"It's okay." He smiled, but it didn't reach his eyes. "I've got big shoulders. You have claustrophobia, right?"

"A touch, yes, along with a dash of acrophobia." Agoraphobia, too, if she'd admit it, but she'd already unloaded too much on him for one day.

"It was very brave of you to get in the elevator at all. Especially after getting stuck in here yesterday," Hank said.

"At least Willow isn't trapped with us too. I had to hold it together for her yesterday." Flannery shook her head. "If it wasn't for her, I'd completely fall apart."

"You had her when you were pretty young."

"I was."

"She's a cool kid."

"She is." Pride flushed her body in a warm heat.

"It's gotta be hard on you, her being in a wheelchair."

"You know what?" Flannery said. "Not really. It's all we've

ever known. She doesn't consider herself different from other people. She's so resilient."

"Just like her mom." This time, Hank's soft smile crinkled the corners of his right eye. The left one was stiffened by scar tissue.

Flannery felt overwhelmed again and dropped her gaze. "I need to get out of here. I have to check on Willow."

"She's with your sister. She'll be all right. Eventually, Harper will come looking for us."

"So we're stuck here until then?"

"It's not so bad," Hank said, shifting from his knees to his bottom, angling his legs out in front of him.

"Tell that to my pulse." She managed a chuckle.

A long silence filled the cage. There was nowhere to go. Nothing to do.

"Do you want to talk about it?" Hank invited.

"What?"

"The abusive husband. You don't have to. Just offering in case you think talking might help."

"I packed up everything and hit the road when Grayson Cooper called me. I didn't tell my husband about the inheritance. He doesn't know I have any family beyond Harper and my dad, who I haven't seen since Willow was born. I had no idea my grandmother Campbell was alive all this time. My mother told us she died before Harper was born."

"What about Jonnie?"

"I only told him about her once since I didn't even know her myself, and I don't think I even knew where she lived."

"I see."

What are you doing? Why are you opening up to him? You know better.

"What do you know about my family?" she asked.

"Not a lot."

"But more than me, clearly."

"The Campbells were . . ." Hank paused. "Different."

"How do you mean?"

"They were clannish and secretive. Except for Jonnie. She wasn't like the rest. She's the only Campbell left in Moonglow Cove now that Penelope is dead. Unless you and Harper decide to stay."

"It all depends on if we can keep that sourdough starter alive."

"You'll do it."

"I don't even know how to bake. Neither does Harper."

"You're both smart. You'll figure it out."

"Thanks." She smiled at him, sheepish that his confidence made her feel good. "How long has it been?"

"Since the elevator stopped?"

"Yes."

"Ten minutes, give or take."

"It seems much longer. I suppose Harper and Willow are still exploring the lighthouse and haven't given us a second thought."

"You're probably right."

"Wow." She rubbed her palms over her thighs.

He watched her anxious movements with curiosity, and no judgment in his eyes.

Flannery looked away. She had an urge to keep blabbing about herself but managed to quell it. From a distance, she could hear the faraway sounds of Paradise Pier. The chugging of roller-coaster cars, the excited screams of passengers, pipe organ music.

It was so tranquil. Why was she nervous and afraid?

Hank slanted his head back and peered up at the sky. "The clouds are so beautiful here. On days like this, it reminds me of home."

"Where is your home?" she asked, happy to get the conversation off her and onto him.

"Baton Rouge." He put more Cajun seasoning in his voice, elongating the vowels.

"The red stick."

"You know French?"

"Only the kind you get from four years of high school French."

"That ain't Cajun at all, woman." He laughed.

"Are you a good cook?" she asked.

"Are you stereotyping me?"

"I guess I am."

"I put on a mean crawfish boil. Maybe I'll do that sometime while you and your sister are here."

"Don't go to any trouble on our account."

"No trouble a'tall. Cajuns love any excuse for a party."

"Playing to the stereotype now?"

"I'm speakin' da truth."

"How did you end up in Moonglow Cove, Hank Charbonneau?"

"Story old as time. A woman." His smile was wry.

"What happened to her?"

"We parted ways. She wasn't into a guy with a burned-up face."

"Oh, Hank," she said. "I'm so sorry."

"T'was for the best. We're both happier now."

"You sure have a positive attitude for someone who's been through so much."

"That's how I know it's possible to heal from PTSD." Kindness was written all over him. It was in his smile and his relaxed way of being.

She liked him too much. This was so dangerous. *Please, Harper. Please. Turn the switch back on.*

"I don't mean to give you advice, Flannery," he said. "So feel free to tell me to mind my own business, but it seems to me you could be gentler on yourself."

"What?"

"You're pounding on your forehead."

Good heavens, she was. Smacking the flat of her palm against her noggin. She dropped her hand.

"You beat yourself up a lot."

"You can tell that about me?"

"It oozes from your pores."

This was all so dangerous. She needed out of this elevator. Fresh panic started nibbling at the edges of her mind.

"You know what," Hank said. "Uncomfortable feelin's are just uncomfortable feelin's. They go away unless you tamp them down and pretend that they don't exist. Ignorin'em is when you get into trouble."

Flannery thought of all the emotions she'd ignored. All the feelings she'd buried to get along with people—her mother, Harper, Kit, Alan.

"Just go easy on Flannery, will you?" he asked. "She's a good woman who deserves to be cherished and cared for."

Tears pressed against the back of her eyelids. She closed her eyes and swallowed hard. *Please don't start crying.*

"Look a there," he said. "A high-stepping pony."

"What?" She opened her eyes.

Hank was leaning back, propping himself up on his elbows and crossing his ankles. "Those clouds there."

She followed his gaze. Indeed, the clouds in question resembled a pony taking a big step.

Hank shifted the luggage and cardboard box around, making a little more space in the tiny cage. "Stretch out if you want," he invited. "Watch the clouds. It'll help pass the time."

She shouldn't. She wouldn't. She stayed where she was.

He returned his attention to the sky, and several minutes passed before he asked, "Whatcha gonna do?"

"About my husband?"

"Uh-huh."

"I'm not going back."

"Atta girl." He swung his gaze to hers again and smiled bigger than she'd ever seen him smile.

Seriously, you've known the man less than twenty-four hours. Stop depending on the kindness of strangers, Blanche DuBois.

"Flannery," he murmured in a somnolent voice.

"Yes?"

"You look to me like a woman who could use a friend. If you let me, I'd like to be your friend."

"I . . . I . . ."

"Don't get me wrong. I'm not looking for anything but friendship. No need to answer now. If you want my friendship, it's there. If you don't, I understand. No harm, no foul."

Flannery let out a long, slow breath, her lungs fully functional again. Slowly she eased her body into the small space that Hank had made. She settled in and they lay side by side, hip to hip and elbow to elbow. Not touching, just close.

It felt wildly comfortable, and it should not have.

They lay like that, not speaking, just watching the clouds roll by, waiting for Harper to come looking for them. For the longest time, it felt nice.

Hank had calmed her down and put her on an even keel.

Danger. Danger. Danger.

This was how it had felt with Alan at first. After Kit was killed drag racing, his best friend, Alan, had been there for her. Stepping in. Taking over. Helping out. She'd seen it as strength. Now she knew it had been about power and control. Alan had been looking for someone to dominate and she'd been ripe for the picking.

Terrified, Flannery sprang to her feet. She couldn't trust her judgment. Didn't know a good man from a bad one. "We've got to get out of here. Harper and Willow are going to be so worried."

Hank said nothing. He stayed stretched out, eyes on the clouds. Not reacting to her anxiety.

Her muscles tensed all over again. "Get us out of here!"

"One day," Hank promised, "what you're goin' through right now is all going to feel like a bad dream. One day, you'll pop out of bed with a song on your lips and a smile on your face and you'll wonder who that person was that you used to be."

Sighing, she sank back down beside him. "I wish I could believe you."

"I understand. You have to find your own way. No one else can do it for you."

"How did you get so calm?"

"I work on it," he said. "Every day."

"You work hard at being easy?" She laughed, but it was a mirthless sound, parched and desperate.

"Bingo."

"How?"

"I was just tellin' you. Feel those hard emotions, let 'em wash over you like ocean waves. They come and they go. They change. You'll be happy one minute and sad the next. You'll be angry and scared. It's all perfectly normal. Where people go wrong is thinkin' we're supposed to be happy all the time, but that's not how life works. It took a big trauma to get me to see that. Sometimes I think God was tryin' to wake me up, and I was so hardheaded it took a fiery explosion to get me there."

"Do you believe in God?"

"This conversation is gettin' a little too deep for one elevator ride, dontcha think?"

"I'm sorry," she said. "That was prying. I shouldn't have pried."

"I wasn't judgin' you, Flannery. I wasn't stonewallin', either. It just takes a while to get to know someone and I like a slow journey."

"But you just offered to be my friend. That's not particularly slow. You've only known me a day."

"I suppose you have a point." Hank started humming, a familiar song that she didn't recognize immediately.

It was soft and low and lulling, and she found herself humming along. She recognized it now. "Down in the Valley."

They hummed together, the old cowboy song. They hummed and rested. Just breathing together and watching the clouds roving the sky over the top of the elevator cage.

"Know what I like about you?" he said after a bit.

"Right now? Honestly, no. All I've shown you is a skittish woman who freaks out too easily."

"I like how open you are."

"That trait has gotten me into a lot of trouble in the past. I wish I could shut it down."

"Don't do that," he said. "Don't close down, Flannery."

She laughed but it sounded wobbly.

"Go ahead and feel it," Hank said.

"Feel what?"

"The feelin's. How are they sittin' in your body? Which muscles are clenched? Which ones can you willingly relax? Sink into the feelin's, but don't build a story around them."

"What does that mean? Don't build a story around it?"

"Most of the time when people feel an emotion, let's take anger for an example, they start picturin' the thing that made them angry. For instance, say it's your mailman."

"My mailman?" She giggled.

"Yep. He delivered a package that was damaged. It's somethin' you really wanted. Now this fragile and beautiful thing is smashed to pieces. You start tellin' yourself how rotten that lazy mailman is. The story feeds your anger. Builds up the bad feelings. You remember the time when he pepper-sprayed your dog because it ran out to greet him and he thought it meant to bite him. Now you're really startin' to hate him, and the anger gets bigger and bigger, and you decide to get him fired. You stew on it and you go to his boss and you rant, and you rave, but it don't change nothin' and you feel like you've eaten poison."

"My goodness, I see what you mean."

"But if you don't build a story and you just feel the anger in your body and you watch it, soon it'll shift and change, and you won't be angry no more." He paused. "Then again, that's just my advice as a small-town maintenance man. You get to decide what's right for you. If buildin' up your anger helps you get away from that abusive man, then you go ahead and build it up. You do whatever you need to protect yourself and your daughter."

She liked that he was giving her agency in his story. He wasn't saying that he would come rescue her from Alan. He didn't promise to sweep her away and take care of her. That was good.

"I think we can do it," Flannery said.

"Escape the elevator?"

"No," she said. "Be friends."

"That's somethin' you need to sleep on for a month or two before you make a firm decision."

"What is this? Bait and switch? You offered to be my friend and then take it away?"

"I'm not seein' it that way. But if that's how you view it, then yeah. Put my friendship offer on hold until you're *really* ready to accept it. How's that sound?"

"Perfect."

They turned toward each other, smiling into each other's eyes. At the same moment, the elevator jerked and whined to life.

CHAPTER 14

Harper

FERMENTATION: A process that occurs when the yeast and bacteria in dough convert carbohydrates to carbon dioxide and alcohol.

"Are you sure you're all right?" Harper asked, guilty that she'd inadvertently turned off the electricity to the elevator and stranded Flannery with Hank.

She knew how fragile her introverted sister was around strangers. Then again, six years had passed. She had no idea what Flannery was like these days. Flannery wasn't a shy kid anymore. She was a mother now, and from what Harper could tell, a damn good one. She was proud of her sister for that, overcoming their sorry parental legacy. Willow was a cool kid who didn't let her physical challenges hold her back.

You should tell Flannery that.

Yes. There was so much they needed to talk about, but right now, she was desperate to get to the Historical Society before Grayson left at noon. She wanted to know about those hash marks in the tower room.

"It's okay." Flannery smiled at her. "You didn't know about the elevator electrical switch being in the lighthouse anteroom."

Hank, who'd just brought in the last of Flannery's belongings, shuffled his feet and tugged his baseball cap down lower over his face. "With you ladies living here now, I'll get that electrical box moved away from the light switch right away."

"Thank you," Harper told him. "We appreciate it."

"Well . . ." He darted a quick glance at Flannery. "I'll let you get on with your day."

Flannery gave Hank a soft smile. "Thank you so much for all your help."

"Anytime." He bobbed his head and scooted out the back door.

"You're claustrophobic," Harper said, still worrying about her sister's emotional health. "I bet you were freaking out suspended in that tiny cage for twenty minutes."

"Initially," Flannery admitted, "but thankfully Hank was there to talk me down."

Harper studied her sister. She seemed to have an unexpected peacefulness and that was surprising under the circumstances. "I'm glad he was there."

"Me too."

"Mommy," Willow said, tugging on Flannery's sleeve, "Auntie Harper and I s'plored the lighthouse."

Flannery crouched in front of Willow's wheelchair. "I want to hear all about it in just a second, okay, puddin' pop?"

"I wanna live in the tower."

"Honey, it's not wheelchair accessible." Flannery smiled kindly at her daughter.

"Is it possible to make it wheelchair accessible?" Harper mused, her mind clicking with ideas.

"It's possible to make just about anything wheelchair accessible if you have enough money." Flannery straightened.

"Mommy, my arm is strong." Willow flexed her biceps built up from propelling herself in her wheelchair. "I could pull myself up the steps."

"Honey, no. Do not even try it. Do you understand me?" Flannery said with a hint of panic in her tone.

"Yes, ma'am." Willow nodded.

"If you want to go up the steps again, just ask me and I'll carry you, Willow Pillow," Harper offered.

Willow giggled and explained to her mother. "Auntie calls me Willow Pillow."

"That's because you're so cuddly and squeezable." Flannery leaned over to hug her daughter. "Auntie Harper loves giving people nicknames. She used to call me Flan Can."

Willow giggled louder. "A pillow is better than a can."

"It is better. But Harper didn't mean like a can of green beans," Flannery explained. "She meant I can do anything. Like Flan can win the race."

"You *can*, Mommy." Willow gave her a thumbs-up.

"I can't believe you remember that," said Harper.

"How could I forget?" Flannery met her gaze. "You called me Flan Can whenever I needed a pep talk. You were determined to remake me in your image. Epic fail by the way."

Troubled, Harper blinked at her. "What are you talking about? I wasn't trying to remake you in my image. I was trying to pump up your self-esteem."

"Oh." Flannery looked embarrassed. "In my head I thought you wanted me to be just like you and I felt like I could never measure up."

"Flan, I never meant that. *Ever.*"

"I know, I was a silly kid."

"I meant to convey that you *can* do anything," Harper said, feeling wretched that Flannery had misunderstood her intentions. "You know that, right?"

Flannery dropped Harper's gaze and reached over to run her hand through Willow's hair. "Uh-huh."

"Just like Willow can do anything she sets her mind to."

"Yes!" Willow agreed.

Flannery bit her bottom lip as if holding back something she wanted to say. It was all Harper could do not to prod her to speak up. But if she was going to talk to Grayson, she needed to get a move on. It was 11:40.

"I was planning on running to the Historical Society before Grayson left at noon. Would you like to go with me?"

Harper wasn't sure why she invited Flannery along; she really wanted to see Grayson by herself. Those hash marks on the shutters had unsettled her and she was looking for explanations.

She couldn't shake the uneasy feeling that once upon a time someone had been locked in that tower and had been marking time until their escape.

"Can we beg off?" Flannery said. "I need to help Willow do her physical therapy exercises."

"Oh, sure. It'll also give you time to unpack. I'm going to drop by the phone store afterward and get a new phone."

"Okay. Would you like to take my van?" Flannery pulled her keys from her pocket.

"No, I don't want to strand you. His office isn't that far from here. If I jog, I should be able to make it in time."

"Have fun. I can't wait to hear what you find out about our family."

"Even if it's unsavory?"

"Even if."

* * *

It was two minutes after noon when Harper got to the Historical Society. She pushed open the door of the office that was housed in an old train depot. Just walking inside and smelling the old-book scent felt like stepping back in time.

"Good morning!" The receptionist smiled bright as a new dime. She was a dashing senior citizen with fuchsia hair and outlandishly large, purple-framed glasses. "Or I suppose I should say, good afternoon. Welcome to the Moonglow Cove Historical Society. I'm Dixie-Lee. How may I help you?"

"Is Grayson here?" Harper asked.

"Oh dear, you just missed him."

Disappointment was a roundhouse kick to the gut. Oh well.

"Would you like me to text him and see if he can come back?" the receptionist asked. "Or would you like another docent to show you around?"

"No, no. That's okay. I've got errands to run. Thank you, Dixie-Lee."

"I don't mind texting him." She picked up her phone.

"Thanks for your offer, but I've got to scoot."

It wasn't until she was out on the sidewalk that Harper realized just how much she'd been looking forward to spending time alone with Grayson. She hadn't known the man twenty-four hours. Why was she so interested?

He's hot and you're sex starved. Two plus two.

She was shaking that off. She had a phone to buy. Glancing down the street, Harper tried to figure out the direct route the phone store was from here and that's when she saw a gray Porsche Panamera pulling from the parking lot of the train depot with Grayson behind the wheel. At the sight of him, her face broke into a helpless smile.

Grayson put the car in reverse and backed up.

Suddenly, Harper was breathless.

He stopped and rolled down the window. His icy blue eyes shimmered in the noonday sun. "You came!"

"I'm late."

"Better late than never. I was just on my way to lunch. Wanna come with?" he invited.

"Yes."

"Hop in."

She ran around to the passenger side of the vehicle.

Harper, what are you doing?

Tia was the type to hop willy-nilly into some guy's car, not her. She hesitated with her hand on the door handle.

"Change of heart?" Grayson asked, ducking his head so he could meet her gaze through the open window.

"I . . ."

"I promise not to bite," he said.

Why did he have to be so gorgeous? Returning his smile, she opened the door and slid onto the plush leather seat.

"What kind of food do you like?" he asked, putting up the windows and pulling to the parking lot exit again.

"I'm not picky."

"Shrimp? You like shrimp?"

"Sure." Right now, the last thing on her mind was food. Her gaze was hooked on his powerful legs encased in the same khaki cargo shorts he'd been wearing in the coffee shop that morning. He had very nice legs. There was nothing unappealing about this dude.

"I know this great little hole-in-the-wall off the beaten path, right on the beach," he said.

"Sounds perfect." She shouldn't have been so excited. She was here to find out if someone had been locked up in her family's lighthouse tower during some point in history. Not to flirt with the most handsome man she'd ever seen. Although who said she couldn't do both?

Grayson merged with traffic and guided the car down Moonglow Boulevard, heading south. On the way to the restaurant, he narrated about points of interest, giving her a brief rundown of the town's past.

"Did you know that Moonglow Cove once served as a hideout for Jean Lafitte?" he asked.

"I did not."

"Pirates settled this town," he said. "Following Lafitte, many sailed here from New Orleans, in the early 1800s."

"That was before Texas was even a state?"

"It was."

"They must have run into some tough difficulties settling this area."

"They did." He glanced over at her.

She could feel the heat of his gaze on her skin. She met his eyes, and he gave her a big grin.

"Both of our ancestors came over on the same ship. The *Bastard Seadog*."

"You've got to be kidding me." Harper hooted. The name appealed to the marketer in her. "How colorful."

"Every pirate on the ship was an illegitimate son from noble Scots or Englishmen."

"Really? That sounds so *Pirates of the Caribbean*."

"Where do you think the filmmakers got the idea? The *Bastard Seadog* was one of the ships they researched for the movie."

Oh, her little advertising heart went pit-a-pat. "I'm charmed."

"Yep. My four times great-grandfather, Edward Cooper, was a sixteen-year-old indentured servant from Penzance."

"No! Get out of here."

"For real."

"Next you'll be telling me your great-grandfather was the inspiration for *The Pirates of Penzance*."

"That's the rumor."

"Shut the front door. No way."

"Moonglow Cove has a colorful history. Why do you think I kept urging you to visit the Historical Society?"

"Wow. I had no idea."

"Your mother never talked about it?"

"Never. We barely even knew about Aunt Jonnie."

"Your five times great-grandfather was the one to whom *my* grandfather was indentured. Captain Ian Campbell from Argyll, Scotland."

"How did your grandfather end up a servant to my grandfather?"

"Back then, boys seeking a better life in America would sign on as a servant in exchange for passage to the new world."

"There's so much I don't know."

"Stick with me," he said, pride in his voice. "And I'll give you all the deets you can learn."

"I think what I've discovered already is enough for one day. I need time to let it sink in." Harper noticed the traffic had lightened considerably as they reached the outskirts of town. "It sounds like you really love history."

"I do. Once upon a time I had ambitions of being a history professor at some Ivy League school."

"What changed your mind?"

"My stepfather convinced me it's better to be a big fish in a small pond."

"Are you considering a political run in the future? I mean, seeing that your stepfather is the mayor."

"Nah. I'm happy doing what I do. I love teaching high school history and writing history books on the side." He took a dirt road off the main highway that led to a secluded part of the beach and pulled into the parking lot of a disheveled hut with a wind-and-salt-battered sign that read: SEA CAPTAIN NED'S.

Grayson wasn't kidding. The place was definitely a hole-in-the-wall and Harper loved it.

She'd discovered the best food eating in out-of-the-way places like this. Actually, Tia had been the one to turn her on to mom-and-pop joints that concentrated more on the food than the decor. Her mother had sought out things that were quirky, off-beat, or unique.

Harper couldn't wait to taste the shrimp.

Grayson escorted her into the building and the owner—who appeared to be the cook and waiter as well—waved a hand. The man had ginger-colored hair and a matching beard covered with a see-through facial hair net. He looked quite piratical, even with the dorky beard guard.

"Morning, Gray, although I suppose it's afternoon now," the man said easily. "Your usual spot?"

"Good morning, Ned. Yes, we'll eat on the patio."

"I see you've got company today," Ned gave Harper a warm smile and big wave. "Hi there. Welcome to Ned's."

"Nice to meet you." She returned his wave. "I'm Harper Campbell."

Ned's smile evaporated instantly, and a flicker of distaste passed over his face. "The Lighthouse Campbells?"

"Yes," Harper said, taken aback by his reaction to her name. "I'm Jonnie's niece."

"Jonnie's a good woman." The way Ned said it sounded as if her aunt was an exception to the rest of the Campbell clan.

"I've only recently met her."

Ned arched an eyebrow at that and studied her up one side and down the other. "You're the one who lives in New York."

"Yes."

"Jonnie's talked about you."

Anxiety pinched the center of her chest. What had her aunt said about her? In Harper's experience, when family "talked about you" behind your back it meant you had a lot of knives to pull out.

"Jonnie's proud of what you've made of yourself," Ned said. "She can't stop bragging about what a splash you've made in advertising."

That comment slapped her with a cold dose of reality. Her thoughts stumbled into the quicksand of the mess she'd left behind in Manhattan. If she hadn't been trying to fix Kalinda and make her over into her own image, she wouldn't be in this pickle. Why was she always rushing in to rescue people? Especially when they'd never asked for her help in the first place? The chest pinch tightened and yanked her belly into it.

"Jonnie doesn't even know me."

"Seems like that's something you'd want to rectify." Ned sank his big hands on his hips and stared at her.

"Excuse me?" Was this stranger giving her advice?

"Get to know your aunt," he ordered. "She cares about you."

Who was this big brute to tell her what to do? Harper rankled and was about to tell him to mind his own damn business, when Gray took hold of her elbow and gently urged, "This way."

As soon as they'd navigated the short distance from the front door to the back patio, Grayson let go of her elbow. The patio had a spectacular view of the ocean and a beach that was thin on tourists. This was such a beautiful spot that the food could be utter garbage, and no one would mind.

He pulled out a wrought-iron cafe chair for her, and once she was seated he took the spot opposite her.

"Don't mind Ned. He had run-ins with your . . ."—he paused and caught her eye—"grandmother."

"His demeanor sure changed when I told him I was a Campbell."

"It's not the most popular name on the island. Besides, Ned's got MacDonald family roots."

"And?"

"Back in Scotland, the MacDonalds and the Campbells had a long-running feud."

"When was this?"

"In the sixteen hundreds."

"And it's still a thing five hundred years later?"

"In a town like Moonglow Cove, which was settled by clannish Scots, yeah."

"Wow." Harper leaned back in her chair and studied Grayson. He had the most perfect nose—classic, masculine, proportionate to the rest of his features. She had a crazy urge to trace the tip of her finger over the bridge.

"You don't know anything about your heritage?"

"No. My mother tried to rid herself of all that."

"There's something to be said for escaping a situation you can't improve, but I've found you can't outrun yourself. Might as well face the hard truths and deal with them." He sounded philosophical. She wondered what hard truths he'd faced and put to rest.

"Where's the menu?" Harper asked, knowing it was better to keep her distance than to find out. His issues were his. She had enough issues of her own without trying to crack that nut.

"There isn't one. All Ned serves is Gulf shrimp. Your aunt Jonnie is his supplier. You can order shrimp gumbo, shrimp po'boys, shrimp scampi, shrimp salad, shrimp—"

"I get the idea, Bubba Gump." Harper laughed. "What do you recommend?"

"It's all good," Grayson said, "but my favorite is the shrimp po'boy. Ned's got this secret sauce for the bread that's orgasmic."

You shouldn't be eating all this bread, nagged a voice at the back of her mind.

"Orgasmic, huh?" She grinned at him.

His answering smile sent goose bumps over her skin. "Well, as close to orgasmic as food will ever get."

"That sounds lovely," she told Grayson. "Go ahead and order for me. This is your town. You know the ins and outs."

"It's your town too, Harper."

It wasn't. "Why do you keep saying that?"

"History's roots are real. You can't separate yourself from what's gone before. It's best not to try. Embrace your past, warts and all."

"No need. I'm returning to New York as soon as everything is sorted out with Granny's will."

"I assumed." He dropped his smile. "But I'm betting that if you let it, Moonglow Cove will charm you, and you'll be eager to return often."

"You've been around," she said. "I can see it on you. You've gotten out of here and come back. Swam in that big pond."

"Yes, you're right. I did escape Moonglow Cove when I was young. Despite my stepfather's advice, I thought I was too big for this small pond. I got my bachelor's degree in history from Rice and then I was accepted into Columbia for my master's degree and I got a job as a research assistant to a prominent Scottish historian, and after graduation I worked on programming with PBS."

"No kidding? What happened? Why did you come back to the tiny puddle?"

He lowered his eyelids. "I'd rather not discuss that."

Oh-kay.

Ned came outside with two glasses of ice water. "Did you want the usual, Gray?"

"Yes, thanks."

"Her too?"

Gray looked at Harper. "You still up for the po'boy?"

"I am." *When in Rome . . .*

"Fries okay?" Ned asked.

"That'll do. May I get a glass of red wine as well?" she asked.

Ned grunted and folded his arms over his chest. "I got beer."

Harper looked to Gray. "Would you like something to drink?"

"I'm good."

"You sure?" she asked. "It's Saturday afternoon and—"

"Harper, I'm an alcoholic," he said it so abruptly she was taken aback.

"Oh." *Aww, damn it.* She should have gotten a clue when he said he was good and left well enough alone. "Never mind then, if Gray's not drinking, neither am I."

"Harper, if you want a beer, get one. Be yourself. You don't have to change who you are because I have a drinking problem."

"I just thought . . . it's been really stressful this past week and sitting out on the deck feels like a vacation. I don't drink a lot. I mean, I can do without it," she babbled.

"I'll put your order on," Ned said and went back inside.

Feeling embarrassed, Harper tucked a strand of hair behind her ear, then dropped her hand on the table, uncertain what to say to ease the tension.

"Why didn't you get a beer?" he asked.

"I couldn't drink in front of you. I wouldn't want to tempt you." And she didn't want him to judge her for drinking.

"Harper," he said, settling his palm over hers. "You don't have to rescue me. I've been in recovery for six years. I'm clean and sober and haven't backslid once. I go to weekly AA meetings and I like the life I've created. I'm not about to screw it up because my lunch partner has a beer."

"Oh."

A long, uncomfortable silence stretched between them. Harper couldn't take it any longer and rushed in to fill it. "You know, I saw this program on alcoholism and it said that—"

He tightened his fingers around her hand just enough to get her to stop talking. "May I offer you a piece of advice that I learned in recovery?"

She pressed her lips together and nodded, but what she really wanted was to say no. If she could think of a way to say it without looking like a jerk, she would. She wasn't the one with an addiction, why should she take advice from him?

"Mend your own fences before you start stringing wire on your neighbor's."

CHAPTER 15

Flannery

SECOND BUILD: The second starter refreshment can be used as is for cakes, pastries, crackers, and biscuits.

At three P.M., over six hours after they'd fed it, the mother dough had doubled in volume. Flannery didn't know if she should be pleased or worried. Not just about the bread, but her relationship with her sister.

Were things developing too fast? Too slowly? She didn't know. They hadn't even had a chance to talk . . .

Or mend fences after six years of radio silence. So far, they'd been tiptoeing around that land mine, but eventually, they'd have to reconcile their falling-out.

Flannery had a million questions for Harper, but asking them had felt like too much, too soon, and threatened to stir up too many emotions. She was already wobbly after getting trapped in an elevator with Hank.

During Willow's physical therapy session, her daughter had told Flannery about her adventure in the lighthouse with Harper. "Auntie Harper told me I can be anything I want, Mommy. *Anything.*"

Flannery bit her tongue. She didn't want to discourage her daughter, but she didn't appreciate Harper putting unrealistic ideas in Willow's head. Harper didn't have children. She couldn't understand.

At loose ends after settling her daughter down for an afternoon nap and irritated at Harper for filling Willow with impossible dreams, Flannery had busied herself cleaning the rest of the dusty house.

An hour after she started, the cottage was spick-and-span, and Flannery curled up on the window seat at the kitchen bay window to watch YouTube videos on sourdough breadmaking.

The back door opened at a quarter to four and Harper waltzed in, her arms loaded with shopping bags.

"My goodness." Flannery shut off her phone and got to her feet. "How did you carry all that stuff up the hill?"

"She had a pack mule," Grayson said, coming into the mudroom behind Harper, laden with more bags.

"Thank you again for giving me a ride." Harper set her purchases down on the kitchen counter and turned to take the rest of the packages from him. "And for a delicious lunch."

"You're most welcome," he said. To Flannery, he gave a casual wave. "Good to see you again."

"I'm glad you had a good time," Flannery said.

"We brought back saltwater taffy for you and Willow." Harper waggled a small white paper bag. "With extra portions of licorice."

"You remembered licorice is my fav." Flannery was touched.

"Of course I did. I remember everything about you, sissy." Harper's smile was so sincere and bright.

Flannery's hopes sank. How could she bring up their hot-button topic now that Harper was in such a splendid mood?

"I'm going to take off," Grayson said. "Y'all have a good time with the sourdough."

Harper's smile widened. "Thanks again for a lovely time."

"You're welcome." Grayson was grinning, too, as he pulled the back door closed behind him.

"Is something cooking between you two?" Flannery asked after he was safely out of earshot.

Harper's cheeks flushed pink, and she dipped her head. "Hardly. I barely know the guy."

"Did you find out anything interesting about our family history?"

"Hold on to your hat, there's so much to learn. Our five times great-grandfather was a for-real pirate."

"No kidding? Willow is going to eat that up. She loves *Pirates of the Caribbean.*"

"Where is Willow?"

"Napping."

"Good for her. Could you help me stow away these packages? I'll tell you what I learned about our dark and tortured family past."

"Sure thing."

They carried Harper's purchases upstairs to her bedroom and Flannery helped her hang things up while her sister relayed what she'd learned from Grayson.

"You know that story Mom told us about *her* mother committing suicide by tying an anchor around her neck and walking into the Gulf?"

"Why do you suppose she lied about that?" Flannery mused.

Harper took it for the rhetorical question it was. "It was actually our five times great-grandmother, Levicia Campbell, who did it."

"How tragic."

"According to lore, she hated Texas, fell into deep melancholia over being so far from her beloved Scotland, and she took her own life. That, and—this is just my speculation here—she had a fierce warrior pirate for a husband and thirteen kids. I mean that's enough to send anyone flying off their rocker. The town rumor says Levicia haunts the lighthouse to this day, pacing the widow's walk in the middle of the night." Harper paused to hold a red sundress up to her neck and survey herself in the mirror. "I might wear this to Missy Sinclair's Memorial Day party. What do you think?"

"Wait, what? The lighthouse is haunted?"

"It's just a legend, Flan. There's no such things as ghosts."

Flannery didn't believe in ghosts, not really, but she did believe in energy and if Levicia Campbell's sad life had been energetically charged with negative emotions, it might explain why the lighthouse seemed so lonely and desolate at the top of the bluff.

"So . . . the dress?" Harper prodded.

"It's perfect. It'll look amazing with your golden skin and blond hair."

"We need to buy you something pretty to wear, as well."

"I'm a bit short on cash right now. I can make do with something I already own."

"Oh." Harper snapped her fingers. "There's something else weird about the lighthouse I haven't had a chance to tell you." Quickly, she told Flannery about the tower room and how she'd found hash marks carved into a shutter as if someone had been locked inside and was marking time.

"That's a bit of a stretch, don't you think? From hash marks on a window shutter to being held prisoner? Could have just been a kid with a new pocketknife itching to carve something."

"You sound like Gray." Harper twirled before the mirror. "Hey, you cleaned up in here. That mirror was so grimy I could barely see myself in it this morning. That was sweet of you."

"I have trouble staying idle. Cleaning clears my mind."

"Yeah, I get that. Me too. Remember how Tia used to yell at us whenever we dared lounge around?"

Flannery nodded. "If we didn't hop up and immediately start doing something, the belt came out."

"Little wonder we don't know how to relax." Harper hung up the red dress.

"That's all over now," Flannery said, hungry to pave the way for the conversation they needed to have. "Maybe we could have a talk—"

"Oh my, the sourdough! I forgot all about it. We need to feed the damn thing." Harper, looking animated and energized, blitzed down the steps two at a time.

Blowing out her breath, Flannery followed. Maybe Harper had the right idea. Fly past their differences, ignore the rift, and pretend it never happened.

That was the easy path.

Why couldn't Flannery just take it?

Why? Because she'd been hiding from reality for too long. The days of lying to herself were over. Time to face the music. Just as she'd done with Alan.

At the thought of Alan, she closed her eyes. Maybe he would just accept she'd left him and not try to find her. It was a possibility, although far-fetched. Tucking her husband out of her mind for now, Flannery entered the kitchen after her sister.

"Whoa!" Harper exclaimed as she peered at the clear plastic container with measuring marks. "That thing has doubled in size. It's really bubbly. That's good, right?"

"It means it's time to feed it." Flannery pulled her phone from her pocket and consulted the website she'd found on how to handle sourdough.

"It makes me think of that old B-movie horror flick *The Blob*." Harper giggled.

The effervescent sound coming from her all-business sister surprised Flannery. "We ought to watch the movie. Willow loves cheesy horror movies."

"Really?" Harper sounded shocked. "You let her watch horror movies?"

"Not truly scary ones, just the goofy ones."

"That sounds like fun, but there's no Wi-Fi here. I tried to get online with my computer last night and couldn't."

"You're right. I had to use mobile data to get online to search for sourdough recipes. That can get expensive."

"Guess Grandmother Penelope never got into technology. We gotta fix that. I'll call the internet company with my brand-new phone." Harper pulled a top-of-the-line iPhone from her pocket for Flannery to see.

"Nice."

"What now?" Harper asked.

"Huh?" Flannery blinked.

"With Blobby." Harper nodded at the mother dough that had indeed doubled in size. "You're the one who's read up on sourdough."

"Oh, I guess we feed her again." Flannery consulted the website. "After it rises a second time, we can use that discard to start baking things like crackers and pancakes and biscuits."

"Good grief, this stuff is complicated." Harper jammed her manicured nails through her sleek glossy hair.

If Flannery tried to imitate her sister's flawless move, her fingers would get jammed in the mass of curls. "Since we can't discard the dough, and it's not yet ready to bake with—or so I gather, I could be wrong—I suppose we just add flour and water to the starter."

Harper crinkled her nose. "At this rate, Blobby will soon outgrow her container."

"We'll just have to bake with the next batch."

"Which, if it doubles in size every six hours, means we'll be baking after ten o'clock at night," Harper said. "We're hostage to the schedule of bacteria."

"It's like having a baby in the house." Flannery chuckled.

"Gee thanks, Grandma," Harper muttered and rolled her eyes heavenward.

"Why do you suppose Penelope put us up to this challenge?"

"Who knows?" Harper shrugged and set a bowl on the kitchen scales so she could measure out the water to add to the mother dough.

"Why do you think she never contacted us when she was alive?"

"One word."

"Tia?"

"You know it. She might have tried to contact us, and Tia blocked her. You know how Mom was. What was it she used to say? 'Once I'm mad at someone, I stay mad,'" Harper said.

"Why didn't Penelope contact us after Mom died?"

"Gray said she'd been in the nursing home after a stroke for the last five years."

"It's been six years since Mom died. There was that year she could have reached out, but didn't."

"Who knows." Harper sighed.

"Let's talk about Grayson. You like him."

"He's all right."

"Gray and Harper sitting in a tree . . ."

"Oh, don't even." Harper shook a kitchen spoon at her.

"Did you ask him to call you Harp?" Flannery teased.

"You're the only one who gets to call me Harp."

Aww, that was sweet.

Harper dumped the water in with the bubbly starter, dried out the bowl with a kitchen towel, and proceeded to measure an equal amount of flour. "I hope we're doing this right."

"What's the worst that can happen?" Flannery muttered. "We kill a hundred-fifty-year-old tradition."

"Well, when you put it like that."

"We'd lose the cottage and the lighthouse." Flannery leaned against the counter and watched her sister.

"Would that be the end of the world for you?" Harper stirred the flour into the rest of the dough and didn't glance up.

But Flannery could see her sister's shoulders tense. "I *do* need this."

"Me too."

That surprised her. She thought her sister had the world on a string. Heck, Harper just purchased a new iPhone. Not the actions of a woman on a strict budget. "Things aren't going well for you?"

"Not at the moment."

"Me either," she confessed, bursting to tell Harper what had gone wrong in her life. But first, there was something more pressing to discuss. Flannery folded her arms across her chest. "I think we should talk about what happened at Mom's funeral."

Harper froze.

"It's important."

"We don't have to talk about it. It's over. Let's just start fresh and go from here," Harper said. "Okay?"

"I need to discuss it."

"Please, let's just drop it. No point fanning dying embers."

"I'm sorry, but I really don't see how we can move forward without settling this."

"Flannery, I don't want to fight with you. There's nothing to settle."

"I don't want to fight either. Let's not fight. Can we just talk?"

"Let's start at the edges and see how that goes first."

"Start at the edges?" Flannery asked.

"I tell you something safe and bland about my life, then you do the same with me. If things get heated, we agree to back off before it turns ugly."

Flannery nodded. "I can do that."

"Do you want to go first?" Harper asked.

"Um, okay." Stalling, Flannery reached for the bag of saltwater taffy, dug out a black one, and popped it into her mouth, chewing slowly and savoring the anise flavor.

Harper waited, watching her.

Swallowing, Flannery said, "Thanks for taking Willow on a tour of the lighthouse. She really liked it."

"She's a great kid. I enjoyed spending time with her."

Flannery cleared her throat, the taste of licorice strong on her tongue. How to begin without sounding like she was criticizing Harper? She needed to set boundaries but didn't want to rock the boat.

"She told me how encouraging you were to her. Telling her she could do anything she set her mind to," Flannery said.

"I believe in her." Harper's tone was heartfelt.

"While I appreciate the sentiment, it's not quite that easy."

"What do you mean?"

"There's a fine line between encouraging your children and setting them up for a fall."

"I just wanted her to know she's not limited to the confines of that wheelchair. I know this world class pediatrician we could take her to in New York. Get a second opinion. Not that I'm denigrating your doctor, but Kansas City compared to Manhattan?" Harper shook her head. "We'll get Willow set up right."

A spark of anger flared inside Flannery. Here was Harper, thinking she knew what was right for Willow, thinking her way was the best way, as usual.

"You don't have children so there's no way you can understand." Flannery worked to keep from snapping at her sister.

"Understand what?"

"For mothers *nothing* matters but your child's welfare."

"Unless you're Tia." Harper raised her eyebrows.

Oh boy, this conversation was already off to a rocky start. "Mom did the best she could. She had serious emotional limitations that we have to make allowances for."

"If Willow's welfare is what matters most, then why not consider the doctor I know? He's doing cutting-edge medicine. Trying things other doctors won't take risks on. I would have thought you'd jump at the chance."

"Because you don't know what you're talking about," Flannery said, losing her battle to keep anger from her voice. "There's more to consider than whether this top-gun doctor can perform some kind of miracle treatment on her. How painful will it be? What if it doesn't work? There's so much to consider, and I won't have Willow be anyone's guinea pig."

"I get it." Harper held up both palms. "I'm not a member of the Mommy Club. I have no right to weigh in on how you're raising your daughter. There's nothing to talk about. I'll keep my big mouth shut from here on out. I promise."

Flannery nibbled her bottom lip. "I don't want that, Harper. Your opinion matters. You're smart, you've been out in the world, and you certainly know how to get things done. You're a go-getter and problem solver. And Willow has some of that same high-flying energy. I'm proud of her." Flannery paused and met Harper's gaze head-on. "And I'm proud of *you*. If things were different, I'd cheer you both on as you raced to the top, but Willow has a disability. You have to respect that. She's not like other children."

"Will Willow ever walk?" Harper asked. "Is there a surgery that can help?"

"Not currently, no. She has what's called a myelomeningocele. It's a form of spina bifida. Willow's is higher up her back, so that means she can't move her legs."

"This is a birth defect?"

"Yes."

"What caused it? Do you know?"

Flannery winced. "The doctors aren't really sure. There was something to do with low levels of folic acid in my body when I was pregnant but there's also a genetic component, and spina bifida runs in her father's family. But his family members who are affected with the disorder have mild cases and no problems with mobility."

"Who's her dad?"

"Kit." Flannery's tone thinned and turned brittle.

"Where is Kit now? Didn't he want to come with you?"

Flannery knew what her sister was thinking. Harper had disliked Kit. Flannery's relationship with him was part of what they'd had a falling-out over. Harper trying to tell Flannery how to live her life. Thinking *her* way was the only way. Of course, in the end Harper had been right about Kit. That was a hard pill to swallow. Kit had been an irresponsible rebel who liked drinking and racing fast cars.

To Flannery he'd been exciting. In reality, this edginess had become exhausting.

"Kit died two weeks before Willow was born." Flannery kept her voice monotone.

"Flan, why didn't you tell me?" Harper looked hurt. "I would have been there in a heartbeat."

That's precisely why Flannery hadn't called her. Harper would have swooped in and taken charge like she always did. Tried to fix the situation. Tried to rescue her.

Instead, Flannery had turned to Alan.

In retrospect, Harper would have been a far superior choice.

"Oh, Flannery." The air left Harper's lungs on a huge sigh. "You've been taking care of Willow by yourself all these years? How do you work a full-time job and care for her as well?"

"I don't work outside the home. I'm married."

"To whom?"

"Kit's best friend." Flannery shook her head.

"Alan Franklin?" A look of distaste crossed Harper's face.

"Yes."

"Why didn't *he* come with you?"

"I don't want to get into that right now."

"I'm so sorry I wasn't there for you. I've failed you."

Flannery shook her head. "Please, Harper, don't make this about you."

Looking as if Flannery had slapped her in the face, Harper stepped back, palm splayed over her chest. "I-I . . ."

"You don't know how many times I wanted to reach out to you," Flannery whispered. "To pick up the phone and call you."

"Why didn't you?"

"After the way we left things?" Flannery shook her head. "No way was I sticking my hand in that beehive."

"What does that even mean?"

"You would have swarmed me. Smothered me. Taken away what little autonomy I had left. Face it, Harper, you would have charged in and completely taken over and at twenty, I would have let you."

Harper's eyes were the size of half-dollars and her mouth was hanging open.

"The reason I never contacted you wasn't because of the way you yelled at me for letting Tia get so obese. *That* I probably deserved. It was because I needed to be free from you, too, Harper.

I wanted the right to make my own mistakes. I needed to find my own way and I knew you wouldn't let me." And boy, had she made those mistakes. Flannery rubbed her left wrist.

"You would rather blow up your life than accept my help?" There was the tiniest quiver in her sister's voice that should have warned her off, but Flannery didn't take the hint, she just plowed right ahead, finally brave enough to say what needed to be said.

"Yes, yes. One hundred percent. I'd rather make mistakes and have them be my own than have a cushy mistake-free life that someone else constructed for me. I'd had enough of living in a gilded cage."

Ironically, it's what she'd done anyway, only with Alan instead of Harper. At least her sister loved her and had her best interest at heart. All Alan wanted was someone he could control.

Harper looked staggered and it was only when Flannery stared into her sister's eyes that she realized that in speaking her truth, she'd cut Harper to the quick.

CHAPTER 16

Harper

FOLDING: A technique for aiding gluten development in a dough.

Flannery's comments were a slap in the face, especially arriving on the heels of Grayson telling her to mend her own fences. Even though Harper knew neither of them had meant it in a hurtful way, she felt judged . . .

And misunderstood.

"I-I . . . only wanted to help," Harper sputtered, struggling against the pain crowding her chest.

Flannery notched up her chin, looking braver than Harper had ever seen her look. "I know, but I don't *want* or *need* your help. That doesn't mean I don't love you, because other than Willow, I love you more than anyone in the entire world. But I'm a grown woman. I'm not a child anymore. I'm in charge of my own life. I'm not saying this to hurt you. I just want you to understand it's not your place to 'fix' me. What you see as broken, I see as the places where the light gets in."

Stunned, Harper blinked, trying to absorb her sister's words.

It felt as if a giant scoop had scraped her insides out and left her hollow and empty.

"You're smart and ambitious and you've made something of yourself and I'm so, so very proud of you, but what's right for you and your life isn't right for me. If you have a problem to solve, your instinct is to charge fearlessly ahead and move heaven and earth to make things turn out the way you want them. Some of us have a softer approach to life. And there's nothing wrong with that."

Harper stared at her sister, feeling more lost than she had when Roger told her she was fired.

"As a survival mechanism, you developed a sense of certainty about the world. That you knew what was best. I get it. Mom abdicated her responsibilities and put you in charge when you were just a kid. But, Harper, your way *isn't* better. It's just different. Which is fine for you. But it's not *my* way."

"How did you . . . where did you get this?"

"I've spent the last six years trying to make sense of our childhood and how it caused each of us to take an unhealthy path. If we ever want to have a happy life, we have to look inside and accept ourselves as we are, not some idealized fantasy versions of who we should be."

Harper's mind whirled.

When had her little sister gotten so wise? All these years as a child struggling to be the adult in the room, Harper had formed strategies, rules, and justifications for how to proceed when she'd had no road map, no plan to follow. She'd created a way of being in the world that meshed with her identity of herself as the savior. The fixer. The rescuer. The one who made things right.

It was all an illusion.

She was no more together than anyone else. She wasn't special. Working her ass off wouldn't save her. Amassing money wouldn't save her. Being the best at her job wouldn't save her. Giving bone marrow to children wouldn't save her. Hiring disadvantaged young women because she felt sorry for them wouldn't save her.

In fact, her behavior was slowly destroying her.

Nothing would save her. Nothing, except facing the truth. Harper was addicted to rescuing others, and in that addiction, she'd lost her true self.

It was the hardest thing she'd ever faced. Harder even than accepting who and what Tia was. *That*, she had suspected from an early age. But this knowledge that she was just as messed up in her own way—especially when she tried so hard to fix others—shook her to her core.

Flannery eyed her as if she was a tripwire time bomb. "Harp? You okay?"

"Uh-huh."

"You sure?"

"Just fine," she lied. "Absolutely fine."

But inside, Harper's heart was breaking for the last six years she'd lost with her sister. How had she let her stubbornness, anger, and fear keep them apart for so long? Even if Flannery had told her that she never wanted Harper to contact her again, she should have called anyway. Flannery had only been nineteen when Harper left, just a child. It was Harper's responsibility—

There you go again, thinking you know best.

Shame blistered her ears. To combat the emotion that scared her the most, she started pacing.

"Harper!" Flannery gasped softly.

"What?"

"You're crying. I've *never* seen you cry."

A bluster of denial spread goose bumps across her chest, up her shoulders and down her spine, but she could taste the salt on the back of her tongue and feel the dampness on her cheek.

Flannery flew across the room, arms outstretched.

Harper was not a hugger. Her initial response was to tense up and resist the overture. If Flannery hugged her, she would full-on bawl. Something she'd spent a lifetime avoiding. She tried her best not to cry in front of anyone. Her inability to cry had been a sticking point between her and Sawyer, the only serious romantic relationship she'd ever had.

The thought of Sawyer made things worse.

He was a good guy and she'd been head over heels for him, but he'd wanted to get married, leave the city for the suburbs, and raise children. Something she'd been unwilling to do. Her career had been on the rise and she was still supporting Tia and Flannery. Their timing had just been off.

In the end, he'd made her feel as if something was wrong with her for not wanting the same things he wanted. Ever since Sawyer ended it with her, she'd gotten her physical needs met through casual relationships and it had been enough. She'd had no need for snuggles and cuddles, spooning and sappy sentiment.

Now here was Flannery with her arms extended.

How could she refuse her little sister's embrace?

Flannery enfolded her in her arms and Harper blubbered like a big old baby. From her pocket, her sister produced a travel pack of tissues and Harper made good use of them.

"I'm sorry, I'm sorry." She dabbed at her face with a fistful of Kleenex, knowing she was smearing her mascara.

"Harper, you're kinda freaking me out," Flannery said. "I didn't mean to hurt you. I'm just trying to stand up for myself."

"Oh, I understand, I understand and that's such a good thing. It's just . . . I feel so damn flawed."

"But you're *not*, Harper. You're amazing. You're the best big sister. And as painful as our rift was, we needed time away from each other to grow as independent people. I depended on you too much growing up. I was scared of my own shadow and you were so brave."

"You were seven years younger, Flan. I had to protect you from *her*."

Flannery's own eyes filled with tears. "But who protected you, Harper? Who protected you?"

No one had and they both knew it. That was the reason she'd been so devoted to championing the underdog.

"You've done so much for me. For Mom. For so many people. It's time you took care of yourself." Flannery hugged her tightly and then stepped back.

Could she do it? Could she let go of her need to chart the lives of those she cared about and start cleaning up her own act instead? For the truth was staring her right in the face. She'd used rescuing others as a way of avoiding fixing herself.

Not a pleasant realization.

"You're absolutely right. My own life is so screwed up. Who am I to tell you how to do anything, much less raise your kid?"

"Your desire to take over comes from a place of love." Flannery smiled softly and squeezed Harper's hand. "I do know that. You're not like Mom. Your goal isn't to control and manipulate other people."

"But it's the same result, and for that, I am deeply ashamed."

"No, no, Harper. There's a world of difference between you and Mom."

"Thank you so much for saying that." Harper buried her face in her hands. "But I've made such a mess of things."

"It's okay. You and I are going to be all right."

"Hey, look at you, comforting me."

"So I am." Flannery lifted her chin and winked. "Don't worry. We'll figure this out."

"My issues aren't just with you." Harper sighed and shook her head. "I've destroyed my entire career."

"Destroyed?" A concerned frown knitted her sister's brow. "Things can't be *that* bad."

"Yes, they can."

"Do you want to talk about it?"

"I don't want to burden you."

"Hey, hey, that's what sisters are for, right? Let me make us a cup of tea and we'll sit and talk the way we used to. How does that sound?"

Like sheer heaven.

"Go sit at the window seat," Flannery instructed as if Harper were Willow's age. "While I put the kettle on."

A few minutes later they were sitting with the windows open letting the sea breeze inside, sipping hot tea with lemon and honey and watching sailboats glide by the lighthouse.

"Okay, now that we're nice and cozy, please begin." Flannery wrapped both hands around her mug and gave Harper her full attention.

Harper hesitated. Now that she was feeling more in control of her emotions, she wasn't so sure she wanted to do this.

"I'm listening," Flannery prodded gently.

"Honestly? My life is a train wreck."

"Does it have something to do with why you pitched your cell phone into the ocean?"

"Yes."

Their eyes met, and a long moment passed before Flannery whispered, "My life's a train wreck too."

"I figured when I saw your car packed down with your belongings. We both know what being on the run looks like."

"You didn't even bring clothes," Flannery said. "Now that's really on the run. What's that all about?"

"I trusted someone I shouldn't have, *duh*." Harper thumped her forehead with an index finger.

"Who was that?"

Harper blew out her breath. "A young woman who reminded me of myself. I gave her a job and took her into my confidence. I didn't realize she was using me as a stepping-stone. I should have known. She was so charming. So bright and ambitious. We clicked right away. It all happened so fast. Too fast. She seemed so perfect. Everything anyone could want in an assistant. I should have gotten an inkling, though. I met her when I was asked to give a talk to a group that helped disadvantaged young women get a leg up. She'd grown up on the streets. Her parents were killed, but she was whip-smart and managed to get her GED and enroll in night school."

"You rescued her," Flannery said.

"Yeah." God, she'd been so damned dumb. "And Kalinda neatly slit my throat work-wise at the first opportunity." She told Flannery about the Twitter post Kalinda had made on Harper's account. "All my fault. I gave her access to my password. I had her post things for me occasionally. She was my representative.

I have no excuse. I let it happen. I lost my job over it and it's unlikely I'll find another one in New York advertising."

"Oh, Harper," Flannery's sympathetic tone stoked Harper's wobbly emotions and she wanted to cry all over again. "You *loved* that job."

"It's just a job. So what if I'm not working in the heart of the advertising industry? Things are much cheaper here in Moonglow Cove. I'm sure I can do online marketing of some nature."

"That's such a comedown from Madison Avenue."

"Nobody stays on top forever, right?" Harper shrugged past the tightness in her throat. A part of her kept thinking Kalinda would be revealed for the deceptive little snake she was, and Harper would somehow manage to get her job back, but another part of her feared that lifestyle was over forever.

"What are you going to do now?"

"Win a bake-off. Keep some flipping mother dough alive. Inherit a lighthouse."

"And you will, too! You've got the drive."

"I can thank Tia for that. I spent my entire life trying to win her validation. Hey, Mom, watch this. Look at me. Straight As. Not good enough? I'll get into an Ivy League school. Not good enough? I'll move to New York. Everything I've ever done has been an effort to prove myself worthy of her love."

"You never could."

Harper blew out her breath. "I know."

"Thank you for agreeing to share this place with me when you win our competition," Flannery said. "I need it."

"Why do you assume I'll win?"

"Harper, you *always* win."

"Not by a long shot."

"You're so much more together than I've ever been. Even in your defeat." Flannery gave a nervous laugh. "You're so accomplished and I've done nothing with my life."

"Are you kidding? You've got Willow. That kid is pure gold. I have nothing except a talent for convincing people to buy things they don't need."

"You've got me," Flannery said. "And Willow, too. We love you."

"Oh, Flan, I've missed you so much."

"I've missed you, too." Simultaneously, they set down their mugs of tea and hugged each other hard.

"What about you?" Harper said. "I want to hear about your troubles."

"Not now." Flannery shook her head. "There's plenty of time for that later."

"You sure? I'm all ears."

"Uh-huh. I need to go wake Willow up. If she naps too long, she won't sleep tonight. Maybe we can take a walk, then come back and make dinner."

"That sounds nice."

"Fresh slate." Flannery squeezed her extra hard and sat back against the cushion of the window seat.

"New start. We'll live in the moment." Harper held up her palm for a high five.

Flannery slapped it. "The Sourdough Sisters."

"An appropriate name. There has been a lot of sourness in our lives."

"But we're learning how to take that fermented bacteria and make bread out of it."

"Watch out Moonglow Cove, the Sourdough Sisters have come to town." Harper laughed.

"Can I be a Sourdough Sister too?" Willow asked, appearing in the doorway in her wheelchair.

"Absolutely," Flannery said. "Want to go for a stroll?"

"Yes!" Willow said with so much cheer that Harper begin to believe that maybe everything would turn out all right after all.

CHAPTER 17

Harper

SHAPING: Folding, rolling, and sealing the edges of dough to produce the final shape of a loaf.

After their walk, the sisters made tacos for dinner and washed dishes, and then sat on the front porch rocking chairs watching the tide come in and listening to the distant party sounds coming from Paradise Pier. Before they could go to bed, they still had to feed the sourdough and use the discard in a recipe, but it wouldn't be ready for another feeding until ten.

"I'm going to give this one her bath and then I'll be back to help you tackle the discard recipe," Flannery said, nodding at Willow.

"No worries. Take your time. I need to set up my phone anyway."

"See you in a bit. C'mon, puddin' pop, we have to wash your hair tonight."

"K, Mommy," Willow said easily. "Night-night, Auntie Harper."

Smiling, Harper waved as Willow wheeled herself to the door. "Sleep well, Willow Pillow."

Once they were gone, Harper pulled her cell phone from her purse and started setting up the features she preferred. She almost downloaded her social media apps, but then stopped herself. Who needed that noise?

Instead, Gray popped into her mind.

No, she wasn't going to think of the man as "Gray." That's what his friends called him, and she wasn't his friend. He'd charmed her late grandmother enough for her to make him executor of her will, and that was that. He was a friendly, devastatingly handsome guy, and nothing else. She liked him, but so what? Her future was too shaky for any kind of a relationship. Even a casual one.

Fiddling with the setup, she recalled the way he moved, self-assured, confident, comfortable in his own skin.

Stop it.

She liked the way his hair was cut short on the sides and a bit longer on top. The way his open, inviting smile urged her to smile back. How he'd latch his gaze onto hers and hold it for just a second too long.

As if he was interested.

You're imagining things. Knock it off.

Harper lifted one leg and curled it underneath her in the chair, her thumbs flying over the phone's tiny keyboard. She could hear the rhythmic sounds of the surf pounding against the rocks below the bluff and she got lost in the task as her mind spun sexy fantasies about Gray.

What did he look like underneath his clothes? What did his mouth taste like? How would it feel to have his strong arms—

A passing boat blasted its horn.

Harper blinked. The spell broke. Clearing her throat, she wandered inside to find her purse, took his business card from the side pocket, settled on the window seat in the kitchen, and texted Gray her new phone number.

The second she hit send her entire body flooded with dread and if she could have snatched it back, she would have. She was just about to text—oops wrong number—when he replied.

Gray: How's the breadmaking going?

Her heart skipped a beat. Then another one. *Don't answer. Wait. You'll look too eager.*

Harper answered immediately. I'm contemplating sourdough discard recipes. Do you like sourdough crackers?

Harper Lee Campbell what are you doing? Stop flirting with the man. Are you insane?

Gray: I do like sourdough crackers. Try adding rosemary 2 the recipe if you've got any.

Harper: Thanks for the baking tip. I don't know if we have rosemary. How about garlic powder?

Gray: Even better.

What should she say now? *Just leave it. Don't text anything more.*

Gray: I enjoyed our lunch 2day.

Harper: Me 2.

Gray: We should do it again.

Her cheeks heated. I'll see you at your mother's dinner party.

Gray: That feels like forever away.

Holy crap, he *was* interested.

Harper: Thxs for helping me with my shopping.

Gray: My pleasure.

She paused. Not knowing what else to text. Waited.

Gray: Did I scare you off?

Harper: Still here.

Gray: I'm talking about when I told U I was an alcoholic.

Harper: Recovering.

Gray: Still, there's always a risk I could relapse. I can understand if that gives U pause.

Harper: I thought U didn't believe in absolutist words.

Gray: Got me there. But I had to tell U. I believe in honesty in my relationships.

Well, who didn't?

Harper: You 4get, I'm in advertising where truth-stretching is an artform.

Gray: Hmmm.

Harper: What does that mean?

Gray: Can you separate your personal life from your career?

Harper: Don't know. Never tried.

Gray: Honesty. I like it.

He added a smiley emoji and Harper's heart fluttered.

"Ready to bake?" Flannery called from the doorway.

"Eep!" Startled, Harper tossed her phone across the table, feeling like a kid caught with her hand in the cookie jar. Recovering quickly, she turned off her phone, and stuck it in her pocket.

"I'm sorry. Didn't mean to startle you."

"No worries." Harper got to her feet. "Is Blobby ready for feeding yet?"

"She's doubled in size. Have you decided what we're going to bake our first time out?" Flannery waved at the recipe box on the counter.

"Gray likes sourdough crackers," she said inanely.

A knowing smile crossed Flannery's face. "Ahh, that's who you were texting."

"Why are you grinning? There's nothing to grin about. I was just giving Gray my new cell phone number. He might need it to tell us something about the will."

"Uh-huh." Grin widening, Flannery bobbed her head.

Honesty, Harper. Best policy. That was one hundred percent Gray inside her head. "And flirting with him a little bit."

Flannery's eyebrows went up on her forehead. "I'm surprised."

"About what?"

"I can tell you two have chemistry, but you have such a hard time being vulnerable in romantic relationships."

"A woman can change, can't she?" Harper gave a wry smile.

"That's the hope."

Harper rubbed her palms together and smiled brighter than she felt. "It's almost ten, let's get down to it while I can still keep my eyes open. You read the recipe and I'll make it. Unless you want to swap roles?"

"If you're gung-ho, have at it."

While Flannery found a recipe for sourdough discard crackers in Aunt Jonnie's recipe box, Harper took the portioned amount of starter and then doled out water and flour to feed the mother dough. The recipe was simple—sourdough starter, butter, garlic powder, and salt. Measure, mix, spread out on parchment paper, transfer to a baking sheet, bake for ten minutes, take it out, score the crackers and put them back in to finish baking for an additional fifty minutes. Following Flannery's directions, five minutes after she started the recipe, Harper popped the dough into the oven.

"Ta-da!" Harper set the kitchen timer for ten minutes, washed her hands, and dried them on a kitchen towel. "Our first attempt at baking. Fingers crossed it's not a fiasco. What shall we do while we wait?"

Flannery hid a yawn behind her palm.

"Why don't you go on to bed?" Harper said. "I'll stay up to finish this project."

"No, no. I can hang in there with you."

"You've got a daughter to look after. You need your rest more than I do. I'll catch up on my email."

Which absolutely wasn't true. She wasn't up to tackling *that* Herculean task, but she didn't want to admit she was just going to watch goofy TikTok videos. Maybe she'd see if there was anything on there about sourdough.

"All right." Flannery gave in easily and yawned again.

As her sister left the room, Harper's heart filled with hope. Maybe the mess of her life had a purpose. Maybe it was leading her here all along to make things right with her sister.

It was a worthy goal and until this moment, one she hadn't even realized she was desperate to pursue.

Instead of worrying about how she was going to reclaim her status in Manhattan, for now, she'd focus on reclaiming her family and figure out the rest later. Surrounded by the aroma of garlic and toasting sourdough crackers, she settled in at the table, turned on her phone, and saw Gray had texted again.

Just two words.

Sleep well.

Smiling, she almost texted back but resisted the impulse. Leave him wanting more.

Through the open shutters she could see the lighthouse, looming unlit, a tilted tower seemingly poised on the precipice of something monumental. She wondered what it had been like when it was a functioning lighthouse warning boats from the rocky shoals. Her ancestors the keepers of the lantern. That thought surprised her; she was a forward-facing woman who'd never had much use for history.

She thought about the George Santayana saying Gray had quoted to her yesterday. *Those who cannot remember the past are condemned to repeat it.*

Pushing back her chair, Harper walked over to the window and peered out into the thick shadows. Beyond the lighthouse, the ocean glittered in the dark. A peaceful, serene nighttime scene.

And then from those shadows, she saw a ghostly figure pacing the widow's walk and her tranquility evaporated.

CHAPTER 18

Jonnie

TEMPERING: Slowly raising the temperature of an ingredient that is sensitive to heat.

Restlessly, Jonnie paced the wooden platform of the widow's walk, knowing Harper was watching. She could see her silhouetted in the kitchen window of the keeper's cottage.

Question. Would Harper investigate?

Jonnie certainly didn't want to scare her. From what little Jonnie had seen of her intrepid relative, Harper just might come charging up to the lighthouse to confront her.

On the surface, it seemed Harper was afraid of nothing, while Flannery was terrified of her shadow. But Jonnie knew looks could be deceiving. Flannery was a mother and from what Jonnie could tell, a darn good one. A good mom would do anything for her child. Run through fire if needed. She'd never bet against that.

Unable to sleep, and feeling the itch of the old temptations, Jonnie had climbed the lighthouse to get some perspective. Over the past two decades her addiction had been quelled and unless she was attending a meeting, she rarely thought about drinking, but along with the arrival of her kin had come a stirring of the old anxieties.

And the raw fear.

Fight.

Her sobriety was too important to throw away. Not for herself, but for Harper, Flannery, and Willow. They were too important. She had to be present for them. They needed her more than they knew.

And she needed them.

Jonnie shoved a hand through her hair, felt the cool breeze against her face, sucked in a deep breath, and ignored the arthritis aching in her knees. Time to head back down the steps before the pain worsened.

Why had she come up here?

It was a rhetorical question. She knew why, but the answer would sound ridiculous to anyone but herself . . .

And Tia.

Tears pressed against the back of Jonnie's eyelids, and she just let them fall. Allowed the sorrow and grief to fill her up. The tears had been a long time coming. They were cleansing.

Wrapping her arms around herself, she held on tightly while the emotions pounded at her like the waves against the shoreline. Just as she had as a teen, sleeping in the top room of this leaning tower.

No. Not going there.

Jonnie squelched the memories, crushing them out. Reliving the stories served no purpose. But feeling the pain? Ahh yes, fully letting the emotions embody her until they rolled on through was cathartic.

Just as long as she didn't wallow.

Hauling in a deep breath, she swiped at her eyes and felt a hard shudder run down her spine.

Was she wrong in what she was doing? It was certainly manipulative. Too much like her mother for Jonnie's comfort. Grayson was unhappy with her over it and she couldn't blame him. She'd asked him to compromise his principles for her and he'd done it because he cared about her.

A savage stab in the center of her gut told her she'd hit the crux of the problem. The thing that in the past had urged her to get her hands on alcohol by any means and drown her shame.

You have to do this. There's no other way to mend your family.

How about the truth? Wouldn't that work? Just come right out and say it?

But no. They weren't ready to hear the truth. She had to get them to trust her first before she lowered that boom. You couldn't suddenly turn up the heat on an egg dish. It would curdle. You had to temper it, slowly adding a little bit of heat until the egg adapted.

Because if those girls curdled, that was the end of the line for the Campbells of Moonglow Cove.

This was her one and only chance to right past wrongs and she had to proceed with caution. Slow and steady.

Temperance. Her touchstone.

The end justifies the means, the end justifies the means, she chanted inside her head—as she had been since she'd set this whole thing in motion—*the end justifies the means.*

But did it really? In the end, wasn't she just trying to make herself feel better about her sins?

It was a question she'd explored with Grayson and they'd both arrived at the same conclusion. As unsavory as her deception was, there really wasn't any other way.

Switching on the flashlight that she'd brought with her, Jonnie descended the steps in the darkness with only the thin beam lighting her way. How many times over the past sixty-three years had she traipsed down this spiral, vertigo-inducing staircase? Tens of thousands for sure. Maybe a hundred thousand. Her mother used to make her climb the stairs as punishment. Climb until her legs cramped up and she crumpled at the bottom.

Her legs ached just thinking about it.

As she left the lighthouse, a figure came toward her out of the dark, and icy fingers clutched her heart.

Harper!

Her mind scrambled for an excuse for why she was here, but then she registered the height, build, and gait.

"Hello, Jonnie," called the steady, familiar male voice. "Glad it's you and not an intruder."

Hank.

Until she'd recognized him and relaxed, Jonnie hadn't realized just how much her body had tightened.

"What are you doing out and about this late?" she asked.

"I'm the caretaker." He walked closer. "I'm taking care."

She could see his scarred face in the dim glow of her flashlight. He was a protector to his core, and she respected him for that. He'd lost so much in his thirty-eight years on the earth, almost as much as she had.

Suffering.

The thing that linked them. The tie that bound. It was the reason he worked for her in the first place.

"Thanks for keeping such a close eye on everything," she said.

"Of course. How are they doing, by the way?" he asked.

"Adjusting . . . slowly."

"The younger one's carrying a heavy burden."

Jonnie nodded. "They both are."

Hank stood there, blocking her path, watching her intently. She could feel the heat of his gaze on her face and his intensity had her squirming.

"You need a meeting?" he asked.

"I could . . . probably should." She hesitated. "But the closest one this late is in Houston."

Hank nodded. While he wasn't a recovering addict himself, he understood. "C'mon," he said, holding out his hand. "I'll drive you."

"It's not an open meeting."

"I'll wait in the truck."

"I'm all right." She drew in her breath and pulled up her spine. "I promise."

"You sure? You *were* haunting the widow's walk. I saw you through my window when I got up to let Vixen out." Vixen was his mixed-breed shelter rescue, who was as big as a reindeer, but had a bladder the size of a pea.

"It's under control," she assured him.

"How about coffee and pie at the While Away Diner? I'm wide awake."

Jonnie did like pie and Hank was the best listener she'd ever met. Plus, the man could keep a secret, which had a lot of value in this gossipy town.

"My treat," he added.

"That'd be nice." She smiled.

As Hank led the way toward his truck, Jonnie couldn't help thinking how lucky she was to have broken at least one thread of the family curse. She'd learned how to make, and keep, trustworthy friends.

CHAPTER 19

Flannery

LEVAIN: A French term for sourdough bread. May also refer to the sourdough starter itself when used as a pre-ferment in a recipe.

On Sunday morning, May 22nd, Willow woke at dawn, chirpy as a bluebird, and peered over the side of the bed to shake Flannery's shoulder.

"Mommy, why you down there?"

While Flannery loved her child to pieces, Willow was not an ideal bed companion, especially in a full-size bed. Frankly, her daughter was a bed hog, sleeping sprawled out, all elbows and knees, and she'd disturbed Flannery several times during the night.

Eventually, Flannery surrendered, took her pillow and a blanket, and curled up on the floor to get some rest.

"Mommy?"

"Huh?" Flannery rubbed her bleary eyes.

"Can we have doughnuts for breakfast?"

Yawning, Flannery sat up and stretched big. Normally, she kept an eye on Willow's sugar consumption, but whenever they traveled—which granted wasn't often—she permitted her a sweet indulgence, usually in the form of doughnuts or waffles with maple syrup and whipped cream.

They did have to do something with the morning sourdough discard. Maybe she could find a sourdough doughnut recipe. Failing that, they could make waffles. She'd seen a recipe for discard waffles in Jonnie's recipe box.

And today was the day she and Harper needed to start their first loaf of bread. If they had any hope of competing in the bake-off, they needed to get up to speed as fast as possible. The thought of tackling that task had her wanting to flop back down on the floor and cover her face with a pillow. She'd read enough about sourdough to understand this was not a casual undertaking. The process of going from freshly fed dough to baked loaf spanned over twenty-four hours.

Ugh.

Instead of giving in to inertia, Flannery reached for her phone, googled "sourdough discard doughnuts," and boom, a plethora of thirty-minute recipes popped up. This she could handle.

"Doughnuts," she said. "You got it, sweetheart. Let's get this party started."

"Yippee!" Willow gifted her with the biggest smile that warmed Flannery to the soles of her feet.

* * *

An hour later, Flannery, Harper, and Willow sat in the breakfast nook scarfing down the best doughnuts Flannery had ever eaten. She couldn't believe her low-carb sister had decided to share in the carb-heavy breakfast, but she didn't comment.

Harper was in charge of her diet and she could eat whatever she chose.

Harper took a second doughnut, met Flannery's gaze, and said with a shrug, "When in Rome . . ."

Flannery liked that her sister seemed to have loosened the reins on her strict self-control. Harper had always been far too hard on herself, terrified that if she ever let up, she'd end up like their mother.

"Can we make these every day?" Willow asked, licking her fingers after she'd polished off every last crumb.

"Why not?" Harper said. "We'll have plenty of discard."

"How about we restrict the doughnuts to a Sunday morning treat?" Flannery suggested.

"Aww, rats," Willow said.

"Appreciate what you have," Flannery said gently. "Doughnuts could disappear from the menu completely."

After breakfast, they cleaned the kitchen and turned to tackle the big challenge. Making their first loaf of sourdough bread.

"How about I read the directions this time, while you're hands on?" Harper said, sounding so cheerful that Flannery wondered if she'd missed something. It was as if their six-year estrangement never happened.

They were healing.

Her heart filled with hope. "Taking turns sounds like an excellent idea."

Flannery dug around in a kitchen drawer, found two well-worn aprons, tied one around her waist and tossed the other to her sister.

"I don't need one," Harper said. "You're the one doing the work."

"In case you haven't noticed, sourdough sticks to *everything*." Flour and water made such a gooey paste they'd had to soak the utensils they used to stir the dough in hot water to get the gunk off. "And you look pretty in that snazzy outfit."

"What?" Harper glance down. "Not snazzy. I'm wearing a tank and shorts."

"High-end tank and shorts. Protect your investment, sis."

Harper waggled her head in a movement that said Flannery had a point and she put on the apron.

Willow wheeled herself over to watch the proceedings. "Canna help?"

"Not right now, sweetie. Auntie Harper and I have to figure out how this whole thing works ourselves. Later, once we get good at it, you can help."

"Oh." Willow's curiosity lost steam. "Canna play a video game?"

Biting back a sigh, Flannery pulled her cell phone from her pocket, switched it on, opened the gaming app that Willow favored, and passed it to her.

"Thanks, Mommy." Willow wheeled back to the breakfast nook and was instantly engrossed in the screen.

"I feel bad using my phone as a babysitter," she mumbled to Harper.

"Hey, a mom's gotta do what a mom's gotta do. After this, we'll go do something fun."

"Thanks," Flannery said.

"What for?"

"Not judging me."

"Why would I judge you? I'm not a mom. I have no idea how to parent and if I do ever offer a flip opinion, completely ignore me. I sometimes spout idiotic things without first thinking it through."

Flannery lifted a shoulder. "I guess I'm overly sensitive. I often feel like I'm not doing a good enough job."

"Well, you know where *that* comes from."

She did.

"You're doing the best you can, sis, and that's all anyone should ask of you." Harper's eyes were kind.

"It's an ongoing battle, isn't it? Overcoming a rotten childhood. People tell you to just move on, to let it go, as if it's that easy."

"Those are the people who have no idea what it's like to be raised by a mentally disordered parent. They assume their experiences of a loving mother are yours. It's normal, really, to project our experiences, thoughts, and beliefs onto others."

"Regular people often don't appreciate that when your childhood is unstable, the entire world feels forever unsafe."

Harper put a hand on Flannery's upper arm and gave her a reassuring smile. "It's safe here. I'm safe. Or at least I'm trying to be."

"Me too. I want to be there for you as well."

"Let's just be honest, okay? We're survivors. Let's try not to forget that and be gentle with ourselves and each other."

The conversation Flannery had had with her sister yesterday seemed to have shifted their relationship in a positive way. If things kept going at this rate, they might even become a real family again.

No, not again.

They'd never been a family. Not really. Tia's constant triangulation of her daughters saw to that. But maybe, if they both worked at it, they could find a way to love and accept each other for who they were, flaws and all. It had been Flannery's greatest wish since childhood.

A loving and intimate connection to family.

They had a few hurdles before they could get there. Make-or-break hurdles. Flannery could hope for the best, but she wouldn't fully let down her guard until those hurdles were cleared. Eventually, when she felt safe enough, she'd tell Harper about Alan; she really didn't want to get into it right now, especially with Willow in the room.

Harper bit her bottom lip and knotted her fingers together. She looked so vulnerable that Flannery couldn't resist hugging her as she'd done the night before.

"Alrighty." Harper took a deep breath and stepped back. "Ready to tackle this thing?"

"Yep." A sudden effervescent joy feathered inside Flannery. This was going to be a good day. She could feel it in her bones.

Harper consulted the recipe. "Oh boy, this is *not* a piece a cake."

"We can handle it . . . together."

"The Three Musketeers," Harper declared.

"Three?"

"Willow's part of this too."

The fact that her sister had included Willow touched Flannery's heart. She was so glad she'd come here and wondered why she'd been so worried.

"What about Jonnie?" she asked. "Where does she fit?"

"I'm not sure about her." Harper shook her head.

"What do you mean?"

"Something's going on there. I can't put my finger on it, but it feels like she's hiding something from us."

That ruffled Flannery's guilt. She had secrets too. "Doesn't everyone have skeletons in their closet?"

"Yeah." Harper got a faraway look in her eyes. "I suppose you're right."

That triggered Flannery's curiosity, but she didn't ask about her sister's secrets because she wasn't ready to reveal her own. Instead, she rubbed her palms together. "What's the first step?"

"Oh dear," Harper muttered. "Since we fed the starter again after we made the doughnuts, we've got to wait between four and six hours or more, depending on the temperature, before we can start the bread baking process. Unless I'm misinterpreting this." Reading aloud, Harper described the process. "We fed the levain an hour ago, it's nine now, so six hours from now . . ."

"It'll be three P.M. I have a feeling we're going to be up late again."

Harper groaned. "I hardly slept last night."

"Me either. That full-size bed is too small for both me and Willow. What kept you up?"

Harper cast a quick glance in Willow's direction. "I saw something . . . or thought I saw something . . . last night that worried me."

"What was it?"

"Someone pacing the widow's walk at the lighthouse. But it was late and dark, and I couldn't be sure. Maybe it was just my overactive imagination."

Goose bumps popped up on Flannery's arms. So much for feeling safe. "Who could it be?"

"Hank Charbonneau maybe?" Harper suggested. "Keeping an eye on things. Or Jonnie."

"We'll ask her." Flannery reached over and squeezed her sister's hand. "One for all and all for one."

"Yes." Harper paused. "What do we do for the next several hours while we wait on Blobby?"

"Do you want to go see Aunt Jonnie?" Flannery suggested. "I'd love a tour of her houseboat."

"I'll text her and see if she's up for a visit and then maybe we can take Willow to Paradise Pier. By the time we get back, the dough should have doubled in bulk."

"And then we begin this process in earnest."

* * *

THEY FOUND AUNT Jonnie on her houseboat in the marina. She was swabbing the deck with a mop, wearing mom jeans that hung loosely on her hips and a red-checkered men's shirt with a black tank top underneath and sneakers with no socks.

She stopped working as Flannery rolled Willow's wheelchair down the wooden dock toward her boat slip and shaded her eyes with her hand. She broke into a big smile, dissolving her inherent seriousness with a warm welcome.

"Good morning, good morning!" Jonnie waved them aboard. "It's good to have you visit."

"What's that?" Willow pointed at the Jolly Roger flag fluttering from the flagpole, the wind whipping through it. *Whup, Whup, Whup.*

"A nod to the Campbell family's pirate heritage." Aunt Jonnie laughed. "If you can't beat 'em, join 'em, right? Y'all come on in." She propped her mop against the side of the house and waved them in with an arching motion.

"I don't think Willow's wheelchair will fit through the door," Harper said.

"It will if we collapse it. Can one of you guys do that while I hold her?" Flannery asked.

"May I hold her?" Aunt Jonnie asked.

"Ask Willow."

"You gonna let your old aunt Jonnie hold you?" Jonnie held out her arms.

Without hesitating, Willow went to her great-aunt, open and accepting.

Trusting.

It concerned Flannery to see her daughter so easily go to a stranger, but another part of her said, *Look how confident she is, you haven't screwed Willow up too much.*

Yet.

But she had to get away from Alan if she had any hope of keeping the damage to a minimum.

"Oh, my goodness, child," Jonnie said lifting Willow out of the chair. "You're light as a feather."

"I'm not a feather," Willow denied. "I'm heavy."

"You're right." Laughing, Jonnie pretended to stagger under Willow's weight as she led the way inside her small houseboat. Flannery collapsed the wheelchair and pushed it ahead of her as she followed and Harper brought up the rear.

The living room was stuffed with belongings and smelled of the sea as the floating house swayed gently underneath their movements. Flannery opened the wheelchair and motioned for Jonnie to settle Willow into it.

Aunt Jonnie eased Willow down and invited, "Have a seat, have a seat."

Flannery noticed that her aunt repeated phrases just as their mother had. It made her nostalgic and sad, longing for things she'd never had to begin with.

Aunt Jonnie sank into a plush chair upholstered in a seahorse-patterned fabric.

"Seahorses!" Willow exclaimed.

"Do you like seahorses?" Jonnie asked.

Willow nodded vigorously. "They are *sooo* cute."

"She's loved them since I took her to the aquarium," Flannery explained.

Willow made horse noises, curling her lips back to neigh, and everyone laughed.

"I've got something for you, Willow." Jonnie went to a large wooden chest in the corner. It was old and heavy and looked like a pirate's treasure chest.

"What is it?" Willow asked.

Winking, Jonnie dug in the trunk, pulled out a stuffed seahorse, and passed it to Willow. "You can have it."

Her daughter's eyes widened. "Really?"

"Absolutely, absolutely."

Willow clutched the stuffed seahorse to her chest and let out an awed breath. "Thank you."

Her aunt's generosity sewed up Flannery's favorable opinion.

Harper was investigating the room, not taking a seat. Prowling. It seemed a bit rude to Flannery, but she was not in charge of Harper's behavior.

Stopping in front of the bookcase, Harper studied the shelves. "You've got annuals from Moonglow Cove High School."

"Yes. I kept them all. I don't know why. I can't bring myself to throw them out," Jonnie said.

"Not just *your* annuals," Harper said. "There are three here from the years our mother would have been in high school."

Jonnie nodded and pressed her lips together. "Those are Tia's yearbooks, yes."

"Why only three?" Harper turned to meet Jonnie's eyes.

"Tia didn't finish high school. She left Moonglow Cove before her senior year," Jonnie explained.

Flannery blinked. That absolutely could not be true. Their mother had a master's degree in literature. She loved learning and reading and research to the point where her interests became all-consuming, overshadowing everything, including the care of her children.

"Tia got her GED when she came back home, with Harper in tow, two years after she left. She showed up out of the blue one day, never explaining where she'd been or why she hadn't contacted us." Jonnie sounded wistful and sad.

Flannery wanted to wrap her arms around her aunt and hug her tight. She didn't, of course. She wasn't as spontaneous as Willow. Her needy impulses had led her astray too many times.

Harper jumped and looked alarmed as she set down the annual she'd been leafing through. "What are you talking about?"

"You lived here with me for a year between the ages of two and three and you were the cutest kid I'd ever seen . . ." Jonnie shifted her gaze to Willow and smiled. "Until this one came along."

"I'm the cutest now?" Willow asked.

"Indeed." Jonnie leaned over to pat Willow's knee.

Willow beamed and wriggled with happiness.

"Wait, what, back up." Harper stopped pacing and came over to plunk down on the couch in front of Jonnie. "Grayson mentioned something yesterday about us playing in the sandbox together, but I was sure he'd mistaken me for someone else. Now, you're telling me he was right?"

"He was right."

"What happened? What caused Mom to leave high school and Moonglow Cove?" Harper grilled her. "And then why did she later return only to take off again?"

Jonnie squirmed in her chair, hauled in a deep breath, and then on one long gush of air, as if she couldn't wait to get it out, said, "Tia got pregnant with you at the end of her junior year and our parents—your grandparents—came unhinged. They were superstrict, and Tia ran away, and I don't know where she went or what happened to her during those two years she was gone. My father died at sea during the time Tia was gone when his shrimp boat sank in a squall."

"Whoa." Harper raised both palms.

"That must have been so hard for all of you," Flannery said.

"Mom never said anything about any of this to us." Harper crossed her legs. Uncrossed them. Crossed them again as if uncertain what to do with her restless limbs.

"What did Tia tell you about your early years?" Jonnie asked.

"Honestly? She refused to talk about it. She said my father didn't want me and that her family didn't support her decision to keep me, so she left." Harper jammed her fisted hands between her knees and pressed her thighs together, a sure sign she was holding in the emotions that she was afraid to express.

"And you don't remember *anything* about coming back to Moonglow Cove?" Jonnie's voice was thick with melancholia.

"No." Harper locked eyes with Jonnie. "Not a thing."

Flannery watched the interaction between the two of them, feeling left out. That wasn't uncommon, though. People often overlooked her.

"I suppose you were too young. You were only a toddler when she left you here for thirteen months. I don't imagine that you would remember it. You lived here on the houseboat with me and—" She broke off, inhaled deeply, and then continued. "In fact, that seahorse I gave Willow used to be yours."

Stunned, Flannery felt her jaw unhinge. "You raised Harper for over a year? All on your own?"

Harper's face was completely blank. She seemed in shock.

Jonnie nodded, her chin clenching as if she were struggling not to cry. "It was the best year of my entire life . . . and the very worst. When Tia took you away from me, it killed my soul. I . . . well, I made some pretty bad mistakes in the aftermath."

Tears misted their aunt's eyes and Jonnie turned her head so they couldn't see her cry.

Flannery ached to hug her hard, but it wasn't her place. She reached in her purse for tissues and passed several to Jonnie who scrubbed at her face.

Harper hopped to her feet, pacing like a restless lion. "Could I speak to you outside, please, Jonnie?"

Flannery didn't know whether to feel hurt or encouraged that her sister wanted a private conversation with their aunt, but this wasn't about her. She wouldn't get in the middle of it.

Mutely, Jonnie bobbed her head, pushed up from her chair, and walked outside, leaving Flannery feeling left out again and abandoned as she had for much of her life.

CHAPTER 20

Harper

AUTOLYZE: Sometimes called for in recipes where the flour and water are mixed just until combined and allowed to rest before adding salt, leavening, or other ingredients.

Once the door had closed behind them and they were standing on the deck underneath an overcast sky, Harper rounded on her aunt.

"Was it you? Were you the one on the widow's walk late last night?"

Jonnie didn't meet her gaze; instead she picked up the mop she'd left propped against the side of the houseboat and went at the deck again with stiff determined strokes. What? Jonnie was just going to ignore her?

"Was it?" Harper prodded.

After a long moment, Jonnie said curtly, "It was."

"Well, you scared the daylights out of me. Was that your intention?"

"No, not at all." Jonnie looked up from her mopping and briefly met Harper's gaze before returning her attention to her work. "I couldn't sleep. Sometimes, when I can't sleep, I drive over to the lighthouse and climb the stairs to the tower."

"Why?"

Jonnie's eyes were on the deck, the strands of her mop flicking over the surface.

"Why?" Harper persisted. She was fed up with subterfuge and wanted answers.

"The lighthouse is haunted."

Harper groaned and leaned the back of her head against the houseboat, peering up at the clouds as if she might find salvation there. "Please do not tell me that you believe in ghosts."

"I do," Jonnie said with such conviction that Harper jerked her head around to stare at her aunt. "But the place isn't haunted by otherworldly spirits."

"What then?"

"It's haunted by history and lineage."

Harper thought of the hash marks on the shutters in the tower room. There were too many festering secrets in this family, and it was time to drag them out into the light. "If the place is haunted by bad memories, I'd think you'd want to stay as far away from it as possible."

"I visit the lighthouse to remind me of who I was and how far I've come." Jonnie was pushing the mop so vigorously it was a wonder she didn't rub a hole in the deck. "And to keep me from backsliding."

"Backsliding into what?"

Jonnie kept scrubbing.

"Into what?" Harper persisted.

Jonnie stopped mopping, looked weary to the bone. "I'm a

recovering alcoholic, Harper. I've been sober for twenty years and I intend on staying that way."

"Oh." Harper paused, absorbing this information. Grayson had a problem with alcohol too. He'd told her Jonnie had saved his life. Did that mean she'd helped him get into treatment?

"The three of us being here is putting a strain on your sobriety," Harper murmured.

"It is, but I can handle it." Jonnie met her gaze.

"Can you?"

Jonnie narrowed her eyes. "You look after you, Harper, and I'll look after me. Okay?"

"Maybe Flannery and I shouldn't be here."

"No, no." Jonnie looked stricken by the thought of them leaving. "I'm thrilled you're here. It's a very good thing . . . for us all."

"Are you sure?"

"Having you girls here together is the best thing that's ever happened to me."

"I'm thinking maybe it is for us, too." Harper smiled gently at her aunt. "But I do have one request and I hope you can honor it."

"What is it?" Jonnie asked, the strong woman looking suddenly vulnerable and uncertain.

"I'd appreciate it if you'd stop coming to the lighthouse in the middle of the night as long as we're staying at the cottage." Harper braced herself for blowback. She'd learned the hard way that setting boundaries didn't always go over well. "It's disconcerting."

To her surprise—and relief—Jonnie nodded. "You're absolutely right. It's past time for me to let go of that self-soothing ritual."

A long moment passed. They studied each other, not speaking.

Jonnie went back to mopping. The Jolly Roger clanged against the flagpole. From inside the houseboat, Harper could hear Flannery and Willow singing "Under the Sea."

Harper took a deep breath, plowed ahead. "So you kept me for a year when I was little."

"I did."

"What did your parents think of you keeping me?"

"My dad was dead by then and I didn't ask my mother's opinion."

"And you have no idea where Tia went during the period when she left me with you?"

"No. Who knows?" Jonnie shrugged and sighed on a long exhale. "That girl always had a snout for trouble. She was a moth to the flame."

Mixing her metaphors, Harper noticed but said nothing. Tia *had* been both moth and snout, ethereal and heavy, refined and crude, literate and illogical.

My mom, the paradox.

It had been confusing as a child, but as an adult, she'd come to understand her mother had been mentally unwell and dragging her kids along with her. Harper used to think kids made you crazy, now she realized crazy had made kids. Sadly, she wondered what might have happened if she'd stayed with Jonnie.

Her aunt sniffled and stopped mopping to swipe at her eyes with the back of her hand, wet marks streaking the wooden deck in a haphazard pattern. She'd missed a few spots in her agitated state.

"Are you okay?" Harper jammed her hands into her pockets and hunched her shoulders. *Dear God, don't let her start crying.*

"Allergies," her aunt mumbled and turned her head away. "Ragweed."

"On the ocean?"

"In the air."

Good. Great. Fantastic. Harper was taking Jonnie at face value and leaving things alone. She pressed her palms downward, and then swung her elbows around to plant her hands, fingers splayed, over her hipbones.

Her aunt's shoulders shook.

She *was* crying.

Aww, damn it. Harper raised a hand, jabbed it through her hair. Moved closer. Backed up. Opened her mouth and bit her tongue.

Do. Not. Say. A. Word.

If she said something, she'd get sucked in. She was a recovering "fixer" who took it upon herself to solve other people's problems when she should usually let them work things out on their own. She had to tiptoe lightly.

"Can you remember *any* good times with her?" Aunt Jonnie asked, sounding mildly desperate for positive news about Tia. "Any time at all that you felt emotionally connected to your mother?"

"Sure, of course." It was easy to be gracious under the circumstances. Jonnie needed something upbeat and honestly, so did Harper. "She loved to dance and sing. Get her in front of a camera and she'd light up . . ."

"But?" Jonnie arched her eyebrows.

"Life with Tia was complicated. When times were good, she was more fun than anyone I've ever known, but she could turn on a dime and when she raged, it was the worst thing ever." Harper interlaced her fingers. "And she raged a lot."

Aunt Jonnie made a squeaky noise of distress. "I hate that you and Flannery had to experience her shadow side so often. It breaks my heart."

"Yeah. I saw a therapist for a while and she said from my accounts, Mom exhibited a pattern of behavior that suggested borderline personality disorder or maybe a bipolar one." Harper shrugged, acting as if it was no big deal. "The labels don't really matter. Either way, she never got the help she so desperately needed and that breaks *my* heart."

"It's the family curse," Jonnie muttered and ran the toe of her sneaker over a dark spot on the deck, trying to dislodge stuck gunk that looked like tar.

"That pirate DNA?"

"Maybe, perhaps, who knows? All I know is all the way back to Ian Campbell, people in our family struggle with interpersonal relationships."

Just like her and Flannery.

"Is that why you've stayed single?"

"In my younger days I attracted the wrong kind of people."

"And now?"

"Now? I have good friends and a solid reputation in the community."

"And that's enough?"

"Now that you girls are here it is."

"We might not stay."

"Maybe not, but at least we've started building a relationship. At least you and Flannery are reunited."

Yes, that was something.

"Still, you don't want someone to love?"

"I've done my best to counteract those counterproductive genetic tendencies, but it's often a struggle and I don't want to drag other people into my personal battles. I work hard every day to be the best person I can be and that works for me. I've been in love before, and it's never ended well. I figure not everyone is meant to have a lifelong partner."

"You're scared to give your heart away again."

"Terrified," Jonnie said with so much stark frankness it left Harper speechless.

"Aunt Jonnie?" Flannery called, coming out of the houseboat holding an open yearbook in her hand. "Which one of these fellas is Harper's father?"

Harper sidled over to get a look at the page. There were four guys and Tia horsing around on the football field. The boys were in football uniforms and Tia wore her cheerleader outfit. They were lifting her in the air above their heads while she lounged in their upturned palms like she was Cleopatra, and they were her minions.

Aunt Jonnie glanced briefly at the book, went back to her stress mopping, and spoke from one corner of her mouth. "It could have been any one of them. I don't think Tia herself knew for sure."

* * *

After the weird visit with Aunt Jonnie, they went for lunch on Paradise Pier and then took Willow through the House of Mirrors and on the few rides that could accommodate wheelchairs. On the surface, they had a good time, but Harper couldn't really enjoy herself. She'd learned too much about her past from Aunt Jonnie and she needed time to digest it.

She was already starting to obsess over who her father was and nothing healthy could come of that. He had no place in her life then or now. That was a rock better left unturned.

They browsed the shops. For fun, she bought matching T-shirts for herself and Flannery that said, MY SISTER HAS A FREAKING AWESOME SISTER. TRUE STORY.

The T-shirts put a smile on Flannery's face.

"Now we need a shirt for Willow," Harper said. "Something that matches her badass personality." She leafed through the clothes on a circular rack. "What color do you like, Miss Willow Pillow?"

"Pink!" Willow exclaimed.

Harper found a pink T-shirt with FEARLESS BRAVE GIRL embroidered with cheetah print lettering. "This is perfect."

She flipped it around so Willow could see the slogan.

"Yes!" Willow pumped a fist.

That kid was priceless, and Harper was falling unabashedly in love with her niece.

"That's sweet of you to buy us T-shirts," Flannery murmured.

"I thought we needed a bit of fun. Are you buying anything?"

Flannery shook her head. "I'm on a budget."

"You sure? That dress you were admiring would look really good on you."

"I shouldn't splurge."

"Suit yourself." Harper made her purchases, and by the time they got back to the cottage, the sourdough had risen enough to begin the process of baking their first loaf of bread.

Flannery set Willow up with crayons and a coloring book at the dining room table and returned to the kitchen.

"How are you feeling?" she asked Harper as she dug out the bread recipe again.

"About what?"

"What Aunt Jonnie told us this morning about our family." Flannery tied an apron around her waist.

"I don't have any feelings about it. Do you?"

"It makes me sad, but I'm not surprised." Her sister sighed. "Tia didn't occur in a vacuum. I mean, we always knew something was off with her. Now we have a small window into why."

"Does it really matter?" Harper asked. "She's dead. It's over."

"Except that pirate DNA is inside of us, too," Flannery said.

"But we can overcome the negative aspects. Jonnie has and she's a terrific example. Why not us?"

"I agree."

"Now, about the sourdough. What's next in this multistep process?"

"Autolyze."

"Meaning . . . ?"

"First we gather all the supplies." Flannery ticked off the items needed on her fingers. "We need a dough scraper, a bench knife, proofing baskets, cloches—"

"I don't even know what half those things are."

"Baby steps," Flannery said with infinite patience. "We'll get there."

Once they'd gathered the supplies, Harper rolled her eyes when she discovered that "autolyze" simply meant they mixed together the flour and water that would form the basis of the loaves. The resulting dough felt dry, rough, and shaggy and Harper had serious doubts about the bread's viability. Then, they covered the bowl with plastic wrap to keep it from drying out and let it rest for an hour.

"Good grief," Harper said after Flannery finished reading off the instructions. "With sourdough, it's all hurry up and wait."

"The next step is more active," Flannery said. "You'll love it."

"What step is that?"

"Stretching and folding. That process takes two and a half hours according to the recipe."

"Ugh." Harper groaned. "Why couldn't this challenge include something I'm good at, like public speaking?"

"I'm no good at baking either."

"Maybe not, but you have infinitely more patience than I do."

"Patience, immobilizing fear." Flannery shrugged and laughed. "Potayto, potahto."

Her sister's casual joke, and nervous chuckle, brought Harper up short. "What are you afraid of, Flan?"

"Everything. Shorter list, what am I not afraid of?"

"Aww, sis. That's rough."

"You were always the rebellious one," Flannery said. "It got you into a lot of trouble with Mom. I learned to lie low, and it kept me from getting hit as much."

Harper rubbed her cheek. "Mom did have a swift backhand."

"I wanted to stay off her radar. You went with her toe-to-toe. I just craved peace."

Studying her sister, Harper felt a tug of sadness yank at her heart. "Like I said, that's all over now. We get to make our own future from here on out. There's nothing holding us back."

"Except," Flannery said. "Mastery of sourdough."

CHAPTER 21

Flannery

EXTENSIBILITY: A property of dough that allows it to be stretched.

They baked their first loaf of sourdough on Monday morning after the dough had proofed overnight in the fridge, and it was an epic fail. The bread turned out dense and hard as lighthouse bricks, but they had so much fun, playing music and dancing around the kitchen as they worked, that neither one of them cared. Willow played DJ, picking out their playlist, which was a hodgepodge of musical genres.

"Oh well," Harper said with cheerful efficiency that Flannery admired. "One little stepping-stone on the path to ultimate success."

Flannery appreciated the positive attitude, and she was determined to get to the bottom of what had gone wrong. She consulted the internet and unearthed the cause. "We didn't sufficiently develop the gluten. A longer autolyze should increase the extensibility."

"English, please." Harper laughed.

"The stretching and folding part."

"We'll correct it next time," Harper assured her. "After all, we're the Sourdough Sisters."

"What'll we do with the bread?" Flannery asked. "It's too heavy to make sandwiches with."

"How about toasting it up, throwing it in the food processor, and making breadcrumbs?"

"Smart idea."

Aunt Jonnie dropped by before heading to work, bringing with her two entry forms for the Moonglow Cove Fourth of July annual bake-off contest. "Get this turned in soon. The registration deadline is Friday."

"Will do," Harper said.

"Try again tomorrow with the bread. You'll nail it in time," Aunt Jonnie encouraged and left with a wave.

Not long afterward, Hank popped by to see if they'd discovered anything in the house that needed maintenance before he started working on moving the electrical switch to the elevator. When they assured him that all was fine, he offered them a tip of his baseball cap and ambled out the door.

"He seems like a good guy," Harper said, watching Hank through the bay window as he headed for the lighthouse. "A basic, decent person. I like him."

Flannery liked him, too, but she didn't tell her sister that. She was in no position to have feelings about any man. Her life was in shambles. Well, except for reconnecting with her sister and slowly getting to know her aunt. Those were blessings beyond measure, and she was deeply grateful for them both.

Hank reminded Flannery a bit of her father, Matt, who'd been a kind and loving man, always ready to lend a hand to anyone in need. A positive parental role model in stark contrast to her mother.

Tia had made mincemeat of Matt's kindness though. Her dad stuck it out for as long as he could, but when Tia cheated on him a second time, he'd had enough and left her. He'd tried to get custody of Flannery, but the court ruled in Tia's favor. He'd stayed in Flannery's life all throughout her childhood, but his job relocated him to the West Coast when she was a teenager and as he remarried and started another family, she and her dad slowly drifted apart, seeing each other mainly at holidays and family functions. Especially as Tia's failing health made her more dependent on Flannery.

Flannery hadn't heard from Alan, and she was starting to relax, praying he'd decided to let her go and get on with his life. She needed to have a talk with Grayson soon to see if he could recommend a divorce attorney since she respected his opinion. Then she'd have to worry about funding the divorce. Maybe if she could win the $5,000 prize from the bake off contest . . .

Oh now, that is a pipe dream, Flannery. From sourdough novice to bake-off queen in six short weeks? Not gonna happen.

In between their baking schedules, Harper helped Flannery with Willow's physical therapy. The two were good for each other, Flannery admitted. Willow's easygoing nature softened the sharp edges of Harper's intensity. Whereas Harper's tendency to turn everything into a competition motivated Willow to try harder.

"Do twenty arm lifts and we'll go for ice cream," Harper enticed. "Come on, you can do it. Push yourself."

Gamely, Willow complied.

* * *

Throughout the week, the sisters and Willow fell into a comfortable routine—getting up early, having breakfast together, baking, doing Willow's physical therapy, spending time at the beach, returning to the cottage for lunch and then baking again, exploring Moonglow Cove, having dinner, and baking some more. The three of them became inseparable. The bond Flannery and Harper once shared as children regenerated and grew stronger with each passing day. Sipping mugs of hot tea on the window seat in sight of the lighthouse or on the front porch rockers, they discussed how they'd redecorate the cottage once it was theirs.

In between the bread folding, proofing, shaping, and baking, they inhabited the beach. Harper and Flannery took turns giving Willow piggyback rides. They became a common sight on Paradise Pier, sometimes going on the rides, sometimes just strolling the boardwalk, sometimes browsing the shops. People grew to recognize them and greet them with smiles and waves.

"Hello, Sourdough Sisters," townsfolk would call out and ask how the bread-making challenge was going.

This level of people knowing their business was new to both Flannery and Harper. Tia had moved around so much, they'd never been part of a community growing up; and as adults, Flannery had been so isolated in her marriage to Alan, while Harper had been in a city too big and diverse for anyone to care much about other people's business.

It was kind of nice, Flannery admitted, having the denizens of Moonglow Cove take an interest in them. In less than a week, she was already starting to feel as if they belonged.

The rhythm of their days matched the rhythm of sourdough—feed, rest, rise, stretch, shape, proof, bake—it was a cycle that lulled as surely as the ebb and flow of ocean waves.

As they worked, they talked about their childhood, both the good and the bad. Because indeed, there was a good side to having grown up with a complicated mother like Tia. They hadn't been bound by convention and that had stoked their creativity. Their mother would take them out of school on a whim just to do fun things—go to an amusement park, dress up in Halloween costumes in February, and hang out at the mall, getting free makeovers at department store makeup counters. She gave them a love of literature and her infatuation with books was their ticket out of her control. Between the pages, they found guidance and new worlds to explore. Inside books, they found loving mothers and shining examples of the way things could be.

There was no regular bedtime in their mother's household. No schedules to follow. No hidebound rules. Except for one—*don't set Mom off.*

The problem with that single rule was that they were never certain what would set her off. It could be something as simple as leaving the lid off the peanut butter, which could earn them a slap across the face, or she might force them to sit down and eat the entire jar until they got sick. Other times, she wouldn't even notice their oversight. The unpredictability made them anxious, yes, but along with the anxiety came flexibility. They could adapt and change with short notice, quickly adjusting to whatever environment they found themselves in.

* * *

By Thursday, May 26, six days after they'd arrived in Moonglow Cove, Flannery and Harper were no longer afraid of the sourdough. It was sturdy and readily bounced back if they'd accidentally skipped a feeding. Thin flakes of dried flour and water inescapably ended up on the counter every night and Willow took special delight in sweeping away what she called "sourdough dust."

The only sticking point was in the amount of food they produced. Under the rules of their grandmother's codicil, they couldn't throw away any of the dough for any reason. They had to use it all. The bread they'd made from the first days became croutons or French toast or bread pudding. Since starting this challenge they'd made sourdough crackers and sourdough pancakes, sourdough cookies and sourdough biscuits, sourdough doughnuts and sourdough cake.

And, of course, the bread. Loaves and loaves of bread.

Their second loaf was better than the first, but still not great. They studied and adapted their techniques. They knocked it out of the park with the third loaf, but then stumbled again on the fourth and fifth. Throughout the process, they learned mistakes were just part of it and nothing to be feared. Instead of problems or challenges, they started seeing opportunities. Everything was a chance for growth.

Willow took to this concept like a sponge to water, eagerly soaking up the secrets of sourdough like a natural. The child got to where she could eyeball the dough, shake her head, and diagnose the consistency before they'd bake.

"Sticky," she'd say. Or poke out her tongue, acting as if her mouth was too arid to spit and announce with a giggle, "Dry."

Based on Willow's analysis, they'd adjust the water-to-flour ratio and soon, they were popping out perfect loaves every time. That success gave them the confidence to try rye and wheat breads.

Willow got so invested in the process, she played her video games less often and Flannery discovered she herself didn't spend as much time on the internet either. Real life was happening all around them and there was no need to escape into a screen. Flannery was proud of them both, and it was only here on the bluff above the ocean that she began to realize how much she'd used the internet to hide from the real world.

The sourdough stacked up, far more than they could eat. At first, Harper took extra loaves to Grayson and the Historical Society. Once, Flannery walked the half mile to Hank's house and left a basket of bread on his front steps with a note telling him to enjoy. She added with a flourish *your friend, Flannery*.

They took bread to Aunt Jonnie and her employees, and when Jonnie nodded her head in approval over their efforts, they were thrilled.

"Good job," Jonnie said. "Keep it up and you'll stand a real chance of winning the bake-off."

That excited Flannery. She could definitely use the prize money that went along with satisfying the conditions of their grandmother's will. Although, if she won, she would split everything with Harper, fifty-fifty.

Soon, however, even Jonnie, Hank, and Grayson couldn't keep up with the baked goods. The sisters hated to waste the food and didn't know what to do with the volume of bread they churned out.

That day, Hank showed up with a middle-aged woman in tow. She had her silver hair pulled back into a messy bun and carried a big wicker basket. He introduced her as Ms. Gimble.

"Edith," the woman said, extending a friendly palm to shake first Flannery's hand and then Harper's. "Hank told me you have more bread than you know what to do with. I run the community restaurant in town where your aunt Jonnie volunteers on Thursday evenings. If you'd like to donate some—"

"You're a godsend!" Harper ushered Edith into the kitchen and loaded her wicker basket with bread. "Please come back every day and we'll have more for you."

"How wonderful." Edith smiled at the bread in her basket. "You can bet I'll be back."

"Thank you," Flannery said to Hank. His kindness touched her heart. "That was thoughtful of you to connect us with Edith."

Hank blushed, ducked his head, and tipped his cap. "You're welcome, Ms. Flannery."

After they completed their morning baking and fed the mother dough, they were just in time to attend the 10 A.M. Thursday morning story hour at the library. Aunt Jonnie had told them about the event and Willow was excited for it. Who was she kidding? Flannery was excited too. She loved oral readings. On the slate for today's story time was Hans Christian Andersen's *The Little Mermaid*.

The librarian, who introduced herself as Joan Marsh, welcomed them with a bright smile and invited them into the storytelling room where folding chairs were assembled for the adults and cushions for the kids. The place was packed with moms and kids and a few dads, too. Joan cleared a path for Willow and some of the other children came over to talk to her, curious about her wheelchair.

Willow lit up at the attention, and it was only then that it hit Flannery how truly isolated they'd been in Kansas City. Every time she or Willow tried to make a friend, Alan would nitpick the person's flaws, until in an effort to keep the peace, they'd drop the relationship. Now, seeing a circle of kids surrounding her animated daughter, Flannery understood not only how much of an extrovert Willow really was, but also how stunted their lives had become.

She was never going back to Alan. *Ever.*

Feeling more confident than she'd felt in a very long time, Flannery left the library with her head held high.

They took an early lunch, ordering shrimp salads for Flannery and Harper and a loaded baked potato for Willow at the outdoor patio seating of the While Away Diner on Moonglow Boulevard. It was a sweet day, filled with storytelling and delicious food, sea and sunshine, laughter and love.

Every day could be like this, Flannery thought, *if only they had a way to make money.*

As if reading her mind, Harper speared a shrimp on her fork and said, "You know, I've been thinking, there must be some way to make a living from this sourdough thing."

"You're seriously thinking of not returning to New York?"

Harper shrugged. "There's nothing for me there anymore."

"Surely your issues there will blow over and someone will come to their senses and snap you up."

"I'm not sure I want that life anymore. Not after being here with you and Willow. I don't want to be that far away from you again."

"Really?" Flannery scarcely dared hope.

"It's too soon to make a permanent decision, but my mental cogs have been whirling. What if there was a way to start a small business?"

"You mean like a bakery?"

Harper waved a hand at the boulevard. Directly across the street from them was a store with a sign that read: MOONGLOW BAKERY. "We'd have competition and when I looked up the Moonglow Bakery online, I saw that it's been in business for years. The owner, Anna Drury, has a decade head start on us, and we're those odd Lighthouse Campbells. I'm not sure we could give Anna a run for her money."

"So what are you thinking?"

"Instead of creating a retail storefront, what if we developed an online business."

"Selling baked goods?" Flannery crinkled her nose. "That hardly seems sustainable since fresh baked goods are not shelf-stable. I hate to think about pumping our products with preservatives to make them last longer."

"I've got something else in mind."

Flannery leaned forward, captivated by her sister's enthusiasm. Had Harper discovered a way for them to create a thriving business from home? "Yes?"

"What if we opened an online artisanal store that sells baking products. Not just that, but we create an online community based on bread making with an emphasis on sourdough. The lighthouse will be our branding, the hundred-fifty-year-old mother dough as our anchor, and the pirate legend as our family legacy. We could call our website the Sourdough Sisters."

"Harper, that's genius!"

"We could sell flour and mills and kitchen gadgets."

"Scales and oven mitts and thermometers." Goose bumps spread up Flannery's arms.

"Bread bags and parchment paper and mixing bowls."

"Earthenware crocks and measuring utensils and rolling pins."

"To create an active community of sourdough enthusiasts, we can teach people how to use the products. We'll film tutorials and offer recipes."

"Recipes from Aunt Jonnie's discard box!" Flannery sang out, fully getting into it.

"We'll write a weekly blog—"

"We could call it From the Lighthouse Kitchen," Flannery brainstormed.

"Encourage customers to share their recipes and creations on a forum."

"Oh, Harper." Flannery breathed. "That's a magnificent idea."

"Do it, Mommy, do it!"

Harper and Flannery looked over at Willow who was perched on the edge of her wheelchair, her golden hair glowing in the sunlight, a wide grin on her darling little face. And Flannery knew they had to try. She had to set a good example for her daughter. Teach Willow how to pursue a dream with grit and determination.

It was time to show her child what she was made of.

"It's something to keep tucked in the back of our mind for the future," Harper said and consulted her iPhone. "But for now, it's time to autolyze."

They paid the bill and headed back to the keeper's cottage.

Because Flannery kept her minivan parked under Hank's carport half a mile from the lighthouse, and the library was just a mile away, they'd walked instead of taking the vehicle. In fact, they hadn't driven the minivan since she'd parked it at Hank's on the second day. Walking was such great exercise, and everything was so close, driving didn't seem worth the bother and she saved on gas.

They skipped the elevator and pushed Willow up the incline. Flannery was still nervous about the lift, even though Hank had relocated the switch so it wouldn't be accidentally shut off.

Willow started singing "Under the Sea" and Harper and Flannery joined in, singing at the top of their voices as they danced their way up the bluff.

As they crested the rise, Flannery, doing a little hip twist, glanced up to see a man standing at the back door, with his arms folded over his chest and a stern scowl on his face.

Flannery stopped in midsong, dropped her purse, and froze.

"Flan," Harper said, "what is it?"

She was trembling from head to toe. Couldn't speak.

"Who is that guy?"

Through clenched teeth and stiff lips, Flannery pushed out his name. "Alan."

CHAPTER 22

Flannery

RHEOLOGY: The study of how materials deform when a force is applied. The rheological properties of sourdough are mainly determined by water absorption.

At the sight of her husband, all the blood left Flannery's body, leaving her shivering and breathless.

"Mommy," Willow said, her high scared voice piercing through Flannery's iced-up brain. "He found us."

Alan replaced his frown with a slick smile, pasting on that false charm that had fooled Flannery once upon a time. He was so very good at sucking people in. "Well, well, so this is where you've gotten off to, sweetheart. Why didn't you tell me you were hankering for a seaside vacation? I would have brought you here."

To the uninitiated, he sounded calm and friendly and reasonable. Ahh, but Flannery knew better. Beneath that false grin, he was seething.

Alan stalked toward them.

Beside her, she felt Harper tense. Her sister was an ace at confronting conflict head-on, but this wasn't her battle to fight.

Flannery moved in front of Willow's wheelchair, protecting her daughter. "What are you doing here, Alan?"

He flicked a gaze over her. "You look good. Have you lost weight?"

She had, with all the walking they'd been doing, but she wasn't going to give him the satisfaction. "What do you want?"

"Why," he said in a helpless voice designed to paint himself as the victim, "to find out why my wife up and left me out of the blue without a word of explanation."

"You know why I left."

"I don't."

She wanted to say something tart and provocative, but not in front of Willow. "I'm not going to argue with you."

"I'm not arguing. You're the one who's being argumentative."

Oh boy, here it came, the gaslighting.

Alan cast a glance at Harper. "Do I sound argumentative to you?"

Harper glared at him. "Flannery obviously left you for a reason. I'm on my sister's side."

"Of course, you are," Alan said. "It's to be expected. She is your flesh and blood. But you haven't had contact with her in six years. You have no idea what she's capable of."

Harper clenched her fists and looked as if she'd enjoy punching him.

His eyes narrowed to slits and with the noonday sun gleaming off his face, he appeared reptilian as he assessed her sister. Flannery was still trembling so hard she didn't think she could take a step. She stayed rooted. She had to keep her wits about her. He could be a formidable adversary.

Alan strolled closer, still smiling that creepy smile. He cocked his head, peering around Flannery. "Hello, Willow, aren't you glad to see your dad?"

Flannery looked over her shoulder to see Willow jut out her chin. "You're not my real daddy."

She'd told Willow from the beginning about Kit, but Alan was the only father she'd ever known. He'd never spent much time with her, unless he was trying to impress someone. She'd never said anything disparaging about Alan to her daughter. She didn't want to be the kind of mother who bad-mouthed people.

Oftentimes, Flannery had wondered why he'd ever married her. What he'd seen in her. She wasn't a fashion plate like her sister. Nothing eye-catching about her. She was pretty enough, in a bland girl-next-door way kind of way, but certainly no beauty. She didn't have a college education or work skills beyond caretaking her mother.

Now, she understood the truth. Because of the way she'd been raised—enmeshed without any personal boundaries and nursing a desperate need to have someone love her—she'd been left vulnerable to an abusive manipulator. Alan had wanted her because she'd been easy to control. He got his kicks from wielding his power. And in theory, Willow, too, because of her health issues, would be easy to control.

He didn't love her. Had never loved her. He was just one of those awful men who took satisfaction in finding people who would knuckle under his authoritarian rule and help him keep up his false mask of being a great family man.

Alan faltered, his smile dropping, but he quickly picked it back up again and drilled Flannery with a hard stare. "I see you've poisoned her mind against her own father. For shame, Flannery."

Harper stepped between her and Alan.

Flannery felt both irritated and deeply grateful for her sister's support. This was her battle, but she wasn't sure she was strong enough to fight it without Harper by her side. Harper was the one person in the world she could depend upon to have her back and she deserved to have some help. She'd gotten so isolated she'd forgotten that sometimes it was okay to ask for backup and support. She didn't have to handle everything on her own.

But Harper was working on letting go of her need to rescue people. It wouldn't be good for her best growth if Flannery allowed her to intervene. It was time she learned to stand up for herself.

"This is private property," Harper said. "And you're trespassing. I'm inviting you to leave. If you're not out of here in two minutes, I'm calling the police."

"Sure thing, lady. We'll get right out of your hair," he said to Harper. To Flannery he said, "Go gather your things. We're leaving."

"Not so fast," Harper said, her fists clenching tighter. "She's not going anywhere with you."

Alan's grin turned into a full-on smirk and he stepped even closer, toeing off with Harper. "I don't know what she's been telling you about me, but your sister is mentally unwell. She's not to be trusted. Just like your mother."

"You think my sister is crazy?" Harper said. "Dude, you have no idea what crazy looks like until you mess with *my* family."

Flannery had to de-escalate this before things got out of hand. "Harper," she said softly, "it's okay. Alan is my husband and I owe him an explanation."

"Damn straight." Alan gave a cocky wiggle to his spine. "It's high time you knew your place, Flannery."

"Alan, I'm not putting up with your abuse anymore—"

"*My* abuse?" Alan growled. "*You're* the one who took off without a word. *You're* the one who took my child. *You're* the one who—"

"You just forfeited your two minutes." Harper pulled her cell phone from her pocket. "I'm calling 911 to tell them we have a menacing intruder."

Before she could punch in the numbers, Alan leaped forward and knocked the phone from Harper's hand. Then he quickly flashed his startlingly white teeth and said in a sarcastic tone, "Oops. My hand slipped."

"You just bought yourself a load of trouble, buddy. I don't put up with that kind of behavior and neither does Flannery. I want you off our property right now!"

Harper didn't give an inch. Alan didn't scare her. But that's because her sister didn't know what cruelties he was capable of. Alan sure as hell scared Flannery, especially when he delivered that cool shark-tooth smile.

Alan and Harper stood glaring at each other.

Willow did not need to see this. Flannery had witnessed far too many altercations between her mother and the various men in her life. She knew firsthand the damage this kind of thing could do to a kid over time.

"Harper," Flannery said, keeping her tone as calm as she could, "would you please take Willow inside while I have a discussion with my husband?"

Stubbornly, Harper shook her head. "I'm not going anywhere. I'm not leaving you alone with this creep."

"You best do what your sister asks." Alan's tone was smooth and even. His controlled voice frightened Flannery more than his raised voice. When he yelled, he was just popping off, but when he got quiet, he was scheming.

Her sister sank her knotted fists onto her hips. "Is that a threat?"

"Harper, please. For Willow's sake, take her into the house," she whispered urgently. "Let me rescue myself. I need to do this on my own." She could call the cops as easily as her sister if need be. She stuck her hand in her pocket and wrapped her fingers around her cell phone.

Glowering at Alan, Harper raised her fist under his nose and for one horrifying moment, Flannery feared she was going to haul off and punch him.

"Keep your hands off my sister. I'll be watching from the window and if you so much as twitch wrong, I'll call 911."

"I'm not a violent man," Alan said. "I don't know where you get that idea. If she's been telling you that I hit her, she's lying."

Growling at him, Harper bent to scoop her phone off the ground and then released the brakes on Willow's wheelchair and straightened to push her into the cottage.

Leaving Flannery alone with the man who made her life a living hell for nearly six years.

The second the door closed behind Harper and Willow, she said, "Alan, I want you to walk away and never come back. If you leave quietly, I will not ask for anything. You can have the house, keep all your retirement, everything. Just go, sign the divorce papers when my lawyer sends them to you, and we'll be done. You can marry your mistress and live happily ever after."

"Divorce?" He looked so shock she couldn't tell if it was an act or if he was truly surprised that she was leaving him. "What are you talking about?"

"You cheated on me. You did this . . ." She pushed up the sleeve of her sweater and held up her arm splotched with the bruises now a mottled yellow green.

"What are you talking about? I never did that to you. You're so clumsy." He offered an oily laugh. "You knocked into something and forgot all about it."

It was hard to believe that not so very long ago, his gaslighting could so easily cause her to question her own reality. Well, no more. She wasn't putting up with that kind of behavior ever again.

"It's not up for debate. We're getting divorced. We can do this the easy way—you let me go and everything is yours, or you fight me, and I hire a high-powered lawyer to take you for every cent I can get."

"Flannery, baby," he wheedled. "What's happened to you? It's that sister of yours. She's poisoned your mind. This isn't you. You're a sweet person. You're a devoted mother. You're so loving and kind."

So damn codependent. Groomed by her mother to put up with abuse. Well, this was the end of the line. She was owning her responsibility in this mess. She hadn't put up any boundaries with Alan. She'd allowed him to run over her.

"Honey, honey," he said. "Let's just get out of here. We'll go home. We'll figure this out. I'll go to counseling. I promise. Just give me another chance. I'll become the man you need for me to be."

She knew this pattern too. Love bombing. Hoovering.

"No," she said.

"You're gonna throw away five years of marriage? After all we've been through? The ups? The downs? Who was there for you when no one else was? Who took care of you after Kit died? Your sister certainly wasn't there. She washed her hands of you."

"No, *I* was the one who broke things off with Harper. She never turned her back on me."

"But she didn't even try to convince you to mend things, did she? I was there for you when Willow was a baby. Just me. I was the only one who was willing to take a risk on someone like you."

"Someone like me?" *Watch out. He's luring you into a fight. Ruffling your emotions. Don't rise to the bait.*

"Damaged goods. Crazy." His upper lip curled in a harsh snarl.

Okay, they were past the love bombing and coaxing now. Flannery waited, knowing too well what came next.

Here was the cycle—love bomb, devalue, discard. It went endlessly like this. In the love bombing phase, he offered up the sincere promises to change. In the past, traumatized empath that she was, Flannery had wanted to believe him. She'd given him second chance after second chance. But no longer. Now she fully understood what she was dealing with. A deeply damaged soul with the emotional maturity of a toddler.

Just as Tia had been.

And she'd rather die than let Willow live one more day under the roof of such a man.

"Alan," she said. "I was wrong."

He puffed up his chest and strutted a little. "I'm glad to hear you say that."

"I shouldn't have run away without an explanation. I owed you that."

But she'd been too afraid Alan would convince her not to leave as he had so many times before. She hadn't been strong enough then, but now that she had Harper and Aunt Jonnie in her corner, she felt braver, more courageous. Getting stranded in the elevator with Hank had helped too. She'd faced her claustrophobia and come out better for it. She could face this as well.

"I should've told you where I was going. I should've told you that I was leaving you. I shouldn't have snuck away in the night. That was wrong of me."

"Damn straight," he said, back to that cock-of-the-walk attitude.

"I messed that up and I apologize for not handling the situation like a mature adult."

"That's better. You know where your bread is buttered, don't you?"

"Let's get something straight," Flannery said, amazed at her level of calm. She wasn't sure where this new strength was coming from, but she was holding on to it. "I *am* leaving you."

He made a dismissive noise, blowing a raspberry. "You've never had a job. How do you think you're going to support yourself? How are you going support Willow? Her medical expenses aren't cheap."

It wasn't the first time Alan had made these arguments and for too long she'd let financial fears control her, but no more. She would figure something out. There were organizations that could help her with Willow's expenses, plus, she could get social services for her daughter. She had family now. She had support. She wasn't alone anymore.

Flannery hauled in a deep breath. "There is nothing you can say or do that will change my mind. I'm no longer going to be your emotional punching bag. I'm done. This marriage is over."

"Oh no, bitch, that's not how this is going down," Alan said, his face contorted with rage. "You don't get to discard me. I discard *you*."

It used to scare her, his fury, but now? It was like watching a three-year-old have a meltdown when told that he couldn't have a coveted toy.

The back door to the cottage opened.

From where she was standing, Flannery couldn't see the door, but she heard it creak on its hinges.

Harper, no, please, please, stay in the house with Willow.

She feared Harper would stir the pot and escalate this mess with Alan. Flannery's goal was to set a firm boundary, let him have his fit and then storm off. It was the Alan Franklin way. If Harper came out at this point, it would only agitate him more.

Flannery cast a quick glance over her shoulder, hoping to give her sister a look that would warn her off. But it wasn't Harper coming from the house.

It was Hank.

Harper must have called him, and he'd come up in the elevator to the lighthouse and gone on through the front door of the keeper's cottage. Unless he'd already been at the lighthouse doing repairs.

Seeing Hank's scarred face lifted her hopes. The man radiated serene self-control. He ambled toward her in a slow, easy gait, a neutral expression on his face.

Her heart thundered. What would happen between the two men next? Oh! She didn't like this. Tension had her tied in knots.

Alan scowled at Hank. "Who are you, Scarface?"

Hank said nothing. He just strolled up to stand behind Flannery, his muscled arms folded over his chest.

"This your new boyfriend?" Alan jeered.

She didn't answer either.

"Trust you to hook up with a freak." Alan's upper lip curled.

Hank stepped closer. She could feel the heat of his body behind her, and just having him there bolstered her courage.

The back door opened again. It had to be Harper this time, unable to quell her rescuing tendencies, but now Flannery didn't mind. She needed all the help she could get, although she did worry where Willow was and if she was watching all this unfold.

Glancing over her shoulder again, she spied Aunt Jonnie determinedly stalking toward them in her *Starry Night* rubber boots, looking as if she'd just stepped off one of her shrimp boats. Where had she come from? Aunt Jonnie came to a stop beside Hank. Now it felt as if Flannery had two bodyguards standing behind her.

Flannery lifted her chin and met Alan's piercing gaze.

"What's going on here?" he asked.

"Our thoughts exactly," Aunt Jonnie said.

"I'm here to get my wife," Alan said.

"She doesn't want to go with you," Hank said. "I think it's for the best if you leave town and don't come back."

Hate glittered in Alan's eyes and he gnashed his teeth.

The back door opened a third time. Now, it *had* to be Harper.

Another peek over her shoulder and Flannery saw that nope, it was Grayson. She grinned, unable to contain herself. How had Harper rallied the troops so quickly? He joined the ranks of Jonnie and Hank.

"Are you living in some hippie commune or something?" Alan asked. "What is this? Are you having orgies with freaks and geeks? Is that the appeal?"

"I thank you not to speak to Ms. Campbell in that tone of voice," Grayson said.

"Her name is Franklin," Alan said. "*My* name. She's *my* wife."

Grayson opened his briefcase and took out a sheaf of paper. "Not anymore. She's filed for divorce and I'm serving as her intermediary."

What a bluff! He made it sound like he was a practicing attorney instead of a history teacher and author. Grayson should have been a professional poker player. He had *her* believing she'd already filed for divorce.

Alan was a bully, but as most bullies were, he was also a coward. He wasn't going to do anything in front of three people. That would make him look bad. He abused in private. In public he put on that fake persona that fooled so many.

"Fine. Good. You can have her. She was lousy in bed anyway." With that, Alan turned and walked away.

CHAPTER 23

Harper

BENCH REST: Dough rest period after fermenting and before shaping, which allows gluten to soften, making bread pliable for shaping.

Flannery was in the living room with Gray and a lawyer friend of his who'd shown up twenty minutes ago. Flannery was anxious to get a restraining order against Alan and divorce proceedings for real while Harper served Hank and Aunt Jonnie sourdough toast with honey butter and strawberry jam.

Harper was still flabbergasted at the timing of the arrival of the cavalry. Just as she'd been about to dial 911, she'd seen Hank and Jonnie walking around the grounds together. They'd come to discuss a fence Jonnie wanted Hank to put up between the lighthouse and the bluff drop-off, now that there was a child staying on the property.

It felt as if the universe was looking out for them.

She had run out the front door to tell them what was happening at the back of the keeper's cottage between Flannery and Alan and asked for their help while she stayed with Willow. The moment Hank had walked out the back door, Gray had shown up on the front porch. He'd come to bring Harper an advanced reading copy of his book that prominently featured their grandmother and the history of the Moonglow Cove Lighthouse. He'd just gotten the copies in the mail and had wanted to share it with her.

Before he could even knock, she ushered him inside, quickly summing up the situation. "I promised to stay inside with Willow and out of Flannery's business, but—"

"I didn't promise that," Gray had said with a determined set to his jaw and he headed right out to join Jonnie and Hank standing behind Flannery.

Harper watched him stalk out the back door to help her sister and she thought unabashedly, *I could so kiss that man right now.*

To keep Willow occupied while it all went down, Harper used her computer as a babysitter since they didn't have a TV yet and set her up to watch cartoons in the bedroom that Willow shared with her mother, before Harper had hustled back to nervously pace the mudroom.

When Alan finally left, and the others came into the house, Harper threw her arms around Flannery and hugged her so tightly, her sister squirmed.

"You're squeezing the air out of me, Harp."

Once Flannery started talking about her husband's controlling behavior, Harper had been horrified by the mental and emotional abuse her younger sister had endured at his hands. Guilt perched on her shoulder like a vulture pecking at her head. *You should have been there. You should have rescued her. She's in this situation because of you.*

"Flannery is an adult," Jonnie said, totally reading Harper's mind. "I know it hurts to see her suffering. I know you want to rush in and rescue her, but this is her problem to solve. It's not your pain to carry and it's not your fault."

Harper had a dozen retorts to those arguments, but the idea that she wasn't to blame for Flannery's domestic situation provided her so much relief, she clamped her mouth shut and said nothing.

Jonnie reached across the bar to touch Harper's hand and give her a soft smile filled with tenderness and empathy.

"I should have maintained regular contact with her," Harper said mournfully. "I shouldn't have let our disagreement keep us apart. I've already missed five years of my niece's life."

"You're here now," Jonnie said. "That's all that matters. We can't change the past. All we can do is work together to make a brighter future and that future can start now."

"I feel like I've failed her."

"Harper, it's okay to be human," Hank said, contributing to the conversation for the first time. "Beating yourself up doesn't help Flannery in any way and only lowers your self-esteem."

"So what do I do?" Harper asked.

"Listen to her. Don't try to fix things for her," he suggested.

"Give her possible solutions, but don't push anything on her," Jonnie added.

"Let her know you love her and support her." Hank swept toast crumbs off the counter and onto his plate.

Talking to them was helping her calm down. "Thank you both so much for being here."

"Of course." Aunt Jonnie offered that soft smile again. "That's what a healthy family does for each other."

"The way you're supporting me is the way I should be supporting Flannery."

Jonnie and Hank nodded in unison.

Harper pressed her palms together and touched her chin with her fingertips. "Thank you, thank you."

"Any time." Jonnie pushed back from the bar. "That was excellent sourdough toast. Keep this up and there's a real possibility you could win that bake-off."

"Really?" Harper said, surprised at how much pride she felt at Jonnie's compliment.

"She's not pullin' your leg," Hank said. "You nailed the perfect loaf."

"Flannery baked this one," Harper said. "I can't claim credit."

"You didn't help at all?" Jonnie asked.

"I did the stretching and folding."

"See there? Team effort. Getting the best out of that mother dough." Aunt Jonnie straightened and pulled a credit card from her back pocket and handed it to Hank. "For the fencing supplies. And while you're at it, buy some security cameras . . . just in case."

* * *

"I DON'T WANT to go to Missy's party," Flannery told Harper the next evening, standing in the doorway of Harper's bedroom where she was putting on her makeup, getting ready for the Memorial Day event.

"Um, you were the one who accepted the invitation for us all."

Flannery looked contrite. "It's too much for me after the thing with Alan yesterday."

Harper was about to say, *Aww, are you going to make me go alone?* But she stopped herself. She didn't want Flannery to feel obligated to attend. It was the kind of controlling thing Tia might have done.

"Still shaky after yesterday?" she asked instead.

Flannery nodded and offered a faint smile. "Thank you so much for understanding. I'll call Jonnie and tell her I won't need her to babysit Willow after all."

"I'll give Missy your regrets," Harper said, suddenly wanting to stay home too. She'd been looking forward to meeting Grayson's family and friends, but now, she felt awkward about walking in alone.

"Thank you," Flannery said, looking relieved.

"Are you nervous about staying here alone?" Harper asked.

"I feel safer since Hank installed the security cameras and he's also monitoring the grounds from his house," she said. "Although I really don't think Alan will come back. Once he's washed his hands of someone, generally he's done with them. And while he is controlling, he never hit me."

Harper noticed her sister rubbing her left wrist. She bit down on her bottom lip. "But he did grab you hard enough to leave bruises. That's not nothing."

"There is always the possibility he could try to win me back. He can really turn on the charm when he wants to, but since he has a girlfriend, I think the only reason he came looking for me is he hates that *I* left *him*. He likes to be the one to drop people."

Harper shook her head. "I hope you're right, but what I've learned about abusers is that when you reject them they often become more violent."

"We'll stay aware and alert. And that's one of the reasons I'm giving Alan everything in the divorce even though Grayson's lawyer friend is against it. I just want to make it as easy as possible for Alan to let us go. I *have* thought this through, Harper.

"Okay then, I support you whatever decision you make." Harper dabbed contour makeup on her temples.

"Thank you so much. If it weren't for you, I don't know if I'd have the courage not to be convinced into going back."

"Yes, you would," Harper said. "You're a Campbell. You've got warrior blood pulsing through your DNA. Our Scottish ancestors might have been nuttier than fruitcakes, but they were brave as all get-out."

Flannery laughed. "I'll keep that in mind."

"You should read Gray's book. It's an eye-opener. There's a lot of pretty colorful stuff in there."

"Maybe later. Or you can just tell me what you find."

"That'll work."

Flannery came to stand behind Harper. "Would you like me to braid your hair like you used to do for me when we were kids?"

"Sister," Harper said. "I would love that."

* * *

HARPER TOOK AN Uber to the mayor's house. It was one of those grand old family mansions in an area of town dubbed The Grace where the wealthy and influential of Moonglow Cove lived. Grayson had told her the house itself was named Sinclair Manor and it had been in his stepfather's family for four generations.

"Fancy," the Uber driver said as he dropped Harper off in front of the mansion. "Have a great time."

"Thanks," she said and stood staring at the impressive home, feeling a little intimidated by the grandeur. She knew a bit about architecture, having developed a love of old buildings from living in Manhattan.

She gauged that the house had been built sometime in the late nineteenth or early twentieth century, in the Beaux-Arts colonial style more common to public buildings than private residences. The elegant symmetry, impressive columns, pediments, and balustrades, and eye-catching balconies, terraces, porches, and porticoes immediately swept visitors back to a magical time in Moonglow Cove's history. Well-dressed couples were streaming toward the house while more people exited Ubers and taxis or passed their keys to valets.

Harper had dressed simply, in navy blue slacks and a patterned, sleeveless silk blouse and understated jewelry and now she was glad she'd decided against the casual sundress she'd bought when she'd gone shopping with Flannery. Her conservative attire suited the elegance of the Sinclair Mansion far better. Her only notable article of clothing were her stilettos. She held back a little, waiting for a lull in the flow of foot traffic. Snippets of pleasant conversation rode the early evening air, along with the scent of gardenias and honeysuckle in bloom.

Walking up the palm-tree-lined sidewalk, Harper had to quell a strong urge to flee. Flannery had had the right idea. Harper felt out of her element in this genteel, coastal environment.

Tia, on the other hand, would have embraced the Faulkner-esque splendor.

From inside the mansion, Harper could hear laughter and sounds of piano music, Scott Joplin's "Maple Leaf Rag." Someone was going all out to create a particular mood and tone. It felt like a carefully orchestrated endeavor.

A group of people entered before her to excited exclamations and enthusiastic welcomes. Again, Harper shrank back, letting others go ahead. She wasn't an introvert, but sometimes when faced with the unknown, she'd hold herself back until she was surer of her surroundings. She stepped around one of the white columns to draw in a deep fortifying breath. She was safe. It was a party at the mayor's house. Nothing to fear here.

"This is my stepfather's ancestral home," drawled a familiar voice from the veranda porch swing. "Not mine. Just FYI, in case you were feeling overwhelmed. My dad owns a modest beach condo in Port Aransas."

Grinning, Harper swiveled her head to catch Grayson's eyes. He was slouching like a lazy favored son in beige linen slacks and a short-sleeved aqua shirt. He looked the epitome of southern cool.

Her heart did a little hip-hop.

"Joplin on the player piano is just for the first fifteen minutes as the guests arrive," he said. "When the party migrates to the backyard, the DJ will play Gulf Coast songs."

"I see."

He scooted over and patted the seat beside him.

She pointed a thumb in the direction of the front door. "Shouldn't I go say hello to your mom first?"

"She's in her element. She'll just hug you warmly then pass you off to an underling. Might as well hang out with me until the crush of arriving guests passes and she starts looking for you."

"This is some dinner party," Harper said, watching as more guests arrived. "I thought it would just be a few people."

"When Missy Sinclair throws a party, it's a minimum head count of fifty."

"Wow. You grew up like this?"

"What can I say? Mom's a social butterfly. I'm sure it's one of the reasons Ward married her. He needed someone who loved entertaining as much as he does, and she adores playing lady of the manor."

"She neglected you when you were growing up?"

He shrugged. "I'm not complaining. When you've got a popular mom, it's hard for her to put her kids center stage. But you know what? I kind of like it here in the shadows."

"Me too," Harper said, finally sinking down beside him.

"There's no pressure to be 'on' in the shadows."

"I understand that compulsion." Harper gave a rueful shake of her head. "It's only now, since I've been in Moonglow Cove and I'm starting to finally relax a little, that I've come to realize just how jacked up I was in the world of Madison Avenue advertising."

"It is the apex. You were in the middle of the hive, honeybee."

"I'd forgotten how to chill," she said and paused. "If I ever even knew how to begin with."

"You'll get there."

"Why are you *really* hiding out?"

"I promised to put in an appearance, but since I got sober, I'm not much for parties with alcohol."

"Temptation too great?"

"No, drunk people can be pretty silly."

"They can, can't they?"

"The part I miss about drinking is how it lowers your guard and helps you get to know people quicker."

"You know, you can do that without alcohol," she said.

"Oh?" His eyebrows went up on his forehead and his grin deepened. "What's your method?"

"Rapid-fire questions. You just answer off the top of your head."

"Questions like what?"

"The Colbert Questionert."

"I'm not familiar."

"From Stephen Colbert. Not a fan of late-night talk shows?"

"I do get up pretty early."

"Do you want to play?"

"For sure." He lowered his lashes and studied her.

"I'll steal a few from Colbert and add some of my own."

"Game on."

"Best sandwich?" she said.

"Ham and cheese on whole wheat. You?"

"Pastrami on rye from Katz's deli." She sighed longingly. "I do miss the food in Manhattan."

"Moonglow Cove seems pretty pedestrian in comparison."

"A turtle's crawl."

"Next question."

"One thing you own that you should really throw out?" Harper asked.

"I'm a minimalist, but I'd have to say a flannel shirt I've had since college. It's just so soft. You?"

"Worn-out attitudes about small towns," she said.

"Interesting." He smiled and she felt uplifted. "What else?"

"Scariest animal?"

"Sloth."

"A sloth?" She giggled.

"Have you ever seen one crawling on the ground?" He shuddered. "They're creepy."

"For me, I'd say rattlesnake. I have reoccurring nightmares about rattlesnakes."

"My reoccurring nightmare involves being naked in public."

"You don't say. Hmm." She held his gaze. "Country or rock?"

"Don't make me chose. You?"

"Rocker chick."

"Somehow I knew that instinctively. Can I ask a question?"

"Sure."

"Number one deal breaker in a relationship with you?" His gaze lingered on her lips.

"I loathe deceptive and manipulative people," she blurted without thinking. "Like my grandmother Penelope."

He shifted away from her. It was slight, but she noticed. "And your mother as well?"

Harper didn't answer. Instead, she dropped his gaze and glanced toward the street where more guests were arriving. It was a lively shindig.

"What's *your* deal breaker," she asked, hearing her tone drift lower.

"People who don't know how to forgive."

Well, that was a conversation killer.

Gray moved his legs, setting the swing to gently rocking. Overhead the ceiling fan churned, cooling off the heated air.

"Feels like a storm's coming," he murmured.

"What?" she asked, thinking he meant a figurative storm of some kind.

But he was leaning his head forward to peer up at the sky. "Hurricane season officially starts June first; that's only a few days away."

Harper, too, cast an eye toward the sky. The clouds looked balmy to her, like cottage cheese against the darkening palette of gathering twilight.

"Are you borrowing trouble, Cooper, or as a lifelong Moonglow Covian, do you just feel something brewing?"

Gray turned his head to lock gazes with her. "Oh, I *definitely* feel something brewing."

Harper stared into those hypnotic pale blue eyes and her pulse thundered. "Are we still talking about hurricanes?"

Almost as if on some celestial cue, the Joplin music cut off and from the back of the house came the sound of Neil Young's "Like a Hurricane."

"That's cosmic," she said.

"Not as coincidental as it might seem," Grayson said mildly. "I got a look at Mom's playlist."

"Ahh. You brought up hurricane season on purpose."

"I did."

"As a lead-in?" She leaned closer.

For a moment, they sat listening to the lyrics about a man so blown away by a woman he was afraid to love her as they peered into each other's eyes.

"You're just a dreamer?" she asked, referring to a line from the song.

"And you are just a dream."

"No, I'm not. I'm real, Grayson. Very real."

"Harper," he said.

"Yes?"

"I don't want to scare you, but . . ." He planted his feet firmly on the porch, stopped the swing from rocking.

Her heart was pounding so hard and fast she couldn't hear herself think. "But?"

"It seems I'm making you nervous."

"No, not nervous. Unsettled maybe." She quelled the urge to jump up and start pacing.

"Why are you unsettled?"

"Because I like you too much and I'm in no position to like you so much. My life is in turmoil. I don't know what the future holds. Honestly, I'm confused and conflicted and—"

"I feel the same way."

"Conflicted and confused?"

"No," he said. "The other thing."

"Your life is in turmoil?"

Slowly, he shook his head. "No, the other thing. My life is more settled than it's ever been."

"Does that mean you like me?" She heard her voice rise, felt her stomach clench with hope.

"It does."

She shook her head. "This is inconvenient."

"I know." His steady gaze never left her face.

"I can't promise you anything."

"I know that, too."

"It's really bad timing. I—"

"Harper?"

"Uh-huh?"

"Could you please stop talking now because I'd really like to kiss you?"

CHAPTER 24

Harper

MAILLARD REACTION: A chemical reaction that occurs during baking, giving baked goods their golden-brown color and caramelized flavor.

The minute Grayson's lips touched Harper's her entire body caught fire.

The kiss was gentle, light, a sweet, tender brushing of their mouths. It shouldn't have felt so exciting.

But it did.

She leaned into the kiss and closed her eyes, desperate for him to continue, to take things deeper.

Instead, he pulled away.

What was wrong? Harper opened her eyes.

Gray was staring down at her with an expression so tender it stole all the air from her lungs. "We have an audience."

"What?" She was still dazed, dazzled. "Where?"

He inclined his head toward the mimosa tree in the side yard.

Harper craned her neck to see twin boys about Willow's age sitting on one of the branches watching them and giggling.

"Hey, you two," Grayson called. "Aren't you supposed to be in bed?"

"No way, Unca Gray!" the boys called. "It's not even dark yet."

"Your nephews?" Harper asked.

"Yep. My half sister Desiree's kids."

"They live with your parents?"

"Desiree's going through a divorce. She's moved in temporarily with Mom and her dad until she can figure things out."

"What does she do for a living?"

"She's been a stay-at-home mom since those two little chuckleheads were born. Before that she worked as a buyer for Williams-Sonoma."

"Wow."

"Yeah, Moonglow Cove is a bit of a comedown from a job like that."

"Tell me about it," Harper said ruefully.

"You miss Manhattan?"

"I lived there for ten years, so yes, but Moonglow Cove has its charms."

"Desiree said something similar."

"We should get her and Flannery together. It sounds like they have a lot in common—getting divorced, kids about the same age, starting new chapters in their lives . . ."

"Flannery couldn't come with you?"

Harper shook her head. "She's still rattled over what happened with Alan yesterday."

"My lawyer friend, Jim Conroe, is working on the restraining order. Hopefully, her soon-to-be ex will get the hint that our community has Flannery's back."

"It's weird how loyal you and Hank and Jonnie are to us," she said. "You don't even know us."

"You've got Moonglow Cove DNA, Harper Campbell. Like it or not, you're one of us." His eyes crinkled when he smiled that wide.

"Do you live in this area of town?" she asked, feeling intimidated by the idea that she had a group of people ready, willing, and able to be her tribe. It was something she'd never had and, until now, hadn't realized she'd longed for.

"No way. I'm a high school teacher. This neighborhood is too rich for my blood. I live in a bungalow a few blocks behind the Historical Society. 612 Lee Street." He paused. "Just in case you ever want to drop by for a visit."

"Thank you for the invitation."

"Anytime." He grinned.

"Unca Gray! Watch this." The twins were now hanging upside down, their legs wrapped around the branches as they swung several feet above the ground.

"Come on, you little monkeys, get down before you fall on your coconuts." Grayson got up and sauntered down the porch steps to his nephews in the mimosa tree.

Harper trailed after him, her stilettos sinking in the soft, thick Saint Augustine grass. She could see part of the backyard from here. People were gathered around a large lap pool while a man in an apron manned an oversized grill. The smell of mesquite wood and conversation carried over on the breeze underscored by a Jimmy Buffett tune.

Fingering her lips and hungering for more of Gray's kisses, she watched him help down one twin and then the other.

"This is Chaz and Chad," he introduced the boys who were

both missing the same bottom front tooth. "Kids, this is my friend Harper."

"Hi, Harper," they said in unison.

"Hello, fellas." Harper winked at them. "You two are pretty good tree climbers."

They got self-conscious at her compliment, ducking their heads, and toeing the ground with their matching sneakers.

"Hamburgers and hot dogs are ready," announced the man at the grill.

"Yay!" the boys hollered and took off toward the pool.

"Now," Gray said. "Where were we?"

He slipped an arm around Harper's waist and pulled her away from the party and toward a small garden maze.

Oh, now this looked delicious.

Once inside the garden maze, amid the sounds of people splashing in the pool and "Gulf Coast Girl" from the speakers, Gray pulled her into his arms.

"Rarely have I ever wanted to kiss someone this badly," he murmured. He held her gaze and she wondered what he saw when he looked into her eyes. Could he see her damage? Did it scare him off?

"I feel the same way."

"It's electric, our chemistry."

"Powerful," she admitted. *Dangerous even?*

"The last time I felt this way I was with my wife."

That put a damper on things. She stepped back, held up her palms. "I'm not ready for anything that intense, Gray."

"Me either."

"Then what are we doing?"

"How can we leave feelings like this on the table? Don't we

owe it to ourselves to explore the possibility of something monumental?"

"I don't want to get hurt, and I don't want to hurt you, either."

"Ditto."

The yearning in his eyes matched the longing in her heart. He stepped closer. She didn't back up.

"Harper," he whispered her name and slid his palm up her nape, forking his fingers through her hair. His other hand cupped her cheek and she rested there, savoring the feel of his masculine palm.

"You have strong palms for a desk jockey," she murmured.

"I didn't tell you? I'm an avid windsurfer."

"Really? I've always wanted to learn that sport."

"I can teach you. Name the time and place."

"That would be amazing."

"Done." He stroked her bottom lip with his thumb.

She shivered, and goose bumps spread over her skin.

"I'm going to kiss you again, unless you have an objection."

"Only that it's taking you so long," she said, closed her eyes, parted her lips, and waited.

His mouth came down on hers, firmer than before, and he kissed her. A kiss filled with heat and pressure.

Harper lost herself in the man. She folded her arms around him and held on for dear life, wriggling closer, making encouraging sounds deep in her throat.

He groaned and got the hint, his tongue teasing past her parted teeth. He tasted so good, like salted caramel, and he smelled even better. His scent of sandalwood and myrrh tangled up in her nose. A fragrance she would forever label *Grayson*.

"Mmm," he murmured against her lips. "You taste yummy."

"My thoughts exactly."

"You kiss as good as you look, Ms. Campbell."

"Why thank you, Mr. Cooper."

"I wasn't expecting anyone like you to walk into my life."

"Thought you had everything figured out, huh?"

"No. Life has taught me that I know absolutely nothing. I just try to stay curious and open to possibilities."

"And I'm a possibility?"

"Oh, I'm afraid you're much more than that."

She loved that grin of his. It had magical powers to lift her spirits right up to the sky.

"Want to kiss some more?" he asked.

"You know I do."

He reached for her, but a noise in the bushes stopped him. "Those ornery twins. They love spying on people."

But it wasn't the twins who appeared at the entrance to the maze. Instead, it was Gray's mom.

"There you are," said Missy Sinclair, looking pampered and polished in a stylish summer jumpsuit, with her hair and nails freshly done. "The twins told me they'd met a pretty lady named Harper. I see that my rascal son has absconded with you." To Gray, she said, "Shame on you for hiding our guest."

"We had things to talk about, Mom."

Missy's eyes lit up. "I'm sure you did. Ward and I had our best 'talks' inside this garden maze when we were courting."

Grayson blew out his breath and jammed his hands in his pockets. Harper noticed his cheeks reddened. Embarrassed by his mother? That idea amused her.

"Where's Flannery and Willow and Jonnie?" Missy asked. "Are they here?"

"Flannery had a little incident yesterday and she's a bit shaken up," Harper said.

"I do hope she's okay." Missy seemed genuinely concerned, but Harper wasn't going to spread her sister's business.

"She'll be fine. She just wasn't up for a celebration. Jonnie stayed behind to keep her company."

"What a diplomatic way of putting it. I know Jonnie doesn't approve of me. She always thought I was a bad influence on Tia."

"Jonnie doesn't dislike you, Mom," Grayson protested. "She just has a different lifestyle than you do."

Harper appreciated him taking up for her aunt and sent him a grateful smile.

"Well," Missy said to her son, coming over to link her arm through Harper's. "Because you were selfish, my son, and took Harper from our party, I'm going to steal her from you. Ward needs some help with the grill, so be a dear and give him a hand. I'll bring Harper back soon enough."

"Okay," Gray said in that easygoing way of his, but he apologized to Harper with his eyes, winked, and silently mouthed, *Later.*

* * *

"Let me give you the grand tour," Missy said, sweeping Harper up the steps and into the Sinclair mansion.

Harper cast a glance over her shoulder to see Gray standing on the lawn behind her, his hand raised and a "good luck" smile on his face.

His mother was a force of nature, and Harper could see why Missy and Tia had been friends. Both colorful and expressive with a need to feel special, but whereas Tia's larger-than-life personality had taken her down a toxic path, Missy seemed to have struck the proper balance between her strengths and flaws.

People kept interrupting them on the tour to talk to Missy and she soaked up the attention. Tia would have immediately launched into how wonderful and unique she was, while Missy truly listened to others, asked lots of questions, and showed empathy. She took the time to introduce Harper to everyone, compliment the person she'd just introduced, and then gently remind the other guests she was giving Harper a tour. Once the person had gone on their way, Missy would tell Harper something kind about them instead of running them down behind their backs as Tia would have.

Harper found herself gravitating to Missy. This was how her mother could have been if she'd been emotionally healthy.

A deep pang of sorrow and regret punched her solar plexus at her mother's self-induced suffering. Instead of doubling down when she flubbed, if Tia could have just admitted she was human, owned her flaws, and tried to change her negative behavior, her life could have been so very different. When life went her way, Tia had been fun to be around, but things could turn on a dime, and as kids, Harper and Flannery had never known what would flip her switch from cool mom to witch-on-wheels.

"You missed out on so much, Tia," Harper murmured under her breath, watching Missy charm people with her interest and concern.

"What's that, sweetie?" Missy wrapped her arm around Harper's shoulder.

"Just admiring how good you are with people."

"Everyone just wants to be recognized and respected."

"You're adroit at it."

"Why, thank you. That's kind of you to say. I work hard at it. Now, this is the master bedroom." Missy opened the door to a room straight out of *Town and Country*.

Why had two people with such similar personality styles as her mother and Missy turned out so differently? What had guided Missy to choose a healthier path to self-actualization while Tia had devolved into self-destruction?

That pirate DNA? Or was it more nurture than nature? It dawned on Harper that she knew absolutely nothing about Penelope Campbell, beyond what she'd started reading in Gray's book, or what her mother's early life had actually been like. All she had to go on was Tia's distorted lens of the past.

The sadness washing through Harper was overwhelming.

Smelling of Chanel No. 5, Missy fondled the geometric Alexander Calder necklace at her throat as she shut the door behind them. "There's something I wanted to give you. Something of your mother's. Have a seat."

Wincing at the intimacy of the room, Harper perched on the edge of a Queen Anne chair in the sitting area on the opposite side of the bed as she watched Missy turn to the dresser and rummage in a jewelry box.

"I'm actually glad now that Flannery, Willow, and Jonnie couldn't make it," she said. "I'm grateful for this private time with you."

"Me too," Harper said because she really didn't know what else to say.

Missy turned back to Harper. In her hand she clutched a small stack of letters. "Your mother wrote these to me during that year she left you with Jonnie."

Harper's heart slid into her Christian Louboutins.

Missy came over to sit on the sofa next to Harper's chair. "I debated on whether to give them to you or not. Reading them is bound to stir up powerful emotions. They certainly did in me."

Shaking her head, Harper sank back in the chair suddenly feeling boneless and breathless. She'd found it odd that her mother, an avid reader who dabbled in writing poetry, had not left behind any personal correspondences for her daughters. She'd decided it was because Tia didn't want to leave behind a paper trail to chart her mental imbalance. Harper had felt a bit robbed that there'd been nothing left behind that gave any insights into Tia's skewered thought processes.

But now, with her mom's best high school friend sitting here, holding out letters from Tia, she felt terrified.

She did not want to read them. Did not want her childhood fears exposed as truths. That her own mother *had* hated her as she'd always suspected. That Harper never had been nor ever would be worthy of unconditional love.

"I . . . that's personal between you and Mom. I don't want the letters."

Missy kept them extended. "You don't have to read them now. You can wait until you're strong enough. I don't know if they'll make you feel any better, but they'll explain some things about your mother."

Harper kept shaking her head.

"Flannery might want them."

"Why? Tia wrote them before she was born."

"In an attempt to understand her, perhaps?"

Harper buried her face in her hands, blew out her breath, and raised her head to face Missy's kind gaze. "What does it matter?

She's gone. She led a miserable life and made our lives miserable as well. I don't need any insight."

"Oh, sweetheart, but you do. Until you can forgive her, you can't move on with *your* life; and from the way my son talks about you, I'm worried that you're going to break his heart. I haven't seen him look at a woman the way he looks at you since Stephanie."

CHAPTER 25

Flannery

POOLISH: A pre-ferment made using a mixture of flour, water, and commercial yeast that has a consistency more like batter than dough.

It was just after nine when Flannery tucked Willow into bed, checked the security cameras to make sure all was well outside and tiptoed into the kitchen to feed the sourdough starter.

While the conditions of their grandmother's will prohibited them from throwing away the discard, or refrigerating the mother dough, Aunt Jonnie had convinced them it was perfectly legitimate to refrigerate the discard and use it at a later time as long as they kept the mother dough fed and happy on the counter. No more staying up late to bake.

Thank heavens. Flannery was still exhausted after her encounter with Alan the previous day. As she measured out the flour and water, she heard a key in the lock at the back door and the sound of her sister's footsteps. Straightening, she turned toward the kitchen entrance.

"Hey," she called. "I didn't expect you back so soon. I—"

At the sight of her sister, Flannery's heart somersaulted. Setting down the measuring cup of water, she rushed across the room.

"Harper? What is it? What's wrong?"

Harper's face was ghostly pale, and her forehead was beaded with perspiration.

"Come in, sit down." Flannery put an arm around her shoulder and guided her to the kitchen table.

Meekly, Harper followed.

"What's happened?"

Harper shook her head.

Fear squashed Flannery's chest. "Please," she begged. "Talk to me. Did something happen at the party? Did you get bad news? Has something happened to Jonnie? What is it? What's wrong?"

Harper didn't answer. Instead, she stared with glazed eyes out the window at the lighthouse. That's when Flannery saw that her sister was clutching three envelopes, the once-white paper yellowed with age. She reached to take the letters, desperate for answers.

"No." Clinging tightly to the envelopes, Harper moved them from her grasp.

Flannery tried to read the return address, but Harper pressed the letters against her heart with both hands.

"Where did you get those?" she asked.

"Missy Sinclair," Harper answered in a robotic tone.

"Who are they from?"

Still shaking her head, Harper pressed her lips together.

"Mom?"

Harper nodded.

"Oh dear." Flannery flopped down into the chair beside her sister.

Harper fisted her hands around the letters, crumpling them.

Wincing, it was all Flannery could do not to yank the envelopes away from Harper. Her sister was having some kind of breakdown.

"What's in them?"

"I don't know."

"Then why are you reacting so strangely?"

"She wrote them to Missy the year I lived with Aunt Jonnie from age two to three."

"And you're scared to read them?"

"Terrified."

"That's understandable. Would you like for me to read them and give you the CliffsNotes of what's inside?" Flannery wasn't so sure that she was ready to read her mother's letters, either, but they were written before she was born so they couldn't contain any information about her, which provided some level of emotional safety for her.

"No."

"Why don't we put them away for now and head to bed? You can read them tomorrow when your feelings have calmed."

"No." Growing agitated, Harper pushed back from her chair, got up, and started to pace. Her skin still looking wan and clammy.

A pacing Harper was not a good sign. Worry burrowed into Flannery's back jaw.

Harper stalked to the kitchen junk drawer, dug inside, and pulled out a grill lighter.

"No." Flannery rushed to stop her. "Don't burn them. You can't burn them."

"Why not?" Harper lifted her chin, holding the lighter and the letters away from Flannery.

"Because you can't undo it. Once you burn them, they're gone."

"Good riddance."

"You don't mean that."

"I do. When Missy gave them to me, it was all I could do to keep from ripping them to pieces in front of her."

"I'm glad you didn't do that. What did you say?"

"I split as soon as Missy gave the letters to me. I couldn't face her, knowing she'd been keeping Tia's secrets all this time. Knowing she knew things about us that I didn't know myself. I barely said good-bye to Gray."

Flannery sat perfectly still when what she really wanted to do was rush over and hug her older sister. "I'm sure he'll understand. Gray is a smart guy."

"This has nothing to do with him."

"You're upset with his mother."

"No, I'm not. I'm upset with *me*. I'm not fit company to be around."

"Why?"

"Because I care about what's in here." She shook the letters at Flannery. "Because despite how horribly she treated us, despite everything, I still love her. Why do I love her, Flan? What's wrong with me?"

"She's your mother. We're hardwired to love our mothers. It comes with the territory."

"Then why wasn't *she* hardwired to love us?"

It dawned on Flannery then, just how different her experience of Tia was from Harper's. She couldn't ever remember having loved her mother with her sister's passion. Her primary emotion in regard to Tia had been fear. Then again, Flannery had had her dad and Harper to balance out Tia's tirades and she'd transferred her love onto them instead. Harper hadn't had anyone to mitigate the abuse.

Except maybe for that one year with Aunt Jonnie.

"My earliest memory of Mom is when I was around three. She was hanging out clothes on the clothesline and I was sitting in the laundry basket watching her. The morning sun peeped over her shoulder and bathed her in a golden halo of light and my heart just about burst with love for her."

Harper's pacing intensified, her fingers still clutching the letters so tightly that her knuckles had turned white. "She finished pinning a towel to the clothesline, looked down at me, and smiled so big I thought my heart was going to split right open with love. She bent down and picked me up and swept me into her arms and told me how much she loved me."

"Aww, that's so sweet."

"No," Harper said. "It's not, because now I realize it wasn't Tia. It was Aunt Jonnie."

Her sister stopped pacing abruptly, closed her eyes, and gulped so hard that Flannery could hear her halfway across the room.

"I've held on to that memory for many years to remind me that Tia *did* love me back. At least once upon a time. But now I don't even have that anymore. My love for my mother was unrequited. Not only that, she actively *hated* me."

Harper *had* been the family scapegoat even as Tia also often treated her as the golden child for her accomplishments, blaming her oldest daughter for all her problems. Harper had taken the brunt of Tia's abuse. She'd been their mother's punching bag. Flannery had mostly been neglected and ignored until Tia needed her for something and then she'd been her handmaiden.

Her heart wrenched for her sister, and she wished there was something she could do to wash away all the pain they'd suffered at the hands of the one person who was supposed to love them unconditionally.

"Maybe there's some kind of explanation in the letter?" Flannery offered hopefully. "A reason why she left you. The reason she came back."

"I wish like hell she'd left me with Aunt Jonnie." The words ripped from Harper's throat, jagged and heartfelt.

"Selfishly, I'm glad she didn't. If you hadn't been there for me, Harper, I don't know how I would have survived. You're the one *I* loved. You were *my* shero."

"Oh, Flan." Harper sighed. "Oh, sister. I'm a hot mess."

"No, you're not. You're smart and resilient and determined."

"And fired because I stupidly trusted the wrong person."

"What about me? You got a gander at Alan. I'm no slouch in the stupid decisions department."

Harper sighed again, but this time it was less angsty. "Boy, we're a pair."

"We're no more messed up than anyone else. Look at Hank. He's got serious scars. And Aunt Jonnie. She's a recovering alcoholic. Grayson too. Everyone has demons, Harper. Although some of us have more than our share. No one gets through life unscathed. We're all struggling to get by. Just like Tia was."

"I know." Finally, Harper put down the lighter.

Relieved, Flannery's shoulders sagged. She hadn't realized how much tension she'd been holding. "Would you like for me to read the letters now? I don't have to tell you what's in them if it's hurtful."

Harper slowly blew out a long-held breath. "I don't know."

"Surely Missy wouldn't have given them to you if there had been meanness in them."

"I can't guess Missy's state of mind," Harper said. "I barely know her."

"She raised a great son," Flannery said. "Sure, she's flamboyant and a bit over the top, but I feel like we can trust her."

Closing her eyes briefly, Harper held the envelopes out to Flannery.

She took them and instantly caught a whiff of their mother's signature scent. *Opium* by Yves Saint Laurent. "Because I'm addictive," Tia had once laughed to Flannery as she spritzed some behind an ear, readying herself for a date. The spicy fragrance of clove, cinnamon, black pepper, and sandalwood tangled up in Flannery's nose along with the memory of their mesmerizing, fascinating, outrageous, and far too often very toxic, mother.

Harper trailed back to the kitchen table and plunked down, looking like a deflated balloon, shoulders slumped, head down. Flannery followed, checking the dates on the letters, and started with the one postmarked the earliest, June 15, 1991. Harper had been born in 1989.

Teasing the letter from the envelope, Flannery opened it and began to read silently.

"Go ahead and read it out loud," Harper said. "Let's just get this over with."

"You sure?"

Harper nodded.

Clearing her throat, Flannery started to read.

Dear Missy,

Please don't be mad that I took off and left Harper with you. I needed a break. She was driving me bonkers. She's as clingy as that guy I dated freshman year, Melvin Maites. Remember him? God, what a mouth-breathing loser. I deserved so much better.

Did you turn Harper over to "she-who-shall-not-be-named" or do you still have her? I can try to send you some money if you've got her. If she's *got her, then fine and dandy. Let* her *pay for Harper's care. The kid cramps my style anyway.*

Seattle is the bomb! You'd love this place. People read like crazy here. Partly because of all the rain and partly because there are a lot of supersmarties around. My kind of people. We both know my IQ is off the charts. Who doesn't want to curl up with a good book on a rainy day? I got a job at a bookstore, yay me. It's only minimum wage and I deserve so much better, but it'll do until I can find some place that recognizes my greatness. Ha. Ha. I do get a ten percent discount, although I just read the books in the store without breaking the spine or creasing the covers and put them back on the shelf. What they don't know don't hurt 'em, right?

Peter is such a sweetie pie. He wants to take me to Vegas for a quicky wedding, but I'm not having any of that. It's the full Monty or nothing for this girl. I made that perfectly clear. You want the best, you gotta fork out the dough.

Wowza! Peter just showed up in the bedroom doorway, buck naked and beckoning. He's taking me to dinner at the Space Needle later. I'll order your fav, lobster bisque, and we'll share a toast to you, my BFF and personal savior. Thanks so much for everything. You rock. Gotta go now, hot sex is about to happen.

Toodles,
Tia

P.S. Let me know about Harper. Oh, and FYI, she's allergic to peanuts, which is superannoying because PB&J is the easiest thing to feed her besides goldfish crackers, but her face will swell up like a toad if you do and no one wants a toady kid.

Cringing, Flannery lifted her head and met her sister's gaze, trying to gauge her reaction to the letter.

Harper's face was bland, showing no emotion at all. "Sounds like Tia."

"Were you expecting something else?"

"Not really. I suppose maybe there'd be some kind of explanation about why she dumped me and took off. I guess it was just my resemblance to the unfortunate Melvin Maites."

"I'm sure she wasn't as callous as the letter makes her sound."

"Still making excuses for her, Flan? You can stop now. The truth will set you free."

"Maybe, but I don't want to be like her. Saying tacky things about people behind their backs."

Harper's cheeks flamed red.

"Oh, my goodness, I didn't mean that's what you were doing. You are completely justified to be upset with how she treated you. I just meant, for me, I want to avoid being like her in—"

"Flan," Harper interrupted.

"Yes," Flannery said, hating that she'd just spouted off without considering the effect her words would have on her sister.

"It's fine. I understand."

"Do you want me to keep going?" Flannery held up the other two letters.

"Why not? In for a penny, in for a pound."

Flannery so admired her sister's ability to keep a tight lid on her emotions. She didn't know if she could be that strong if the letter was about her, and she was starting to regret not letting Harper burn the stupid things.

"I'm so sorry."

"Not your fault," Harper said. "And it's nothing I didn't expect."

"I wonder why Missy even gave you the letters."

"Maybe there's something in the other two that will shine a light on the deep mystery of our mother."

"Maybe," Flannery echoed, but she didn't feel the least bit hopeful. Holding her breath, she took out the second letter, this one written on pink notepaper with red hearts along the border. Looking at their mother's childish paper choice sent a pang through her heart. "You know, she was only nineteen at the time she wrote this letter."

"The same age you were when Tia died."

"She never changed," Flannery said.

"Never grew up."

"As a mom, I don't understand that. Once Willow was born, *everything* changed for me. I can't begin to wrap my mind around what Tia did. Abandoning you with Missy. Just taking off without a word to anyone from the sound of this letter."

"I'm assuming Missy gave me to Jonnie," Harper said. "Although I wonder why Aunt Jonnie and not our grandmother?"

Flannery glanced down at the second letter, saw dark words that leapt off the page at her. Hateful words about Jonnie. Ugly words about Harper. Her sister did not need to hear this. Flannery did not need to read these toxic words out loud.

"You know what? You were right the first time. Let's burn these letters. Make a ritual of it. Let Tia go once and for all."

"Is it that bad?" Harper asked.

"It's just too sad," Flannery said. "Seeing the words of a mentally disordered person. Knowing how much she suffered. Knowing she was the cause of most of her suffering and couldn't see it. There's no need for us to wallow in toxic sludge."

Hopping up, she retrieved the lighter and marched into the living room. Harper followed her.

They sat on the fireplace hearth, and Flannery settled the letters on the grate, then gave her sister the lighter.

"Burn it," she said. "Burn up the past."

"Why the sudden change of heart?" Harper asked, curiosity in her eyes as she held on to the lighter.

"I've been doing a lot of self-reflection, trying to be a better mother for Willow, trying to figure out how I let myself get tangled up with Alan. And reading that first letter, I just realized something important."

"What's that?"

"The *why* doesn't matter beyond recognizing the patterns and changing the bad habits. And that can be done with awareness and mindfulness. What does matter is forgiving myself, correcting my mistakes, and moving forward."

"Wow, look at you, baby sister." Harper smiled for the first time since she'd come into the house. "Being all wise and everything."

"I reached that conclusion because of you."

"Me?" Harper looked surprised.

"You're not a broody ruminator like me. You go after what you want. You make decisions quickly and you bounce back from setbacks just as fast. I mean, look, you lost your job two weeks ago and you've already come up with a plan to start your own business. That's an amazingly swift turnaround."

Harper looked as if a lightbulb went off in her head. "I forgot to tell Gray about the Sourdough Sisters. That was the main reason I went to Missy's party, to pick his brain about the best way to incorporate the lighthouse into our branding since he knows so much about the place. Thank you for the reminder."

"Where are you going now?"

"To see Grayson."

"Tonight? We haven't burned the letters."

Harper handed Flannery the lighter. "You do the honors. Burn, baby, burn."

"Seriously? You're going over there at ten o'clock at night?"

"Carpe noctem," Harper said, pivoting on her heel, picking up her purse from where she'd dropped it on the mudroom counter, and walking out the door into the bright, starry night.

CHAPTER 26

Harper

LAME: A tool consisting of a handle with a sharp blade, used to score the top of a loaf just before it is baked.

Truthfully? Harper left, not to go talk to Grayson—although she did give the Uber driver his address—but to get away from Flannery. One more minute in her little sister's company and she was terrified she'd start crying again.

She was running scared and that's all there was to it. No longer able to keep her emotions in check. What was happening to her? For years she'd been able to tamp down her feelings and sweep them under the rug, but no more. She had to find a way to shut them down again. Over the years, sex had worked wonderfully for that.

Harper wanted Grayson with a powerful need and from the way he'd kissed her in the garden maze, she had a pretty good clue that he wanted her too. The man had given her his address after all. Would he do that if he minded her showing up unannounced?

Besides, she had a good excuse for her visit. To get his opinion on the viability of the Sourdough Sisters business.

At ten twenty at night, Harper? Lame excuse.

Panic rushed through her as she stood on his doorstep. What was she doing here? This was stupid.

Go! Get out of here!

The door opened and a sleepy-eyed Gray in pajama bottoms and nothing else appeared, disguising a yawn. "Harper, what are you doing here?"

One look at him and Harper's pulse took off at a gallop. It was the dumbest thing in the world. She knew it the second she did it, but Harper raised her shirt and flashed him her black, lace, push-up bra.

Grayson's eyes popped wide open. "Holy cow, woman!"

The appreciative look in his glacier blue gaze thrilled her to her bones. "Like what you see?"

"Get in here." He grabbed her wrist and hauled her over the threshold.

Laughing, she didn't resist as he tugged her into his living area.

The room boasted midcentury modern decor—clean lines, organic curves, simplicity, and functionality. Which, come to think of it, was a perfect metaphor for Gray himself. Harper undid the top two buttons on her blouse, giving him a clear view of her cleavage.

Sweat pearled on his upper lip and he looked as if he wanted to eat her up in one big bite. "What the blue blazes is this all about?"

Harper sauntered toward him, seductively moistening her lips with the tip of her tongue, and murmured, "What do you think?"

"I think something is out of whack." He crossed his arms over his bare chest. "You hardly said good-bye to me before you fled my mother's party and then you show up on my doorstep two hours later looking like you're aiming to spend the night."

"You did invite me to drop by for a visit." She held her arms outstretched. "Ta-da. Here I am."

Gray whistled long and low, his gaze fixed on her breasts. "Yes, you are," he said. "Yes, you are."

She crooked a finger at him.

He shook his head. "Something's up."

She fixed her gaze on his crotch. "I hope it's what I think it is . . ."

"Harper, what if I had company?"

"Do you?" She lifted an eyebrow.

"No, but that's beside the point."

"I wanted to surprise you," she said and undid another button, giving him a glimpse of her flat belly. "Surprise!"

"Dang it, woman." His face flushed. "Stop doing that."

"You don't like what you see?" She was coming on too strong. She should back off. This wasn't like her. But she desperately needed something to soothe the ache in the center of her heart that had started when Flannery read the letter out loud. She wondered what awful thing had been in the second letter that caused her sister to want to burn them.

"I like it." Gray bobbed his head. "Very, very much. That's the problem."

"How's that?" She struck a coy pose, peeping at him from underneath her eyelashes.

"Harper, you're damn sexy and it's been a really long time since I've wanted a woman the way I want you."

"Great. I want you, too, Gray."

"But it's not happening."

"What?"

"Don't get me wrong. I want to sleep with you more than I want to breathe, but we're not doing this tonight."

She sauntered closer, putting an extra sway to her hips and a smoky tone in her voice. "Doing what?"

"Harper . . ." He dragged her name from his throat. "I can't."

"Can't?" She cocked her eyebrows and dropped her gaze to the fly of his pajamas again.

"Won't," he said adamantly.

"Why not?" She stepped closer, crowding his personal space.

"It's too soon."

"Too soon for this?" She wrapped her arms around his neck and dropped a kiss on his warm lips.

He did not kiss her back.

Hot shame swept through her and burned the tops of her ears.

"No," he murmured, giving her a look of infinite patience as he gently disentangled her arms from around his neck. "It's not happening. Not tonight."

She licked the tip of her finger, touched his bottom lip.

Gray let out a groan and said in a guttural tone, "Please."

"Please what?" she teased.

"Please don't do that. I'm hanging on by a thread here."

Her equilibrium was off. After the sparks that flew between them in the garden maze, she'd thought that the bedroom was a logical place to end up. Apparently, they were not on the same page. "Is that how you really feel?"

He nodded. "It is."

"You're not just playing hard to get?" She gave him her best smile.

"No."

He *was* rejecting her.

"Oh," she said in a rush of air. "I'm sorry. I'll go. I shouldn't have come." She spun on her heels, grappled for the purse she'd dropped when he'd dragged her inside.

"Harper," he said, taking her hand. "Shh, shh. You've got nothing to be ashamed of. You took a chance. You were brave. I admire you for that."

"Really?" she asked, feeling far too vulnerable. She didn't do vulnerability. She wanted out of here to go stew in her shame.

But Gray was gently leading her to his stylish modern couch in white vegan leather, and he was too charming to resist.

"There now," he crooned, easing her down beside him. "There now."

Feeling confused, she stared into his mesmerizing blue eyes. No man ever turned her down for sex. This was a new wrinkle. She could've *sworn* he was interested in her. Had she misread the signs that badly?

"Harper." His tone was low and filled with sympathy.

He felt sorry for her? Fresh shame flooded her body. Quickly she started buttoning up her blouse, her cheeks burning hot.

"Please, don't feel embarrassed. There's nothing wrong with your seduction. I want you to know that. There's nothing in the world I'd like more than to take you to bed. In fact, I can barely keep my hands off you." He was rubbing his thumb along her knuckles, and he looked so earnest her body literally ached.

She felt a sudden sharp pain deep in the center of her chest. "I'm sorry, so sorry. I'm an idiot."

"No, no you're not. You're bold and you're brave and you went for what you wanted. There is nothing wrong with that."

She ducked her head but couldn't shake off the shame. She

hadn't thought this through. She was hurting from Flannery reading that damn letter and all she wanted was to feel good.

"I want you to listen to me, not just listen but hear me, fully hear me." He hooked two fingers underneath her chin and tilted her face up to meet his gaze. "Can you do that?"

She nodded. She could hear him out, but she couldn't hold his gaze. Closing her eyes, she swallowed hard and licked her lips.

He didn't say anything.

Opening her eyes, she found him studying her with an expression so tender that panic gripped her hard and it was all she could do not to bolt up from the couch and run away. This was *not* what she'd bargained for.

"I like you, Harper. Very much. And I think we have something we can build on if that's what you want. Something special. But I won't ruin that by hopping into bed with you too soon. I've done that too many times in the past and nothing good has ever come of it. And something tells me you've done the same thing. Is that right?"

"Yes," she mumbled.

"Something sent you here tonight and that something isn't just a desire for sex."

She opened her mouth, but he laid a finger over her lips.

"You might think you want sex, but you're just using it as a pacifier. I won't be your pacifier, Harper. If we have sex now, it's the end for us. Do you understand?"

She nodded, her pulse pounding hard and fast through her veins.

"I'm past that point of casual sex in my life. I want an honest, intimate relationship like I had with my late wife, Stephanie."

"I understand."

"Do you want to tell me the real reason you came here tonight?" he asked.

Did she? "I came to talk to you about a business Flannery and I want to start. The Sourdough Sisters will be an online artisanal store for bread enthusiasts. We're using the lighthouse as our logo and since you know all about the Moonglow Lighthouse, I wanted your expert input."

"That sounds like a fantastic idea for a business, Harper, and we can discuss that tomorrow," he said, low and comforting, "but I'd like to know the *real* reason you're here."

His face was so kind, so caring that Harper couldn't speak. She pressed a palm to her mouth. Tasted salt. Felt something warm and wet trickle down her cheek.

Damn. She was crying.

He reached for a tissue from a box on the end table and dabbed away her tears.

She smiled at him through a watery film. "Thank you."

"Anytime."

She told him then about the letter her mother had written his mother over thirty years ago. How she and Flannery had burned the remaining two letters without reading them. "The letter confirmed what I'd always suspected about my mother. She was basically a toddler in an adult body. She had no idea how to be a mom. Then or later. She had no idea how to change. Had no desire to change. I don't know if she was even capable of it. She had some kind of undiagnosed mental disorder."

Grayson offered no advice, no comment. He just listened as she spilled it all out. Talking to him in a way she'd been unable to talk to anyone, not even her therapist.

"That's what's so damn sad about the whole thing. Tia was

a terrible person, but she couldn't help it. She had no idea why her life didn't work out and no one could offer her any advice. Heaven knows Flannery's dad tried. I tried. I'm assuming your mom and Aunt Jonnie tried too. No one could reach her. She thought she was perfect and everyone else was to blame for the problems in her life. No, not just thought it, she believed her own self-aggrandizement with all her heart and soul and if you tried to talk her out of her delusion, she labeled you the enemy." Harper took the tissue from him and wiped away fresh tears.

He said nothing, just listened attentively.

"I kept hoping for some glimmer of kindness in her, some indication that she loved us at least on some small level . . . but that letter? It cinched it for me. The truth I've spent my whole life denying. She was incapable of loving anyone but herself and my heart just breaks for her. She was a human being and she deserved to be loved, but she demanded that people worship her and when they didn't, she discarded them. Everyone who tried to love her ended up damaged. Some of them beyond repair."

"But not you. Not Flannery."

Hiccuping, Harper swiped away the last of her tears and stuffed the tissue in her pants pocket and gave him a weak smile. "Thank you for saying that."

"It's the story of your family tree, Harper. You have a legacy of multigenerational abuse. Part of it is genetic, but part of it is environment too. Life was harsh back then. Your ancestors had to be tough to survive, both in Scotland where they came from as borderland warriors and then out there on that isolated, craggy, lighthouse bluff. They self-isolated from the rest of the town and the mean ones subjugated the loving ones. That abuse cycle, that toxicity, is part of the fabric of America. Hell, it's the fabric of humanity."

"So you're saying there's no hope for any of us?" Her chuckle came out harsh and ragged.

"No," he said. "Quite the opposite. That's the value of history and why I love it so much. Paying attention to the past gives us a path out of so much suffering. Facing the truth of multigenerational abuse and doing our best as a society to put a stop to it *is* the way out. As Oscar Wilde said, 'we are all in the gutter, but some of us are looking at the stars'; those of us looking at the stars can start to climb out of the gutter. We do that through kindness, love, and patience."

"I tried all that with Tia, it didn't work. The kinder we were, the more she ran over us."

"Sometimes life just breaks your heart, Harper. At some point, you have to let go and save yourself. You have to set boundaries and when those boundaries are violated, you have to walk away from abuse. It's that simple and that hard. The best way that those of us who've gained a little perspective can help those still struggling is by example. Show others how to live a happy, healthy life by doing it yourself. You don't have to rescue anyone but yourself. It's more than enough."

"Wow," she said. "How did you get so smart?"

"Stephanie," he said in an unequivocal tone. "*She* showed me the way out. Of course, I did a lot of backsliding first when I lost her, trying to drown myself in alcohol. It was your aunt Jonnie who showed me the way out of that."

"Life sucks."

His own eyes turned a bit misty. "I did lose Stephanie way too soon, but I'm so grateful to have had her for the short time that I did. She made me promise to find someone special and to love again."

"And that's what you're waiting for. Someone special to love."

"It is." His eyes shone as he looked at her.

Harper teared up again. What was happening to her? She'd cried more since she'd been in Moonglow Cove than she'd cried in the last twenty years.

Grayson wrapped his arms around her. "Shh, it's okay, you're all right. It's all right. You're here with me now. Everything is going to be just fine."

He murmured the words she'd longed her entire life for someone to say to her. That she was safe. She was cared for. That everything was going to work out.

She buried her head on his shoulder, and he held her close. Gently, he kissed her forehead and cradled her against him. Rocked her softly in his arms. The next thing she knew, he was scooping her up and carrying her into his bedroom.

"I thought you said we weren't going to sleep together."

"No," Grayson corrected. "I said we weren't going to have sex. It's late. You need some rest. And so do I."

She didn't argue and when he laid her down on the bed and climbed on the mattress beside her, tucked her against his strong body and wrapped his arms around her, she felt as if she was snugged inside a warm cocoon.

For the first time in forever, Harper finally felt safe enough to lay down her burdens and just sleep.

CHAPTER 27

Flannery

SCORE: Cuts made on the surface of the dough just prior to baking.

Her sister changed after Flannery read Tia's letter and Harper spent the night with Grayson.

Harper had come into the keeper's cottage the morning after Missy's Memorial Day party happily singing "Under the Sea."

Willow immediately joined in and Flannery stood at the kitchen counter feeding Blobby and watching her sister dance with her daughter, twirling Willow in her wheelchair. Utterly relieved that her sister's mood had shifted overnight, Flannery joined in the impromptu party until they were all three laughing and breathless.

After that wonderful moment, the weeks leading up to the Fourth of July Weekend Bake-off unfurled in a delightful, leisurely pattern. Their days filled with baking, food, and community. Days chock-full of family and making new friends and developing their fledging plans for their online business.

They got up early to start the bread-making process, branching out and trying new varieties of sourdough—San Franciscan style, Danish rye, Camaldoli, desem, and New Zealand. They experimented with different grains—whole wheat, spelt, gluten-free, brown rice, rye, potato, honey wheat, and soda bread. After the day's batch of bread was set aside to rise, they'd gather the freshly baked loaves from the previous day's proofing and start their deliveries, dropping off the free bread to Edith Gimble at the community restaurant kitchen and then making their rounds to Aunt Jonnie's office and her shrimp boat employees, to Missy's house and the Historical Society, then completing the loop by visiting Hank.

When they returned to the cottage, it was time for lunch and the second rise. In the afternoon, Harper worked on the Sourdough Sisters website and other details about getting a business started such as obtaining a license to run a commercial kitchen, while Flannery helped Willow with her physical therapy and hung out with her daughter until it was time to stretch and fold the bread. After that process, they'd go for a walk together or tend the flower garden Willow and Flannery had planted around the cottage and the lighthouse.

In the evenings during the week, more nights than not, Aunt Jonnie would drop by the cottage or they would go to the marina for a shared meal. During these dinners they kept the conversation light and fun, often playing music themed with whatever they were eating. The practice started when Jonnie cooked shrimp paella, put on "La Macarena," and they wriggled around her tiny galley kitchen in time to the music.

Harper, competitive soul that she was, took up the challenge and the next time served spaghetti to the tune of Dean Martin crooning "That's Amore," and afterward they watched *Lady and the Tramp*. When it was Flannery's turn to cook, she picked the song first and the meal second. "Cheeseburger in Paradise" with cheeseburger sliders followed by a dessert cake fashioned to look like a cheeseburger. Jonnie stewed coq au vin with red vinegar instead of wine and cued up Édith Piaf's "Non, je ne regrette rien." On steak night, it was "Home on the Range" and a showing of *Shane*.

One evening, Hank finessed jambalaya and played the Hank Williams song of the same name. Having Hank join their group added an air of gentle masculinity and they invited Grayson to join their dinner parties as well. Declaring that he didn't cook, Gray brought KFC and Peeps and played "The Chicken Dance" on an endless loop.

Next, they invited Grayson's sister, Desiree, and her twins to dinner for taco night with Santana on the sound system and a showing of *Coco*. Flannery and Desiree hit it off, and Willow was thrilled to have a playdate with kids her own age.

Willow had never really had playmates. Alan had kept them so isolated and dependent on him. But she thrived on suddenly having a peer group. Flannery couldn't wait for her daughter to start kindergarten in the fall. Alan hadn't wanted to send her to preschool, and Flannery had deferred to keep the peace. Now she saw that had been a mistake. Her daughter needed a social life as surely as she did.

Quickly, the Campbell household's pairing of food and music became synonymous with joy. The sight of Willow's happy little face during these precious moments filled Flannery's heart with so much happiness and love, she could scarcely get her breath. This was the kind of family life she'd always dreamed of and it was finally coming true. She craved it so badly but was still afraid to hope such bliss could last.

With the help of the divorce attorney, Jim Conroe, who'd known Grayson from high school, Flannery served Alan with divorce papers. Now, the wait was on for him to sign them. But still, she was encouraged since she hadn't heard a peep from him since the day he'd shown up at the lighthouse.

All the bad stuff seemed to fall away as good things and people filled her world. Flannery crossed her fingers and prayed hard that they could sustain the life that they were building. It was everything she'd ever dreamed of.

Of course, her future hinged on winning that darn baking contest and fulfilling the conditions of her grandmother's will, but she was determined to make that happen.

On June 25, over a month after they'd arrived in Moonglow Cove, Harper went out on a date with Grayson while Flannery and Willow decided to have a tea party in the flower garden beside the lighthouse. Her sister and Grayson had been going out every weekend since Memorial Day, and Flannery was thrilled to see Harper bloom under Grayson's attention.

Aunt Jonnie had given Willow a tea set that had belonged to Grandmother Campbell, telling her that Penelope had enjoyed setting a lavish table for the holidays even though, for the most part, only family members attended her gatherings. Flannery tucked that in with her minuscule knowledge of her grandmother. Generally, when the topic of Penelope arose, Jonnie steered the conversation to other subjects.

The tea set pattern was a lovely Royal Albert rose design and they couldn't wait to use it. Flannery made sourdough scones and boiled water in the teakettle.

Willow helped her set the folding table, covering it with a

white lace tablecloth that Flannery found in the linen closet, and topping it with dishes, marmalade, honey, milk, and loose-leaf tea with tea strainers. They strewed the tablecloth with rose petals from the bushes growing by the door of the lighthouse and the air smelled heavenly. Her daughter was so excited. She'd been begging to have a tea party ever since Flannery read her *Tea for Two* from the Fancy Nancy series.

They dressed for the party in sunhats and gloves that Flannery had purchased at the Dollar Store for the occasion. Willow looked so adorable in her floral dress and pink patent leather shoes. Flannery had a blast taking her picture as she posed with the tea set.

"Put your pinkie out like you're hoity-toity," Flannery said.

Mugging for the camera, Willow stuck her pinkie finger in the air as she sipped from the delicate cup.

"You are so darned cute, child of mine!"

"*Mommy.*" Willow good-naturedly rolled her eyes.

"I love you to pieces." Flannery came around the table to rain kisses on her daughter's forehead.

Giggling, Willow wriggled away.

From behind them, Flannery heard the whirl of the elevator as it engaged on the beach level. She glanced over her shoulder to see who would disembark at the top. Harper would be out late, and Jonnie was at the hospital sitting with a friend who'd just had major surgery. They didn't get many other guests up here on the bluff. She and Desiree had just started their friendship, and she hoped Grayson's sister would soon visit often, but so far only one other person was a regular visitor.

The elevator door opened, and that one person stepped out.

Hank.

The minute she saw him, Flannery broke into a smile and her spirits soared.

"Well, well," Hank said strolling toward them. "What big event do we have going on here?"

"A tea party," Willow said.

"Nicely done." He nodded, circling the table like a dog show judge assessing the contestants.

"Want some tea?" Willow asked.

He lifted his baseball cap and scratched the top of his head. "Well, that's a mighty nice invitation, Miss Willow. Thank you for asking."

They had set up four place settings because Willow had insisted on spots for her favorite stuffed animals.

"But where am I gonna sit?" Hank asked. "All the seats are taken."

"Miss Giraffe and Miss Piggy can sit together." Willow leaned over and moved the stuffed giraffe to settle her in beside Miss Piggy on the opposite chair.

"Where is Kermit?" Hank asked.

Willow laid a finger to her lips. "Shh, they broke up and Miss Piggy doesn't want to talk about it."

Hank shot Flannery an amused grin. "The kid has got some imagination."

"She does indeed." Flannery chuckled.

Hank perched on the spindly-legged chair that Miss Giraffe had vacated. He looked so comical, the sturdy, rough-hewn man balancing on the delicate piece of furniture.

Flannery tried to disguise her grin behind her hand, but he caught her.

"Don't make fun," Hank grumbled playfully. "This is my first tea party. I don't know what's expected."

"Oh, you'll get the hang of it fast." Willow waved a hand. "Let me teach you how to stick out your pinkie."

Flannery watched Willow and Hank interact. He was so patient and kind with her daughter. She caught his eye and mouthed silently, *Thank you*.

He winked with his unscarred eye and Flannery's heart fluttered crazily. What was wrong with her? Hank was just a friend.

"Have a scone," Willow invited with a grand sweep of her arm at the plate of scones. "Try one with clotted cream."

"I think I shall, m'lady," Hank said mimicking Willow's fancy tone. To Flannery, he whispered, "What the heck is clotted cream?"

"It's the butter," Flannery whispered back. "We're pretending it's clotted cream to be more British."

"Ahh, I see." Hank settled his baseball cap on his knee and reached for a scone. He studied it closely. "So what's the difference between a scone and a biscuit?"

"Pretty much the same thing. There's some baker's differences that I could bore you with, but bottom line they're cut from the same cloth."

"Huh. You learn something new every day," Hank mused and took a bite of the scone he'd buttered. "This is so good. I can't believe you didn't know how to bake before you got here."

"I want to learn something new today," Willow said. "Teach me something new."

Hank glanced around, his gaze landing on the stuffed animals. "Hmm, let me think. Did you know that a group of giraffes is called a tower?"

“Yes. Mommy and I watched a program on giraffes.”

“You’re pretty smart, Miss Willow. I don’t know if I can teach you much.” Hank picked up one of the rose petals lying beside his plate. “Did you know you can eat rose petals?”

“You can’t eat flowers.” Willow shook her head, confident in her opinion, but then she met Flannery’s gaze and asked, “Can you, Mommy?”

“Hank is right. You can eat certain flowers like roses, but you have to be careful because some flowers aren’t edible and other flowers could even make you sick if you ate them.”

“I’m sorry,” Hank mumbled. “I shouldn’t have taught her that.”

“No, no, it’s fine. The more she knows, the better off she’ll be. Knowledge is power, after all. It’s fine to snack on rose petals,” she said to Willow. “But please don’t eat any other kind of flower without asking Mommy first, okay?”

“Okay.”

Flannery picked up one of the soft pink rose petals and nibbled it. “Hmmm. It tastes just like roses.”

“I wanna taste.” Willow picked up a red rose petal, shoved it into her mouth, and chewed pensively.

“My granny used to make rose petal butter cookies,” Hank said. “They tasted pretty good with all that sugar on them.”

“Do you like the rose petals?” Flannery asked Willow.

Willow made a face and shook her head.

“It’s okay if you want to spit it out,” Hank told her.

Looking grateful, Willow spat the petal on the ground and then scrubbed her tongue with a napkin.

“Let’s just stick to scones for today, how about that?” Flannery said.

“Good idea, Mommy.”

They drank tea and ate scones with peach marmalade and butter masquerading as clotted cream and had the best time together. Hank took their picture and then they snapped selfies with the three of them in it.

When Willow got to the bottom of her tea, she made a face. "Mommy, there's leaves in my tea."

"That's because we used loose-leaf tea instead of teabags, like we usually do."

"I don't like it."

"Do you know what's nice about loose-leaf tea?" Hank asked.

Willow vigorously shook her head.

"You can use the leaves to tell your fortune. My granny was good at reading tea leaves."

Willow let out a long peal of giggles. "You can't read tea leaves, silly. They're not books."

"Willow," Flannery corrected. "It's not nice to call people silly."

"Sorry," Willow apologized to Hank.

"You're right. It does sound silly to say you can read tea leaves, but you just have to know what you're looking for. You can read all kinds of things besides books."

"Like what?" Willow asked.

"Like people." Hank's gaze was locked on Flannery.

"No kidding?"

"No kidding."

"Show me."

"Drink your tea down without swallowing the leaves and I'll read your fortune just like my granny used to read mine."

Looking skeptical, Willow finished off her tea and then handed him her cup.

Hank got a serious expression on his face, as if he was actually reading tea leaves. He swirled the cup between his palms. "Tasseography."

"Huh?" Willow rubbed the bridge of her nose, a gesture she used whenever she was confused about something.

"Tasseography is the practice of reading tea leaves," Hank said.

Flannery reached for another rose petal to nibble on. "See there? I learned something new today too."

Hank grinned at her and then shifted his attention to the tea leaves in Willow's cup and studied them intently. "Hmm . . ."

Willow was on the edge of her seat. "What is it? What did the tea leaves say?"

"They say you got a very beautiful mommy."

Flannery felt her ears burn and didn't dare look at Hank in case he was studying her. She liked him a lot and she was afraid it would show on her face. She wasn't ready to like anyone in that way. Friendship was the best she could offer.

Willow sounded impressed. "The tea leaves told you that?"

"They sure did. They also tell me that you are smart as a whip and you're going places."

"Like where?"

"Anywhere you want to go."

"Like the zoo?"

"Sure thing. They also tell me you're a very lucky little girl to have such a loving family."

"I am! I am!"

"And reading the tea leaves, I can see that you're going to have a very happy future."

"Yay! Will I get a pony?"

"Sadly," Hank said with a slow shake of his head. "A pony can't live in the lighthouse."

"Rats."

Hank raised his head and met Flannery's gaze. "Do you want me to read your tea leaves?"

Flannery knew it was all in fun, but her pulse picked up at the idea of Hank reading her future. "No. I'm good."

"Aww, c'mon, Mommy. Do it."

Flannery wanted to tell Willow that there is no such thing as tea leaf divination, but she didn't want to spoil the party. It was natural for children to believe in magic because they didn't understand the natural world.

Instead of ruining things, she finished off her tea and passed the cup to Hank. "Have at it, mister."

"Hmmm," Hank said as he stared into her cup. "I see here there's been a lot of sorrow in the past."

Flannery shifted uncomfortably. Where was he going with this?

"And your future is still a little hazy. But the present moment, aah well, it's spectacular. You've got friends who care about you. And a roof over your head and a darling daughter."

"I can't argue with that," Flannery said, lightly catching Hank's eyes and holding his gaze.

His smile was reassuring. "Everything is just peachy, except there's a little bump in the road up ahead."

"What's that bump all about," she asked, feeling unsettled all over again.

"Storm brewing."

Her pulse quickened. That sounded ominous and not at all like kind Hank. "What sort of storm?"

Hank pointed at the clouds that Flannery hadn't noticed were darkening the horizon in the distance.

"Oh," she said. "You meant a real storm."

"Yes, ma'am. That's what I dropped by to tell you. The National Weather Service has upgraded the tropical storm that's been brewing off the coast of Mexico for the last couple of days. No reason to be alarmed yet. It could die off the same way it picked up. We'll keep a close eye on the sky, though. I just wanted you to be ready in case we need to evacuate."

CHAPTER 28

Harper

THIRD BUILD: A third build is needed for enriched doughs and boules. The more a starter is refreshed, the higher the microbial activity; the higher the microbial activity, the more the fermentation will take place.

Harper and Grayson had been seeing each other for four weeks and tonight was officially their ninth date—if she included his mother's Memorial Day party. Harper had never dated anyone for this long that she hadn't already had sex with. By the third date she'd usually figured out whether she wanted to break up with the guy or sleep with him.

Ahem. She *had* slept with Gray.

And how terrific had that been? He was a grade A cuddler. Spooner extraordinaire. Harper wanted more.

Today, Gray had planned on teaching her to windsurf, eager to take advantage of the waves whipped up by the tropical storm brewing in the Gulf, but when she arrived at his house in her swimsuit, cover-up, and flip-flops, he met her at the door with a rueful head shake.

"Change of plans," he said. "The weather service has upgraded the tropical storm and we're under a hurricane watch. At the current rate the storm is traveling, it could hit landfall by tomorrow night. We need to prep. Normally, I try to stay stocked up here, but I'm sure the cottage and lighthouse need hurricane survival supplies."

"Oh wow. We've been so busy that we rarely check the news these days. I had no idea a storm was coming." Harper felt foolish for not having kept an eye on the weather.

"That's understandable. This one spun up pretty quickly," Gray said.

It was kind of him to excuse her ignorance. "Should we evacuate?"

"It's just a level one and as fast as it's moving, it's not likely to gain much power. The really dangerous hurricanes are the ones that sit out in the Gulf brooding for days. Although losing power and water is always a possibility with any storm and there are the tornadoes that hurricanes spawn to watch out for as well. I'm no meteorologist, so I can't predict the severity, but we need to get you stocked with flashlights, batteries, bottled water, zero-prep food, and other essentials. Just in case."

Great. More expenses. Harper's small savings had already taken a hit while paying for the costs of starting a small business and she didn't want to run up her credit cards unless she had no other choice, but Gray was right. They weren't prepared to ride out a hurricane.

"Good thing I brought a change of clothes, huh?" She held up the tote bag she carried.

"I was so looking forward to admiring you in that swimsuit," he said with longing in his eyes.

"I'm not going anywhere." She winked. "There will be other chances for you to ogle me in a bikini."

"I'm counting on it." His gaze fixed on her body beneath the gauzy cover-up and his face lit up.

Feeling her cheeks burn, she said, "May I borrow your bathroom?"

Their eyes met and Gray's soft smile warmed her from the inside out. "Please, be my guest."

* * *

In the short time it took Harper to change, the weather had grown moodier. The clouds thickened and darkened and as they drove along Moonglow Boulevard, she could tell the ocean waves were coming in faster and higher. Her thoughts on her sister and niece, she dug out her phone to text Flannery and let her know what was going on. Her sister and mother had been in a hurricane once when they'd lived in Maryland—Harper had been in college on the West Coast at the time, attending the University of California at Berkeley—and Tia had chosen to ride out the storm instead of evacuating. Her mother and sister ended up having to be rescued from the rising floodwaters. Ever since the incident foul weather stirred Flannery's anxiety.

Harper: Heads-up. We're under a hurricane watch.

Flannery: Thanks. Hank dropped by 2 tell us. He's still here.

Whew. She was glad Flannery wasn't by herself.

Harper: Gray and I are buying supplies. We'll be back in a bit.

Flannery: Okay. Take care.

Harper: U 2

The stores were packed with people who had the same idea about stocking up on supplies and the shopping trip took far longer than it should have. By the time they reached the keeper's cottage, it was five o'clock in the afternoon and the gloomy sky made it seem much later. The air was sticky and oppressive, and inside the house they found a jumpy Flannery struggling to stay composed for Willow's sake.

Hank was with them, providing a calming influence. He went back outside with Gray to help him unload the car.

"How are you holding up?" Harper asked, coming over to where her sister was sitting in the window seat watching the sky.

"Worried."

"Have you spoken to Jonnie?"

Flannery nodded, the movement sending the mermaid earrings she wore dancing about her earlobes. "She and her crew are busy battening down the hatches on her shrimp boats and her houseboat in the marina. She's coming here as soon as she's done."

"Should we go help?" Harper asked Gray.

"We've got our hands full here," Gray said. "Jonnie's weathered more than her share of storms. She can handle herself."

"I'll go check on her when Gray and I get done boarding up the lighthouse," Hank assured Harper. "But knowing how efficient Jonnie is, she'll be finished with her tasks and over here long before we're through."

From the radio that Hank had set on the kitchen counter and tuned to the local weather report, the announcer issued an update. "Hurricane Blythe is moving faster than expected with wind speeds of up to ninety miles an hour and should make landfall between Corpus Christi and Galveston by noon tomorrow."

"That would make Moonglow Cove dead in Blythe's path!" Flannery blanched.

"Those in the way of the storm surge are urged to take caution and have an evacuation plan in place," the weather forecaster continued.

"We should go." Flannery hopped up. "Why chance it?"

"You want to evacuate?" Hank asked, looking surprised.

"I think so." Flannery chewed her bottom lip.

"At ninety miles an hour Blythe is a category one hurricane," Gray said in a reassuring tone. "We should be able to ride her out just fine."

"But the storm could speed up, right?" Flannery put a hand over her heart.

"It could," Gray agreed.

"There's more than just wind damage to consider." Flannery clenched her hands. "There's flooding and tornadoes and there's no storm cellar."

"All legitimate concerns." Gray nodded.

Flannery cast a glance at Willow who was at the kitchen table playing a video game and whispered, "I have a child to consider."

"We can evacuate," Harper said, recognizing her sister's rising anxiety. From the time Flannery was small, she was oriented toward safety and away from risk-taking. If all people were like her sister, places like Las Vegas would go out of business. "If that's what you want."

"*Please.*" Flannery pressed her palms together and thrust a beseeching gaze at Harper. "I know we'd have to pay for a motel and things are tight right now, but I'd feel much better if we didn't take chances."

"My sister runs an Airbnb in Austin," Hank said. "I could see if she has a room open. It'd be cheaper than a motel."

"Could you, please?" Flannery's voice was strained.

"Sure thing," Hank soothed and pulled his phone from his pocket. "I'll contact her now." Giving Flannery a comforting smile, he stepped into the living room to make the call.

Flannery let out a pent-up breath and sagged against the counter.

"I'll get started boarding up the windows," Gray said.

"I'll give you a hand." Harper tucked her fingers into the back pockets of her denim walking shorts and ducked her head to eye the troubled skies through the kitchen window.

"While you guys do that, I'll pack our bags," Flannery said, relief on her face.

Giving her sister an encouraging thumbs-up, Harper followed Gray outside.

An hour later, with all the windows in the keeper's cottage boarded up, Hank and Gray prepared to secure the lighthouse. Hank's sister had said she had a spare room they could use for free and to come on up.

"Go ahead and get on the road," Gray said. "I don't think there will be a mass exodus out of the Cove for a cat one cane, but you don't want to get caught in a traffic snarl. The later you wait, the more likely that is to happen."

"I wish you could come with us."

"I'll be waiting for you when you get back."

"I'm counting on it."

"It's a sweet thing you're doing for your sister," he said. "Accepting that she's right to want to leave. Many coastal residents would make fun of her for running from such a mild hurricane."

"It's not about being tough enough to weather a storm. She's got a child in a wheelchair. It's just practical to leave. Things would be so much more difficult for Willow to get around if the power went out."

"Excellent point."

"Besides, I owe it to her not to second-guess her decision." Harper glanced over her shoulder at the keeper's cottage behind them, the rapidly rising wind whipping her hair into her face. "I basically abandoned her for the last six years. Right when she needed me most."

"You know one of the things I like most about you?" Gray's loose cotton shirt filled with air and billowed around him.

"What's that?" she asked.

"Your sense of responsibility. You don't shirk your duties or run from your mistakes."

"Look who's talking." Harper smiled and leaned toward him.

He wrapped his arm around her waist and pulled her to his chest, the lighthouse casting a long shadow in the gathering darkness.

"Thank you so much for everything you're doing for us."

"Hey," he said and gently kissed her. He tasted like the salty air. "That's what friends are for."

"Gray," Harper said solemnly. "When we get back, you and I need to talk."

"Uh-oh." His smile faded. "That sounds ominous."

"It's not. I want more than friendship from you. That's what I want to discuss."

"Me too," he said, kissed her again, and then lightly swatted her fanny. "Now scoot while the getting is good." Turning to Hank, who was waiting at the anteroom door of the lighthouse, he said, "Ready to get this party started, Charbonneau?"

"Yep." Hank tipped his hat and headed into the lighthouse.

Gray stole one more kiss and this time Harper was the one who swatted him on the butt. Grinning, she turned to walk back to the keeper's cottage just as Aunt Jonnie stepped off the elevator.

"How are things here?" Jonnie asked.

"We're headed to Hank's sister's B&B in Austin."

"You're evacuating?"

"Flannery lived through a hurricane with Mom when she was a teen and the house flooded and they ended up on the roof waiting for rescue. It was pretty traumatic for her and she doesn't want to take chances."

"My goodness. I never knew. I'm so sorry she and Tia went through that experience. Leaving is smart, anyway, since you have Willow to consider as well."

"We're loading up now."

"Would it be all right if I went with you?" Jonnie asked shyly.

"Sure," Harper said, surprised that her stoic aunt wanted to come along. "The more the merrier."

"It's rough riding out a storm on the water," Jonnie said.

"You could hang out here at the cottage."

"I'd rather be with y'all if that's okay."

"You bet! It'll be fun," Harper said. "Like a big old slumber party."

Jonnie looked so happy to be going with them that it touched Harper's heart. "I'll just run home and pack a few things."

"We'll swing by and pick you up on the way out of town."

"Sounds like a plan."

"See you in twenty minutes," Harper shouted to be heard over the wind.

Jonnie gave her a wave and went back down the elevator.

Inside the house, she found packed bags in the mudroom ready to be carried to the minivan. In the kitchen, Flannery was filling a brown paper bag with food, including sourdough loaves, almond butter, cheese slices, apples, and bananas.

"In case we break down somewhere," Flannery said.

Harper almost said, *You know there are stores and restaurants along the way*, but she didn't want to pooh-pooh her sister's fears. If being prepared helped Flannery feel more secure, then prep away.

With the windows boarded up, the kitchen felt like a cave. Honestly, Harper wasn't sad to be leaving.

"Oh, by the way, Jonnie's coming with us."

"Oh, that's good." A smile replaced the worry furrow between Flannery's eyes. "I'm so glad she's coming. I wish Hank and Grayson could come too."

"They'll be all right," Harper assured her. "They're accomplished at riding out storms."

"This is more than a storm, Harp. This is a *hurricane*."

"It's just a category one—"

"For *now*."

Okay, her sister wasn't in the mood to be appeased. "Let's get loaded up. Where's Willow?"

"Here I am!" Willow announced gaily as she wheeled her chair down the hallway toward them, her lap filled with pillows and stuffed animals. "I'm ready."

"It sure looks like." Harper bent to kiss the top of her niece's little head.

"I'm not scared of the storm. I like wind," Willow declared.

"That's because you are braver than brave," Flannery told her daughter. "But sometimes you've got to do the practical thing."

"Is the minivan at Hank's or in the cul-de-sac?" Harper asked.

"Cul-de-sac. Hank moved it for me."

"I'll head on down with one load, then come back to help you with Willow and the rest of the things."

"Sounds good. I'm almost done here." Flannery added carrots and celery sticks to the bag of food.

"Oh, don't let me forget that Blobby needs to eat," Harper said. "I want to feed her before we pack her up in the minivan."

"Don't forget the mother dough, don't forget the mother dough, don't forget the mother dough," Flannery mumbled under her breath in her nervous habit of repeating things when she was stressed.

"Hey," Harper said, resting a hand on her sister's shoulder. "It's going to be okay. We're bugging out. You're right to want to go. There's no shame in leaving, even if the hurricane doesn't turn out to be that threatening. Better safe than sorry, right? Plus, road trip!"

Flannery looked at her with grateful eyes. "Thank you for saying that. It's just that I don't want Willow to have to go through what I did with Mom during Hurricane Danielle . . . or worse."

"It's completely understandable."

"You don't think I'm overreacting?" Flannery picked at her nails.

Harper did think she was overreacting a little, but her sister needed encouragement, not judgment. "You're doing what you think is best for your child. No one can blame you for that. I'm behind you one hundred percent."

"I appreciate you so much." Flannery gave her a harried smile.

"Whatever happens, we're together through thick and thin. No more rifts. If we hit turbulence, we work it out. I won't walk away from you ever again, sister."

"And I won't push you away ever again."

They clasped each other and hugged hard.

When they broke apart, Harper felt as if they had truly repaired their rift and despite the impending storm, hope buoyed her heart. Everything *would* be all right.

Flannery took Willow to the bathroom before they got on the road and Harper hauled the two suitcases down to the minivan. Once she got back, Flannery and Willow were out of the bathroom and helped her gather the rest of their belongings.

They waved good-bye and thanked Hank and Grayson who were securing the shutters on the lighthouse and they took off for Jonnie's houseboat. Their aunt was waiting for them on the dock with one efficient overnight bag and she slipped into the back seat beside Willow.

It was only later, when they were settled in Hank's sister's house in Austin that Harper realized they'd left the unfed mother dough sitting on the kitchen counter.

CHAPTER 29

Flannery

HYDRATION: The ratio of water to flour in a bread dough.

They spent two nights at the Airbnb, waiting for the hurricane to blow itself out and avoid any flooding. Hank and Grayson texted them reports from Moonglow Cove. Hurricane Blythe decided to piddle along when she got closer to land, lollygagging, and then finally shifted toward Houston before she stumbled to shore more than twenty-four hours after the Campbell family left Moonglow Cove, downgraded back to a tropical storm.

Harper fretted about the mother dough they'd left behind, and Jonnie assured her that while it might turn hoochie, the starter would be fine. Nothing that a healthy feeding wouldn't cure.

To lift everyone's spirits, they made an adventure of the trip. Singing carpool karaoke on the way up. Playing board games in the Airbnb because the rains that spun off from Blythe kept them indoors. Aunt Jonnie told ghost stories and Harper led them all in some CrossFit exercises. Aunt Jonnie could keep right up with

Harper, but Flannery was soon huffing and puffing. The four of them worked on a thousand-piece jigsaw puzzle. They visited with Hank's sister, Leeanne, and her husband, Dodge. Leeanne made out-of-this world enchiladas and told stories of her and Hank growing up in Louisiana. It turned out to be a really nice visit, but by Monday, Flannery was more than ready to go home.

Home.

Yes, she'd come to think of the keeper's cottage as her home. She'd never considered the house in Kansas City as hers. Alan had bought it from his parents before he and Flannery were married. And for a kid who'd bounced around the country with a nomadic mother who changed men as often as she changed her hair color, it felt nice to think that soon, after she and Harper competed in the bake-off and met the condition of their grandmother's will, the place would be theirs for real.

A home of her own.

That's all she'd ever wanted really. A place to call her own. A child of her own. A real family who loved one another. A family that she and Harper were building together, erasing the pain of their childhood as they learned to love with open hearts and strong boundaries.

It was a beautiful time, and Flannery savored the sweetness of it. Everything was within her grasp. The only thing holding them back was the competition and that was just a week away.

Flannery had driven on the way to Austin, and Harper drove the three hours back, rain still dogging them. Jonnie sat in the passenger seat with Harper, while Flannery sat in the back with Willow, braiding her hair and singing softly.

Harper told them funny stories about her life in Manhattan.

She was so animated when she talked about the city, Flannery couldn't help wondering if she would miss it too much to stay in Moonglow Cove for long. But her sister seemed fully committed to starting the Sourdough Sisters business and Flannery wouldn't doubt her. Whenever Harper committed to something she went all in, and nine times out of ten, accomplished her goal or something even better.

They arrived back in Moonglow Cove just before noon to find minimal damage done by the storm. Some trees had been uprooted, and debris littered the grounds. Hank was busy cleaning up the yard when they arrived via the elevator.

The minute he spied them, he dropped the trash sack he was carrying and rushed over to greet them with a welcoming grin. "How y'all doin'?"

"We're doing great," Flannery said. "It turned out to be a lovely trip."

"We missed most of the storm," Hank said. "Just a minor cleanup."

Jonnie stretched, raising her long arms over her head and walking around the property to survey the damage. Willow's wheelchair got stuck in the mud, and Flannery went to help her pry it loose. When she looked up, she saw Jonnie holding a piece of wood. It took her a minute to recognize her aunt was holding one of the wooden shutters that had been blown loose from the lighthouse.

It was a shutter from the tower room. The shutter with the hash marks on it that Harper had told her about.

There was a strange look on Jonnie's face, and she tucked the shutter underneath her arm as if saving it was important.

"I'll unload the car," Hank said. "And drive the minivan back to my place, then I'll come back and give you a rundown on the storm damage."

"Thank you," Harper said. "I'm going to feed the mother dough. It's been almost three days since she was fed."

"We'll come with you," Flannery said, leaning over to knock the mud from Willow's wheelchair tires.

All of them except Hank, who went down in the elevator, entered the house through the front door, Aunt Jonnie still cradling that shutter. Inside, the house was dark and stuffy from the boarded windows.

"The first order of business after the mother dough is fed is to get those boards down," Harper said. "I need sunshine."

They walked into the kitchen together. Flannery flipped on the light while Harper made a beeline to the sink to wash her hands. Willow wheeled past them, headed for the kitchen table, Flannery's phone in her hand, eager to play her video game. Aunt Jonnie sat down at the bar, stared at the shutter, and traced her finger over the hash marks. She had a faraway look in her eyes.

"Auntie J?" Flannery called.

"Huh?" Jonnie blinked as if waking up from a long dream.

"Are you okay?"

"Yes." Jonnie forced a smile. "I'm fine. My mind just got hung up in the past for a minute."

Harper was at the pantry, taking out a canister of flour to feed the dough. She brought it to the counter where they'd left the mother dough sitting in the ceramic crock. Harper popped open the lid, looked into the crock, and gasped. Her sister's sharp intake of breath was so startling, they all turned to stare at her.

"What is it?" Flannery asked, rushing over.

"Something's terribly wrong." Harper's brown eyes were huge and seemed to engulf her entire face.

"Are you okay? What is it? Are you in pain?"

"It's not me," Harper said with a tremor in her voice. "It's Blobby."

"It looks bad when it's hoochie," Jonnie said. "Honestly, don't worry about it, just pour off the liquid and feed her."

Flannery peered inside the crock and heard her own gasp. "It's not hoochie, Auntie. Blobby's pink!"

* * *

"We killed the mother dough," Harper said in a voice so controlled and robotic it scared Flannery.

"What happened?" Flannery glanced at her aunt for answers. "How did this happen? We only left it unfed for three days. How could this happen?"

"I don't know," Jonnie said, getting up from the bar to come over, still clutching that scarred, weathered shutter. "I've never seen a dough turn pink."

"We failed, that's what happened." Harper capped the lid. "It's all over. We didn't meet the conditions of the will. We're bust. Back to zero."

"Look it up, look it up. Google it. Maybe there's something we can do to save it." Flannery waved at Harper. In her heart she knew it was useless. There could be no rescuing dough the color of Barbie's Dreamhouse. One hundred fifty years of starter, destroyed in just three days.

Harper tugged her cell phone from her pocket as they all three peered into the crock like *Macbeth* witches evaluating a spell gone wrong. Feeling sick, Flannery placed a hand to her stomach and willed herself not to throw up. They'd killed the mother dough. The one major rule that could not be broken.

"It says here, if it's turned pink, it's contaminated and should be thrown out," Harper said mournfully.

Jonnie picked up the crock and took a whiff. Her brow furrowed. "It smells like roses."

"How is that possible?" Harper blinked and shook her head as if doing so could clear up the mystery.

They'd killed the mother, and with it, all their dreams.

"I'll google that, too; hold on." Harper tapped on her phone. "There's nothing here about floral-smelling sourdough."

"Here, you smell it and tell me what you think." Aunt Jonnie stuck the crock under Flannery's nose.

She inhaled and had a sudden, unwanted thought enter her brain. The dough *definitely* smelled like roses.

"Willow," she called to her daughter.

Willow bobbed her head as she manipulated the game on her phone and didn't glance up.

"Sweetheart, please turn off the game, Mommy needs to talk to you."

"Just one minute. I'm about to win."

"Willow, I'm not kidding. Turn off the phone right *now.*" There must have been something in her voice that told her daughter she meant business.

Immediately, Willow set the phone down.

"Please, come here."

Willow obeyed, wheeling freely into the kitchen. "What is it, Mommy?"

Flannery took the crock from Jonnie and held it underneath Willow's nose. "Do you know anything about this?"

Looking happy as can be, Willow grinned at them. "Yes, ma'am. I heard Auntie Harper say that Blobby needed to eat before we went on our trip, so I fed her."

Flannery crouched in front of her daughter, her legs muscles trembling. Willow had meant well. She hadn't known she was destroying Mommy's future as well as Aunt Harper's. They'd put all their eggs in one basket and now that basket was . . .

Pink.

And smelled of roses.

"How did you feed it?" Flannery asked, barely aware of where Harper and Jonnie were standing. Every bit of her attention was focused on her daughter. She was determined not to make Willow feel bad for being enterprising and resourceful. She wouldn't scream at her the way Tia would have screamed at Flannery for a similar offense. Who was she kidding? Tia would have probably slapped her across the face.

Flannery winced. She would rather end her own life than intentionally cause her child harm.

"Why, Mommy," Willow, beaming like she'd done the finest thing in the world, said in her high, sweet voice, "Auntie Harper says Blobby likes to eat flower, so I fed her *rose petals*."

CHAPTER 30

Harper

PROOFING: The final rise of the dough after shaping.

Sister." Looking stricken, Flannery turned to Harper, beseeching with her eyes to be kind in her response to Willow. "*Please.*"

What? Did Flannery think she was going to go off on Willow?

That hurt Harper's feelings. Sure, she was eviscerated by the loss of their inheritance, but she wasn't about to yell at an innocent child who'd simply believed she was helping. That sort of thing damaged a kid straight to her soul. Both she and Flannery knew that firsthand.

For Flannery to believe that Harper would fly off the handle meant her sister didn't know her at all. Even after five weeks of baking bread, sharing a house, and making plans for a future together, Flannery still didn't trust her.

Well, you did trash her pretty good six years ago. Can you really blame her?

Shame blazed a heated trail up Harper's neck. She'd made so many mistakes. There was so much she regretted. So many things she wished she could undo.

"Willow," Harper said, "you have got to be the smartest kid I know. Who would think to substitute *flower* for *flour*?"

"I would!" Willow's innocent face glowed up at Harper.

"And that's the best marketing spin I've ever heard." There were grateful tears in Flannery's eyes as she met Harper's gaze.

"I'm thinking maybe we shouldn't call our store the Sourdough Sisters after all," Harper said. "I'm kicking around the idea of Lighthouse Flower, in honor of Willow's impressive discovery that flower and flour can be interchangeable. Although Flourtopia is in the running as well. Thoughts? I've lost my edge since I left Manhattan and I can't tell if these ideas are good or just silly."

Flannery was staring at Harper as if she'd lost her ever-loving mind.

"Oh, oh, I've got it!" Harper snapped her fingers. "The Flower Dough Sisters! People will be instantly intrigued, wondering what the heck is flower dough. We could tell the story of how we got our name in the 'About Us' section of our website."

"Harper, are you in shock?" Her sister looked concerned for Harper's mental well-being.

"What do you mean?"

"It's over. We blew it. We didn't meet the conditions of the will. The lighthouse and keeper's cottage will go to the Historical Society. We're out on our ears. We killed the mother dough."

"No, you didn't," Aunt Jonnie said, speaking for the first time since Willow announced she'd fed rose petals to the starter.

Simultaneously, they turned to look at their aunt who still had her hands wrapped around that broken old shutter, holding it close to her heart.

"What do you mean?" Flannery asked.

"We should sit down for this conversation." Jonnie's voice was leaden, and she looked absolutely exhausted.

From outside there came a pounding at the window and then a screeching sound and suddenly the kitchen flooded with light. Blinking, Harper saw Hank standing in front of the window, taking down the plywood that had been used to board it up.

"Better yet," Aunt Jonnie said, using the wood shutter as a shield. "Let's go to the top of the lighthouse. I have a story you need to hear, and the setting will help me tell it."

Goose bumps raced up Harper's arms. From the expression on her aunt's face, she wasn't so sure she wanted to hear this.

Flannery glanced at her daughter. "I can't leave Willow."

"The topic isn't for young ears anyway," Jonnie said. "We'll ask Hank to watch her."

"Is that okay with you, honey?" Flannery put a palm to Willow's head.

"Sure! I like Hank. He's my friend."

Hank waved at them with a cheerful smile. Indeed, he was their friend. "Bring her outside," he hollered from the other side of the glass. "She can sit on the porch and play her game while I finish taking down the boards."

They left Willow on the porch with Hank keeping an eye on her and the three of them headed toward the lighthouse. With each step, Harper's heart grew heavier. She didn't know where this conversation was headed, but she had an uneasy feeling it had something to do with that shutter that Jonnie couldn't seem to let go of.

Their footsteps echoed against the metal as they climbed the circular staircase to the top. With each footfall Harper's pulse pounded louder and louder in her ears until by the time they reached the tower room, her entire head thumped with the sound of her own blood, and sweat was ringing her collar.

The rest of the lighthouse was dark from the boarded-up windows, but in the tower room where the winds had ripped off the shutter, light poured in.

Harper and Flannery entered the room, but Jonnie hung back at the door.

Flannery cast a worried glance at Harper and silently mouthed, *What's going on with Aunt Jonnie?*

Harper shrugged, went to the window, and stared down through the open hole to the grounds below. There was glass on the floor, and she carefully trod around it, and then turned back to look at her aunt.

"We're here. What's the story?" Harper asked, uncertain as to why she felt so on edge.

Jonnie stayed in the doorway as if her feet had been nailed to the floor. She gave her head a hard shake. "I-I can't. Not here. I thought I could, but I can't."

"So where to?" Harper struggled to keep a waspish note from her voice.

"The widow's walk." Jonnie headed for the stairs that led to the beacon room and the circular wooden platform surrounding it.

But when they got to the widow's walk, they discovered the glass had been knocked out up on the walk, too, and sharp shards lay everywhere.

"What now?" Harper stared at the turbulent ocean below the bluff, stiff with whitecaps and still agitated from the aftermath of Hurricane Blythe.

"I guess we start cleaning up the glass," Aunt Jonnie said.

"You're stalling." Harper grunted. "Let's just go back to the tower room and you can tell your story. We can clean this up later. From the expression on your face I can see this won't be an easy conversation, so let's just get it over with."

"No," Aunt Jonnie said. "It won't be an easy conversation. I expect it will be the hardest of my life."

* * *

By the time they were seated on the floor in the tower room, far away from the broken glass, Harper's anxiety had sharpened to a razor-thin point and it was all she could do not to jump up and pace.

The three of them sat cross-legged in front of each other, forming a triangle. The breeze from the open window ruffled their hair. Harper wasn't surprised at Aunt Jonnie's flexibility. Their aunt was in great physical shape. The shutter with the hash marks rested across her lap and she had her hands closed over each knee. Jonnie's back was to the doorway and she was facing the window. Harper and Flannery had their backs to the window and were facing Jonnie. Jonnie wore jeans, Harper had on yoga pants, and Flannery wrapped her summery maxi dress around her bare legs.

Harper's throat was tight, her stomach jittery, and her heart spiked harder than when she did burpees. The buildup of tension was killing her.

"Just say. Just tell us what's going on," Harper blurted, unable to stand the suspense one second longer. "Rip off the Band-Aid."

Aunt Jonnie inhaled deeply, held her breath, and then slowly exhaled. Marshaling courage? Harper wondered.

Flannery reached over to take Harper's hand and squeezed it. "Please, Aunt Jonnie, take your time. We understand that whatever you have to tell us is important to you and deserves to unfold naturally."

That was her sister. Kind to the bone.

Feeling like a jerk for pushing her aunt, Harper said, "Flan is right, do this at your own pace."

"There's nothing natural about what I have to tell you," Jonnie said in a voice as creaky as a rusty hinge. She was absentmindedly tracing the hash marks on the shutter again, as if counting each one. "It's all twisted. Every bit of it."

Harper and Flannery exchanged glances. Her sister looked as alarmed as Harper felt. Aunt Jonnie's behavior was scary, but at least Harper and Flannery were on the same page. At least they had each other.

"I was going to wait until after the bake-off to tell you all this," Aunt Jonnie said with a sigh. "But with Willow feeding rose petals to the mother dough, there was no point in keeping my secrets any longer."

"The truth about what?" Harper prodded, knowing she did not want to hear this but also knowing she had to know the truth.

"The Campbells have a dark history," Aunt Jonnie finally began, her brown eyes, the same color as Harper's, latching onto her gaze.

"Yes," Harper said. "Gray wrote about Ian Campbell being a pirate in his book."

Aunt Jonnie shook her head. "It runs much deeper than that. Gray only really knows what my mother told him and the town gossip."

"Meaning?"

"He knows little of the unhealthy dynamic in our family that's been passed down through the generations. Whether it's DNA or culture, trauma, or environment, or all of it rolled into a toxic stew, the members of this family fall into two groups. You're either an abuser or a victim, and it's damn near impossible to crawl out of those roles. The cycle keeps repeating over and over and over . . ."

Harper thought of Tia and closed her eyes, unable to bear the weight of Aunt Jonnie's open stare. She knew where her mother fell in the family hierarchy, but Harper bridled under the label of victim. She considered herself a *survivor.*

Just like Flannery.

Just like Jonnie herself.

"Unless," Jonnie continued, "you have a moment of clarity, accept reality, start working on yourself, and let other people sort themselves out."

That last part had always been so hard for Harper. Letting go. Stop trying to save everyone else. Fixing herself.

She'd tried for years to rescue Tia. Nothing ever worked. That had been the worst part. Knowing that no matter how much she tried, she couldn't change her mother. Harper pulled a palm down her face and opened her eyes.

From outside the window, far below at the keeper's cottage, they heard the sound of Willow's laughter carried in on a gentle wind.

"My mother, Penelope," Jonnie said, "was the abuser and my father, Douglas, was the victim who propped her up and enabled her abusive behavior. His father had been the abuser in his family, and he'd vowed to never be like his dad. He overcorrected, went the other way, and ended up marrying an abuser himself."

"It was a familial pattern he couldn't shake," Flannery murmured.

"Exactly." Jonnie looked so forlorn. "If we grow up in an abusive household and don't understand trauma bonding . . . if we can't see the pattern and come to realize it for what it is, then we end up following the same emotional grooves worn by the previous generations. Playing out those same awful roles. And society encourages us to stay in toxic families. It's incredibly hard to break free."

"It takes a lot of effort to jump the track," Harper said.

"Indeed. And most people don't ever escape their own mental torment," Jonnie mused.

"But you have," Flannery pointed out.

"Somewhat," Jonnie said. "I'm a work in progress."

"How did you manage to change your mindset?" Harper asked. "Especially with the odds stacked so highly against you?"

"I'm getting to that." Jonnie paused, inhaled deeply, held her breath for a long moment, and then gave a deep exhale and resumed her story. "To get away from my mother's abuse, my father spent ninety percent of his time at sea."

"And left you alone with her," Harper guessed.

Jonnie nodded.

"That must have been so difficult," Flannery said in a soothing voice and squeezed Harper's hand again.

"She was a cruel woman. In those days," Jonnie said, "they just called it meanness, but now they'd probably say she had antisocial personality disorder."

Harper heard herself gasp. "Y-y-your mother, our grandmother, was a *sociopath*?"

"Labels only help to identify those patterns of behavior," Jonnie explained. "People are so much more complex than that, but yes, most likely my mother was a sociopath."

Flannery pressed a palm to her chest. "Jonnie, that's shocking."

"My mother used strict religious views as a weapon of manipulation and control. She beat me whenever I was too worldly or went against what she declared as 'God's will.' Worldly could mean anything from wearing too-tight clothes or talking to boys or even something as innocent as whistling. Dad went along with her harsh rules because he was terrified of her."

"Whistling?" Flannery frowned. "What's wrong with whistling?"

"Unladylike behavior, but you have to understand. It wasn't really the whistling. She used whatever she wanted as a justification for her abuse."

"That's awful," Harper said. "I'm so glad we never met her."

"You didn't meet her because Tia was brave enough to go 'no contact.'"

"She might have been bold enough to leave, but she didn't know how to change her pattern of behavior either," Flannery added. "So the cycle kept going."

"No, she didn't," Jonnie said in a tone so filled with sadness and grief that it broke Harper's heart right in two. "When I was younger, I accepted my mother's view of me. I felt I was worthless and bound for hell. I jumped through hoops to please her, but she was impossible to please. No matter what I did, it wasn't good enough."

Jonnie paused again, looking first at Flannery and then meeting Harper's gaze. "Sadly, I have a feeling you two are all too familiar with what that feels like."

Harper clung to Flannery's hand like a lifeline. Jonnie had been just as abused as they'd been, if not more so, but she'd managed to come out of it. She'd turned her life around and so had they. In five short weeks they'd cobbled together a little family that was kind and loving and loyal. This tragic story could have a happy ending.

Except she was not getting happy vibes from Jonnie. "Are you going to tell us about the shutter?"

"I'm getting there. It's hard for me to talk about it." Jonnie was back to fingering the carved shutter.

"Then don't tell us. Don't put yourself through that," Flannery said.

"I must. You have to know the truth." Jonnie bit her bottom lip.

Silence filled the small room. They waited.

Finally, Jonnie started up again. "When I was thirteen, I began to rebel. I snuck out of my bedroom in the keeper's cottage. The bedroom you're now in, Harper. I'd climb down the trellis and meet boys. Mostly, it was innocent fun. And then I got involved with an older boy . . . a young man actually. He was nineteen to my thirteen." With faraway eyes, Jonnie peered at the window and gulped.

Jonnie was stroking the worn shutter so hard that Harper was certain she would get a splinter. It took every bit of control she had not to reach out and take the shutter away from her. If rubbing the shutter soothed her aunt, though, who was she to intervene? If Jonnie got a splinter, Harper would pull it out for her.

"My mother caught me having sex on the beach with this boy."

Their aunt was sexually active at thirteen? Harper couldn't wrap her head around it.

"That must have been mortifying," Flannery said.

Jonnie's nod was terse. "She grabbed me by the hair, called me a whore, and she didn't let go until she'd dragged me up to this tower room and locked me in. I could only go from here to the beacon room and the widow's walk. I felt like Rapunzel and kept dreaming the guy I'd thought I was so in love with would rescue me. He did not. I can't blame him for that. My mother was a formidable enemy. He disappeared from Moonglow Cove and I never heard from him again."

"Do you think your mother had him done away with?" Harper asked, feeling truly shocked.

"No," Jonnie said. "Although I wouldn't put it past her. When I was going through Mom's things after she died, I found a canceled check made out to him for ten thousand dollars."

"She paid him to leave town?"

"Yes," Jonnie said. "And she'd stapled the canceled check to a copy of her will. So that I'd be sure to find it."

Flannery gasped. "That's so mean."

"That was my mother." Jonnie shrugged. "Your grandmother. Our family legacy."

"The hash marks on the shutter were you marking time," Harper said, horrified that Jonnie had been put through such abuse. She'd suspected someone had been locked in the tower, but she'd never guessed it was her aunt.

"At thirteen? Oh, Jonnie." Flannery reached for Jonnie with her other hand. "That must have been so hard."

Jonnie shook her head, drew back, and held up the wooden shutter as if to keep Flannery at bay. "I don't deserve your sympathy. Please, save it for each other."

"Of course, you deserve sympathy! You have our empathy, too. Mom used to lock us in closets and basements and attics. Whatever was lockable in the houses where we lived."

"Dear God, no." Jonnie put a palm over her mouth and looked as if she might vomit.

"But not for months on end," Flannery rushed to add. "Never longer than a few hours. Maybe overnight once or twice."

Jonnie dropped the shutter and buried her face in her hands. Her entire body shook from the force of her sobs.

"Shh, shh," Flannery, always the sweet one, the gentle one, soothed. "You were a child. What your mother did to you was rotten to the core. You deserved love, kindness, and understanding, not hatred, mistreatment and self-righteousness."

Jonnie raised her head, the stark anguish in her eyes was bleak. "No, no. You don't know what *I've* done."

"We won't judge you," Flannery said. "I promise."

"You can't say that. You don't know." Jonnie let out a mournful wail so different from the strong woman they'd come to know.

"So tell us," Harper said, sounding sharper than she intended. "Tell us the terrible things you've done and help us to understand."

"I lied to you girls."

"What did you lie to us about?" Harper asked, feeling weirdly detached as if she was in a dark tunnel a long way from her sister and her aunt. Things weren't adding up, but she couldn't quite put her finger on what was off-kilter.

"I'm not your aunt."

"Huh?" Harper wasn't sure she'd heard her correctly.

"How can that be?" Flannery looked confused. "I don't understand. Were you adopted or something?"

Harper stared at Jonnie, dread pressing in on her chest as she felt Flannery squeeze her right hand tightly, and she just knew in her heart what Jonnie was about to say. "Then who are you?"

Jonnie straightened her spine, held Harper's hard gaze, and answered in an unwavering tone, "*I'm* your grandmother."

CHAPTER 31

Harper

ASH: A measure of a flour's mineral content. The higher the ash count, the more minerals are present in the flour.

"Wh-what? How can this be true?" Mouth agape, Flannery blinked at Jonnie.

Jonnie laid the shutter on the floor in front of her with the hash marks facing Harper and Flannery. Harper counted the groups. Seven and a half bunches. Jonnie had had her baby a month early.

"The night that my mother caught me with the young man I'd sneaked out to meet, I got pregnant."

"What happened to the baby?" Flannery asked, apparently still struggling with the implications of the bomb Jonnie had just dropped.

"Sweet sister," Harper said. "Don't you get it? The baby was our mother."

"Tia?" Flannery slowly shook her head, her gaze latched to Jonnie. "Tia was your baby?"

"Yes." The one terse word was jam-packed with Jonnie's pain.

"Tell us what happened." Flannery's eyes were wide, incredulous. "How did this happen? Tia was your *daughter*?"

Harper couldn't speak. She was shaking all over. If she spoke, she'd tear into Jonnie. Yell and throw around cruel words. She wouldn't do that. She refused to respond the way an abuser would. The way Tia would have.

And apparently, the way their great-grandmother would have too.

This multigenerational abuse thing was heartbreaking, and somehow it seemed that no one was capable of learning from the past. That made her think of Gray and his love of history. That George Santayana saying he'd quoted on the day they'd met.

Those who cannot remember the past are condemned to repeat it.

Fresh anger bit into her. Grayson was just as culpable in this charade as Jonnie. He'd been in on the deception with her. He was the executor of Penelope's will. He had to know it was all a sham. His underhanded behavior changed the way she thought of him and she didn't know if she could ever see him in a positive light again.

Hot sickness washed over her, and for a moment she thought she would vomit.

"When my mother locked me in the tower, she didn't know I was pregnant. I didn't know I was pregnant. She was just trying to keep me away from the town boys. But then I began to show, and she hatched a plan to take my baby away from me. She started wearing loose clothing and she told my dad *she* was pregnant. He was out to sea for so much of the time that it was easy for her to pull off a fake pregnancy."

"No one in town noticed that you were missing? No one questioned your disappearance? What about school?" Flannery ironed her palm across her forehead.

"Our family didn't mingle much with the community and

she told people I'd gone to stay with relatives in another state. Whenever she went out, she strapped a pillow to her waist. I can't speak to my dad's role in all this. I suppose he accepted her at face value. Lying to himself to survive the marriage was his M.O."

"Surely, he must have had some kind of inkling that things weren't right," Harper said. "He must have."

"Probably, but he was so browbeaten and henpecked he went along with everything she said and did. When he was home, he would come visit me in the tower, but when I tried to tell him she was holding me prisoner, he would tell me not to speak ill of my mother. So we'd play chess together and then he'd go out on his boat, and he wouldn't return for weeks."

"Good Lord!" Flannery clasped both palms to her chest. "How awful."

"Your dad couldn't tell that you were getting bigger?" Harper asked.

"She told him I was getting fat and during that time period, he stayed away even longer than usual."

"In his heart, he knew," Flannery said.

"Most likely." Both of Jonnie's hands were plastered against her belly.

"That's pretty damn sick," Harper said. "Of both of them."

"Our entire family history is littered with stories like that," Jonnie said. "I'm not unique. Not by a long shot."

Flannery put her palms over her ears. "Please, don't tell me any more. I can't stand it."

"And here we thought Tia was bad." Harper let out a mirthless laugh. "By comparison she was a peach."

Flannery dropped her hands to her lap. "No joke."

"What happened when it was time for you to deliver?" Harper asked.

"Tia was born in this tower room," Jonnie said. "My mother was my midwife. She took Tia away from me and claimed her as her own."

"You didn't try to fight her?" Harper asked.

"I'd just turned fourteen and I'd been gaslit my entire life, though of course I didn't know what to call it then. What was I supposed to do, Harper? Steal Tia and run away? Go where? How would I support us?"

"You did what you could." Flannery patted Jonnie's knee. "You did your best."

Jonnie looked grateful for Flannery's kindness, but Harper didn't feel so forgiving. She hopped up and started pacing, struggling with her emotional turmoil.

"So you had to live in this house, watching your mother raise your daughter as her own. That must have been so difficult," Flannery said.

"Incredibly difficult. Especially when she started abusing Tia the way she'd abused me." Jonnie's words came out on a ragged sob.

"When did Tia find out who you were?" Harper asked.

Jonnie buried her face in her hands, and it took her a few minutes to compose herself before she could continue. Flannery scooted around to put her arm over Jonnie's shoulder, but Harper stayed stoic, pushing away the urge to tell Jonnie that everything would be okay. There were no easy solutions in this situation.

Finally, Jonnie raised her head and continued. "When Tia got pregnant at sixteen, my mother went off on her and started screaming that she was just like me. Tia asked questions and Penelope told her the truth. That I was her real mother. Outraged that we'd lied to her, Tia left town with a guy she'd just met. He wasn't your father." Jonnie met Harper's gaze. "She was so angry. Much like you are right now."

Harper fisted her hands, clenching them hard. She pivoted and paced to the other side of the room.

"Not that I blame you. You're entitled to your rage," Jonnie murmured.

"Oh, thanks so very much for your permission," Harper sniped.

"Harper," Flannery chided.

Harper pointed a finger at Flannery. "Don't you dare shame me. I don't have to forgive her."

"No, you don't have to," Flannery agreed. "You can choose to be angry for the rest of your life, just like Mom was."

Jonnie got to her feet, looking pale as a ghost. "Your sister is right. If you nurse this anger, it will destroy you."

Harper whirled on her. "Okay, I can excuse the fact that you were a helpless, abused teenager. I can forgive *that* girl. But you know who I can't forgive?"

"Let me have it." Jonnie puffed out her chest and held her arms open wide. "Give me all of your rage." She pounded her chest with her fists. "I deserve it."

"No, you don't!" Flannery jumped up, too, and it was the three of them facing off. "You were just a little girl with horrible parents. You never stood a chance."

"Jonnie wasn't a little girl when I stayed with her for a year." Harper had no idea what she was going to say. The angry words just came spilling out of her. "By my calculations, she was close to the age I am now when Tia came back for me. Thirty-three. You let Tia take me, Jonnie. Knowing what she was, you didn't even try to stop her. You didn't try to hold on to me. If you cared as much as you claim, explain that!"

Jonnie looked as if Harper had slapped her hard across the face. Wincing, she staggered back.

"Why?" Harper cried as thirty-three years' worth of sorrow and pain exploded from her with startling force. "Why did you let her take me back? Why, when you knew what she was?"

Tears streamed down Jonnie's face and dribbled off her jaw. "I couldn't take you away from her because I couldn't do to Tia what was done to me. I couldn't steal her child. If I did, I'd be no better than *my* mother."

"But it wasn't the same. Your mother took your baby away, while my mother abandoned me to you. That's a world of difference."

"I had such hope that Tia would change. That she could break the pattern. That was before I fully understood the dynamics of multigenerational abuse. I was naïve—I admit it—and I've spent my life regretting letting you go."

"You regret it?" Harper lashed out.

"Harper!" Flannery looked shocked. "Be kind!"

"No, no." Jonnie held up a stop-sign palm. "Let her talk. Let her say what she really feels."

"I feel betrayed," Harper howled, startling herself with the truth. "Why didn't you ever come see us? Why didn't you check in to see how Tia was treating us?"

Jonnie hung her head. "I'm ashamed to admit it but to ease my grief over letting you go, I started drinking heavily. I lived in a blind, drunken stupor for thirteen long years. It's no excuse and I let you down in the most fundamental way. It's my fault, and I'm to blame for how Tia treated you. It's why I wanted you to come back to Moonglow Cove so badly. Why I lied about my mother's will. Why I roped Grayson into my scheme. It was the wrong thing to do, but I was desperate to make amends and I knew no other way to get you to show up . . . and stay long enough to learn the truth."

"It's not your fault, it's not your fault." Flannery wrapped her arms around their grandmother. "You were a victim too."

"Yes, I was a victim, but I enshrouded myself in victimhood," Jonnie said bluntly. "I wore it like a badge of honor. Identifying as a victim is what kept me stuck for so many years."

Flannery gave Harper a chiding glance and said to Jonnie, "You did the best you could. You got help. You changed. You—"

"*Deceived* us." Harper glowered, terrified of her own stony heart.

"Harper!" her sister said, clinging tightly to Jonnie. "Where is your compassion?"

"Where was Jonnie's compassion when we needed her most?" Harper asked, so blinded by her own pain she couldn't see past it. "Answer me that, Flannery?"

"Where was *yours* when your mom died?" Flannery looked like a fierce terrier who'd sunk her teeth into an attacker's ankle. "Where were *you* when *I* needed you most?"

It was all too much for Harper to handle. Too damn much to absorb at once. Her emotions beat at her like a hurricane tide—hurt, anger, guilt, pain, regret, sorrow, betrayal, and grief.

So much damn grief.

Overwhelmed, she stormed down the lighthouse stairs, the sound of her tromping footsteps reverberating off the brick walls. Blindly, she blasted out the door, swiping at tears, and ran straight into Grayson Cooper's chest.

* * *

"WHOA THERE, SPEED Racer," Grayson said in a jovial voice and reached out to slip his arm around her.

Harper swatted at him. "Get away from me. Get away!"

His pale blue eyes clouded with concern. "What is it, Harper? What's wrong?"

She had to get off by herself, collect her thoughts, and make plans to leave Moonglow Cove as soon as possible. "I simply can't deal with you right now."

Shoving past him, she ran toward the cottage.

Grayson grabbed the back of her shirt and hauled her backward. "Hold up there, Harper. Instead of running away, stay and talk to me."

She spun and turned on him. "If I stay here, I'm going to say something I'll regret and I really do not want to do that, so get out of my way, Cooper." She paused and added, "*Please.*"

"What's happened? Can you tell me that at least?"

"I *know*, Grayson. I know everything. I know about Jonnie. I know about the fake will and I know about your hand in it as executor. I know you deceived us. You know that deception and manipulation are my deal breakers."

"Just like the inability to forgive those who are truly contrite is my deal breaker," he said, his mouth flattening into a straight line.

"You want me to *forgive* you for lying to me?"

"I didn't actually lie. I did read your *grandmother's* will. I—"

"A lie of omission is still a lie."

"Harper, you have to understand. I didn't know you at the time. But I did know Jonnie. She literally pulled me out of the gutter when I tried to drink myself to death after Stephanie passed away. If it hadn't been for Jonnie, I would not be standing in front of you today. She saved my life, and she earned my undying loyalty."

"To the point where you'd tell such a massive lie for her? And keep lying to me even as we were dating?"

"Life is complicated. It's not all black and white. That kind of thinking is rigid and judgmental and it suggests you think you have all the answers."

Harper snapped her jaw shut. He was stoking the anger Jonnie had lit inside her, dumping gasoline on the fire. "I can't even with you right now. We're done, Grayson. This is over."

Hurt filled his eyes. "Just like that?"

"Just like that. And remember, this is your doing. You brought it on yourself."

Leaving him gaping, she fled up the steps to the keeper's cottage, blasting past Willow and Hank who were playing checkers on the front porch. She thundered upstairs to her bedroom, aching for the sweet happy life she thought she'd been building with her sister, her aunt, and her niece.

But she'd learned too late that it was all a lie.

CHAPTER 32

Flannery

SHAPING: Folding, rolling, and sealing the edges of dough to produce the final shape of a loaf.

I've broken her," Aunt Jonnie said mournfully. "She's shattered."

"Harper is as tough as an old boot," Flannery reassured her. It was going to take a mental shift to start thinking about Jonnie as her grandmother and not her aunt. "She'll rebound."

"She'll never forgive me." Jonnie shook her head. "I could see it in her eyes. She's hard-line, just like Tia."

"Yes, she's determined and stubborn, but unlike Mom, Harper can be reasoned with," Flannery said. "Let me talk to her."

"I hope you're right," Jonnie said. "I hate to think that bringing you girls here was just another one of my unforgivable mistakes."

"This is a bombshell and I know you meant well going about it in the way that you did. But it's a mess. No matter how you told us the truth, hearing it would have been intense. Please don't beat yourself up for not just coming right out and telling us. Because of you, Harper and I have mended fences. And that's no small feat. I don't think that would have happened if you'd been straightforward with us. I think Harper would have just gone right back to New York. So thank you for that gift . . . *Grandmother.*"

"Thank you for being so generous and forgiving."

Flannery gave her grandmother a hug and stepped back, torn between comforting Jonnie and going to her sister. "It's going to be okay. We're all learning important life lessons. We'll fix this."

"Why aren't you angry with me too?"

"Because I have a daughter."

"You get it," Jonnie said, tears shining in her eyes.

"Although no mother is perfect, when you're raised by a woman who has no idea how to love you, there's no template for how to be a mother, no role model." Flannery felt her own eyes grow weepy. "I only know how to love Willow because Harper loved me. Harper was the one who raised me, not my mother. And I suspect that the only way Harper was able to love me was because of the way you loved her during the year that she lived with you. She might not have consciously remembered it, but she imprinted on you."

"Oh, Flannery, what a kind thing to say."

"Where I stumbled was in the aftermath of my rift with Harper, where my low self-esteem and depression led me to marry an abusive man like Alan."

"Plus, you were little more than a child with a new baby. Please don't beat yourself up for making a mistake."

"Ditto, Grandmother."

Fresh tears wet Jonnie's cheeks.

Flannery pulled a tissue packet from her pocket and passed it to her. "We might be broken, but we're trying to mend ourselves, and as long as we can help each other through it, we're a real family."

They clung to each other and cried for a bit. Then Flannery wiped away her tears. "I have to go to Harper. She needs me."

Jonnie nodded, wiped her eyes. "Yes, go find your sister."

Before she left the tower room, Flannery squeezed her grandmother's hand. "Thank you for bringing us here. I'm not condoning the subterfuge, but honestly, it is the best thing you could have ever done."

At the keeper's cottage, Flannery paused on the front porch to check on Willow where her daughter and Hank were involved in a heated checkers match.

"Mommy," Willow said proudly. "I'm winning."

Flannery caught Hank's eye and mouthed, *Thank you.*

He winked and smiled

He was a good man. A kind man. And she was so grateful he was content to be her friend.

"You okay?" he asked.

Flannery nodded. "Long story. I'll explain later."

"Oh," he said. "I forgot to warn you. Stay away from the widow's walk. The boards were damaged in the storm and I haven't had a chance to repair them yet. I figured all the broken glass up there would keep you ladies off it, but I just wanted to make sure you knew to avoid it until I get it fixed."

"Thank you for letting me know," Flannery said, then kissed the top of Willow's head, heaved a deep breath, and headed inside the house to reason with her sister.

* * *

SHE FOUND HARPER yanking clothes off hangers and stuffing them into her duffel bag. Flannery stood in the doorway, arms folded over her chest, still feeling raw and achy with all the upheaval. She hadn't experienced so much emotional whiplash since she'd married Alan and he'd started in with the verbal abuse.

"Harp? Are you okay?"

"I don't even know anymore."

"You're leaving?"

"Yes, I'm going back to New York. I still have my apartment. I can find another job. Scrape together a life. I'm resourceful. I always have been. Tia made sure of that. It was sink or swim on my own."

"But what have you got there? No family. Most of the people you thought cared about you turned on you. Here, you have me and Willow, Aunt . . . er . . . Grandmother Jonnie and Hank and Grayson. Don't forget him."

"I do have other friends that aren't related to my job and c'mon, not everyone is meant to live in a lighthouse. It's a fairy-tale existence."

"What's wrong with that? We deserve a fairy-tale ending after all we've been through."

Harper gave her a look that said *get real*. "Seriously, how can I stay? Jonnie wants to pretend she's different from Mom, but she lied to us. No matter how you sugarcoat it, she deceived and manipulated us."

"And she taught us how to make sourdough bread and she did get us back together."

"Don't make light of her sins, Flannery."

"Why not? Because we're so perfect? Because we're sin-free?"

"I'm not saying that." Harper moved to the dresser and started yanking lingerie from the underwear drawer.

"Harper, have you no heart? Jonnie had a horrible life until she turned it around and got sober."

"Like our lives with Tia were peaches and cream?"

"I know you're hurting. I know you think that Jonnie betrayed you by not fighting for custody after Tia abandoned you."

"Damn straight. I could have had such a better life. Jonnie wouldn't have become an alcoholic if she'd just stepped up to the plate and taken me away from Tia."

"You know that might not be true. She may have become an alcoholic anyway."

Harper paused.

At least Flannery had gotten her sister to slow down her frantic packing. "And there's something else to consider."

Harper raised her head and drilled Flannery with a hard glare. "What's that?"

"*Me.*"

Harper looked confused. "You?"

"If Tia hadn't kept you, I would have been all alone. I wouldn't have had you to look after me, Harper. I wouldn't have survived without your strength and courage. Can't you find that same courage now to forgive Jonnie and Grayson? They did have our best interest at heart."

"Did they?"

"Yes, I believe that with all my heart. It would have been so much easier on both of them not to bring us here."

Harper slammed the dresser drawer and sank down on the mattress. Her shoulders slumped and she let out a long sigh.

"I've got something I think you should see, but I don't want you to be upset with me," Flannery ventured.

"What is it?" Harper eyed her suspiciously.

"Don't be mad, but I only burned two of Mom's letters to Missy Sinclair. I kept the third one because I thought one day, when you were ready, you might want to read it."

Harper blew out a long breath. "It's not going to change anything, Flan."

"I know, but when I read it I thought . . ." Flannery's voice stumbled, clogged with tears. "It was as close to closure as you're ever going to get from Mom."

"Okay." Harper sounded resigned. "I'll read it."

"I'll run get it." Flannery hurried downstairs and as she passed the kitchen saw through the window Hank and Willow sitting on the front porch. Willow was walking her little fingers up Hank's ropy forearm and singing "Itsy Bitsy Spider."

Hank was so patient with Willow . . . and with Flannery. He'd become a dependable friend and maybe, someday if their feelings for each other grew, they could be more than friends. It was something to hope for, but for now, she had to strengthen things with her sister. Nothing mattered more in this moment than convincing Harper that their relationship with their grandmother was worth saving.

She hurried to her room, retrieved the letter, and took it back upstairs. Harper was still sitting on the end of the bed, looking forlorn.

"Should I read it to you, or do you want to read it in private?"

"Go ahead and read it." Harper flapped a hand.

Encouraged, Flannery unfolded the letter and started to read.

Dear Missy,

My life has been a train wreck since I left my baby. I might not be good for Harper, but she is sure good for me. She kept me grounded. Responsible. Without her, I'm flying off the handle, bouncing from guy to guy, job to job.

When I look at her little picture my heart breaks right in two. I love that kid so much. I had a good thing, and I threw it away. I know you had to give her to Jonnie. You have your own life to live. I get that. I don't blame you, but now you've got to help me get her back. Leaving Harper behind is the worst thing I ever did. I don't know if I can ever be whole without her. Can you and Ward help me afford a good lawyer? I promise I'll pay you back.

Love bunches and bunches,
Tia

"I know it's all about Tia and what you could do for her, and we both know her idea of love was transactional, but, Harper, it was the very best that she could do. She could no more help being the way she was than Willow can help being born with a crippling form of spina bifida." Flannery hauled in a deep breath. "And you did save her for a long, long time. She wouldn't have been as stable as she was without us. I'm not asking you to excuse her abuse, I'm just saying maybe we should forgive her and accept her for who she was—broken, imperfect, but a woman so ensnared in her own misery she couldn't find her way out. I believe she sincerely wanted to be a good mom, she just didn't know how, and she fell back on the toxic family patterns."

Harper grunted and bit down on a fingernail.

"Most of all, Harp, I don't want you to end up like her."

Her sister whipped her head around, fire in her eyes. "I could *never* be like her."

"You're kind of acting like her right now. Being judgmental. Nursing your hurts and what was done to you, rather than forgiving good people who are trying to live a better life. Don't Jonnie and Grayson deserve a second chance?"

Harper fell back on the bed and stared up at the ceiling and Flannery was so terrified she was going to hightail it back to New York that she just kept talking, pleading her case.

"We're the only ones who can change the future, Harper. The only ones who can end the toxic Campbell legacy. We have to forgive *everyone*. But most of all we have to forgive ourselves. Can you do that, Harper? Can you forgive yourself for being human?"

"Flannery," Harper said in the bleakest voice Flannery had ever heard, "I'm not sure that's even a possibility."

CHAPTER 33

Harper

TRANSFER PEEL: A wooden board used by bakers to move loaves into and out of the oven.

Her sister was absolutely right, and Harper knew it. They couldn't build a brighter future until they confronted the past head-on and made a resolute pact with themselves to change.

And that change started with her.

That change started today.

If she wanted a happy life, she had to start acting like a happy person and a big part of being a happy person was forgiveness.

And accepting people for who they were.

Flawed humans.

That didn't mean she had to put up with abusive behavior. On the contrary, part of self-love was refusing to accept abuse. Boundaries were important, along with vulnerability. It meant not clinging to grudges, magical thinking, or outdated beliefs about what a family was supposed to be and accepting reality as it was.

Including her role in it.

Frankly, it was the hardest part of healing. Admitting her own flaws and mistakes, but still being kind to herself. *Yikes.*

She'd been way too hard on Jonnie. Her grandmother had risen above their legacy the best she knew how, and Harper respected her for that. Jonnie was just like them, raised by a demented mother. In judging their grandmother, she *was* acting like Tia. Lashing out, hurting because she'd been hurt, not thinking about Jonnie's feelings or how much her confession had cost her.

Harper understood why Jonnie had done what she'd done, and she had no moral high ground to blame her for her decisions. Harper had made plenty of bad choices of her own. Like trying to rescue people who didn't want or need saving.

It was time to save herself.

As she mulled this over, her cell phone rang. Pulling it from her pocket, she saw that the call was from Roger.

What did her ex-boss want? For Harper to claim her belongings? She'd already gotten two messages from HR to that effect, but she'd ignored them, not wanting to deal with the clutter she'd left behind amid the sourdough challenge.

A fake challenge constructed by her grandmother.

There it was again, that resentment over being deceived. How could she move forward until she cleaned up her past? Now was the time. Going back to New York would give her much needed distance from her emotions and help her make better decisions.

"Excuse me," she told Flannery. "I need to take this. It's my old boss."

"Sure, sure." Flannery gave her an encouraging smile and slipped out the door.

Harper answered her phone and, keeping her tone cool and noncommittal, said, "Hello, Roger."

"Harper! Thank God you answered." Her former boss sounded harried. She could hear the anxiety in his voice, felt her own muscles tense in response.

Until this moment she hadn't realized how her own body had been dialed at that same intensity for years—*go, go, go, do, do, do, get, get, get*. It was only as she'd experienced a slower-paced life in Moonglow Cove that she'd started to relax on a deeper level.

"What do you want?" she asked evenly.

"It's Kalinda. She's a loose cannon and she's wreaked havoc on the company."

Harper would be lying if she said she didn't feel vindicated. Perhaps it was petty, but she couldn't help the urge to gloat. She did manage to tamp down her glee though. "I'm sorry to hear that."

"Elise gave her your old job and she's made a mess of it. Things are falling apart here without you. We've lost sixteen accounts in five weeks! We let her go, but the place is utter chaos. We need a fixer. We need *you*."

Her old instincts to rush in and repair everything swept through Harper. She could fix this. She knew that, but should she?

"I don't mean to be rude, Roger, but how is that my problem?"

"Kalinda destroyed your legacy. She killed everything you built."

"No, Roger, you did that when you fired me."

"Come back," he pleaded. "The company is prepared to offer you a big raise and a bonus." He named a number so high it shocked her. They must truly be desperate. What on earth had Kalinda done?

Her mental cogs churned, enlivened by the challenge. Did she want to do this? Did she want her old life back? Considering everything Jonnie had revealed to her today, Harper had no idea. Her life was in turmoil and there wasn't an easy answer.

"Please," Roger said. "Please consider it."

"I was just about to return to Manhattan to handle my affairs and wrap up my life in New York."

"No," Roger said. "Please, no wrapping things up. At least not until you've given us a chance to make amends and welcome you back home."

Home.

That was the thing. Where was home? In New York? Or Moonglow Cove? Or maybe somewhere else entirely?

* * *

When she told Flannery about the call from Roger and that she was flying back to New York on the next available flight, her sister took the news with resigned acceptance.

"You aren't coming back, are you?" Flannery asked softly as they stood on the upstairs landing. Harper's luggage sat at her feet. She'd packed everything she'd bought since she'd been in Moonglow Cove.

In the distance, she heard the sound of a tugboat horn and her chest tightened all over again. "Of course, I'll come back to see you—"

"But not to live."

"I don't know," Harper answered honestly.

"And the Flower Dough Sisters?"

"I don't know."

"The bake-off?"

"I won't be back in time for that."

"I see."

"The mother dough is dead anyway."

"We could just bake regular bread for the bake-off."

Harper felt a hard ping inside her chest. "I've got a lot of things to sort out."

"I get it." Flannery nodded and tacked on a mournful smile. "I understand."

And yet, Harper couldn't help feeling she was letting her little sister down in a fundamental way.

"What about Aunt [illegible] our grandmother?" Flannery asked.

"I'll talk to her before I leave."

"And Grayson?"

"Him, too."

Flannery shifted her weight and dropped her gaze. "I better go check on Willow."

"Don't I get a hug before I go?" Harper asked.

"Oh yes." Flannery rushed to crush her sister in a heartfelt embrace and held on for too long.

Finally, Harper broke the hug and stepped back. "Did Jonnie leave yet?"

"I'm not sure. She was still in the lighthouse when I came inside."

Hoping to catch Jonnie and apologize to her before she left—she didn't want to get on that plane filled with anger and regrets—Harper went running from the cottage, bursting out the front door so fast she almost crashed into Willow and Hank who were coming inside.

"Everything okay?" Hank asked.

"We're working through some family stuff today," Harper explained. "Have you seen Jonnie and Grayson?"

"I'm right here," Jonnie said, coming out of the lighthouse, her eyes red-rimmed from crying.

"Could we talk in private?" Harper asked her.

"Yes, of course." Jonnie headed for the rocking chairs as Hank followed Willow inside and shut the front door behind them.

They settled into the rocking chairs and Harper braced herself as guilt knocked around inside her. Harper scooted her chair over so that she was facing her grandmother.

"I'm sorry," she apologized. "I had no right to speak to you the way I did."

"You had every right."

"No, I was selfishly thinking about how your revelation affected me without giving a second thought to you or your feelings. I let myself down and I let you down too."

"Harper, you had a normal response to an upsetting discovery. I'm the one to blame."

They stared at each other and simultaneously burst out laughing.

"Well," Jonnie said. "There's that. We both enjoy beating ourselves up."

"I want to do better. I want to be a better person."

Jonnie offered up a soft smile. "That's all anyone can ask."

Harper held out her hand to her grandmother. "I hate that we killed off the mother dough. That's a blow for us all."

"The mother dough isn't dead," Jonnie said.

"But the rose petals Willow fed Blobby—"

"I freeze-dried some of the dough years ago. We can just reconstitute it and go from there."

"Really?"

"You didn't think I'd keep some of it in reserve?" Jonnie asked with a laugh. "It is a one-hundred-fifty-year-old tradition, after all. Even toxic families have their good parts, and that mother dough is ours."

"Oh, Jonnie . . . Gramma . . . er, what do I call you?" Harper asked.

"When you stayed with me that one beautiful year, you called me Nonnie because you couldn't say your Js. I think that might work if it's okay with Flannery and Willow."

"Thank you, Nonnie." A lump welled in Harper's throat. "Thank you for breaking the cycle of abuse."

"Thank you for forgiving me."

"Thank you for forgiving *me*."

They smiled at each other.

"I think everything is going to be okay," Harper declared and leaned over to hug her grandmother.

"I think so too."

"Flannery will be so happy that she can still be in the bake-off with the Campbell family sourdough."

Jonnie's happy smile faded. The rocker creaked as Jonnie began to rock. "You're not going to bake in the contest?"

Harper shook her head. "I won't be here."

"You're headed back to New York?" Jonnie guessed.

"Yes." Harper told her about the call from Roger.

"I wish you didn't have to go."

"Me either."

"Then don't go."

"I have to."

"You're a fixer," Jonnie said wistfully. "It's what you do."

"It's my mess to clean up," Harper said. "I trusted the wrong person and gave her too much power. Now the company is in turmoil because of me."

"You don't think you're taking the blame for some things that weren't your fault? You might have hired this Kalinda woman, but she's the one who did the destructive acts. I know Tia indoctrinated you into thinking that everything that goes wrong is always your fault, but that's not true. You're not responsible for someone else's behavior."

"Maybe I am assuming too much of the blame," Harper conceded, touched by her grandmother's grace and kindness. "But I still have to go back."

"It's not just because of the job, is it?" Jonnie looked heartbroken.

"No." Jonnie's astuteness impressed her. "I have to figure out who I want to be and where I really belong."

"And New York City could win."

"It has been my home for over a decade."

A single tear trickled down Jonnie's cheek. Whisking it away, she whispered, "Whatever choice you make, I'll support you one hundred percent."

CHAPTER 34

Flannery

THERMAL DEATH POINT: The temperature at which yeast is killed as the loaf is baked.

The house felt so darn empty without Harper in it.

It was early Saturday morning, July 2, two days before the bake-off and Flannery couldn't sleep. Even though there was no longer any need to compete in the contest since Penelope's will was a fake, Flannery was determined to win that five-thousand-dollar prize.

Without Harper to depend on to start the Flower Dough Sisters business, Flannery had to find her own path to success, and the prize money would go a long way in helping to provide for Willow.

Every creak of the old house yanked her eyes wide open. On the mattress beside her, Willow was completely sacked out. Flannery's thoughts churned on an endless loop between fear and excitement, anxiety and elation.

Eventually, she'd need to get her daughter her own bed. Her own room. Their arrangements here were no longer temporary. Jonnie was waiving her inheritance from her mother and gifting the keeper's cottage to Flannery and the lighthouse to Harper—*if* Harper even wanted it. They would sort all that out when Harper returned from New York. For now, Flannery was happy to have her child breathing softly next to her.

Willow's warm little body was comforting and soothed Flannery's night terrors. She was still working on feeling safe and secure after a lifetime of hypervigilance. Change did not come swiftly or easily, but each day that she'd been in Moonglow Cove, she progressed just a little more toward the person she was truly meant to be.

Lying in the dark, Flannery realized she'd never lived by herself. She'd gone from living with her mother to Kit to Alan to Harper. It should feel freeing being on her own.

It did not.

She felt isolated. Completely alone except for a five-year-old.

Flannery knew her emotions were in flux from finding out about Jonnie, and from Harper leaving for New York so abruptly. But her feelings would shift and change. In the morning things wouldn't seem so gloomy.

But now? This minute? Uneasiness settled heavily over her like a weighted blanket.

She closed her eyes and willed herself to fall asleep. She had to be up at dawn to start the prep a day ahead of time for the contest. While searching for a recipe to help her stand out in the Fourth of July Bake-off, she'd discovered the Shooting Star Sourdough Bread among Jonnie's recipes that would serve perfectly with the holiday theme.

The problem?

The technique was quite complicated, and she wasn't sure

her budding skills were good enough to execute it properly. The recipe called for not only expertly twisting the dough into a star shape, but successfully lacing strawberry and blueberry jam into the bread without accidentally mixing the two before finally topping the finished results with white icing for the Fourth of July effect.

It could be an epic crash and burn or win her the grand prize.

Too bad Harper wouldn't be there to compete against her. She'd been looking forward to pitting her skills against her sister's.

She'd only heard from Harper once in the last days since she'd left Moonglow Cove. Just a quick text to tell Flannery she'd landed. She knew her sister was busy, and she hadn't wanted to bother her, but she couldn't help worrying. It couldn't be easy for Harper, going back into the lion's den. Then again, Harper had always thrived on chaos. A gift from growing up with Tia? The ability to adapt quickly. Except Flannery hadn't gotten the same gift. She shut down under pressure.

And yet, here you are, planning to bake in front of a live audience.

More doubts nibbled at her, keeping her awake. Would Harper return? Or would she realize how much she loved New York and want her old job back? What would Flannery do without her older sister's driving force?

"You'll be fine," she whispered into the dark. "You can do this."

Flopping over onto her side, she saw the digital clock on the dresser glowing green.

One A.M.

Sighing, she got up and went to the bathroom. On the way back to bed, she thought she heard a noise in the kitchen.

Pausing, she canted her head, listening for the sound to repeat. Probably just the oven cooling off. Except it had been hours since she'd finished baking for the day.

Unless she'd forgotten to turn the oven off.

Oh dear. She needed to go check.

Pulling on her bathrobe she kept on a hook by the door, she paused to peer over her shoulder at Willow who had her head buried under the pillow. An involuntary smile touched her lips.

Heavens, how she loved that child! Leaving Alan was the best thing she could ever have done for her daughter.

Yawning and tying her bathrobe sash, she padded into the kitchen. Moonlight streamed in through the open shutters. She glanced at the oven and saw that it was turned off.

Okay, she'd just been imagining things. Nothing amiss here.

She turned and from her peripheral vision caught movement in the shadows of the mudroom. The hairs on her nape lifted, and she sucked in a deep breath just as a hand snaked out of the darkness and closed over her mouth.

"Miss me?" hissed an ugly, all-too-familiar voice.

Terror struck her heart. Her worst nightmare coming to life in front of her.

Alan.

Stalking her in a seething rage. Somehow he'd managed to circumvent the security system that Hank had installed and gain access to the house.

Flannery's survival instinct was to shut down, make herself small, act passive, submissive, make him think she wasn't a threat.

His palm was still plastered over her mouth. She wanted to scream and yet there was no one to hear her high on the bluff. No one to come to her rescue.

She had to save herself and her daughter.

But how?

Get him out of the house. Get him away from Willow. The command throbbed in her brain.

How? How? How?

Escape plans hatched in her head, popping in and out as she discarded one after another. *Grab an iron skillet and bash him in the head. Kick him in the groin. Slam the back of your head into his face.*

No, no. All those solutions would leave her fighting him in the kitchen. Willow could wake up and enter into the middle of this and Flannery could not allow her daughter to witness the attack. Could not let Alan use Willow as a bargaining chip. She knew firsthand how such trauma affected a child.

In the end, she bit his hand.

He yelped.

Flannery jumped and spun out of his reach but didn't run. Couldn't run until she made sure he was going to follow her.

Her back was now to the mudroom door and he was in front of her, standing in the hallway between the mudroom and the kitchen. He was wagging his head and leering at her, his eyes glowing like coals in the moonlight.

He was dressed all in black and wore a ski cap and, horror of horrors, in his hand he held the fillet knife he used to gut fish.

Her blood froze icy cold.

He meant her the utmost harm. He'd gone completely over the edge. Before this, he'd been domineering and controlling. Had been verbally and emotionally abusive, but until the day he'd bruised her arm, he hadn't ever gotten physical.

But this? This was a whole new level of danger.

She had to get him away from Willow.

Now!

"You want me?" she taunted, fighting off her terror.

"I want to make you pay for what you did to me," he said. "You left me. You took my child from me."

"Willow's not your child."

"I provided for her. I paid for her medical care. I've helped you raise her for the last five years."

"Yes, you did those things and I thank you for it—"

"Oh no, you're an ungrateful, selfish bitch. You don't get to weasel out of what you've done."

Anger flared inside her. "And what have I done, Alan? Other than take your abuse for far too long."

"Abuse?" He howled. "You think I've been abusive? Woman, you haven't begun to experience abuse."

What a mistake! She shouldn't have challenged him. She knew better than to challenge him.

He lunged for her.

In an instant, she understood how she could use her mistake to her advantage. He was so enraged he would follow her anywhere.

Away from the caretaker's cottage, away from Willow.

Jerking back just in time to prevent him from grabbing her wrist, she whirled and tore out the mudroom door, Alan following step for step.

Flannery sprinted, running as hard as she could straight for the lighthouse with no clear plan in mind, just a single thought driving her.

Get him far away from her daughter.

But that singular-minded focus caught her in a trap. There

was nowhere to go. She could either try to pivot and run past Alan and make a break for the incline to the cul-de-sac. Head toward the bluff that dropped off into the ocean. Or run to the lighthouse.

She feinted to the left and he followed and then she dodged right, but he was faster than she and blocked her escape.

He came toward her, slashing at her with the knife. He called her names. Ugly names.

She backed up, arms raised.

"You thought you could discard me," he snarled, clouds passing over the moon and momentarily plunging them in darkness. In his black clothes and ski mask she could barely see him. "No one discards *me*."

Her heart battered her chest and her lungs clamped down, spilling air from her body, tightening with spasms. She couldn't catch her breath.

"I've been waiting . . . watching." His voice was thick, ominous with innuendo. "Five weeks. Waiting for that pushy sister of yours to finally leave."

"You've been in Moonglow Cove all this time?" She gasped.

"You didn't think I was just going to let you go, did you?" The look in his eyes was maniacal and Flannery saw pure evil.

In that instant, she knew he planned to kill her. Her heartbeat pounded so hard and loud her entire body was a singular throbbing pulse.

He lunged.

She jumped, turned, and ran as hard as she could toward the lighthouse. The clouds parted, illuminating her path with moonbeams.

His taunting laughter rang out in the night air as she pried open the anteroom door and scrambled up the circular steps to the tower. The metal steps cold against her bare feet.

"Dumb idea," he called. "Unless you plan on flinging yourself off the tower. If so, I'd be delighted to help with that."

Panic shoved her forward; she stumbled on the stairs, fell, and banged her knee. The pain was blinding, but she couldn't afford to give in to it.

But he was right. She was on a path to destruction. Her exit was blocked by Alan behind her. She had nowhere to go but up. Her feet felt as if she had ten-pound weights strapped to each ankle.

"You can run, but you can't hide," he said in a singsong voice, his footsteps echoing on the stairs behind her.

She scaled higher, knowing there was only one destination. One outcome.

"You know," he said, his eerily calm voice echoing in the stairwell, "it's not too late."

Frantically, she darted into the tower room.

"You can still come home. Pack Willow up and go back to Kansas with me. We can be a family again."

"Over my dead body!" She whirled around.

Alan was standing on the landing in front of her. Just a few feet away. Out of arm's reach, but not by much.

He shrugged, shifted the knife from his left hand to his right, and stared at her with vacant eyes. "Have it your way."

Her entire body went as cold as an iceberg. Her heart was a hammer, pounding her chest. She was good and truly trapped.

In stark despair, she slammed the door in his face and locked it.

"You think that flimsy door is going to stop me?" Alan kicked the door.

If only she had her phone! If only she hadn't left it on the table in her bedroom. She could call 911. Where was her mind? What had she been thinking? Why hadn't the phone been the first thing she thought of?

Because you were trying to get him away from Willow.

Mission accomplished, but now what?

Kick, kick, kick.

The ancient door creaked and groaned against Alan's assault.

Another forceful kick and she heard the wood splinter, saw it shudder on its hinges.

She backpedaled fast, running to the window. Hank had cleaned up the mess, replaced the glass and repaired the boards on the widow's walk as well. Any fleeting thoughts she'd had about luring him to the widow's walk and pushing him off vanished completely. She wasn't sure she could have done it anyway. He was much bigger and stronger than she.

Bam, bam, bam

He was coming for her. This was it. Time to take a stand. If he tried to throw her off the lighthouse, she was taking him with her. She wasn't about to let Willow fall into his hands. Even though she knew Harper and Jonnie would fight him with their last breaths, the law could be fickle. He could get custody of Willow since she was his legally adopted daughter.

No. No. She would not allow that to happen under any circumstances.

The door collapsed inward, and Alan's body filled the doorway. The moonlight pouring in through the curtainless window glinted off the knife in his hand.

She cowered against the wall beside the window, her body bathed in sweat. How many times had this awful man terrorized her with his verbal abuse? She was frozen with dread and shame that she'd allowed herself to be with such a man, to accept his abuse.

"This is it, bitch. Now you die," he declared.

She thought of begging for his mercy but couldn't bring herself to do it.

He stepped over pieces of splintered wood, crossing the threshold.

"You're going out that window and the sad story will be that in your despair over your beloved sister abandoning you, you flung yourself from the lighthouse. After all, mental illness is a Campbell family tradition. Any townie will tell you that."

Not the only damned family tradition.

With a Scottish pirate warrior's guttural scream, Flannery charged at him. Startled, Alan jumped back, stumbling over the busted door, surprise and fear in his eyes.

It was now or never.

With every ounce of strength that she had in her body, Flannery headbutted him in the gut.

Hard.

"*Oof.*" Alan grunted and flew across the landing.

The impact knocked Flannery to the floor and sent her head spinning.

He came for her, slashing the knife like a madman.

Moaning, she tried to roll away, but she was too late. His knife hit her neck, and she felt hot blood bloom down her back.

He raised his arm to strike again.

She clamped a hand around his ankle and threw all her weight into knocking him off balance.

The knife fell from his hand. Fiercely, he cursed her and grabbed for the blade.

Missed . . .

And went tumbling backward down the stairs. Just as the urgent sound of sirens shredded the dark night.

CHAPTER 35

Harper

REFRESHMENT: Feeding of the sourdough starter for the first time after a period of dormancy.

A sense of unerring urgency fisted Harper's spine in a tight grip. She didn't know where the feeling came from or what specifically had triggered it, she just knew she had to get back home as soon as possible.

Home.

To Moonglow Cove.

On Friday evening, July 1, she'd been in her apartment packing up boxes, eager to return to Texas on Monday the Fourth, in time to watch Flannery compete in the bake-off.

She couldn't wait to give her sister the happy news that she had decided against returning to her old job. She'd wanted to surprise Flannery, so she hadn't alerted her sister of her return. Her heart, she'd discovered over the last four days she'd been in Manhattan, belonged in the coastal community with her sister, grandmother, and niece. In Moonglow Cove, she'd found what she'd never known she'd been searching for.

A family.

Sure, they were screwed up. Sure, they would have many more ups and downs. Sure, they still had a lot to sort through, but one thing was crystal clear.

They loved each other and they wanted the best for each other, and they were all trying to be better people. Love and forgiveness were their watchwords and that's what made all the difference.

Together, they could end this family legacy of power, abuse, and control. Together, they could free future generations. They had such power, the four of them. *If* they banded together. If they united against the anger, hatred, and cruelty of their traumatized ancestors.

To make this change happen it took the ability to admit when they were wrong, have empathy and compassion for others, and use kindness as their guide. It also took courage to set strong boundaries and to love themselves first so that they would have an abundance of love to give to others.

And Harper was committed to this change. To making their world a better place. She'd told Roger that while she appreciated his offer, she was starting her own business in Texas with her sister, and he'd sincerely wished her the best. Then he asked her to forgive him for not having her back.

Willingly, she forgave him, and she forgave Kalinda, but most of all, she forgave herself for her mistakes and foibles.

Once she'd made her decision, she felt freer than she'd ever felt in her life. She had a mission. A life's purpose. Bring more love into the world. And her vehicle to that goal was through the Flower Dough Sisters where she planned on building a community of like-minded people.

Sure, she would make more mistakes. Sure, she would fumble.

She was human and that was okay. Tia had made her feel as if she had to be perfect in order to earn love, and that distorted belief stemmed from Tia's own insecurities and inability to admit she wasn't perfect.

Harper felt deep sadness that her mother had died forever searching for some perfect image of love that had never come, unable to accept the wild, messy love that her daughters had so desperately ached to give her. It broke Harper's heart but strengthened her resolve to shatter the Campbell family curse.

As she'd sat on the floor, applying shipping tape to boxes, a strong feeling had come over her. A feeling that something was amiss in Moonglow Cove and that she should return home immediately.

She phoned Flannery, but her sister didn't answer, then she realized it was the time of day when Flannery and Willow took their evening stroll. She left a message and tried to settle back down to her work, but the nagging feeling wouldn't go away.

Not one to put much stock in intuition, she shoved the feeling aside for a while, giving Flannery time to call her back.

By seven, she could no longer sit still and messaged Jonnie who texted back that everything was just fine in Moonglow Cove. She told her grandmother she'd be back in time for the bake-off on the Fourth and got a screenful of heart emojis in return.

But she couldn't shake her feeling of dread no matter how much she tried. An hour later, she called Flannery again and once more got her voice mail.

That's when she called the airline and changed her flight from Monday to the next available plane out of Manhattan to Houston. She got to the airport just in time to catch the last flight of the night.

Now it was one o'clock in the morning and she was in the Uber headed for Moonglow Cove, feeling a little foolish, but no less urgent. Anxiety was a whip urging her to lean forward and tell the Uber driver there was an extra fifty dollars in it for her if she could get Harper there any faster.

"Sorry," said the driver. "It's not worth the risk of a ticket. This gig pays for my daughter's college."

"No," Harper apologized. "That was inconsiderate of me not to think of the consequences for you."

"Something going on?" the driver asked.

"No, no. Just eager to be home."

"Long journey back?"

"Yes." Harper stared out the window into the night illuminated only by a crescent moon. The lights of Houston were behind them, Moonglow Cove still thirty minutes away.

Her sense of panic was completely illogical, and she knew that, but Flannery had never called her back. Sure, there could be a simple explanation. The most likely being that Willow had used her sister's phone as a gaming console and had run the battery down and Flannery had yet to check her cell.

Calm down, you're making a mountain from a molehill.

Still, she couldn't shake the sensation of impending doom. She quelled the desire to phone Flannery again. If nothing was wrong, she didn't want to wake her at this hour of the morning. And odds were everything was absolutely fine.

After what felt like an eternity, they finally reached Moonglow Cove and Harper could at last take a deep breath again.

Her relief didn't last long.

As soon as the driver turned off Moonglow Boulevard onto Comfort Road, Harper could see the flashing lights of a dozen emergency vehicles converged in the cul-de-sac, and among the mix was Grayson's Porsche.

"Holy crap," the Uber driver said. "Now I understand why you wanted me to rush."

But Harper barely heard her. She was already out of the car and flying toward the elevator, a million terrifying thoughts in her head.

A police officer posted at the elevator stopped her. "Crime scene, ma'am. Please turn back now."

Crime scene! Oh, dear God, what had happened?

Even before Grayson appeared out of the darkness, reaching for her with outstretched arms and somber eyes, Harper already knew the answer. The single, terrifying word reverberating in Harper's mind.

"*Alan*," he said.

Sobbing helplessly, Harper fell into Gray's steadying embrace.

* * *

AMBULANCE. POLICE. THE coroner's van. Flashing lights and sirens. A trip to the hospital for Flannery to receive stitches for the wound on the back of her neck. Interviews with law enforcement until dawn.

Throughout it all, Grayson was at her side.

And Hank was at Flannery's.

Jonnie stayed behind in the cottage with Willow who'd remained miraculously asleep throughout the chaos.

Alan was dead. His neck broken from the fall down the stairs.

Hank had been the one to call the police, having put in a feed to the lighthouse's security cameras that he had sent to his home via Wi-Fi. He'd gotten up to use the bathroom in the night, passed by the room where he kept the monitoring equipment just in time to see Alan pursuing Flannery into the lighthouse. He'd called 911, jumped into his pickup, and screeched over to the lighthouse, arriving immediately after Alan plummeted to his death.

There would be follow-up with law enforcement, but the evidence and the restraining order that Flannery had taken out on Alan satisfied them that Alan had been stalking his wife and she was lucky to have escaped with her life.

Flannery's wound was superficial and would heal in no time. They considered keeping the truth about Alan's death from Willow but decided she should know—secrets were toxic—and, with the help of a trained counselor, told her what had happened.

"He'll never come back?" Willow had asked.

"No," Flannery had told her in front of the therapist.

"Good," Willow had said staunchly. "I'm glad he won't hurt us ever again."

Flannery scheduled regular appointments for herself and Willow while the three Campbell women also decided to have family therapy once a week. It would take a while to sort out the legacy of their dark past, but they were determined to conquer it.

With a stubborn bent that reminded Harper of herself, Flannery insisted on competing in the bake-off on the Fourth of July despite her neck wound. Harper offered to help as her assistant, but Flannery lifted her chin and said, "This is something I need to do on my own, sister."

Harper raised her hands and stepped back, letting Flannery do what she needed to do, and Harper cheered the loudest when Flannery won first prize.

And when Flannery accepted the oversized five-thousand-dollar check in the photo op, she looked like exactly what she was—not just a survivor, but a thriver.

"Do you feel that?" Harper whispered in Flannery's ear as they got out of the minivan, and she wrapped an arm around her sister's waist as they gazed up at the lighthouse.

"What's that?" Flannery asked.

"The shackles of the past breaking."

"I do indeed," Flannery said, her eyes misting with happy tears.

"It won't be easy, and we've lost so much, but we're ready to do the hard work to mend our lives and we love each other."

"We do," Flannery whispered back and rested her head on her sister's shoulder.

Then Harper, Flannery, Willow, and Jonnie made their way back home together.

EPILOGUE

Jonnie

OVEN SPRING: The increase in volume of the loaf during the first few minutes of baking as the heat of the oven speeds up the yeast's production of carbon dioxide.

Two years later . . .

Grayson and Harper were married on the bluff overlooking Moonglow Bay, the oddly leaning lighthouse as a backdrop.

So many people were there. The friends they'd made in Moonglow Cove. Coworkers and family. It was a magical day. Willow served as a superpowered flower girl in her new electric wheelchair and Hank gave the bride away.

Flannery and Hank had just recently started dating but they were taking it slow, both believing that good things took time.

Harper and Flannery's business, the Flower Dough Sisters, had taken off like gangbusters, thanks to Harper's marketing savvy, and they'd just won an award for best new Texas business. The lighthouse had been transformed into the business hub, while Flannery and Willow lived in the keeper's cottage. Harper and Grayson had bought a house not far down the beach and they were looking forward to starting a family.

Jonnie herself had decided to retire to make up for lost time with her granddaughters and sold the shrimp boats to her employees. She still lived at the marina, as she had enough of that pirate DNA in her to enjoy life on the water. But she visited her granddaughters and the lighthouse several times a week.

As she watched Grayson kiss his new bride, Jonnie's heart filled with joy. Turning, she smiled up at the lighthouse that had once been a prison, knowing that while life would always have its ups and downs, the ghosts of their ugly family past had at long last been put to rest.

About the author

About the book

Insights, Interviews & More . . .

Meet Lori Wilde

Tamara Burros

LORI WILDE is the *New York Times*, *USA Today*, and *Publishers Weekly* bestselling author of ninety-seven works of romantic fiction. She's a three-time Romance Writers of America RITA Award finalist and a four-time Romantic Times Reviewers' Choice Award nominee. She has won numerous other awards as well. Her books have been translated into twenty-six languages, with more than four million copies sold worldwide. Her breakout novel, *The First Love Cookie Club*, has been optioned for a TV movie. Also, Hallmark television is producing three movies based on her Wedding Veil Wishes series.

Lori is a registered nurse with a BSN from Texas Christian University and a Master of Liberal Arts from the same school. She holds a certificate in forensics and is also a certified yoga instructor.

A fifth-generation Texan, Lori lives with her husband, Bill, in the Cutting Horse Capital of the World.

A Note from the Author

I got the idea for this book when the COVID-19 pandemic first hit and all these lovely images of sourdough breadmaking began hitting my social media feeds. There was something so comforting about this artisan skill that produced loaves of nourishment for people stuck inside their homes. Bread is the staff of life after all, and although it was virtual, sourdough was bringing people together!

There's something here, I thought. Something that I could use in my book to build and strengthen connections among my characters. The only problem? I'm not much of a baker and I knew nothing about sourdough.

The first step in my research journey was to learn how to make sourdough starter. Little did I know how frustrating, challenging, time-consuming, and, quite frankly, joyful the process would become. Every happy accident, mistake, and success I experienced along the way ended up in the book. The first sourdough starter I made was an epic fail, but the second one took hold. A year later, the mother dough is still alive and producing delicious loaves. Once you get it down to a science, the process of making sourdough bread is Zen-like and soothing.

If you're already an accomplished baker, sourdough shouldn't give you any trouble. If you're a new baker as I was, be patient with the process and give yourself grace. I promise the results are totally worth the effort.

To get you started on your own sourdough journey, I'm including the recipe that my family enjoys most.

I adapted the following recipe from *The Kitchn* (thekitchn.com/how-to-make-your-own-sourdough-starter-cooking-lessons-from-the-kitchn-47337).

SOURDOUGH STARTER

Ingredients

To create the starter:

- 4 ounces (¾ cup + 2 tablespoons) unbleached all-purpose flour
- 4 ounces (½ cup) water

To feed the starter each day (Day 3–7):

- 4 ounces (¾ cup + 2 tablespoons) unbleached all-purpose or bread flour
- 4 ounces (½ cup) water

Instructions

Making sourdough starter takes about 5 days. Each day you "feed" the starter with equal amounts of fresh flour and water. As the wild yeast grows stronger, the starter will become frothier and sour-smelling. On average, this process takes about 5 days, but it can take longer depending on the conditions in your kitchen. As long as you see bubbles and ▸

A Note from the Author ***(continued)***

signs of yeast activity, continue feeding it regularly. If you see zero signs of bubbles after three days, take a look at Day 2, step 2 below.

PROCESS

Day 1: Make the Initial Starter

- 4 ounces all-purpose flour (¾ cup + 2 tablespoons)
- 4 ounces water (½ cup)

1. Weigh the flour and water and combine them in a 2-quart glass or plastic container (not metal). Stir robustly until combined into a smooth batter. It will look like a sticky, thick dough. Scrape down the sides and loosely cover the container with plastic wrap or a clean kitchen towel secured with a rubber band.

2. Place the container somewhere with a consistent room temperature of 70°F to 75°F (like the top of the refrigerator) and let sit for 24 hours.

Day 2: Feed the Starter

- 4 ounces all-purpose flour (¾ cup + 2 tablespoons)
- 4 ounces water (½ cup)

1. Take a look at the starter. You may see a few small bubbles here and

there. This is good! The bubbles mean that wild yeast has started making itself at home in your starter. The yeast will eat the sugars in the flour and release carbon dioxide (the bubbles) and alcohol. It will also increase the acidity of the mixture, which helps fend off any bad bacteria. At this point, the starter should smell fresh, mildly sweet, and yeasty.

2. If you don't see any bubbles yet, don't panic—depending on the conditions in your kitchen, the average room temperature, and other factors, your starter might just be slow to get going.

3. Weigh the flour and water for today and add them to the starter. Stir vigorously until combined into a smooth batter. It will look like a sticky, thick dough. Scrape down the sides and loosely cover the container with the plastic wrap or kitchen towel secured again. Place the container somewhere with a consistent room temperature of 70°F to 75°F (like the top of the refrigerator) and let sit for 24 hours.

Day 3: Feed the Starter

- 4 ounces all-purpose flour (¾ cup + 2 tablespoons)
- 4 ounces water (½ cup) ▸

A Note from the Author ***(continued)***

1. Check your starter. By now, the surface of your starter should look dotted with bubbles and your starter should look visibly larger in volume. If you stir the starter, it will still feel thick and batterlike, but you'll hear bubbles popping. It should also start smelling a little sour and musty. Give it a few more days.

2. Weigh the flour and water for today and add them to the starter. Stir vigorously until combined into a smooth batter. It will look like a sticky, thick dough. Scrape down the sides and loosely cover the container with the plastic wrap or kitchen towel secured again. Place the container somewhere with a consistent room temperature of 70°F to 75°F (like the top of the refrigerator) and let sit for 24 hours.

Day 4: Feed the Starter

- 4 ounces all-purpose flour (¾ cup + 2 tablespoons)
- 4 ounces water (½ cup)

1. Check your starter. By now, the starter should be looking very bubbly with large and small bubbles, and it will have doubled in volume. If you stir the starter, it will feel looser than yesterday and honeycombed with

bubbles. It should also be smelling quite sour and pungent.

2. Weigh the flour and water for today and add them to the starter. Stir vigorously until combined into a smooth batter. It will look like a sticky, thick dough. Scrape down the sides and loosely cover the container with the plastic wrap or kitchen towel secured again. Place the container somewhere with a consistent room temperature of 70°F to 75°F (like the top of the refrigerator) and let sit for 24 hours.

Day 5: Starter Is Ready to Use

Check your starter. It should have doubled in bulk since yesterday. By now, the starter should also be looking very bubbly—even frothy. If you stir the starter, it will feel looser than yesterday and be completely webbed with bubbles. It should also be smelling quite sour and pungent. You can taste a little too! It should taste even more sour and vinegary.

1. If everything is looking, smelling, and tasting good, you can consider your starter ripe and ready to use! If your starter is lagging behind a bit, continue on with the instructions below. ▸

A Note from the Author ***(continued)***

Day 5 and Beyond: Maintaining Your Starter

- 4 ounces all-purpose flour (¾ cup + 2 tablespoons)
- 4 ounces water (½ cup)

1. Once your starter is ripe (or even if it's not quite ripe yet), you no longer need to bulk it up. To maintain the starter, discard (or use) about half of the starter and then "feed" it with new flour and water: weigh the flour and water, and combine them in the container with the starter. Stir vigorously until combined into a smooth batter.

2. If you're using the starter within the next few days, leave it out on the counter and continue discarding half and "feeding" it daily. If it will be longer before you use your starter, cover it tightly and place it in the fridge. Remember to take it out and feed it at least once a week

3. *How to Reduce the Amount of Starter* Maybe you don't need all the starter we've made here on an ongoing basis. That's fine! Discard half the starter as usual but feed it with half the amount of flour and water. Continue until you have whatever amount of starter works for your baking habits.

4. *How to Take a Long Break from Your Starter*
   If you're taking a break from baking but want to keep your starter, you can do two things:
   - **Make a thick starter:** Feed your starter double the amount of flour to make a thicker, doughlike starter. This thicker batter will maintain the yeast better over long periods of inactivity in the fridge.
   - **Dry the starter:** Smear your starter on a Silpat and let it dry. Once completely dry, break it into flakes and store it in an airtight container. Dried sourdough can be stored for months. To re-start it, dissolve ¼ cup of the flakes in 4 ounces of water and stir in 4 ounces of flour. Continue feeding the starter until it is active again.

If this process seems daunting, you can buy a live starter, or if you have a sourdough-making friend, ask nicely if they'll gift you some of their starter.

My favorite sourdough bread recipe is this one from King Arthur flour: kingarthurbaking.com/recipes/extra-tangy-sourdough-bread-recipe. We love extra tangy, so if you prefer a milder taste, you might want to try an alternate recipe. ▸

A Note from the Author ***(continued)***

The three sourdough discard recipes my family loved most were sourdough crackers (warning! you'll get addicted: loveandoliveoil.com/2019/03/sourdough-crackers-with-olive-oil-herbs.html); sourdough discard pancakes (sugargeekshow.com/recipe/sourdough-discard-pancakes/); and cheese and tomato sourdough focaccia (flouronmyface.com/cheese-tomato-sourdough-focaccia/).

From my home and hearth to yours, happy baking!

—Lori 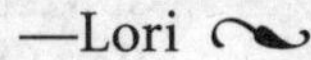

Reading Group Guide

1. Lighthouses seem to capture the imagination of people from all walks of life. What is it about the lighthouse that inspires such fascination?

2. Harper's professional career seems to be interrupted by something posted on social media. Do you think this is fair? Have there been moments in your life when you've regretted what you've said on social media?

3. Flannery and Harper have not spoken in six years. Do you think Flannery or Harper were in the right regarding the argument they had?

4. In what ways are Flannery and Harper each influenced by their unstable upbringing?

5. Often in toxic family situations, the younger siblings resent the elder for "getting out" or "leaving." Do you think Flannery's issues with Harper's escape are valid, or is she blaming her sister for the very natural act of growing up?

6. Baking is often a way to bring people together. Are there traditions of baking or cooking in your family that have been carried down through the years? ▸

Reading Group Guide ***(continued)***

7. Without giving away spoilers, were you surprised at Aunt Jonnie's secret and the way she "coped" with it?

8. Hank says that "Where people go wrong is thinkin' we're supposed to be happy all the time, but that's not how life works." Do you think that as a society we are obsessed with happiness? And is this insistence on happiness ultimately problematic?

9. At one point Gray tells Flannery to "Mend your own fences before you start stringing wire on your neighbor's." What do you think this means? Do you agree or disagree?

10. Harper feels she has always had to be the adult in the room. Do you feel this was necessary for her survival? Were there other ways in which she could have coped better?

11. Family can be sustaining of life, but are there times when family is destructive? In what ways were Harper and Flannery's family life sustaining? In what ways was it problematic? Do you think that we place too much value on keeping family ties together when sometimes they should be cut?